He saw, for an ins... man's hand, wrapped in a towel. It was ... off .22 caliber semiautomatic rifle, converted to fire on full automatic. It had a twenty-shot magazine. The man, stepping to one side of the congregation, had a clear line of fire. The twenty shots, firing at a cyclic rate of six hundred rounds a minute, blasted out in a single two-second burst that tore Feliciano's face to ribbons.

Air. She needed air.

*Also in Mysterious Press
by William Marshall*

MANILA BAY

WHISPER
*A Manila Bay
Mystery*

William Marshall

MYSTERIOUS PRESS

Mysterious Press Books (UK) are published
in association with Arrow Books Limited
62-65 Chandos Place, London WC2N 4NW

An imprint of Century Hutchinson Limited

London Melbourne Sydney Auckland
Johannesburg and agencies throughout
the world

First published in Great Britain 1988
by Mysterious Press UK
Mysterious Press paperback edition 1989

Printed and bound in Great Britain by
Courier International Ltd, Tiptree, Essex

ISBN 0 09 958790 4

Whisper

Tooth and Claw

*B*enigno Feliciano said, "Don't bite my finger!"

Mrs. Gallardo said, with Benigno Feliciano's finger in her mouth, "Oh my God!"

God was everywhere in Feliciano's Faith Healing House on Rio Cocodrilo Street, Manila (Psychic Dentistry a Specialty). He brought His warm glow of love and charity to the establishment. Benigno Feliciano, His humble servant, said, *"Shut up!"*

"O God of Abraham, God of Isaac, God of Jacob, God of Moses, and the Father of Christ—" There was a small, all male, congregation of patients standing in the furnitureless front room of Feliciano's house. Praying, their heads bent, they faced Feliciano's little dais. Behind the raised dais where Mrs. Gallardo sat on the single chair with Feliciano's thumb and finger in her mouth, there was a great staring eye painted on the back wall watching them. It was God's eye. Feliciano did not pull the teeth: God pulled the teeth.

*"—Thou hast revealed to the Prophets what they have written, and to the Apostles the New Testament—*THY DIVINE WILL BE DONE!"

It wasn't going to be. It was a whacking great second molar and it was stuck in there with celestial glue. Feliciano, not tugging—psychic dentists do not tug—twisting, sending vibrations through his hand, massaging the tooth, caressing it, breaking the ectoplasmic bond between this world and the next—*tugging the goddamned thing*—said in a gasp, "Gimme the tooth!"

Mrs. Gallardo said, "Oh my *God!*"

1

For some reason, there was a television news crew in the street, walking up and down outside the front windows of the house looking for something to happen. Feliciano, his eyes not on God or the tooth but them, said in a whisper, "Give me the tooth, I command thee!"

"THY WILL BE DONE!"

It was television. The TV crew was waiting around in the street on a tip. The tip had come from God. It was God's gift to him. Feliciano, starting to shake with effort, said in a whisper, "Listen—listen—"

Mrs. Gallardo said, "Aaarrgggg! Aaarrgghhh! *AAARRRG-GHHH!*"

The TV crew was a cameraman with a camera and lights and one of those female TV reporters with a microphone who smiled a lot on camera and probably never smiled in real life at all. It was fame, success, an audience of two million people. Feliciano, trying to reason with Mrs. Gallardo as blood started flowing from her gums, said in a rasp, "Help me! It's my big chance!" His eyes stayed on the prowling fame-makers. Feliciano said, *"To Thee, I give this sacrifice of my love, for it came from Thee, even as all things come from Thee—"*

Good. That was good. He saw the reporter and the cameraman turn around and look in his window. They looked like they were about to pack up. No riots, no rapine, no multiple pileups. And they still had film to shoot.

Feliciano said at the top of his voice, "MY TONGUE CANNOT EXPRESS MY GRATITUDE TO THEE, GOD, FOR PERMITTING ME TO SEEK COMFORT IN CHRISTIAN SPIRITISM!" If he got famous—if the tourists heard about him—if he could give up part-time taxi driving—*"HERE I HAVE DISCOVERED THOSE GREAT TRUTHS RE-VEALED TO ALL MANKIND BY THE HOLY SPIRIT—"*

The congregation joined him.

"—CONCERNING NEW SALVATION!"

Feliciano ordered Mrs. Gallardo, "Give me the tooth. Oh God, give me the tooth—"

Just one perfect extraction. One glowing testimonial on the six-thirty news. Just half a dozen rich Americans, three or four West Germans, a couple of Australians, little stories in all the back-home newspapers, donations, cars, gifts, gratitude . . . Whatever had sent the camera crew to Rio Cocodrilo Street at seven in the morning wasn't going to happen. *And they had all that lovely virgin film left for a five-minute spot.* Feliciano, seeing them start to pack up, seeing the lady reporter starting to get a snarl on her face, said desperately to God, "Please . . . please . . ." He vibrated the tooth with the gentleness of practice and the power of the cosmic finger.

Mrs. Gallardo shrieked, "Oh . . . *AYO!*"

He softened its hold in the cosmos with the slightest twirl of his thumb.

Mrs. Gallardo, starting to shake, yelled, "*AAAHHHH!*"

He . . .

Mrs. Gallardo said, "EEEEE!"

He didn't do a goddamned thing!

Mrs. Gallardo said, "OHHHH!"

"Give me the tooth!"

"*MIGUEL!*"

Who the hell was Miguel? He saw the lady reporter glance in the window, think for a moment, and then start to shrug. Feliciano said in a tight prayer, "Don't shrug. Think. Think of an angle. Think of—"

Mrs. Gallardo screamed, "Miguel! Miguel! *HELP!*"

"*Thy divine will be done. Amen.*" The congregation stopped praying. They began to open their eyes. They were the usual collection of the ragged and the poor and the aching.

"Miguel! MIGUEL!"

One of them must have been her husband. At the window he saw the lady reporter look in. Feliciano smiled. He gave the tooth his best twirl. Mrs. Gallardo said— He stuck his thumb and finger in her mouth as far as they would go. Mrs. Gallardo said, "Uk!" The lady reporter was looking in, thinking. Feliciano, smiling, gave her his left profile. He smiled. He shrugged as if it were nothing. Feliciano said in the voice he usually reserved for God, "I work humbly for mankind!" It carried out to the street. He saw the reporter turn around and say something to the cameraman. He saw the cameraman think about it for a moment and then rub his nose.

Mrs. Gallardo, sinking in the chair, had turned a strange color. Mrs. Gallardo said, "Uk . . ."

"Thy divine will—" Now or never. Feliciano, using every ounce of his strength, still smiling, said in a last, final, desperate plea to God, "If I was a rich man—" He pulled. He yanked. He saw one of the men in the congregation start to come toward him. Miguel? He heaved. He—

Feliciano ordered the man, "Pray!"

He didn't.

Mrs. Gallardo, running out of breath, said in a hiss, "Ohhh . . ."

"THY—"

The TV crew was still discussing it. They wanted a story. He had one.

He hauled on the tooth.

"—DIVINE WILL—"

Feliciano ordered Miguel—a middle-aged but wiry man in his late forties wearing a manual worker's khaki shorts and white T-shirt, "Pray!"

"—WILL BE—"

He felt it come. He saw the cameraman, at last, nod. He saw him take out his light meter to test the light.

"—THY DIVINE WILL BE DONE!"

He had the tooth.

He saw, for an instant, something in the T-shirted man's hand, wrapped in a towel. It was a sawed-off .22 caliber semiautomatic rifle, converted to fire on full automatic. It had a twenty-shot magazine. The man, stepping to one side of the congregation, had a clear line of fire. The twenty shots, firing at a cyclic rate of six hundred rounds a minute, blasted out in a single two-second burst that tore Feliciano's face to ribbons.

Air. She needed air.

Mrs. Gallardo, released, the finger and thumb and the tooth gone suddenly from her mouth, falling off the chair, shrieked, "Help me! Miguel! Saint Miguel and all the saints in Heaven . . . *help me!*"

The congregation had not moved. In the corner of the room, as far away from Mrs. Gallardo and the dead man as he could get, the man with the gun, pressed in hard against the wall, trying to stand up straight with the reloaded weapon in both hands, shrieked, "Help me!" He was talking to God. "Pray for me!" The congregation—all men—did not look at him. They had their eyes tightly closed. "Save me!" He was not talking to God, but to the television camera, *"Film my face!"* The camera was moving everywhere in the room, getting the body and Mrs. Gallardo by the fallen-over chair. Everything but him. He lowered the muzzle. The man with the gun said, "Emmanuel Ernesto Barrera—B-A-R-R-E-R-A! Fruit vendor, 87 General Vega Street! Married! Aged forty-seven." He ordered the camera, *"Film my face!"* He ordered the camera, "Save me!" It was everywhere but on him. Behind the camera, the cameraman's hands were shaking. He saw the woman reporter with fear on her face. All the members of the congregation had their eyes closed. Barrera yelled, "Film my face! FILM MY FACE!" He was rocking back and forth in the corner, "Emmanuel—Ernesto—Barrera." He ordered the woman reporter, "Write it down! Look at my face!" He brought the gun up toward the camera. "Here! Film here! Put it on television!"

Mrs. Gallardo shouted, "Oh God!" She had no handkerchief. Blood was coursing down her chin from her ruined gums. Mrs. Gallardo said, "He hurt me! He hurt me!"

The cameraman, turning the camera and pressing hard on the *Film* button, said, "Yes! Yes!" He had no idea what to film. The camera moved to the gun.

"Record my face!"

The cameraman said, "Yes!"

Barrera said to the congregation, "Friends . . ."

The congregation was praying, intoning in whispers over and over the same words of prayer.

Barrera said, "Yes?" He had his eyes on the woman reporter. Barrera, nodding hard, said, "Yes? Yes?"

"Yes!"

"Name! My name!"

"Barrera—Emmanuel—"

"Write it down!"

"I—" The woman reporter said, "I haven't got a—" The woman reporter said, "I'll remember!"

Barrera said softly, "They know my name." He nodded to the congregation. "If you forget, one of them—" He looked to the cameraman. Barrera said, "All right? Was the light good enough?" He said softly, "OK." Suddenly, his body went limp. Barrera said with a sigh, "Oh." In his hands the gun was dropping. No one in the congregation turned to look at him or opened his eyes. Barrera said, "Good. OK." Barrera, relaxing, almost letting go, said conversationally, "It was—the feeling of release was—" Barrera said, shaking his head, "I never thought that doing it—that—doing it would—" He saw the woman reporter staring at him. She was very beautiful. He had seen her somewhere on TV. Like the people on TV she did not look the way ordinary people looked. Barrera said, "Stay here. Stay here." He looked down at the floor. He was a man who at one time had done heavy work. All the veins and muscles in his neck and arms stood out. Barrera said to no one in particular, perhaps to God, "I have given up all hope for myself, but it—" Barrera said quietly, "I know the difference between right and wrong—but it was impossible!" He blinked back tears. "It was impossible!" The congregation did not look at him. *"Emmanuel Ernesto Barrera!"* His face changed. Barrera demanded, *"Have you got that?"*

The woman reporter said, "Yes, yes, I've—"

Barrera said, "Fruit vendor." Suddenly, it seemed funny. "Aged forty-seven." His breath was coming in gasps. It was as if he were on the point of telling a joke, of being a joke, of realizing that all his credentials— Barrera said, "Married, fruit vendor, aged forty-seven." Barrera said, *"Oh, Holy Mary in Heaven!"* Barrera said, "What time is it?" He was on the point of tears, on the point of laughter. Barrera said, "Turn off the camera!" Barrera said, "They know my name." He nodded to the silent congregation. Barrera said, "Turn off the camera, please." He saw it come down. Barrera said, "Stay. Watch my face." He nodded as if he had thought of something. Barrera said softly, "Bananas, coconuts, nice fresh green vegetables from the provinces . . ." Barrera said, raising the weapon, "They know my name." He was shaking, coming to something, his hands starting to tremble. Barrera said, "Oh . . . oh . . ." Barrera said, "Oh . . . quickly! Quickly! *QUICKLY!*"

"O God of Abraham, God of Isaac, God of Jacob, God of Moses, and the Father of Christ—" The congregation was praying aloud. Barrera said, *"They know my name!"*

"O God of Abraham, God of Isaac, God of Jacob—"

In the corner of the room, he raised the gun and began turning it. There was a click as it rested muzzle first against his own chest. The weapon had been cut down, shortened with a pistol grip. His thumb reached the trigger easily.

"—God of Moses and the Father—"

Barrera said, "Emmanuel Ernesto Barrera, fruit vendor, aged forty-seven!"

"—Father of Christ—"

Barrera said, "Fruit vendor!"

"THY WILL BE DONE!"

"He—" Barrera said—"He—"

"Thy will be done."

"Fruit vendor!" For an instant, momentarily, in his last moment, he almost laughed.

The muzzle of the gun was pressed hard in against his chest where the heart was.

"Emmanuel Ernesto Barrera, 87 General Vega Street, Manila, fruit vendor, aged forty-seven, married . . ."

With the pistol grip, his thumb reached the trigger easily.

Barrera said—

There were no words left. There was only the trigger of the gun against his chest. Barrera said, *"Oh—!"*

He pushed hard on the trigger—quickly—once.

The Republic of the Philippines lies in the South China Sea midway between the north coast of Australia where there is a population density of approximately one human being per ten thousand square miles and the south coast of China where the statistics are reversed. After four hundred years of colonial rule by Spain and fifty years in the American Commonwealth it is the only Asian country to be almost totally Christian, to use the Western music scale, to speak English as a first language, and to bear no colonial grudges. The country is composed of some seven thousand volcanic islands—more or less, depending on the earth's daily activity—of which Luzon in the north and Mindanao in the south are where most people live.

The capital is Manila on the north island of Luzon where the main interests of the people are cockfighting, basketball, and chess, the combination of which, within the same national psyche, has been known to send sociologists fresh from Western universities back to those Western universities gibbering.

The climate is tropical with a wet and a dry season, the people brown and almond eyed with a propensity for romance and arson. Presently, the going rate for bribing a traffic policeman in the poorer areas is approximately seven pesos or fifty-three cents.

Manila's sunsets are justifiably famous if you can see them around the high-rise buildings or the fires.

There are almost no tourists in Metro Manila these days and if you do go there, everyone—especially the Foreign Currency Deficit Department—is very glad to see you coming.

Each morning, standing on the balcony of his first-floor apartment in Paranaque, south of the city center, Lieutenant Felix Elizalde of the Western District Detective Bureau craned to see the sunrise. Each morning, because of the buildings in the way, he could see nothing.

Some mornings, because of the smog, or in the wet season from July to September, he could not even see the buildings.

Each morning, without fail, smelling Manila, hearing it, knowing it was there, he couldn't wait to begin the day.

It was a little after seven twenty in the morning.

In Feliciano's Faith Healing House on Rio Cocodrilo Street, Manila (Psychic Dentistry a Specialty), softly at first, then louder and louder until it drowned out even Mrs. Gallardo's cries of pain from her ruined mouth, the congregation—all men—began wordlessly, earnestly, to applaud.

1

*I*t was the Gnome Home on Padre Diego Tomas Street.

It wasn't the Gnome Home on Padre Diego Tomas Street, it was the Gnome Home Acrobatic and One-Ring Sawdust Circus Café; Coffee, Meals, and Entertainment Three Times a Day on Padre Diego Tomas Street. It even had sawdust. In the ring, to the blasting of a Chuck Berry record screaming the joys of "Maybelline!," jugglers juggled, clowns fell about, flash powder exploded, breakfasters breakfasted, applause rippled, and, as in all circuses everywhere, everyone was happy.

Well, almost everyone. In the kitchen twenty-five feet above the ring, Detective Sergeant Baptiste Bontoc, contorting himself to lean out a hole the size of the entrance to a dog kennel for small dogs, yelled, "WHAT?" Someone was shouting at him. It was someone hanging upside down on the serving hatch entrance like a human fly. If it was a human fly it had shoulders like a wrestler and wore a set of what looked like gold-lamé long johns. Bontoc, twisting his head up, as below at the tables around the ring people applauded and shouted as a juggler juggled or a clown clowned, yelled, "What did you say?"

It wasn't the jugglers or the clowns in the ring the breakfasters were applauding, it was a papier-mâché dragon (painted pink). It was lighted up in a corner of the ring with a spotlight. It gushed fire breath. The breakfasters at their tables went, "Cooo!" It turned green. The diners went, "Ahhh . . ." It pissed itself. The breakfasters went, "Ho! Ho! HO!"

"Two black coffees and make it snappy!" It was the long-john man. He was a dwarf. He stood about two-and-a-half-feet high.

10

Leaning in, grinning at Bontoc, looking happy, the long-john dwarf asked above the din, "How are you enjoying the show so far?"

The chef dwarf, working at a coffee percolator that looked bigger than he did, shouted to the long-john man, "Ready to go!" They were all dwarves. Everyone. Bontoc, almost putting his back out to peer through the serving hatch opening, shouted to the long-john man, "What are you doing up there?"

" 'Maybelline!' " The long-john dwarf yelled, "Jorge! I'm Jorge Abala!" He stuck his hand in through the opening. He didn't seem to be standing on anything.

"Baptiste Bontoc!" Bontoc yelled as the chef dwarf shoved two cups of steaming black coffee on a tray into his hands, "What do I do with it? How do I get it down to the tables?"

There was a roll of drums.

The spotlight moved.

It illuminated a man and a woman sitting at a table looking up. They looked like tourists. Tourists knew where everything was. They always knew exactly what to do. They looked up.

There was a grinding noise high up in the roof as something mechanical moved. Jorge, glittering in his lamé, got another spotlight on him. Jorge said, "Here!" He disappeared.

Bontoc said, "Jorge—?"

"AND NOW—FOR TABLE SIX—TWO BLACK COFFEES!" It was some sort of ringmaster. He was also only two-and-a-half-feet tall. He wore a top hat and black riding boots.

Bontoc said, "Jorge—?" Maybe he had fallen down. Bontoc asked the chef, "Excuse me—"

They were a friendly lot. The chef, putting out his hand, said, "Ernesto Abala—"

"Oh." It was the same name. Bontoc said, "Is he your—" Bontoc asked, "What happened to the coffee?"

"COFFEE!" The drums stopped. Chuck Berry stopped. The "Skaters' Waltz" began. Bontoc thought he saw, for an instant, Jorge in his lamé long johns go sailing by outside upside down like a bat.

He couldn't have.

"OOOOO—FEEEEE!" He did. He went sailing by upside down on a trapeze like a bat making straight for the spotlighted table. The coffee cups were still on the tray. He was holding them in both hands, hanging down from his ankles on the silver trapeze, going straight for— Bontoc said in a gasp, "Oh my God!"

He came down like a cleaver, missed the table with his knuckles by an inch, dropped the tray neatly dead center between the man and the woman and sailed on by. He must have got great tips. He hit the full length of the arc, dodged the flame-throwing dragon with a quick flip, turned to face the other way, and as the trapeze took him back and up past the breakfasters, opened the lid of their stainless steel sugar bowl, smiled, and shouted, "Enjoy!"

The male breakfaster shouted with an American accent, "Thanks!"

"You're welcome!"

Bontoc said, "Wow!" He turned to the chef—to Ernesto—

Jorge said, "Almost missed opening the sugar bowl that time!" He was back. He was hanging on the ledge not even out of breath. Jorge said, "You were saying—?"

Down in the ring someone had finished his coffee. There was another roll of drums. The Ringmaster, in the spotlight, yelled, "CROCKERY! TABLE *TWO!*"

At table two, a dwarf in a clown's suit took the empty coffee cups and poured the dregs into a little silver dish. The spotlight stayed on the Ringmaster. By the Ringmaster there was a cannon. Bontoc, trying to lean out of the bar and ending up looking up at the ceiling where the winch was that turned the trapeze equipment toward any table in the place, asked conversationally, "What's the cannon for?"

The "Skaters' Waltz" stopped.

The dragon stopped.

The jugglers stopped.

In the ring the clowns stopped hitting each other with slats.

The crowd—there seemed to be lots of them—said, "Aahh—"

"CROCKERY!"

Bontoc, turning to Ernesto, asked, "What's the cannon for?"

Ernesto was moving back to the far end of the doll's house kitchen, cowering.

Bontoc, looking back at the hatch, said, "Jorge, what's the cannon for?"

Jorge was gone.

Bontoc said to no one in particular in the silence, "Um, what's the cannon for?"

The "Skaters' Waltz" had died away.

There was a roll of drums.

The Ringmaster ordered, "HA!"

The coffee cups went sailing across the ring.

One . . . "HA!"

Two . . . "HA!"

Three . . . "HARR . . ."

It must have been a big party.

Four . . . "HARR—HARR—" The Ringmaster ordered, "CROCKERY!"

The saucers went sailing.

Bontoc said, "Jugglers?"

"HAA-RUM!" The Ringmaster shouted, "CROCKERY!"

The cups and saucers went into a sort of papier-mâché ball with a lid that looked like a little cannonball. Bontoc said, "Ernesto, what's the—" Bontoc, sticking his head out and looking around the ledge, said, "Jorge—?" Jorge was up on his trapeze rope like a human fly looking down. Bontoc shouted, "Ernesto!!" He heard a scratch as someone out of sight put the next record on.

It was the 1812 Overture.

In the ring they had a cannon.

Bontoc said in a panic, "Jorge! What do I *do?*"

"READY—"

Bontoc said, trying to turn in the opening, "Ernesto . . . ?"

"AIM—"

He had this letter from the United Nations, see, and this letter said that he was to—

Bontoc said, "I'M A COP! I'M A—"

"FIRE!!!"

"*Catch it!*" It was Ernesto the Craven Coward.

"I'M A—I'M A—EYEMMA—" Thank God it was only a circus spring cannon with a flash powder detonation. If it had been a real cannon, it would have fired the papier-mâché ball of crockery straight in through the kitchen window, hit him in the groin, lifted him off his feet, and propelled him into the back wall.

Fortunately, it was only a circus spring cannon with a flash powder detonation and all it did was fire the papier-mâché ball of crockery straight in through the kitchen window, hit him in the groin, lift him off his feet, and propel him into the back wall.

"THREE WHITE COFFEES! DECAF! TABLE FOUR!" It was Jorge hanging upside down in his lamé long johns at the window. In this world, to get ahead, you had to work for a living.

"Right! Right!"

Bontoc, picking himself up off the back wall clutching the papier-mâché cannonball firmly in his groin, thinking, concussed, that so far he hadn't done too badly, said, "Right! Right!" He went to put the cannonball in the sink.

Jorge, hanging upside down, looking at him with eyes that seemed to go the wrong way, shouted in applause, "Well done!"

"Thanks!"

Bring on the tigers.

Funny. First thing in the morning, on a bright fine day in Manila, in the capital of the Philippines, he thought he was in a circus. Down in the ring, he thought he heard a horse whinny.

He put the cannonball in the sink. He heard a voice. He looked up and the ceiling was only twelve inches above his head.

Jorge said politely, "Baptiste—Baptiste . . . um . . . we have to have our ball back." He smiled.

Sure. OK. He was all right. He was a Bontoc. He was used

to the rough-and-tumble of life. Bontoc, nodding, looking determined, wondering why everything below waist level was completely numb, said resolutely, "Sure." He was a cop as well as a Bontoc: he had been trained for things like this.

Bontoc, smiling, nodding, blinking, clutching his groin by the sink, said pleasantly, well on top of the situation, "Certainly. Of course."

He looked at Jorge looking at him upside down.

Bontoc asked with that politeness that Bontocs and cops were famous for, "Um . . . um . . . um . . ." The room was a doll's house, tiny, but it had in one corner the most comfortable corner he had ever seen. Fortunately, his body happened to be going in that direction. Bontoc said, "Cannon." Bontoc said, "OK." Bontoc, happy to be nearer his corner by the second, said, "Right."

Three white coffees. Decaf. Table four.

Cannons.

Dwarves.

Circuses.

The United Nations.

Wondering just what the hell you were doing there in the first place . . .

It just wasn't the sort of thing you hurried.

In his corner, humming a little tune, Bontoc said, "Fine."

He sat down to carefully, logically think about it for a while.

In the bay there was a forty-two-foot, white-and-blue Crowther Spindrift catamaran lying at anchor. There was no wind and, with her sails furled and protected by matching blue sail covers, a quarter of a mile offshore, she moved almost not at all on the still, full tide.

Inside the boat, with the curtains drawn in the main cabin and in both the hulls on either side of it, there was only the faint light of the digital-frequency readout of a Seaphone HF radio.

In the main cabin of the boat, at the chart table, there was only the shadow of a man.

The boat, according to the twin legends painted on her hulls, at the stern in blue italic lettering was *GOOSEWING.* Below the name, her port of registration read in black roman, MANILA.

"Benigno Feliciano, number 54 Rio Cocodrilo Street, Manila, Western District." The man at the chart table spoke in a whisper.

A voice calling back on the seaphone said, "Yes." There was faint static.

The whispering man, not disguising his voice, but speaking as he always spoke, touching at his throat with his free hand, said, "Good." The boat was lying quietly to anchor, moving only a little in the tide.

The whispering man said into the phone, "Wait." He reached for something on the chart table and looked down hard at it in the poor light.

It was volume one of the Metro Manila Electoral List.

The whispering man said only, again, "Wait."

He clicked off the connection.

On the boat, in the bad light, in the semidarkness, he began carefully to look up a name.

"In the movie *Butch Cassidy and the Sundance Kid,* Butch Cassidy says to Sundance, 'I work like a dog, Sundance, and I just can't get a single centavo ahead.' *WHY?*"

On the beach off Rizal Park Detective Sergeant Jesus-Vincente Ambrosio, walking up and down on the sand, said, "I don't know."

"You don't know?" The voice on the cassette tape said through his earphones, "You don't know?" There was a little click on the tape, "Answer here: *No.*"

Ambrosio said, "No."

"YOU DON'T KNOW BECAUSE YOU'RE A FAILURE! YOU DON'T KNOW BECAUSE YOU'RE A BUM—A NOTHING! WHAT ARE YOU?"

The beach was deserted. A little way out in the water there was a vitna coming in under sail. It was some sort of shell or coral carrier from Mindanao or Cavite province or somewhere. Ambrosio said, "I'm a bum!"

"LOUDER!"

"I'M A BUM! I STINK! I'M A FAILURE! I'M THIRTY-THREE YEARS OLD AND I'VE ACHIEVED NOTHING WITH MY LIFE!"

"Are you physically handicapped? Is that the reason for your bumhood?"

"No."

"Answer: *No.*"

"No."

"*WHAT?*"

"NO!"

"Then you must be too old to succeed even though no one is ever too old to succeed. Is that it—are you too old to succeed even though no one is ever too old to succeed? Answer: NO!"

"NO!"

"Are you out walking by yourself listening to this tape? Have you done what the instruction books tells you? Are you walking somewhere quiet first thing in the morning with only you, my voice, and your total lack of achievement in life, the taste of bitter vetch in your mouth, to comfort you? Answer: *YES.*"

Ambrosio said sadly, "Yes." He watched the vitna.

"You said yes softly. I know. I KNOW BECAUSE I KNOW PEOPLE! THAT'S WHY YOU BOUGHT MY SUCCESS TAPE—YOU MISERABLE, SOFT-SPOKEN WORM! Are you physically unattractive—is that your excuse for failure?"

"I'M AVERAGE!"

"TOULOUSE-LAUTREC WAS PHYSICALLY UN-ATTRACTIVE AND LOOK WHAT HE ACHIEVED! DO YOU CLAIM YOUR FAILURE IS DUE TO LACK OF ED-UCATION—ARE YOU SAYING 'WHO'S TOULOUSE-LAUTREC?' TOULOUSE-LAUTREC WAS A PAINTER—NOW YOU KNOW! HOW DID HE GET AHEAD?"

"I don't know."

"DID HE GET AHEAD BY LUCK? Answer *now!*"

"HE GOT AHEAD BY LUCK!"

"*WRONG!!* HE GOT AHEAD BY WORKING HARD AND CONFIDENTLY TO SURMOUNT HIS FAILINGS! Question: HOW DO *YOU* GET AHEAD? Answer: YOU *DON'T* GET AHEAD! YOU JUST—"

"I JUST—"

"ANSWER: 'LIKE BUTCH CASSIDY, I JUST HOPE FOR A LUCKY BREAK, DO NOTHING ABOUT IT, AND NEVER GET A DOLLAR AHEAD!' "

"*LIKE BUTCH CASSIDY I JUST HOPE FOR A LUCKY BREAK, DO NOTHING ABOUT IT, AND NEVER GET A DOLLAR AHEAD!*"

"Are you easily led?"

"Yes!" Maybe he could throw it all in and become a vitna driver or whatever they called it. Maybe he could dive for shells if he could swim and then sail along through the night watching the moon and take his shells to market and make money and then sail back again watching the moon again or— Ambrosio shouted into the morning, "I'm a bum! I've been given a big opportunity and I just don't know how to profit from it and I'm going to be a bum all my life and—"

"DO YOU SINCERELY WANT TO BE A FIREBALL?"

That was the name of the tape. That was why he had bought it. Ambrosio said, "YES!"

"And you can't." It was a metallic voice. It seemed close and then far away. He had the Sony Walkman cassette tape recorder in his hand as he walked. He gave it a tap with his hand and the voice became stronger. He hadn't put new batteries in the thing. He was a bum. He was so much of a bum that at the turning point in his life he hadn't even thought to put new batteries in the machine. If it ever rained soup he was going to be standing there with a fork. "EVERYTHING YOU DO IS SECOND RATE OR UNSUCCESSFUL! ALL YOUR LIFE YOU'VE MADE EXCUSES AND NOW, BECAUSE EVERYONE YOU KNOW IS DOING BETTER THAN YOU, YOU'VE RECONCILED YOURSELF TO THE NOTION

THAT YOU'RE DOOMED FOREVER TO BE A FAILURE!" The metallic voice said in his ear, "Answer now: What are you?"

"I'M A BUM!" He had read the instruction manual that came with the tapes. He knew the responses.

"YOU STINK!"

"I STINK!"

"YOU STINK BECAUSE YOU'RE A PHILIPPINO—AN AVERAGE PHILIPPINO—"

"I'M AVERAGE!" He was. Everything about him was average. On the beach seen from the vitna he was an average-looking man walking up and down on an average beach on an average sort of morning shouting into the wind. Even the vitna sailor watching him from his boat as it came in looked away without interest. He was average. The vitna sailor was better off looking at the moon. Ambrosio shouted, "I STINK! I'M NOTHING! I STINK ROTTEN! I'M A DISASTER!"

"YOU'RE A PHILIPPINO! YOU THINK GETTING THROUGH THE WORLD WITHOUT INTERFERING WITH YOUR NEIGHBOR, WITHOUT ALARMING YOUR BUSINESS COLLEAGUES, WITHOUT CAUSING ANY TROUBLE—YOU THINK ALL THAT IS MORE IMPORTANT THAN BEING FILTHY RICH AND POWERFUL!"

"I WANT TO BE FILTHY RICH AND POWERFUL!" The vitna sailor, smiling, called out, "Yeah, me too."

"You want to be a Fireball?"

"I WANT TO BE A FIREBALL!"

"DO YOU WANT TO BE A FINE, CIVILIZED, THOUGHTFUL PHILIPPINO LIVING A LIFE OF CONSIDERATION AND CARE FOR YOUR FELLOWMAN OR DO YOU WANT TO BE ONE OF THOSE LOUSY, OPULENT, INTERNATIONAL CUTTHROAT BASTARD YOU SEE ON TELEVISION SERIES, SURROUNDED BY BEAUTIFUL WOMEN AND GROVELING MINIONS?" The voice on the tape ordered, "Answer now."

Ambrosio said, "Minions!"

The vitna sailor called out, "Hey, if you could give me a hand when I come in—"

"LOUDER!"

"MINIONS!"

"LOUDER!"

"MIN-I-*ONS!!*"

"Good." It was the first bit of praise he'd had.

Ambrosio said gratefully, "Thanks."

"YOU CAN HAVE ALL THAT!"

"How?"

"You've taken the first step. You have in your hand the secret of winning all the things you want. You have the means to make all your daydreams come true. You've bought this tape. Maybe you've even stolen it—?"

"Oh, I couldn't do that." The voice, when it stopped shouting, was really quite nice. It was the sort of voice that, when it stopped shouting, you felt you could explain things to. Ambrosio said, "No, I'm a cop, I couldn't—I couldn't steal it. I didn't even pay discount price for it. I paid the full three hundred and fifty pesos with the book."

"IF YOU'D STOLEN IT YOU WOULDN'T NEED IT BECAUSE YOU'D ALREADY BE A FIREBALL! IF YOU'VE STOLEN IT—"

Ambrosio said, "No, I did pay for it!"

"IF YOU ONLY BOUGHT THE FIRST TAPE TO SEE IF THE COURSE WAS WORTH IT, GO BACK TO THE SHOP AND BUY THE OTHER FIVE!"

"No, I bought the lot."

The vitna was fifty yards from shore, its striped sail flapping as the sailor turned it into the wind. The vitna sailor called out, "Excuse me—"

"YOU THIEVE FROM ME, FROM PROFESSOR FIRE-BALL, AND YOUR LIFE WILL BE MADE SO MISERA-BLE, SO RUINED THAT—"

"I DIDN'T THIEVE IT!"

"YOU BUM! PAY FOR THE TAPES!"

Ambrosio shrieked, "I DID!"

"Hey—" It was the vitna man. He was pulling down his sail. The guy on the beach looked like an average, good-hearted Manilan. The vitna man said, calling, "Hey, excuse me—"

"I'M A COP! A DETECTIVE! I'VE GOT A JOB ON FROM THE UNITED NATIONS TO PROTECT DWARVES AND MIDGETS! IT'S MY BIG OPPORTU-NITY TO BE NOTICED! I'M ON MY WAY UP!" There were hissing noises on the tape, then silence. Ambrosio screamed, "I'M A FIREBALL!"

In the vitna, twenty yards from shore coming in unstoppably, the vitna man said in a gasp, "Oh, shit—"

"I'M NOT WHAT I SEEM AT ALL!" There were only hissing sounds on the tape.

The vitna man said in an undertone, "Oh, mother of God." He wasn't what he seemed either. He was a gold smuggler. The vitna man, thinking fast, said, "Half! I'll give you half!"

"Hullo?" Ambrosio, tapping at the Walkman hard with the flat of his hand, said, "Hullo, Professor Fireball—are you still there?" The tape had stopped. Ambrosio, hopping up and down, slapping the tape, said, "Hullo? *Hullo!*"

"Sixty percent! Seventy-five!"

He had forgotten to replace the batteries. Ambrosio, slapping hard at first the machine and then his forehead, said in disgust, *"NO!"*

He should have bought an outboard. He was going to buy an outboard with the profits from the gold. If he had had an outboard he could have outboarded away and— The vitna man, also slapping himself hard on the forehead, shrieked, "Take it all then! Take everything I've worked for and after you've taken that you can take all the shells and coral too!" His wife and eight children were going to starve. Probably best. That way they wouldn't have to make the trip to see him in Manila prison once a month and weep their eyes out for him. The vitna man, knocking his head, starting to throw shells overboard, shouted between sobs, "I work like a dog and I just can't get a peso ahead!"

He was a bum. Slapping hard on the cassette player one last time, Ambrosio said coaxingly to the batteries, "Hullo?"

The vitna man said warily, "Hullo . . . ?" He stopped, for the moment, throwing his shells and his life overboard.

Ambrosio said, "AARRG—*GAH!*"

All his life he had missed his opportunities.

No more.

No . . . *MORE!*

Slapping himself over and over on the forehead to keep the thought uppermost in his mind, Ambrosio began running toward his car on Roxas Boulevard to get to a shop to buy new batteries—the expensive, imported ones.

7:44 A.M.

In Manila, it had been light for over an hour and three quarters.

In the bay, the catamaran was gently rocking in the current and a slight wind was coming up from Bataan.

In his chair at the chart table, the Whispering Man sat silently rocking. He had found the name in the electoral roll and passed his message.

He was a shadow. In the main cabin of the boat, with all the curtains drawn, it was still night.

With the current and the wind, the man rocked gently in his chair.

There was only the sound outside of the slight wind in the rigging.

In the darkened boat—in the awful still silence—the Whispering Man made his hands into fists and waited.

PERSONS OF DIMINISHED STATURE.
United Nations Organization.
Human Rights.
Dwarves.

Gnomes.

One of them was wearing a leopard-skin tutu and was carrying a whip.

Bombs. Black ones, round ones, long ones, square ones with clocks and fuses, incendiary ones with thermite and napalm and phosphorus, ones with trembler switches that heard your heartbeat—he had been up half the night reading about them. In the kitchen, sitting in the corner talking to no one, Bontoc said, "Now listen—!"

Bontoc said, "I'm here at the behest and bequest and behoving of the United Nations and the Metro Manila Police and the tolerance and unprejudicial love and sympathy of all the many colors, creeds, and religions of the seven thousand islands of the Republic of the Philippines to help you." They had only picked him because he was short. Bontoc said, "I am here as a representative of all the caring nations of the world to see you diminished-stature people get a square deal." Ambrosio should have been here too. He wasn't. Bontoc nodded. His head hurt. The room was closing in on him. He said, "I wasn't supposed to tell you this, but I come from a long line of ferocious headhunters and I'm here to give you confidence and protect you from life's hard knocks." Bontoc, happy in his little corner of the asylum, said, *"Small Is Beautiful."* His groin still hurt from the cannonball. Bontoc said, "Now, for a little logic and order—"

In the sink where the cannonball was there was a click.

Bontoc said—

And then a fizz.

Bontoc said—

And the smoke and the faint smell of a gunpowder fuse burning fast.

Bontoc said—

And then—

Bontoc screamed, "DUCK!"

There was a blast. It was something in the pipe in the sink. All the force went upward. So did the crockery-loaded cannonball. It missed his groin. It missed his chest. It flew upward, described without great force a little arc, and then, sailing down as he watched, as he stood his ground—setting a good example to the dwarves—hit him between the eyes and poleaxed him to the floor.

Odd. He had that strange dream again.

Lying full length in a doghouse, he dreamed he looked up and saw a circus. . . .

7:55 A.M. exactly. On the catamaran, the Whispering Man, brushing back his hair with his hand in the faint northwesterly wind, locked the washboard cover on his boat and pocketed the key. He had a two-man inflatable Zodiac tender lashed across the starboard hull at the stern of the boat and he picked his way across to it from the cockpit and, untying it, let it gently down into the water and pulled it around by its mooring line to the stern so he could get into it.

Across from him he could see Manila with all the buildings white in the morning sun along Roxas Boulevard. Here and there, there were beautiful old Spanish-style buildings with verandas and carved stonework slowly, one by one, being pulled down and replaced by glass-and-steel skyscrapers. Only the ocean stayed unchanged. The Whispering Man said softly to himself, "Benigno Feliciano, 54 Rio Cocodrilo Street, Manila." He spoke softly. "Emmanuel Ernesto Barrera, 87 General Vega Street, Manila."

It was 7:57 A.M. exactly. He had to go to work.

Getting down into the Zodiac and starting the Johnson twelve-horsepower engine on its stern at the first pull, the Whispering Man turned the boat toward the shore.

Parked by his own private pier a little down from the Manila Yacht Club on the boulevard, there was a gray Volvo 360GLT, his company car.

He looked back once to the catamaran—to the *Goosewing*—to where he lived, and then, his face fixed, opened the throttle of the little engine and steered steadily for the shore.

He wasn't in a circus; he was in a snowstorm.

In slow motion, turning gracefully over and over above his head, flying to pieces as Bontoc watched, a shower of coffee cups, coffee grounds, spoons, saucers, cakes, and assorted total, complete humiliations began falling down from the heavens to envelop him.

2

"The lost continent of Mú. The great sunken area of land that used to run from near India all the way to Australia and Hawaii." The police pathologist, Dr. Watanabe, bending down over Feliciano's body, said, "The Ancient Motherland. That's where all this faith-healing business stems from—the time when men walked with gods and utilized all the areas of the brain for which, these days, science can't find any explanation." Watanabe said, "The Garden of Eden before the Spanish Christians came to these islands and convinced the natives that the Garden of Eden was in a place they'd never heard of: Palestine." He was Japanese-Philippino. Watanabe said, "They did it in Japan too." There was a priest outside with the congregation and the uniformed patrolmen questioning them: Watanabe saw him go by the open door in black like a bat in flowing cassock. Watanabe said, still on his knees, sounding like the narrator in the opening scenes of a science fiction movie, "They say that in the darkness of prehistory there was no division between the mystic states and the reality of each day's living. They say that men looked up at the stars and were part of them. They say—"

Detective Lieutenant Felix Elizalde, bending down over the body of Barrera in the corner, said quietly, "What do you say?" Barrera had taken all the rounds directly in the chest. His chest was gone. All around him were the little brass fired cases from the gun. The gun was a .22 caliber French Gevarm model A7 automatic rifle, cut down to less than fourteen inches overall: the poor man's submachine gun. All you had to do was buy one over the counter, take a hacksaw and chop the barrel and insert a nail in a drilled hole in the receiver where the trigger and sear contacted, and you had something that would spit out bullets at a rate of six hundred rounds a minute. Elizalde said, "Most of these people are fakes."

"Not this one." Watanabe, moving to one side and lifting up one of Feliciano's bloody hands, said, shaking his head, "Not this one." When he moved he exposed what was left of the head after twenty bullets traveling at a thousand feet a second in a cluster had done to flesh and bone. Watanabe said, "No mica in the fingernails to make phony incisions, nothing concealed in the palms of the hands, and—" He wrenched hard at the thumb. "And no false thumb to hide bits and pieces of chicken gut and putty to look like false cancers or obstructions."

Elizalde said, "He pulled teeth."

"And no preblooded phony teeth hidden in the pockets." Watanabe said, "Magellan mentioned this in the sixteenth century. He said the natives could do it. He said—" Watanabe said, "In Hawaii, where some of my family live there are all sorts of legends about the kahunas, the lost tribe of healers. The Philippino faith healers—the esoteric ones who think about it and believe in Mú—say their powers stretch back in a direct line to them," Watanabe said. "How to pull teeth by astral means: Simple, merely concentrate the bioenergy in the healer's body to his fingertips, take hold of the tooth, dematerialize it while keeping the gum in the real world, gently draw it out on the astral plane, and then materialize it again and it's in your hand. No pain, no blood, no trauma—merely a hymn to whatever god you pray to in your *oración,* your sacred song, and it's done." The head was nothing but pulp and blood. Watanabe, tapping the dead wrist hard with the palm of his hand, said, with mounting excitement, "Felix, I think this guy may have been for real!"

"The woman he was working on when he was killed was still bleeding like a stuck pig when they put her into the ambulance!"

"He was disturbed in his work. Something happened. He saw something or he lost concentration or he—" Watanabe said with sudden vehemence, "You're a mestizo—Philippine-Spanish-American—you've picked up the worst bits of everything! What I'm talking about here is the purity of folk memories that could stretch back as far as—"

Elizalde said quietly, "All right." He was not interested. What he was interested in was what the dead fruit vendor carried in his pockets. He carried nothing. Elizalde, turning the man over a little on his side to get at the hip pocket—and finding nothing—said, "Whatever you say."

"I wish I'd had a chance to talk to him while he was alive." Watanabe, standing up, said tightly, "Felix, if all this is true—if there really are people who can do these sorts of things—" Watanabe said angrily, "It's the goddamned church! They claim to believe in miracles, they say God's power works, but because these people don't say the Garden of Eden was thousands of miles away in a place they've never heard of before the missionaries came to burn and garrote and convert them, the goddamned church says it's all a trick and if it isn't good believers should stay well away! Those people outside, these two in here—they're the poor, the unlettered—they haven't been told they shouldn't do things that are miracles because nobody has ever thought they were worth bothering about! Nobody ever thought—"

Elizalde said quietly, "I'm a policeman, not a—"

"You fool!" Watanabe, reaching down and taking the dead faith healer's hand and holding it up for him to see, said, "Look! Look at his hand! There's nothing hidden! Look at this room! Tell me where all the hidden gadgets and special effects are! Tell me how, day after day, he pulled teeth and healed—not the rich tourists, but the *poor*—and got away with it if he wasn't for real!"

"All I'm interested in is that—"

"My mother is dying of cancer! I can't do a thing for her!" Watanabe, shouting, rounding on him, yelled to the dead faith healer, to the man who had killed him, to the blood everywhere, to God's eye, to the awful pointless extinction of it, "Maybe—maybe—" Watanabe said, "This character—this man—this doctor—maybe he was for real! Maybe he could have done something for her!" He was the police pathologist. He dealt in death. Lately, with his mother, all he had dealt in was hope.

Watanabe said, "It isn't fair, Felix." All it was was a tawdry, usual, sordid little murder-suicide. It wasn't fair.

"I'm sorry."

"It isn't right."

Elizalde, coming across to the man, said softly, "If there's anything—"

Watanabe said, "Bring him back to life. Between us, with everything we know—between us: the educated, the betters, the rich—compared to him—the illiterate, surely to God . . ."

Watanabe said, "We know more than he did with all our degrees and learning and culture. Look at his clothes: he was just scum, a nothing, a peasant, the sort of target the old samurai used to use to test the edges of their swords on—" Watanabe said, "Surely to God, between us, we could do such a little thing as bring him back to life again!"

All night long as he listened in her bedroom, saturated with morphine, his mother screamed with the pain.

Watanabe said, "Us! It's a joke! Between us, *we can't even pull teeth!*"

He reached the private pier. Tying off the Zodiac to a bronze cleat, the Whispering Man undid the two retaining screws on his outboard motor and lifted it up and got out of the boat with it by the pier steps.

He was in good time for work. His suit was in a cupboard, together with clean shirts and underwear and a selection of ties, and he could change there.

Reaching into his pocket for his keys, still carrying the outboard, he went toward his car and unlocked the trunk to put the engine in.

All the way over in the Zodiac, he had been talking to himself, quoting something, or remembering something. Now, he was silent.

Securing the motor carefully to make sure it would not leak on the towel especially laid down in the trunk for it to rest on, the Whispering Man shut the trunk with a bang.

He got into his car and started the engine.

In the street outside the faith healer's house, the uniformed patrolmen were still interviewing the congregation one by one and writing down what they said in their notebooks. There was a black-cassocked priest with them, listening to what they said and nodding encouragement to the man being interviewed or to one of the patrolmen. He had administered extreme unction to Feliciano and done what he could for the soul of the suicide and now he waited to see if he was wanted further. To the *barangay* captain, the neighborhood committee leader, watching the scene from a little way back, the priest seemed to have nothing to do. The woman journalist and the cameraman also waited. They talked in whispers. They seemed to be arguing. The priest glanced at them for a moment, caught a quick glance from the woman that the conversation was private, and went back to nodding and listening with the patrolman and the congregation.

The barangay captain wore a Dunkin' Donuts baseball cap. The man interviewing him had an identification card clipped to his top pocket that said, Elizalde, Felix, Detective Lieutenant, Western District, Metro Manila Police. He wore an expensive safari suit and soft leather shoes. The barangay captain—not a member of the congregation—had only who he was in the neighborhood. The jacket of the safari suit blew back a little in a slight wind coming up from the bay and what the man with the identification had under there was a holstered Walther PPK .380 automatic pistol. He looked, not Philippino, but Spanish. The name said he was from one of the old colonial families. The clothes said the family was probably rich. The barangay captain wore only tennis shoes with his open-neck shirt and slacks. By trade, he was a ticket clerk with the railways. Presently, he was unemployed. He watched, not Elizalde, but his people with the two uniformed patrolmen. Secretly, he was a Communist. One day, he was going to have his place. The man Elizalde, unlike the two patrolmen, was not writing things down. He was educated. He remembered what people told him.

The barangay captain said, "They applauded—probably because they were grateful to be alive." He did not look at the man. He saw some of the congregation, some of his people, watching what he said. "Philippinos, when they're nervous, giggle." He raised his voice a little. "When they're afraid, they laugh. When they—" He felt the man put his hand gently on his shoulder and turn him back again to face him. "When— when someone has made a big, dramatic gesture, they applaud!" The barangay captain said, "Barrera wasn't one of ours. He wasn't from around here. He was just someone who walked in off the streets into people's lives. He was a television character, not known, so therefore not real—he put on a big show— people applauded. Maybe they were praying. Maybe they applauded the tooth coming out." The barangay captain looked at the priest. "Maybe they applauded God." He looked at the man's hands. They were soft. The barangay captain said, "Barrera wasn't from this barangay! He was from General Vega Street!"

"Feliciano was from Rio Cocodrilo Street."

"Feliciano only lived here. He was a taxi driver. He did´his work in Ohio Avenue in Tondo. He only lived here. He was in a private welfare program his company had. He had nothing to do with the barangay."

"He worked his miracles here."

"They were free." The barangay captain said, "Why are you asking me these questions?"

"I'm asking you these questions because he was murdered."

"And the man who murdered him is dead." The barangay captain said, "OK. The end. It makes a break in the monotony of life, but—"

"He was murdered in front of eighteen people!"

"He wasn't from here. He didn't have his roots here and the man who murdered him didn't have his roots here." The barangay captain said, "Television. The poor like us watch television a lot. We see lots of people murdered. They aren't people like us. Barrera wasn't one of us—and neither was Feliciano. They weren't from around here." The barangay captain said loudly, "We care for our own, nobody else's." He said tightly, nodding to the congregation, "These people are the poor. The poor aren't like you. The poor have enough to worry about staying alive!"

"You know nothing about either Feliciano or Barrera?"

The barangay captain said, "No."

"Why were there eighteen men in the congregation?"

The barangay captain said, "Because there weren't eighteen women."

"Not one of them, in all the time I've been watching them, has put his hand to his mouth." Elizalde said, "The Gallardo woman, was she the only person in the entire barangay with an aching tooth?"

The barangay captain said, "It isn't against the law to watch a faith healer pull out a tooth." The barangay captain said, "Mrs. Gallardo has had too many children on the advice of the church: her teeth always have to be pulled out." His face was going hard, "It breaks her monotony too."

"Is that why she was there?"

"Of course it was why she was there!"

He knew. He knew something. He kept glancing at the congregation so they could see what he was saying. Elizalde asked quietly, "Was she supposed to be there or did she just come in off the street and—"

"You're a cop! You're the authorities! You run the place! You get a team in with guns and riot sticks and force everyone's mouth open to see if they've got bad teeth and then you can find out!" The barangay captain, shaking his head, said in a hiss, "Everyone around here has got bad teeth!"

"I'm asking you!"

"And I've told you!" The barangay captain said, "I've told you what my people told me. I've told you what they told me happened! I've—"

"Why did Barrera want his name and face recorded?"

The barangay captain said, *"Because he was a human being!* Because he was—" He looked at the man. It was more than clothes. It was more than money. He had thought when the revolution came that maybe—no, they would all have to be swept away. The barangay captain said, shouting, "Because he was about to die! Because maybe he didn't want to go into the ground as just another nobody in the world! Because— What did you think the poor want from you? Your money? Your clothes? They want your dignity! He wanted his face known because—"

"Did he and Feliciano know each other?"

"No, they didn't know each other!"

"How do you know that?"

"Because they—" The barangay captain said, "Because they—" The barangay captain said suddenly loudly, "Rey Juan Gutierrez, barangay captain, Rio Cocodrilo Street—that's me! Rey Juan Gutierrez, barangay captain, Rio Cocodrilo Street!" He said it facing them so the congregation and the two patrolmen could hear. The barangay captain, holding the priest's eyes for a moment, called out, "OK, Father, did you hear that?" He saw the priest look confused and, smiling, patronizing, humoring him, nod.

The barangay captain, turning back to Elizalde, smiling thinly in triumph, said to end the conversation, "Now try and do something to me. People know who I am!" He said with real, undisguised, naked vehemence, his eyes blazing, *"Cop!"*

"Our Father, Who art in Heaven—"
They were not listening. The police had finished with them and they could go home and they were not listening and they— the eighteen members of the congregation and the barangay captain—began to drift away.

"*Hail Mary full of grace—*" The priest, all the time the police had been talking to them, had stood in the midst of them. Now, he was alone in the street.

"*Hail Mary, full of grace—*"

They went. They went slowly down the street without looking back, without speaking to each other and he was only leading the two patrolmen in prayer. The two patrolmen were fidgeting. They wanted to get on.

"*Hail Mary full of grace, the Lord is with Thee. Blessed art Thou amongst women.*" The priest said to the two patrolmen as the congregation turned the corner of the street and were gone, "Are you very busy these days, boys?"

The bigger patrolman, the one with an ivory-handled butt to his huge holstered revolver, said, "Yes, Father."

"Do you want a blessing?"

"Thank you." The patrolman touched at his gun. He waited.

The priest had been in the parish only two months. No one ever called for him.

The priest, trying to smile, wiping his hands on his cassock, said, "God be with you."

He looked around for something else to do.

There was nothing.

The priest said, "God be with you."

He went toward the faith-healing house to find Dr. Watanabe, the police pathologist.

He thought, in his job, dealing always with the dead, he might appreciate a little religious comfort.

They were the Wildlife Unit. It was on a sticker on the camera and on the woman journalist's notebook above a cartoon of a hippopotamus wearing a white coat and smoking a pipe.

It was a children's program. It went out on the air as *Dr. and Mrs. Hippo's Forest of Enchantment* at 4:00 P.M. weekdays after school.

They had come on an anonymous tip to film a rare Giant Scops owl reported hurt and recovering on a roof opposite 54

Rio Cocodrilo Street, Manila. The tipster had said the owl was best seen an hour and a half after dawn when it tried to hide under the roof from the strong light.

Otus gurneyi: that was its Latin name. It was an owl about twelve inches long that usually lives only on the island of Mindanao and had never before been reported in Manila.

There was no owl.

The cameraman, his voice almost a whisper, said, "I'm sorry." He and the woman journalist had finished arguing and, standing together, did not look at each other.

There was no film.

The camerman said, "I'm sorry." He did not look at Elizalde.

The cameraman, gripping his camera in both hands and trying to squeeze it small, said brokenly, "I'm *sorry!*"

The woman said nothing. She was on her way up.

The cameraman said, "It was the noise from the camera—it was—if I turned it on I thought he might—"

The cameraman said again, "I'm sorry."

He had been frightened.

He turned to the woman and saw her face.

The cameraman, begging, pleading, yelled at the top of his voice, "For God's sake, *please!* Tell them the camera was broken!"

There was only, in the street, the sound of the rising wind on the roofs where he had thought there had been a beautiful, free, wounded owl. There was no owl.

The cameraman, his hands shaking on the camera, said to the woman with ice in her soul and her own ambitions, "Please! *Please!* IS IT SO MUCH TO ASK?"

The name in the electoral roll had been E. R. Beo, with an address in Cavite Street. In his office the Whispering Man tapped out a number on his phone and listened as it rang.

His office, on the third floor, overlooked the bay through an armorglass picture window. As the number rang, he watched his boat swinging gently at her mooring.

He counted the rings. Ten-eleven-twelve, and then hung up.

Goosewing: that was his boat's name. It was what a sailboat did when, with the wind coming from behind, you set the mainsail to one side and the headsail to the other and let them fill.

It was how, unable to sail into the wind with their square rigs, the old sailors had traversed the world. Now, with sail design all different, it was possible to sail almost directly into that wind: in effect, according to the old, the ancient sailors condemned to follow forever the tradewinds, to go backward.

The Whispering Man touched at the automatic last-number-redial button on the phone.

He listened.

He watched his boat.

At night, now, he no longer dreamed. On the boat where he lived he had only—if he slept at all—silent, numbing, dead blackness.

He was a man in his late thirties with a German surname.

His mind, all the time, through the ringing, was full of silence.

8:45 A.M.

In Rio Cocodrilo Street, Manila, there was only silence.

There were only now—the *authorities.*

There was Scientific to come and Ballistics and Photographic and Fingerprints.

There were coffins to be brought.

There were no answers at all.

In Rio Cocodrilo Street, Elizalde, in his expensive suit and shoes, his pistol and his badge under his coat or on it, waited for them to come.

3

"Where did he get the gun?" In the Orchid Gardens in Rizal Park, Elizalde, sitting next to Mrs. Barrera on a bench a little way into the gardens and their profusion of purple-and-white, mauve, pink-and-cream orchids, asked, "Had he had it a long time?" In General Vega Street the Barreras' room had been open. It was a single room with little furniture and, at the bottom of the plywood cupboard in the place, a square of oily sackcloth. The sackcloth had held the gun. Elizalde said to explain, "Your neighbors told me you and your husband used to come here before you were married." She was a tired-looking woman in her late forties with calloused, hard hands. Over her faded, flowered dress she wore an apron. She carried no handbag. By her on the seat, there was only a small, brown, paper-wrapped parcel of what looked like clothing. Elizalde said gently, "Who brought you the news?"

"A priest." Her hair was gray and no longer soft. Mrs. Barrera, looking straight ahead, said, "He was a young priest. He was from another barrio—where it happened. I didn't know him." Mrs. Barrera said, maybe referring to the gun, "I don't know." Mrs. Barrera said, "My husband killed someone. My husband is dead. The priest said—"

"Where did he get the gun?"

"I don't know." She was not crying: her eyes were dry and steady. They merely looked hard at the orchids.

"Did he buy it? Did he meet anyone and buy it?"

Mrs. Barrera said, "Manila is full of guns."

"It was a submachine gun." Elizalde said, "It was oiled, well looked after. Did he—"

Mrs. Barrera said, "I don't know."

"You must have seen him with it in your room!"

Mrs. Barrera said, "No."

"Did you know the faith healer Feliciano?"

Mrs. Barrera shook her head. It was question-and-answer time. If he asked a question, she answered it. She was not grieving. She merely looked straight ahead and from time to time leaned a little to one side as if to touch the parcel in readiness. In readiness for what? Elizalde said, "Your husband is dead, do you understand that?"

"Yes."

"Your neighbor said you had been married for over twenty years."

She blinked. In front of her, the orchids were of such breathtaking fragile beauty it was hard to believe they had no scent. They had none. They merely were. They were merely spots and explosions of color in the world. Without a scent, they merely hung from the trees or grew in rocks or in pots in the place like paintings. They did not seem real. Elizalde said, *"Don't you care?"*

There were no tears. Mrs. Barrera said, "Are you writing this down, Po?" It was an expression of respect. It meant "sir." It meant more. It meant he was not like her. She touched at her parcel. Mrs. Barrera said, "It doesn't matter. No one will read it and say what a good woman or a bad woman I was. I have no one. Anyone who reads what you write down will be a stranger."

"Do you have children?"

Mrs. Barrera said tightly, "No."

"Your neighbor said—"

Mrs. Barrera said, "This morning I awoke and my husband was gone. We had not worked at our business for a long time." She was reciting it for some sort of record. Mrs. Barrera said, "I woke up at dawn. I thought for a moment we still worked at our business, but we haven't worked at our business for some time and I—"

"Where was your stall?"

"Once, here." Mrs. Barrera said, "Then General Vega Street, then, for a year, in the Pistang Pilippino Markets in Ermita—" There was a movement on her face, a twisting. She looked down at the parcel. Mrs. Barrera said, "I have no tears left. The people who will read about me—"

Elizalde said, "No one will read about you—"

"Will be strangers, like him."

"Like your husband?"

"Yes, Po." Mrs. Barrera, her mouth starting to tremble, said tightly, "What I know, you know."

"I don't know anything!"

"What I know, you know!" She moved her head quickly and looked at the orchids. Mrs. Barrera said for the record someone would read, "We were two people. We didn't talk. We were two people. Once we were one person, but that was before—" Mrs. Barrera said, "Before—"

"Before what?"

"—before, when we were one person and we—" Mrs. Barrera said, no longer talking to Elizalde, "Before we—" Mrs. Barrera said suddenly, "Do you have a family, Po?"

"Yes."

She had never spoken to anyone like him in her life before. He had seen her dead husband, perhaps touched him, felt through his pockets. He had been in their room and opened cupboards and doors in it. Mrs. Barrera asked, "Do the rich believe in love?"

"I'm not rich."

"Do they love each other?"

Elizalde said, "Some of them. Yes."

She bit at her lip. Mrs. Barrera, swallowing, said, "How?"

"What do you mean?"

"If they haven't any dreams?"

"The rich have dreams."

"The rich have everything! The rich—" Mrs. Barrera said, suddenly smiling, "When we were young we used to plan and dream about success and being prosperous and—" Mrs. Barrera said, "I've seen it on television: the rich talk to each other across tables about their lives, but they don't huddle together. They—"

"When you and your husband were young, did you have dreams?"

"Yes." She looked down at her hands. They were empty.

"What did you dream of?"

"I don't know." Mrs. Barrera said, "When we were young, we thought we had dreams, but then—now—" Mrs. Barrera said, "They were dreams. They were—" Mrs. Barrera said, "We were together. We only thought they were dreams. We loved each other." Mrs. Barrera said, "Every morning when I woke up at dawn I thought we still had our business, but we didn't. We had nowhere to go together anymore."

"Did you know he had the gun?"

"No." Mrs. Barrera said, "There was nowhere to go in the mornings, nowhere at all." Mrs. Barrera said, "The rich are safe."

"From what?"

"From—" Mrs. Barrera said, "It doesn't matter about the poor. All the poor have is each other. The rich have so many other things. The rich talk and discuss things and have big plans, but the poor—" She turned for the first time to look at him. He was Spanish-Philippino, educated in America or somewhere beyond comprehension. Mrs. Barrera said angrily, "Why are you doing this? What I know, you know!" Mrs. Barrera said, "In our room, where once there was one single person with dreams, there were two people! We no longer talked! We woke up in our bed—two people—and we had that moment at dawn when—but it was two people—" Mrs. Barrera said, "I have no tears left! My husband had no tears left! Once, we—" Mrs. Barrera said, "Po, please, all I want is to sit here for just a little longer and then—" Her eyes, for the first time, were glistening with tears. Mrs. Barrera, pleading, said, "Please, Po, just another five minutes—"

"I don't know what you mean."

"*Roberto Ernesto Barrera!*" Mrs. Barrera, shaking, her hands clenched into fists, said at the top of her voice, "Roberto Ernesto Barrera—that was the name of our son! *He was fifteen years old!* He was fifteen years old! He was our only child!" She was on her feet, shouting, "He's gone, vanished!" There were people in Rizal Park on the other side of the fence that protected the orchid gardens. Mrs. Barrera, shouting as if any moment she would be silenced, yelled to them, "Barrera, Roberto Ernesto, aged fifteen! He's gone, vanished!" Mrs. Barrera said, "*Taken!*" She saw Elizalde stand up and reach for the parcel and feel it. It contained her night clothes. She saw him put it back down again. Mrs. Barrera said in a panic, "Oh, no!" Mrs. Barrera said, "Oh, no, no, no!"

People on the other side of the fence had stopped to watch. Mrs. Barrera said, "I have no one anymore! They took my son!" Mrs. Barrera, rounding on him, shrieked, "The rich don't have feelings! They don't care! My son is gone! All our dreams and—" Mrs. Barrera said, seeing Elizalde coming toward her, "Oh, no, *no!*" The orchid gardens had been where all the dreams were made. Then, outside the gardens there had been a world to go to. For the last six months since her son had gone she had not even looked into her husband's cupboard. Mrs. Barrera said, "We were no longer one person! We were two people living together with separate grief! In the mornings, at dawn, I didn't even know anymore what my husband—"

The parcel of clothes was for prison. She saw him put the parcel back on the seat and come for her. She had nowhere to go. "Roberto Ernesto Barrera, aged fifteen!" She saw him coming for her with his hand out. Mrs. Barrera, shaking, clenching and unclenching her fists, said, "No! No! *No!*"

Mrs. Barrera said, begging, "Oh, please, oh, please, please, before you kill me, please—*someone*—*tell me what happened to him!*"

He didn't hold a grudge. The Bontocs were classified as Igorots. Together with the other minority tribes of the Philippines, the Ifugaos, the Kalingas, and the rest, they were mountain dwellers and, as everybody knew, the gnarled nut-brown mountain-province tribes did not hold grudges.

Well, the Ifugaos didn't anyway. They were social, civilized souls who lived close to nature and built rice terraces and were deep into tourism. And the Kalingas, well, if you offended them you were on the slate for a few water buffalo to be delivered up with a good, long-winded apology.

Bontoc, unsurprisingly, was a Bontoc. He had been educated by the missionaries and in America and transferred to the Metro Manila Police and—lately, today—been tapped by the United Nations as a person of substance. He didn't hold a grudge, he was a Bontoc.

The Bontocs, for a thousand years back, being headhunters, merely shortened you at the neck.

They didn't hold grudges. They held executions.

In the elevated kitchen, still cleaning up the mess from the bomb, Bontoc said softly to himself, "Hmm . . . raaa . . ."

"Detective Sergeant Jesus-Vincente Ambrosio, Metro Manila Police, on special duty to the United Nations!" He was standing at the open side door of the Gnome Home, declaiming, waiting for a gasp of admiration.

Bontoc said in a mutter, "Haaaa . . . !"

He had earphones stuck on his head. He was listening to a music tape.

Bontoc said, "Herrrrr . . ."

Ambrosio said, "Hullo? Baptiste?" He saw Bontoc's face high up in some sort of raised serving hatch. Ambrosio said, smiling, confident, ready, "A good general knows how to take orders from the man on the spot!" He smiled a winning smile. Ambrosio asked, "Well? Where do you want me?"

It was 10:03 A.M.

In the deserted and darkened Gnome Home, Ambrosio, snapping his fingers for the funny little fellow to make up his mind, said, "Come on, now, be decisive, decide what you want to do with me!"

He waited.

He touched at his neck. (For some reason it seemed to have a twinge in it.) Ambrosio, wondering where all the dwarves were, said, "Well? Time is money. Make up your mind." He sniffed.

Moving a little deeper toward the ring, seeing what he thought briefly in the dimness was the outline of a dragon—no, it couldn't have been—Ambrosio asked, "What's that funny smell?"

He couldn't see a single thing.

Ambrosio, primed, ready, no longer the twig of every breeze that blew in life's hard forest, demanded in his best Fireball voice, "Where are the minions?" He couldn't see a single thing.

Ambrosio, sniffing hard, losing confidence, said in a perplexed voice, "Baptiste, why is everyone in here hiding?"

E. R. Beo.

In his office overlooking the bay, the Whispering Man opened his desk drawer and took out something wrapped in linen and laid it on his desk.

He did not open it: he knew what it was. It was a child's rag doll with a noose around its neck. It was his.

E. R. Beo.

The Whispering Man, looking out his window at his boat swinging gently at the midmorning tide change, said softly to himself, "E. R. Beo."

His phone rang and he put the linen-wrapped parcel back in his drawer and picked up the receiver.

He had an outside line, not an extension, so he had no need to identify himself.

The Whispering Man said softly, efficiently, "Yes?"

"BE POSITIVE!"

He was positive. Ambrosio said, "Hullo . . . ?" He smelled that smell.

"AND TRUST IN YOUR OWN JUDGMENT!"

It smelled like a gunpowder fuse burning. No, it couldn't be. Could it?

"BE POSITIVE, RESOLUTE!"

He was positive, resolute. It positively, resolutely didn't smell like a gunpowder fuse burning.

"AND TAKE COMMAND!"

He took command. Ambrosio demanded, "What's that smell?"

"AND, HAVING RESOLVED, SEIZE THE MOMENT, THE DEVIL TAKE THE HINDMOST—AND—AND—"

Where were the dwarves? It was a gunpowder fuse. He heard it hiss.

"AND—AND—"

Ambrosio said, "Oh, *NO!*"

It was a dragon. It was a gunpowder fuse. It was a—

"FIREBALL!"

Wrong. Concussive. The dragon, going up in a sudden roar of ears, eyes, forked tail, and approximately nine hundred thousand two separate pieces of green-painted papier-mâché in the center of the ring, turned the air around him into a solid iron mallet and threw him bodily back out the door through whence he had come with nary a single spark.

"Fireball . . ."

Somebody, when they had made the bomb, had gone easy on the potassium nitrate and held the sulfur. Even the teeth, as they floated down, did not burn.

"Fireball . . ."

Bontocs didn't hold grudges.

He shouldn't have.

He did.

Bontoc, squirmed down in a mass of dwarves on the kitchen floor, watching the teeth, said softly, grudgingly, "Heh."

Bontoc said, "Hee, hee, hee." His groin still hurt from the cannonball.

Bontoc, getting up to see if Ambrosio was all right, said, *"Ouch!"*

On the steps of the Santo Seng Kong Church on Morga Street near Chinatown, Elizalde said, "They applauded. After he'd emptied a magazine of twenty rounds straight into Feliciano's face and then reloaded his gun and blown his heart and lungs out, the congregation applauded." The Santo Seng Kong Church was a pagoda-like building with its ground floor built as a rotunda. It was no recognized church: it was the church of twenty-five major and minor religions of the world inspired, according to the Chinese geomancer who had ordered it built, by a spirit guide from Saturn. It was full of worshipers. They spilled out onto the streets praying to their gods, to Christ, to Buddha, to their ancestors, to secret gods, and gods long thought dead. Against the far wall of the rotunda inside there were, in one corner alone, over two hundred little, various statues of Buddha. And everywhere, there was the smell of incense. Elizalde said to the brown-robed man on the steps beside him, "I don't understand."

Once, before he had become a famous *medium evangelista*— a preaching medium—Molina had been a fisherman in the waters around Mindanao. Now he was Mang Apo Eleuterio: Dr. Father Eleuterio. Seventy years old, his hands still carried the callouses and strength of his first trade. His voice was almost gone: he spoke in a whisper. Mang Eleuterio, waiting as he always waited each day outside the Many Religions Church to give guidance if asked, said, nodding, "Yes."

"Yes . . . what?" The long brown robe—the cassock—was dusty and grimed. When people came to seek advice they sat down together with their mentor on the steps and spoke softly. Elizalde looked at the top step. It was dusty, heavy with grime. He was wearing light-colored clothes, slacks and a safari jacket. Elizalde said, "Did you know Feliciano?"

"I knew of him. He was an *operador*—a surgeon." He was speaking Tagalog with a heavy Mindanao accent. Mang Eleuterio said, "And a taxi driver." He glanced also behind him to the step. Mang Eleuterio said, "A dentist. All my teeth are gone and I never take taxis." Mang Eleuterio said, "He was what he seemed. He had the gift. If he had not been what he seemed God would not have given him the gift."

"And Barrera, the man who killed him?"

"I didn't know him."

"His widow says their son has disappeared."

"I know nothing about that at all. She did not consult me." Inside the church there was the sound of a mantra and then, as a group of Chinese housewives sought out their futures, the clatter of I Ching sticks on the cement floor. Somewhere inside there was the sound of a Catholic catechism at the shrine of the Santo Niño—the Holy Child. Mang Eleuterio said, "I know you, Mr. Lieutenant Felix Elizalde. I know that there is a division between rich and poor—between you and them—that you will never bridge however hard you may want to try. I know you believe in God and you think that—" Mang Eleuterio, shaking his head and looking back into the church, said abruptly, "God does not even bridge it. God merely allocates a place for the poor in heaven they will not have to share with people like you—or what they believe people like you are." He silenced Elizalde with his raised hand. "And the rich believe the same. They do not believe they will have to spend eternity trying to fathom the spirits of the people who, all their lives, they have assiduously avoided—no." He looked down at the step. Mang Eleuterio said, "I know you are a good man. You don't have to prove to me you are any better than you should be. I know your clothes are clean. I know, out of respect, you want to sit on the step and I know you have other people to see—" He saw Elizalde smile. Mang Eleuterio said, "Feliciano wanted to be a famous faith healer. That was what he wanted. He wanted to be rich and prosperous. What he was—what he did day after day—was use his gift without payment. He had the gift. God gave it to him. The rest of what he was or hoped for was only the weakness of his human nature—and God gave him that also. The other man, Barrera, I did not know at all."

"His widow thought I was going to have her killed."

"She thinks you have the power." Mang Eleuterio said before Elizalde could protest, "The educated, the rich, the authorities, she knows nothing about you at all—"

"That's ridiculous!"

"Do you know anything about the poor? When—if you do— you walk down a darkened back street in the slums and you are met by men with tattoos and set faces, do you know what they are going to do?"

"You are talking about criminals!"

"And you deal with them every day. Can you predict their behavior?"

"The laws in this country are codified. Anyone who wishes to know their rights—"

Mang Eleuterio said, "For a start, needs to be able to read." Mang Eleuterio said, "You expect the poor to attack you for no reason. The poor expect the same from the rich. The poor, like you, expect, fear being violently attacked for no reason." Mang Eleuterio said, sighing, as if he had suddenly become bored with the conversation, "What does it matter? They were two people of no importance. One killed the other and then himself. It's over. You must have other things to do. It's finished."

Elizalde said tightly, "They were two human beings."

"And you're curious?"

"The laws are codified. Whether they can read or not, they are codified and part of the code is that—"

Mang Eleuterio said, "Are you rich, Mr. Elizalde?"

"*No!*"

"Do you know anything about the poor at all?"

His voice was tight. Elizalde glanced down at the grimy step. The man was right. There was no purpose to gestures. Elizalde said, "I'm asking you."

There were people coming and going through the front door of the church. For a while, Mang Eleuterio watched them. Many of them nodded or bent their necks to acknowledge him. He was an old man in a grimy brown robe ready to give guidance and advice. Mang Eleuterio, turning back to him, asked suddenly, "Mr. Policeman, are you well educated?"

Elizalde said hesitantly, "Yes. I suppose so."

"Are you, yes or no?"

"Yes."

"And traveled?" Mang Eleuterio said, "I hear in your voice, as well as an accent that tells me you have studied in America, just the faintest trace of the sound of the old Spanish conquerors." Mang Eleuterio said, "And you are taller than me and your face is fine featured and you have strong, but at the same time, soft hands like a woman's." Mang Eleuterio said directly, "Mr. Elizalde, do you believe I can look into your soul and see what is there?"

He had not expected it. Elizalde said, "Yes."

"Do you?"

It was not the time for gestures. Elizalde said, "Yes."

"If I can—"

Elizalde asked softly, "Can you?" He had never understood faith healing. He understood it now. Elizalde said, "Yes, I believe you can."

Mang Eleuterio said, smiling, "And here you are on the steps of this church erected by a madman on the orders of a madman's spirit guide from—from where? Venus? Saturn? Traveled, educated, well dressed and—" Mang Eleuterio said, "I can look into souls. I see yours." Mang Eleuterio said quietly, "Felix, isn't it?"

"Yes."

He smiled.

Mang Eleuterio said quietly, in Spanish—God alone knew where he had learned it—so the people passing by would not understand him, "I know nothing more than I've told you about either Feliciano or Barrera or what happened, but I do know this—I know it to be true—"

Elizalde waited.

"All the barangays, all the barrios, all the neighborhoods and streets of the poor—" He paused, looking around.

Mang Eleuterio said, "I know for a fact that, now, today, this moment, I know they are all arming themselves."

He shrugged. He looked away. At the entrance of the Santo Seng Kong Church, nodding in acknowledgment to his people, Mang Apo Eleuterio Molina, ex-fisherman, looked down at the step.

Bontoc said, "You're late."

"Oh." Was he? He seemed to have got there just in time. Ambrosio, looking up and seeing dwarves, said, "Oh." He said to the dwarves, "Good morning." There were lots of them. They were little. Ambrosio said, "Oh." He looked hard at Bontoc looking down at him. "TAKE POWER! TAKE POWER! *TAKE POWER!*"

He hurt all over.

He looked up at Bontoc.

He looked up at the dwarves.

He saw the look in Bontoc's eyes. He saw Bontoc look significantly at his watch.

He saw—he knew he saw; he thought he saw—Bontoc smile. "AND DESTROY UTTERLY ALL YOUR ENEMIES!"

He hurt all over. Ambrosio, gazing up at the dwarves, said, "They—"

The United Nations—he missed all his opportunities.

"They—" Ambrosio said, with the earphones still on his ears, shouting at the top of his voice over Fireball driveling on about something to do with peer groups and interpersonal interface and screwing the shit out of everybody who even crossed your path while you were putting the trash out, "They—The United Nations—they—THEY ONLY PICKED HIM BECAUSE HE WAS SHORT!"

E. R. Beo. Ermalinda Rosaria Beo. Aged twenty-two. Food packer. Unmarried with no expectations. Not even pretty.

She was nobody.

She had walked a long way.

On Aduana Street, near the ruins of Fort Santiago on the river, she paused to catch her breath. In her left hand she carried a rattan basket, closed at the top with little tinplate clips disguised as colored linen flowers. Some of the flowers had frayed and, as she looked down at them, she saw the cheap metal showing through.

She was nobody.

She had no tears left, not for herself or for anyone.

She was Scream-face. She felt her body tremble.

It was time. It was after 10:30 A.M. on the clock on the Central Treasury building at the end of the street.

She saw the metal show through where the flowers had faded.

She began walking north.

"Mang Eleuterio—"

Mang Eleuterio said, "It's all I know." It was all he could say. Everywhere, on the steps and in the streets and probably inside the church itself, there were people waiting for him.

"Against what? They're arming themselves—against what?"

"I don't know." He had read Elizalde's soul. Mang Eleuterio said, shaking his head, "Truthfully, I don't know."

In the orchid gardens she had thought he was going to have her taken away and killed.

"Felix—" He tested the name. Once, he had been a fisherman. He knew about being infinitely patient. He looked down at the grimy steps where people sat with him and smiled.

It was a smile of intimacy, but the audience was over.

Still smiling, beginning to pray as he went, his eyes half-closed, Mang Eleuterio, his head bowed, went into the open door of the church rotunda and was gone.

In the church, all the time, without pausing, you could hear the faithful praying to their gods.

4

*O*nce, surrounding the walled city of Intramuros along the river there had been a moat. Like the walled city with its churches and chapels, hospitals, houses, forts, and its own printing press and university, the moat had been built by the Spanish conquerors of the Philippines under Conquistador Miguel Lopez de Legazpi in 1571. The moat, over thirty-feet wide and twenty-two-feet deep, mined with hidden obstacles, drowning nets, slashing wires, and spear-pointed tiger traps, had been the only one of its kind in Asia dating from the era of the great Spanish voyages, the Armada, and the reign of Philip the Second.

Behind the moat, inside the three-mile-long walls, there had been seven gates and sixty-four city blocks laid out in the shape of an uneven pentagon representing some numerological talisman for the Castilians who lived there. Indios were permitted to live only outside the walls. The numerological equation, read in conjunction with the Gods of the Inquisition, was designed to keep the Spanish safe in their beds at night.

During the war, the Japanese bombed much of Intramuros, but missed the moat.

After the war, the U.S. occupying forces did not, and sent in the engineers to fill it in as a health hazard.

After the U.S. occupying forces left, as the Spanish had left, and as the Japanese had left, the Indios—the Philippinos— turned the filled-in moat into a nine-hole golf course.

Outside the main western gate, by the first hole of the golf course, there was a *calesa* waiting for tourists and gathering manure. Built as a nineteenth-century-style, single-passenger, horse-drawn carriage with a folding leather tonneau cover, the calesa had a canvas sheet strapped from its axle out under the driver's high box seat directly under the horse's rear. The sheet was for the horse shit, good for gardens. The horse, with nothing else to do, no fares to clop through the streets of Manila, was crapping now. The driver of the calesa, a bored-looking man in his thirties wearing a San Miguel beer baseball cap and striped T-shirt, listened to the sound. He watched a girl carrying a rattan bag walking toward the gate.

He yawned. He looked—a sure indication of whether she was a fare or not—at her shoes. The shoes were flat, old, and, like the bag, frayed. She wore black slacks and a washed-too-many-times blouse.

She was nothing, a nobody.

Listening to his horse making money for him as it passed good, rich sellable fertilizer, the calesa man closed his eyes and dreamed of being a rich Castilian Spaniard in the sixteenth century.

Intramuros: he loved the place.

At the edges of the golf course where he always parked at this time of day there was all that free grass.

Intramuros, Beat Number 38. He hated the place. It was a run-down, rotting museum of empty stone buildings full of rats and squatters and cobbled streets that hurt his feet and had nowhere, absolutely nowhere, for a man to find a quiet, friendly address to pick up a cold drink. The high stone buildings were all turning to dust, to grime. That dust and grime fell down in any weather into the streets and onto his uniform and down his neck and, in the heat of the day, the stone buildings built in whatever crazy pattern the crazy Spaniards had built them, killed even the faintest breeze and made the place a hothouse. Even the plazas where the churches had been or where the cathedral stood now, was nothing but a rain forest of mildewed, smelly buildings with nowhere for a man to get a drink.

He had six children. He also had new police-issue shoes. The shoes were too tight and because he had six children he could not afford to have them stretched. Patrolman Gil, walking at the regulation pace in Real Street inside the walled city, sighed. He brushed at the shirt of his pressed khaki uniform. The pressing had been done by his wife. The unpressing and the gathering grime and the sweat marks under his armpits and probably on his back had been done by the sun and the lousy Spanish and their craziness. He walked. He felt a pang of pity for his wife. She was a good, loyal girl with six children. He touched at his gun butt with the palm of his hand as he walked. The butt of the gun was brown with rust. Some of the unmarried cops got their guns reblued once a year. Once a week—since he had been on the Intramuros beat, once a day—all he could afford to do was oil his. In the Spanish heat, the oil ran. He crossed over Real Street toward the rebuilt Casa Manila—one of the Spanish houses that had once graced the area—trod on a loose cobble and almost twisted his ankle.

His shoes were too tight. They pinched at every step. He thought of his poor good girl doing her best to keep his shirts ironed and he felt a glistening of tears at his eyes.

His feet hurt. It was only eleven o'clock in the morning and he had to keep walking for at least another five hours before he could go home.

He tried not to hobble.

He hobbled.

Crossing Real Street to go into the colonnaded entrance to the tourist attraction of a house built by the crazy Spanish for their upper classes in 1571, Patrolman Gil—poor, sad soul that he was—said, as he trod on yet another unrepaired cobble lying loose in the street, *"Oh . . . !"*

"J'adoube." In the plaza of the Casa Manila, sitting on the edge of the gently bubbling stone fountain, the fatter of the two middle-aged men drinking coffee and smoking cigars raised his finger to show it was not a move. He was merely adjusting the

position of his bishop into the center of its square so he could see better what next move he had to make. He was drinking his coffee black out of a china demitasse, what the Italians called an *espresso*. The fatter man, rubbing his hand over his bald head and looking down hard at the chess board balanced on the edge of the fountain, said in English, "All right?"

"Hmm." The thinner of the two men, rubbing his nose, said, "Hmm." Checkmate in six. The fatter man knew it. The thinner man, making a sniffing noise and drinking his coffee from a larger cup, white, with a little silver spoon on the saucer, said with all the patience in the world, "Sure." He tapped his cigar ash gently into a circular silver ashtray to one side of the board and glanced up at the two-story casa surrounding him. All the latticed veranda windows were closed. The staff were still at their morning coffee—their merienda—down the street. He listened to the gentle burble of the fountain. The thinner man, smiling slightly, puffing gently on his Alhambra Corona Sumatra, said with undisguised contented smugness, "Take your time."

Bishop to knight's pawn . . . The fatter man said, "Hmm." He had his hand ready to make his move. He put his cigar gently down onto the ashtray and rubbed his thumb and index finger together ready. Bishop to . . . The bishop still wasn't straight in its square. *"J'adoube."* I adjust. He moved the bishop straight on its tiny four-sided see. The fatter man said, apologetically, "Sorry."

He limped. His feet were rubbed raw with the shoes and he limped into the Casa Manila thinking nobody would be there.

There were two men there playing chess at the fountain. Gil straightened up. He stopped. He set his face to hide the pain. He looked them up and down in his official police manner. They were two Philippino businessmen in their midforties, well dressed in slacks and traditional embroidered short-sleeved barong tagalog shirts. They smoked cigars and drank their coffee from expensive cups.

His feet were two raw chunks of burning meat. He thought of his poor loyal wife—his good girl—and could have wept.

"J—" The fatter man, smiling, said to the cop, *"Magandang umaga"*—good morning. He saw the cop looking at him. The fatter man, apologizing for the interruption to the thinner man, said with a smile, "Sorry."

The thinner man smiled back. He knew where the game was going and he knew his opponent knew he knew. He glanced at his watch. And he knew there was time to complete the game. The thinner man said in English, "That's OK." He smiled.

"Kumusta sila?"—how are you? The fatter man, nodding to the cop, read the patrolman's name on his ID strip on his creased khaki uniform shirt. GIL, I. L., PATROLMAN. He looked hot. The fatter man said again, still smiling, a little louder, *"Kumusta sila,* Mister Gil?"

He knew them. He could not place them. And his feet hurt. And there was nowhere a man could disappear on duty for a few minutes to get a cooling drink. Patrolman Gil said warily, formally, *"Mabuti naman"*—I'm well. He knew them. He could not place them. Gil said cautiously, *"Salamat"*—thank you.

He saw the thinner man look up, surprised. Maybe he should have added, "Po." He could not place either of the two men. They looked well off, prosperous. They had a little silver ashtray between them and the chess set was not plastic.

They were Pos. Gil glanced up at the stone casa and then down to the fountain and across past the fountain to the other side of the little plazas that featured it to the doorways and colonnades that led back out by other entrances to Real Street.

The thinner man said in English to the fatter man, "It's your move." There was a tone in his voice.

Gil said, *"Salamat"*—thank you, "—po." He had seen them both before, but he could not place them.

The thinner man said to the chess board, "OK." He was someone important. He had certain expectations.

"*J'adoube* . . ."

"Make your move please!"

Gil said, "Po, *salamat* . . ." and he knew them. He knew who they were. Gil said happily, "Chess," and he knew, he knew who they were.

His feet hurt like hell.

"Make your move now, please." They were speaking English and some other language together. They were somebodies and he knew just who and his feet hurt and, at last, he was saved.

Gil, touching at the butt of his rusty gun, looking fierce, said softly to himself, "Good."

He began to walk carefully, unwaveringly, with purpose, like a policeman on his important daily duty, toward the colon-naded exit to the place across the square.

Scream-face. It was coming. At the far end of Real Street inside the walled city, the girl, standing stiff and petrified like stone, felt a tremble start in the back of her legs and travel up her spine.

Her head was bursting. She felt the tremble start. She felt it travel up, she felt her skin turn hot and red with the pressure. She felt her body become a spring. She felt it go hard, then harden again and then, hardening even more, until her head would burst, until her head was the only thing that still made her human and not stone, start to swell, to grow bigger, to pulsate, to start to explode, and then— And then she felt the surge, the paralysis, the calcification, reach her neck and it was coming, coming. . . .

She felt it come.

She felt Scream-face.

She thought for a last, final time before she became stone that . . .

She—

She felt the surge.

She felt it.

She felt the surge. She had the rattan bag no longer clutched

in her hand, but held against her chest in her claws. She
felt . . .

She felt . . .

She felt it close over her head and turn her to stone. She felt
her eyes turn red, become pinpricks. She was at the far end of
Real Street.

She felt the weight of the cut-down submachine gun in her
rattan bag. She felt the bullets in it cry out to be released. She
heard, from everywhere, the sound of every movement in every
crack, every fissure, in every stone in the place. She heard . . .
She heard a long, terrible sigh. Scream-face. She heard someone
crying out in sexual, begging entreaty. She heard.

Scream-face. Released, captured, imprisoned in what had
happened to her body, for one wonderful instant, her head
cleared, she savored the moment, and she was free.

She heard the long, terrible, calling sigh.

It came from her.

She had the gun in the rattan bag with the frayed flowers.

She could have shrieked with laughter at the thought of
something so trivial, so unimportant.

E. R. Beo. Her name was Ermalinda Rosaria Beo. She had
once been a food packer.

Scream-face.

She was an *amok*.

In Real Street, starting to run, she went toward Casa Manila,
pulling at the gun and in a high-pitched sound that in all her
life had never come from her throat before, began laughing and
laughing and laughing.

People who didn't know their places irritated him.

In the Casa Manila plaza, sitting on the edge of the fountain
with his cigar stabbing at the chessboard like a spear, the thinner man ordered the fatter man, *"Make your move!"*

He got under the colonnade where there were a few tourist
shops done up in Spanish colonial style and grinned to himself.

Gil said happily, "Heh, heh." He knew who the two men were.

FLORES DEL ORO. It was the name of their antique shop in the colonnade. They were brothers. He looked at the names over the door of the place. The brothers Yuson—Sonny and . . . There was a dark, wonderfully painted old santos: a wooden saint on display inside the locked shop at the glass where the second name was. Sonny and *Leon.* Leon was the fat one. They were outside. Their shop was locked. There was no one about.

Gil, getting down to sit on their doorstep, safe, unseen, hurting like hell, bent forward with trembling hands and got his shoes and socks off and, in a happy frenzy of joyous relief, began rubbing hard at his feet.

"No one named Roberto Ernesto Barrera was reported missing in the last two years!" Elizalde said, "I checked."

The barangay captain for General Vega Street said, "It was reported." Two doors down from Mrs. Barrera's room he ran a sari-sari shop—a place where everything, cigarettes, sheets of newspaper, plastic bags, anything, could be bought singly. On the plywood wall of the place, among all the pages from magazines for sale, single bamboo skewers, spoons, knives, and un-matching cups and saucers and crockery, there was an autographed photo of John Wayne with an inscription in Tagalog to his friend Emilio of General Vega Street. Wayne had obviously been a man of many talents. The photo had a sign on it saying it was not for sale. Smaller, autographed photographs of someone called General Duglass Macarthur were for sale, with spaces ready for Duglass to write in dedications. The sari-sari shop man said, "She reported it to the police and she reported it to me."

There had been no response when he had knocked at her door. Elizalde asked, "Is she in?"

"No." Emilio said, "No, she isn't." He was a man in his midthirties, the only one on the block who had made it into prosperity, probably also the local bookie and lottery ticket seller. He had a blue sweatband on his head, and hands that stayed beneath the wooden counter facing Elizalde. Emilio said, "Roberto Ernesto Barrera, aged fifteen." Emilio said, "It doesn't matter."

"Did you know her husband?"

"Sure." Emilio said, "Yeah, I knew her husband. He was a nice fellow." He touched something under the counter. There was the faintest click. Emilio said, "I'm not alone here. There are people watching." There was the click again. The sweatband had no sweat on it. He had put it on when he had seen the car coming, to look tough. Emilio said, "Their son's disappearance was reported. She reported it. She told me she reported it and her husband told me he reported it and then they waited and hoped and—" Emilio said, "And then nothing happened." Emilio said, "And now something's happened." He was becoming increasingly nervous. Elizalde, to see what would happen, touched at the butt of his pistol under his coat. Emilio said in a panic, "I'm not alone here!"

Mang Eleuterio had been right. He didn't understand. Elizalde, taking his hand from under his coat and leaning forward a little on the counter, said intimately, "Look, Emilio—"

"*I don't know anything!*" He was not John Wayne, he was merely an ordinary man who wore a sweatband to give him confidence. Emilio said, "Oh Mother of God!" Emilio said, taking his hand away from the counter, "Don't hurt me!" Emilio, starting to shout, looking around desperately, said in a panic, "Oh Holy Mary and Joseph and—"

"*What are you afraid of?*"

There was no one else. He was alone. Emilio, backing to the rear wall, his hands down by his sides as if they had suddenly become paralyzed, said, shaking his head, "Oh, no! People know me! People know my face! I have people!" Emilio, sinking down, going into the corner, starting to draw his knees up to his chest, shrieked, "No! No! *No!*"

There were people coming. Down the street as he looked, there were people running: young men from the neighborhood with tattoos and sweatbands that were covered in sweat. They were running fast, shouting. He saw the hilt of a butterfly knife glitter as it came out of one youth's jeans back pocket and, with a single flick, the youth unlock its blade.

"*What are you afraid of?*" His car was just behind him. Elizalde, losing seconds, shouted to the groveling, whimpering man, "What? *What are you afraid of?*"

"You!" He did not know his friends were coming to help him. He thought he had only words to stave him off. Emilio, on the ground, covering himself, hiding, trying to protect his face with his hands as Elizalde went quickly back to his car and started the engine to get away, yelled at the top of his voice, "You! YOU! I'm afraid of *YOU!*"

He was in the corner of the shop, a grown man, drawn up in the fetal position below his forged personal picture of his hero, John Wayne.

Beneath his forged personal picture of his hero, John Wayne, shaking, trembling, terrified beyond reason by the worst thing in the world, uncontrollably, he began to howl like a stray, starving dog left to die, wounded in a gutter. . . .

> *Dictyopteris membranacea*
> Limu lipoa
> *Description*
> Brown algae. Bushy plant with very thin twelve-inch-long by one-inch-wide flat leaves attached to obvious central veins.
> *Habitat*
> Grows on rocks and a little above the low-tide mark in tropical and subtemperate zones.
> *Uses*
> Employed extensively in tropical Pacific areas either dried or fresh in soups and as a vegetable dish.

Seaweed. At his desk, with the book open at page 141, the Whispering Man was reading Neumeyer's classic of self-sufficiency on a small boat, *Sailing the Farm.*

He marked the page.

In the introduction or the first few chapters, Neumeyer said once you understood what was available around you, once you conquered yourself, once you had your life in perspective, you need never touch land again. All Neumeyer had had when he had done this—to the Whispering Man's knowledge, he was still doing it—was a thirty-foot sloop.

Spirulina. It was another form of algae. Dried, one and a half pounds of it could keep you alive for a month.

Spirulina algae. The Whispering Man, at his desk, wrote it down in a notebook.

He thought, when all this was done—he thought he would never touch land again.

He had no pity or feelings left. Maybe, at sea, his feelings would come back. Maybe, when he was totally, completely, utterly alone, he would . . .

Spirulina algae. He looked out through the window at his boat waiting for him in the bay and, closing the open page, wrote the name down in his notebook, pressing down hard on the pen until it shook.

The doll was in the drawer beneath his hand.

He could not weep.

Spirulina algae.

He wrote the words down hard on the notebook page, over and over and over again.

The pleasure. The pure, wonderful, cool, free, unthrobbing, glorious wonderful pleasure of it.

Sitting on the step, wiggling his toes, Gil, happy beyond reason, said to God, to joy, to feet, to life, to his good girl at home, "Ohhh . . ." The Yuson brothers played chess for hours at a time. They had an exclusive business. If anyone wanted them they would know where to find them.

He would be left alone.

He was happy.

He wiggled and smiled.

Gil said, in ecstasy, "Oh, thank you, God."

Gil said to God, with respect, "Po, oh Po—*salamat*, Po . . ."

In his car stopped at the lights on Roxas Boulevard, Elizalde said suddenly, "*Goddammit!*"

He had the window up and the air-conditioning on against the rising heat.

He had nothing. He knew nothing. There was nothing.

The traffic was snarled. As usual, it was taking forever to get—exactly—nowhere.

Elizalde said hopelessly, "God—*dammit!*"

He heard it. He heard gunfire, shots. He heard a long burst of fire and then the sound of screaming. He heard a woman shriek. He heard people being killed. "*Oh, my God!*" He heard a man yell. He heard the sounds of things falling and being thrown down, crockery and metal. He heard running. Gil, falling over, scrambling to his feet, tripping over his shoes laid out on the ground in front of him, reaching for his rusty revolver, yelled, "POLICE! I'M THE POLICE!" He was barefoot. He heard another fusillade of shots and it was a machine gun. He heard running. He heard. *He couldn't get his socks on!* He found one sock, but it was wet with sweat and inside out. He was barefoot. On his feet, bending, scrambling, getting down onto his knees, Gil yelled to stop the shooting, "Wait! *WAIT!*" He heard people being killed. He heard masonry go flying off the fountain. He heard the sound of water, the sound of something like a dam being broached and then flapping, convulsing. He heard the sounds of a man drowning in the fountain, in blood, in water. He heard a click. Gil, yelling, falling down, getting onto his hands and knees to find the right way for his socks, yelled—

He saw her.

Gil said in a gasp, "Oh, my God—!"

He saw the gun.

He saw her eyes. She was coming toward him.

He saw her put her hands across her face. He saw something come out of the swinging rattan bag. He saw—

He was on his knees. He had lost his revolver. He saw her running. There was blood everywhere. She had it all down her blouse and on her shoes. He got to his feet. Gil, hobbling, his feet icy cold, yelled, "No—*wait!*"

He saw—

He saw her eyes. Gil yelled, "NO!" She was running. He was in his bare feet. She looked for an instant with her work-worn face, just like his loyal girl. She looked—

He saw her put another magazine into the gun and draw back the cocking handle. She didn't even know he was there. He was in his bare feet. Gil, desperate, yelled, "I—I haven't got my shoes on! I—" He saw her face. Her eyes were red. She—

She saw him. She stopped.

He saw her bring up the gun.

His gun was rusty and the oil each day was not like the blueing people without children could afford to buy.

He heard her yell. He knew, outside in the plaza, there were dead people.

He looked for a single mad, sad, humiliated moment at his red, raw feet sticking out under his rolled-up khaki trousers like a clown.

He had never, never, thought if it ever came it would be like this.

He saw the gun come up. Gil said sadly, broken, all his manhood gone in a single moment, "Oh . . . "

He wept. As he did it, he wept.

He wept.

With a single shot to the center of the forehead that smashed her back down the colonnaded arcade like a fragile, bony doll, aiming his rusty revolver with both hands, Patrolman Gil killed her where she stood.

J'adoube.

Make your move.

Magandang umaga. Mabuti naman—how are you? Well, thank you.

Po . . .

In the plaza, around the fountain, for a moment, there were voices, echoes.

Po?

There were no echoes. It was only the movement, the dust, the shifting of the old city in the heat of the day.

In the plaza, their blood soaking fast into the cobblestones, both of them cut in half by the two separate blasts, both the Yuson brothers were dead.

5

UNITED NATIONS ORGANIZATION
Office of Human Rights
United Nations Building,
United Nations Plaza,
United Nations Avenue,
Manila

Cable: *United Nations*

RE: Persons of Diminished Stature

Item First: "Persons of diminished stature" for the purposes of this determination shall be deemed to mean the owner/operators of the establishment known as The Gnome Home Acrobatic and One-Ring Sawdust Circus Café; Coffee, Meals, and Entertainment Three Times a Day located at an address on Padre Diego Tomas Street, Ermita, Metro Manila, Republic of the Philippines.

Item Second: "Bombs" for the purposes of this determination shall be deemed to mean small concussive devices with time fuses encountered in the present determination by the persons defined in Item First at their premises as defined in Item First.
It should not however be limited to this definition and, IT IS DETERMINED, that "Bombs" may also cover antipersonnel devices, Claymores, mines generally, torpedo devices, shrapnel-discharging weapons, napalm, and incendiaries.
UNDER THE RULES OF THE GENEVA CON-

> VENTION, it does not cover chemical bombs, poison-gas dischargers, germ-infecting delivery systems, or snake-venom and other toxin-scattering systems.

Item Third: It does cover Molotov cocktails and petrol igniting improvised weapons and hand guns.

Item Fourth: So far, according to the initial investigation by officers from THE ORGANIZATION, no such weapons have been employed.

He was in the bathroom at the back of the café cleaning himself off. Ambrosio, rereading the letter on the sink top, said in a whisper, "Oh, God." He smelled his shirt. His shirt smelled of disintegrated dragon. He tried using his left foot. His left foot limped. His hands shook. His face was black with burned gunpowder. He ran his hand through his hair. His hair didn't move. Ambrosio, swallowing, said softly, "Oh, God."

Item Fifth: This is not, however, to suggest that such weapons may not be used in the future.

He hardly ever swore. He swore. Ambrosio said, "Oh, shit!"

Item Sixth: The police officers, DETECTIVE SERGEANT JESUS-VINCENTE AMBROSIO, Metro Manila Police, Philippines citizen, and DETECTIVE SERGEANT BAPTISTE BONTOC, Metro Manila Police, Philippines citizen (Bontoc Tribe Protected Ethnic Minority Classification) are granted temporary secondment to the UNITED NATIONS ORGANIZATION to detect, defuse, deactivate, and generally deal discreetly with this matter.

Ambrosio said, "Yeah." He liked that bit. If he lived through it, he was going to have the letter framed. He knew a forger. He could get Bontoc's name faded so indistinctly it was going to look like a flyspeck.

Item Seventh: "Persons of Diminished Stature" as defined
   in Item First carry no special protection under the
   categories of race, color, creed, or political persuasion
   under the CHARTER OF THE UNITED NA-
   TIONS, as defined as dwarves, midgets, gnomes, little people *inter alia,* BUT THIS IS NOT TO
   PREJUDICE SUCH A DETERMINATION
   BEING MADE IN THE FUTURE. The United Nations, therefore, takes an interest in this matter.
   Further, police forces of the world have shown
   a disinclination to become involved in such mat-
   ters.

Nobody liked beating up dwarves.

Item Eighth: The potential opponents of this as yet United
   Nations unprotected classification may be listed as
   the following:
   1. Gangsters
   2. Terrorists
   3. Radicals
   4. Misinformed racists
   5. Tall people with a grudge
   6. Fascists
   7. Disgruntled customers of the establishment
      defined in Item First
   8. Religious zealots
   9. Psychopaths
   10. Mad Bombers

He had Fireball. He still had Fireball. Always, from now on,
what he had was Fireball. Thy headphones and thy tape they
comfort me.
   "WORK OUT A PLAN! BEGIN AT THE BEGINNING
AND WORK OUT A PLAN!"
   "I will!" He would. Ambrosio said into the mirror, setting his
face, "I will!" It was his big chance to make points.

Item Ninth: Re Item Eighth (list of potential opponents), preliminary investigations suggest none of the above.

Final Item: Best possible projections and hypotheses based on placement, construction, and nonlethality as well as total lack of interest previously shown in persons of diminished stature by gangsters, terrorists, radicals, misinformed racists, tall people with a grudge, fascists, disgruntled customers, zealots, psychopaths, and mad bombers suggests that, sadly—making protection by the ORGANIZATION a matter for the most careful, cautious, and well-trained officers on loan to its service—suggests that—

It must have been tough being liberal. You could almost see the tears on the paper.

—suggests that one or more of the goddamned dwarves are doing it themselves!

THIS BACKGROUND IS CONFIDENTIAL.

Ambrosio said into the mirror, "Ha!"

AND WILL BE DENIED IF PUBLISHED.

Ambrosio said, "Ha!"

AND SHOULD BE RETURNED FOR DESTRUCTION.

He had a photocopy.
"ARE YOU READY TO SUCCEED WHERE ALL OTHERS HAVE FAILED?"
He was. He was ready.
Folding his letter along the creases and putting it in his wallet, nodding, his face firm, like a knight girding himself for battle, Ambrosio, using toilet paper, cold water, and spit, began carefully cleaning himself up in the mirror.

On the phone, the Whispering Man said, "Rolly?"

The man he had spoken to by radio from his boat said, "Yes." His voice was toneless, neutral. He simply answered the question.

"And?"

He was three buildings away from the Casa Manila, high up, ringing from a public phone outside a rooftop café. He was a small, portly man in his midthirties wearing slacks and a business shirt. In his top pocket, he carried his money. In his pants pocket he carried a wallet. The wallet was fake, for muggers and problems generally, made by the de Santis Gunhide Company of New York. It held a clipped-in Hi Standard two-shot .22 Magnum derringer that could be fired through a fingerslot with the wallet still folded around it. Rolly said, "They're both dead."

"The Yuson brothers."

"Yes."

"Are you certain they're dead?" His voice showed the strain.

Standing at the public phone, Rolly touched at his hip pocket to feel his gun was still there and smiled. He could see them. He could see people in the plaza far below. He could see how the people stepped around the rivers of blood. Rolly said, "They're dead." They were the poor, the people. They did not walk around the two bodies: like prisoners in an exercise yard, they shuffled. Rolly said, "The people are there now."

"And the staff from the Casa Manila?"

"Still at merienda down the road." They were like a stupid, slow, bovine herd, the poor. They did not look at the bodies or take in the scene—he saw them shuffling—they grazed on it. Rolly said, "It all went well."

"And the girl Beo?"

"She was killed." He waited for the Whispering Man to say something. There was only silence. Rolly said, "A cop killed her." He waited.

There was a silence.

The Whispering Man said only, "Good." He expelled a long breath. The Whispering Man said, "That helps us."

"It doesn't hurt."

The Whispering Man said suddenly, "Did he see you? Should he be killed?"

"No." He was enjoying it. Rolly said pleasantly, "No to both questions."

"What about the photos?"

Rolly said, "I took the one of the Yuson brothers back. She's got the other one with her."

"OK." The Whispering Man said, "The cop on the case—Elizalde—did you get any more on him?"

At the phone Rolly smiled. They were still there, the bovines. He curled his lip in distaste. He had been poor once himself, or at least his parents had. He knew all about the poor. He hated them.

"Are you there?"

Rolly said, "Oh, yes, I'm here." Rolly said, "Elizalde, Felix, Detective Lieutenant, Western District Detective Bureau, Metro Manila Police." He fell silent.

The Whispering Man said, "Hullo?"

"I'm looking for my notes." At the phone Rolly gazed out over the rooftops and down into the plaza. He had no notes. He smiled and waited.

"Rolly!"

Rolly said, "He isn't on the take. He's whiter than white, Philippino-Spanish-American, a mestizo. He's the distant relation of one of the old colonial families here, educated, started off in business but got bored with it and went into the cops, good record, honest, been wounded twice, once seriously, and in the last fifteen years or so he's been on the force killed one man in the line of duty." Rolly said, "It was a good shooting. No problems."

"Political?"

Rolly said, "No, he's honest." He smiled.

"Wife?"

"Marguerita, high school history teacher, no children."

"The people he works with?"

"Two sergeants, Bontoc and Ambrosio. They're not with him at the moment. They're OK. They're out of it."

"They're all dead—the Yuson brothers and the Beo girl? There's no doubt?"

"No."

"How do you know?"

He almost laughed. Rolly said, "Take my word for it—"

"Did you check?"

Rolly said, "They're dead. Maybe you haven't ever seen anyone shot dead. It isn't like television. When someone is shot dead you know they've been shot dead. They don't just fall down, they—"

"I know what happens when someone is shot dead!"

Rolly said, "Then they're all dead. Take my word for it." Rolly said easily, "It's all going very smoothly. I don't know why you're so worried."

"This man Elizalde—"

"Yes?"

There was a silence.

Rolly asked again, "Yes?"

"Can he be relied upon to perform?"

Rolly said, "Yes." Rolly said, "Yes, I think so." He touched at the little hidden gun in its wallet and grinned. He was an anonymous-looking man wearing slacks and a business shirt and no tie. He was the sort of man you might not even notice if he stood next to you on the street. In a crowd on that street, he was totally invisible. Rolly, still smiling, still patting his hip pocket lightly, said pleasantly, trying not to giggle, "Oh, yes, I think so."

Rolly said, "Oh, yes, I think we can properly rely on him to do what's expected of him."

He smiled. He looked across and down to the plaza.

He waited.

———

There were eyes watching him. They were everywhere. There were people. He knew they were there. In the arcade he could see nothing. There was no one there. There were eyes watching him.

Gil, slipping down on the blood and the brains and the terror, yelled, "Help! Help me!" He knew there were people watching. He could see no one.

Gil, slipping, falling down, scrabbling like a child, in tears, blubbering, yelled, "Help me! Someone out there! In the name of the Holy Jesus, HELP ME!"

In the center of the ring, the Ringmaster said, "Pablo." That was him. He wore a morning coat, top hat, and riding boots and carried a long whip. Compared to Jorge standing next to him, he looked plain. Jorge's gold-lamé long johns glittered in the light. Pablo said, "Jorge." Bontoc already knew Jorge. "And our kitchen man and chef, Ernesto." Pablo said, "You already know Ernesto." Know your enemy. Pablo, indicating a clown with a red nose and what looked like calico curtains on his legs, said, "Ignacio." And another clown, this time with a green nose, "Imelda."

Imelda said, "Good morning, Mr. Bontoc." She had a nice voice.

Bontoc said, "Good morning." He was writing it all down. Ambrosio was still in the café bathroom scraping off his sackcloth and ashes with a chisel. Bontoc, reading it back, said, "Pablo, Jorge, Ernesto, Ignacio, and Imelda."

Imelda said, "Yes." Under the nose, she smiled. She had a nice smile. She was about three foot nothing. She had to look up to Bontoc to smile. It was a nice smile.

Pablo said, "Josephine." She was the horseback rider. She wore a leotard. She had long black hair. Bontoc said, "Josephine?"

Josephine said, "Yes."

Jorge said, "My daughter."

Bontoc said, "Oh," He wrote that down.

Pablo said proudly, "I'm her uncle once removed."

Bontoc said with interest, "Oh." He made a note.

Carmel, the dog trainer, said with a touch of pique, "My sister."

Bontoc said, "Who is?"

"Josephine."

Pablo said, "I'm her great-uncle too."

Bontoc said, "Oh."

There was a juggler. He was taller by an inch than the three-foot-high lady. (Which one was she?) The juggler said, "Ricardo." He had another juggler with him. She was also a girl. Also, that was, not like him, but like Imelda and Josephine and Carmel and— The one who was about three-feet high was Imelda. He had it now. Right. Ricardo said, "The strong man in the leopard-skin outfit with the biceps is Rodolfo."

"Who's the girl?"

Rodolfo said, "What girl?"

"The girl with—" Bontoc, turning to the female juggler, asked, "Who are you?"

The strong man said politely, "Sorry, I thought you meant my girl." He was built like a small brick bunker. The strong man said, "I'm a bachelor. I thought you meant Illuminada here."

Illuminada was the only one not in drag. She wore slacks and a blouse, a worried look, and glasses. Illuminada said, "I'm Illuminada. Good morning."

"Um—" Bontoc said, "Good morning." Bontoc said, "Who are you?"

"I'm Ricardo and Jasmine's cousin."

Bontoc said, "Who's Jasmine?"

A voice said, "I am." It was the lady juggler. That was what he'd wanted to know in the first place. Jasmine said, "Ricardo and I are a husband-and-wife team."

"What do you do here?"

Pablo asked, "Who?"

He looked at his notes. He had it all now. He grinned. Bontoc said, "Illuminada."

"I'm the accountant."

Bontoc said, "Ah." He was happy. It was clear. Bontoc said, "Right." Find the sex content and pretty certainly you had—
Illuminada said, "I'm Rodolfo's cousin."

Rodolfo said, "First cousin." He smiled protectively. Rodolfo said, "Ignacio and I are—"

Bontoc said, "Second cousins."

Ignacio said, "Brothers."

"Who's—"

Pablo—the Ringmaster—said, "Yes?"

He had it.

Pablo.

Ernesto.

Ignacio.

Imelda.

Jorge.

Josephine. Who? Oh, the horseback rider—

Carmel.

Ricardo.

Rodolfo.

Rodolfo's wife, Josephine—no, Ricardo's wife, Jasmine.

Rodolfo. And—and—

Illuminada. The accountant.

He had it. Right. He had it all. Right. Right. Bontoc had a degree in business administration. He had a mind honed hard by study and constant persecution. He had it all. "Who's—"

Bontoc said, "Who's—"

He looked at them hard. He saw Pablo the Ringmaster look at him with hope and trust in his eyes. He saw Pablo smile. Jorge, the trapeze man, winked at him. He saw the kitchen man Ernesto nod encouragingly. He was a man. He was a Bontoc. He was—

Bontoc said, "I'm lost. Who are you all again?"

"HELP ME!" He knew they were there. They would not come. They were not coming. He had no shoes or socks. He was out of uniform. He had a wife and children and no money.

Gil, on his knees to God, to the sounds of the people in

the plaza, to the eyes watching, to anyone but the authorities, shrieked, "Help me! Please help me *now!*"

They were going. In the plaza, the poor, shuffling, gazing down at the blood, began, wordlessly, to go. The staff from the Casa Manila and the tourists they served would be along any moment.

There were twenty of them, representatives of their barrio. They had been everywhere in the street outside, moving in. They had heard the shots from the gun, and then they had heard the single shot from a police revolver and not been surprised. They heard the policeman shouting.

Both the Yuson brothers were dead. There was blood and flesh and bone and shiny, brass, expended cartridge cases everywhere on the cobbles.

They had all seen death before. Some of them had seen their children die of hunger and medical neglect. The chess set the brothers had been playing with was ivory. The pawns and pieces were strewn across the plaza with the empty cartridge cases. Most of them had never seen rich people up close before or been so close to their possessions. Thieves would have thieved from them.

They were not thieves.

The Yuson brothers, Sonny and Leon, were dead. That was all. They were satisfied.

In the plaza, the herd, slowly, wordlessly, touching nothing, began filing out.

"Will you continue?" On the phone, the Whispering Man said, "Are you happy to go on?"

"Sure." At the telephone, watching, Rolly said easily, "Sure." He asked, "How much have you got to spend?" He asked, "Six, eight million?"

The Whispering Man said, "Yes."

Rolly said, "Sure. Fine. Yeah. OK." He smiled. He was impressed. Rolly said softly, like the man at the other end of the line, in a whisper, "Wow. Power. Wow—"

Rolly said, "And just poor, harmless little old me, your obedient friend and helpmate—" He made a chuckling noise. Rolly said pleasantly, touching at his wallet, "How could I possibly refuse?"

They were nice people. They gathered around him at a table. Pablo said, "Pablo. P-A-B-L-O. Pablo."

"Jorge. J-O-R-G-E. Jorge."

"Illuminada. I-L-L-U-"

They were all so charming. They all smiled and waited as he wrote it all down.

"My brother."

"My second cousin, once removed."

Pablo said, "My son Ignacio the clown married to Imelda, the first cousin of Josephine and Ernesto—"

So nice, so thoughtful.

As he wrote, each of them, glowing hope and trust and faith in his sworn duty to detect, locate, apprehend, and incarcerate a mad bomber among them trying to destroy a Gnome Home in Manila, showed him all their teeth and smiled.

They had gone. He was alone. No one would come before the police came.

In the empty arcade of the silent and deserted Casa Manila in Intramuros where the Spanish once had kept people like him out, P. C. Gil, on his knees praying, bitterly, uncontrollably, wept.

Right. In the center of the ring, Bontoc, looking hard at his notes, putting his brain to work, said, "Right." He looked up and saw the juggler lady, Carmel. Bontoc said to Carmel, "Thank you, Carmel."

Carmel said politely, "Um, Jasmine."

"Right." Just testing. Bontoc said under his breath, "Tufo!" It meant rice bowl. In Bontoc dialect it was about the worst thing you could say.

"Tufo!"

He didn't care. He said it again.

6

In the Casa Manila arcade Elizalde said quietly, "Go to the coroner's wagon and tell the driver to give you a pair of surgical boots to put on. Carry your shoes and socks. Tell anyone who asks you that your shoes had blood on them and I ordered you to take them off so you wouldn't compromise the crime scene." He had Gil's statement in his notebook. "Then tell the driver to call you a taxi on his radio and go home." Outside, in the plaza, Watanabe was with the bodies of the two dead chess players. With him and the Scientific Team was the General, the Commanding Officer of the Western Police District. As he moved from place to place in the plaza talking to people and giving orders the buttons on his tight military uniform glittered in the sun. Elizalde said, "Don't pay the taxi driver. Tell him you're on police business and to send the bill plus twenty percent to me at the Department." Technical Sergeant Gomez of Ballistics was still bending down over the girl's body in the arcade with a tape measure doing something with the submachine gun. He saw Gil glance at him. Elizalde said, "Sergeant Gomez has your revolver. I'll get a receipt from him for you. He's your witness that I ordered you to take your shoes off." He saw Gil hesitate. Elizalde said, "Go."

Gil said, "Thank you." He nodded to Gomez and tried to smile. He wanted to please. Gil said apologetically, "My gun is a bit rusty, sir, I—"

He was measuring the length of the gun with the tape and writing down the measurements on a clipboard. Gomez said, "I'll reblue it for you." He stopped writing and looked at Gil. Gomez said, "Go."

"Thank you very much, sir." He didn't have anything in the world other than what people gave him. Gil, biting at his lip and trying not to look at the body of the girl, said, "Thank you."

Gomez nodded. He watched as Gil went down the arcade and out into the plaza. Gomez said to Elizalde curiously, "Why is the General here?"

"He knew the victims."

"The girl or—?"

"The two out there." Elizalde looked down at his notebook, still watching Gil. Elizalde said, "Leon and Sonny Yuson, brothers. They owned the antique shop down here." They were both purposely a little to one side and ahead of the dead girl and the blood. Elizalde said, "It's the same sort of gun Barrera used to kill the faith healer." The girl's open rattan bag was by her blown-in face. He had to go through it. Elizalde said, "What is it?"

He smelled of Alox, the wax reloaders used to lubricate their hand-cast bullets. Both the pockets of his brown dust coat were held closed by little padlocks. God alone knew what he kept in there. Gomez said, "It isn't what it is, it's what it was. What it was was a French Gevarm model A7 .22 caliber magazine-fed repeating rifle." Gomez, bending back down to the weapon with his tape still in his hand, said, "What it is now is a .22 caliber magazine-fed submachine gun with a pistol grip and a shortened ten-and-a-half-inch barrel with the main spring adjusted to compensate." He wanted to pick up the gun and feel its weight, but it hadn't been dusted for fingerprints. He turned it over with the end of his pencil. "No apparent serial number, stamped *Carabine Automatique GEVARM 22 L.R. Cal 5.5* on the barrel, plus patent numbers, fitted with an oversized professionally made walnut grip with the number eighteen burned in with die sinking tools." Gomez said, "Two empty twenty-shot magazines out in the plaza, both also stamped eighteen and one still in the weapon, fully loaded, also with the number eighteen stamped on it." He seemed very worried. Gomez said abruptly, as an afterthought, doing his job, "The other ballistics dimension to today is that the girl was killed with one shot from a .38 Special police-issue revolver in poor condition." He looked at the girl's face. There was no face. And then down to her out-flung hand. "Soft-lead, round-nose bullet, entry wound slightly to one side and above the right eye, destroying the side of the skull, large exit wound at the base of the left side of the skull." He had a little glassine envelope on his clipboard with some-thing in it. Gomez said, "Bullet recovered, badly distorted but identifiable lands and groove striations sufficient to make a ballistics comparison." He asked, "OK?" He squatted down again by the gun and took out his tape.

"OK." There were no pockets in the girl's slacks or blouse. There was only the rattan bag with the faded flower clip on it. Whatever the General was saying to the people outside, it was holding them there. No one else was going to come. He and Gomez had rolled the body over slightly to get at Gil's socks. No one was going to come to move it any farther or take it away. He knew who she was. She was one of the poor. The slacks and blouse, apart from the blood and the dirt from the ground where she had fallen, were cleaned, pressed carefully over and over, gently, to protect the fabric. Her hand was flung out by the rattan bag. It was a woman's hand, but with callouses and the tiny abrasions and cuts and long ground-in grime of someone who worked hard and long and dirty to look, on her days off, pretty and light. There was no wedding ring, nor mark of lightness where one had ever been worn. Using, like Gomez, the tip of a pencil, Elizalde opened the bag and took out a small, folded, flowered handkerchief with frayed edges turned in so they would not show too much.

E. B. It was monogrammed on the corner of the handker-chief. It had a label, Rustan, at the corner; it was from one of the expensive shops that threw in monogramming free of charge. The handkerchief was frayed and old and smelled slightly of stale perfume. It had been a gift or an extravagance a long time ago. Elizalde put it into a glassine evidence envelope from his pocket. He opened the bag wider. There was a photo-graph of the girl with a younger man: a boy about sixteen or seventeen walking on Roxas Boulevard, smiling at each other. The photo was a Polaroid done by a street photographer mounted in a square of gold-lined blue cardboard to make a frame. He opened the bag wider. There was a fired .22 caliber case that must have ejected into the bag when she killed the two brothers in the plaza. There was nothing else. Elizalde put the photo into another envelope and put it into his pocket.

Gomez asked, "Anything?" He was still measuring the gun. "No."

Gomez said, "The other gun, the one you found at the faith healer's, was stamped thirty-seven on the butt." Gomez said, not to Elizalde, but as a statement of fact, "In the seventies, when automatic weapons were at a premium for counterterrorism and—and various other things, these guns were imported and converted into short machine pistols as drill weapons for the various security forces. Being .22s they could be used for practice at a vastly reduced cost to the more usual nine millimeters and so they were very much in demand by—" Gomez said, "By all sorts of people." He was not looking at Elizalde, but at his clipboard. He was not reading from the clipboard, he was staring at it to give himself courage. Gomez said, "Then when the Americans converted to nine-millimeter ammunition for their own military submachine guns instead of .45 caliber there was plenty of U.S. Aid nine-millimeter around and the .22 conversions became unnecessary and all the guns were gathered up, recorded, put into sealed boxes, and taken out to the government foundry in Quezon City and melted down." Gomez said slowly, "This one and the one at the faith healer's were part of that meltdown." He said before Elizalde could say anything, "It was all aboveboard! Witnesses saw the sealed boxes go into the furnace!" Gomez said again, "The conversion number on this one is eighteen and the one from the faith healer's, thirty-seven." He paused. He kept staring at the clipboard and would not look up.

"Then—"

"I don't know!"

Elizalde said, "Jorge?"

Gomez said again, "I don't know! I didn't check the sealed boxes because they'd all been in my armory for ages and I—" Gomez said, "Lots of people have access to the armory! Lots of departments have their own ballistics people who use it!" He looked for the first time at the dead girl's face. It was not human. It was merely exploded bone and blood and matted hair. Gomez said, "I don't know! It was years ago! The guns were all melted down years ago! This is the first time any of them have surfaced." Gomez said suddenly in a whisper, "Felix, I did all the conversions myself. I made all these guns. I didn't even keep one back for myself! I—" He glanced down the arcade and saw, for an instant, the General standing with his hands on his hips staring down at him. Gomez said, "Felix, I—"

Gomez said so softly Elizalde had to strain to hear him, "Felix, when the first one surfaced I thought maybe it was a copy or a— All the serial numbers were taken off the guns when I converted them and I thought maybe the number burned into the butt was just a—" Gomez said, "No, they're mine, both of them, number eighteen and number thirty-seven." He looked down the arcade and the General was gone. Out there in the plaza there were two men shot to ribbons and everywhere on the ground, fired, shining, brass cartridge cases. Gomez said, afraid, "Felix—"

Gomez said, "Felix, the conversions—these guns—the cases of them that went into the furnace—" He stared hard down at his clipboard. The weapon, shortened, able to fire at a rate of over six hundred rounds a minute, modified, balanced, adjusted, and fine-tuned with its quality walnut butt and all the new bolts and screws blued and polished, lay on the ground with its twenty-shot magazine still set firmly into the receiver. Gomez said, terrified at the thought, "My God, Felix, numbers eighteen and thirty-seven—that's nothing! There were two hundred and eighty-seven of them!" Gomez said, *"Two hundred and eighty-seven!"* Gomez said, "Oh my God, oh my God—"

He looked up at Elizalde and his eyes were staring.

Gomez said, "Oh my God, Felix, *who the hell's got them?*"

In Cavite Street, each of the possessions the Beo girl had had in her first-floor room had been removed and placed out in the hall. There was nothing much. The furniture was cheap and mainly bamboo and rattan. There were four chairs and a table and, in cardboard boxes in the hall, cans of food and plastic containers of rice and spices and the contents of the ice box. There had been two beds in the room, one curtained off by a cloth. Both the beds were single and made of wood, and they came apart with screwdrivers. They were laid in planks on top of the food and the bedding. There were women's clothes, dresses and blouses and three pairs of slacks and night clothes. They were in another two boxes resting on a dismantled plywood cupboard. The floor of the room had been swept. The dust and trash from the pedal bin by the stove had been gathered up onto newspapers and gone through, sifted, but there was nothing there.

On a separate sheet of newspaper there were bits and pieces of costume jewelery and, in the center, coins and banknotes totaling eighty-three pesos and fifty cents.

In the hall, the bovine herd that had been at Casa Manila waited and did not look at the possessions, did not covet them. They were not a bovine herd, they were people. They were men and women in their thirties and forties and fifties—they were the responsible people of the neighborhood.

They waited.

There was no leader among them.

As one, they went forward and took up all the possessions and began carrying them in their arms, carefully, down the wooden stairs into the street.

The room was empty.

There was no one there anymore.

All the faces of the men and women as they went down the stairs and out into the street were set and expressionless.

It was a wake, a funeral.

Out in the street, in a vacant lot away from the houses, with all the children kept inside for the day, one by one the people of Cavite Street, moving in silence like mourners, deposited the possessions in the center of the lot and stood back to one side to make way.

No one spoke.

There was no leader.

There was no plan and no one had thought to bring kerosene or petrol.

The wood and cane of the furniture in the heat of the day were dry and flammable.

There was no order.

Into the center of the pile, someone merely threw a match.

The doll on his desk had a noose twisted around its neck.

It was a floppy, cheap rag doll wearing a blue dress and a yellow apron and striped, garish, dyed-on-black-and-white stockings and no shoes.

He did not look at his boat through the window. In his office, holding the end of the noose, the Whispering Man looked only at the doll. It had a joyous, painted-on freckled face with wide button eyes and yellow wool hair.

He pulled.

He pulled.

He pulled hard on the end of the noose.

He did what he now did best.

Pulling, pulling, he hated.

His breath was hard, strained, tight in his chest.

He—

He—

He *hated!*

In the Gnome Home, Ambrosio said, "Right!" He saw Bontoc start back in intimidation with his power. They had searched the place for bombs. They had found no bombs in the place. It was still an hour and a half until the lunchtime show. It was plenty of time. (He had all this written down on little, separate, someone-important-called-while-you-were-out telephone message pages in his head.) And, you had to be, now, firm, decisive, resolute, and above all, unafraid to make the big move.

Dwarves. Eleven of them.

They didn't frighten him.

He was going to come down on someone like a ton of bricks.

Make your choice.

Make your play.

Draw!

He thought, wisely, he might start with the woman with bad eyesight, the puny build, and glasses.

It burned. In Cavite Street, everything she had ever had, everything she had ever been, burned.

E. R. Beo. She lay dead in the arcade in the Casa Manila in Intermuros across the city. The authorities, the police, the undertakers, the officials, they all had her there.

That was what she was. What she was now, they had.

In Cavite Street, all she had ever been, piled in the vacant lot safe from the houses and children in the street, burned.

At the fountain, the General said, "I knew them. They were very civilized people." Watanabe and his staff were taking the bodies on stretchers in plastic body bags toward the waiting coroner's wagon. Elizalde had not even been able to examine the contents of their pockets. The pieces and pawns from the chess set had all been picked up and put back on their board. The set lay on a chopped and broken section of the fountain ready for a game. The General said, "I started a little collection of nineteenth-century carved *santos* while I was in the provinces with the army. The Yuson brothers were kind enough to look out for more pieces for me." He still wore his army uniform and ribbons. They were all service and good conduct ribbons. He had been a transport officer. "They kept their prices low for genuine local collectors and made up for it by charging the tourists more." The General asked, "The woman, who was she?"

"Patrolman Gil said she was an *amok.*"

The General said, "I didn't realize it was standard procedure in the police to take your shoes off at a murder scene." He had stopped Gil on his way to the wagon.

Elizalde said, "Yes."

"What about identification?"

"She didn't have any. Her initials may be E. B." The General was not listening. He watched as the two bagged bodies went into the back of the wagon like frozen meat. On the ground, all the fired cartridge cases had been circled with chalk and picked up. There were other, more ragged circles. That was where the bone and flesh had been. Elizalde said, "I'd like their shop opened and searched." Elizalde said, "I'd like to go through their books and papers and accounts."

The General said suddenly, "She was probably a whore used by some petty criminal to get back at the brothers for some real or imagined slight." He shook his head. "Barrio people are like that. The things you and I might pass off as harmless jokes or as—as nothing: the way someone looks at you or inclines their head, that sort of thing—those people in the barrio rat holes take as mortal insults." The General said, "I read about it every morning in the Uniformed Section's reports." He seemed genuinely sad. The General said, "A sawed-off rifle. It's their typical weapon. That murder suicide in Rio Cocodrilo Street, wasn't that the same sort of thing?"

"It was the same sort of weapon." Gomez was still in the arcade doing something with the gun. Elizalde said, "Guns are Gomez's business." Elizalde said, "I'd like to have the Yuson brothers thoroughly checked out."

"No."

"Why not?"

The General said with a smile, "Because I've already had

them checked out." He seemed childishly pleased with himself. He had been vindicated. The General said, "When I started buying valuable antiques from them, of course it occurred to me that here was a wonderful opportunity for someone to worm themselves into a position of influence with a person of importance—" He saw Elizalde's face. "—by selling me stolen items or carvings that the State would consider national treasures." The General said, "Tourists complain every day at the airport that the santos some unscrupulous person has sold them don't have proper museum clearance to leave the country—so before I bought a single item I had both of them run through the police and security computers and the Antique Dealers' Association and—" He was very pleased with himself. "And I suggested in a roundabout way to both the Taxation Office and a few other people, including a very senior member of the church, that they were being considered for high positions in the government and—" The General said, nodding, "And they were squeaky clean. They were two honest men who worked hard, dealt fairly, and lived good, moral, Christian lives." The General, gazing at the wagon as the white-coated attendant in the driver's cab started the motor to take it to the morgue so the brothers could be gutted and dissected and sliced into ribbons by Watanabe's postmortems, said, "They became my friends." He said as an order, "No, their shop won't be searched. We'll leave it untouched as a mark of respect to two honest men." He asked, "What did you find on the girl's body?"

Elizalde said, "Nothing."

The General said, "I know things, Lieutenant Elizalde. Police work isn't unlike a career in the army. You only need to be a good judge of men." The General, turning to him, asked, "Are you a good judge of men?"

Elizalde said with his eyes on the General's, "Yes."

"I hear you spoke to Mang Eleuterio at the Santo Seng Kong Church in Tondo. Why?"

"I thought he could be of assistance."

"And was he?"

"No one in the barrios will speak to me."

"No." The General said, "No, they wouldn't." The General said, "I hate it when good men are cut down by trash. As a Chrsitian I know it must be part of God's plan for us all, but I hate it when it happens." He blinked back tears. The General said, "Those two good men wanted nothing more from life than to give an honest day's work for an honest day's pay and be left alone." They must have given him some wonderful bargains. "They had a terrible habit of parking their truck in a no-parking zone in Real Stret out in front here to load and unload their goods, but it's hardly in the interest of the Parking Police who, after all, like the rest of us only serve the welfare and continued prosperity of the State, to make an issue of it." The General said, "I tell you without shame that I was pleased to be able to convince the Parking Police to turn a blind eye to it." The General said, rehearsing something, "They were ornaments to our society, and people like that should not have to be subjected to the triviality of laws designed for something else."

Elizalde said, "Yes, sir." He touched at the photograph in his pocket.

"You said the woman had nothing on her." The General, eagle-eyed, said, "I noticed there was a rattan bag lying beside her."

"It contained a monogrammed handkerchief." Elizalde, taking it out of his pocket in its glassine envelope, handed it over.

"Probably stolen."

"Yes, sir."

"You said nothing. Now we have a handkerchief. Is there anything else?"

"No."

"We'll probably never get to the bottom of this. At bottom, it's probably something so stupid, so meaningless, so trivial that ordinary civilized people would laugh at it." His mouth was set. The General said, "Barrio insults. Amour propre: the vanity of self-image. I had them in the army." The General said, "You could always tell the barrio scum: they carried knives and had tattoos." He said, "I didn't like them. I—"

The General looked at the setup chess set on the fountain. He said in Philippino, "Taglagás, Tag-araw, Taglamíg, Tagsibul—tag-init, tag-ulán—autumn, summer, winter, spring—dry season, rainy season—" The General said, "That was them. That was what they always said." He sighed. "They were happy here. This was their home. In an old Spanish plaza from a bygone era." The General said, "They were both confirmed bachelors, they were content, they had time to sit and talk and listen to the conversation of civilized men." He said with vehemence, "No, we won't open up their shop and go through it like grave robbers or thieves, we'll leave it as a mark of honor." He saw Gomez coming carrying the gun. Gomez indicated to the Fingerprint Team waiting by the second coroner's hearse that they could go down the arcade. The General said, "I've got work to do now, Felix, very sad work." He was going to tell the relatives or the executor. The General said, "You won't find out, ever, who ordered the filthy little dead whore in there to do it, or why, but—" He was affected. He was blinking back tears. He looked down at his ribbons. "But if you do—" Elizalde's coat was a little open. The General's eyes strayed to his holstered PPK. "If you do—" He was still thinking of little favors like parking.

Elizalde said in Spanish, *"Si, mi General?"*

He received, in return, a sad smile.

The General said with real, undisguised hatred, "If you can, if you can—kill them!" Everywhere, everywhere there were chalk marks. He began walking over them toward the arcade entrance where Gomez waited for him with the gun.

He drew a long, tired sigh.

He looked down and brushed at his ribbons with his wrist.

With his face twisted in distaste, he went to look at the body of the dead, murdering, unwashed whore in the arcade.

It was evidence. In Real Street, away from the Casa Manila, Elizalde, stopping, took the glassine envelope containing the paper-framed photograph from his pocket and looked at it through the plastic.

It showed the dead woman walking in Roxas Boulevard with a young boy and smiling at him as if he had just said something funny. She carried a rattan handbag with something tied to the handle that came out as a soft blur on the cheap print. It was a handerchief. It was new, stiff. It stuck out at one side where it had just been unfolded. *E. B.* It was her. In the street, Elizalde undid the glassine envelope and took the paper frame off the photograph and looked at the back.

Ermalinda R. Beo, Cavite Street.

Santiago Beo, Cavite Street.

It was printed, ornate. They had sat in a café somewhere with the gift—the handkerchief—and the photograph and a pencil and been happy and written their names down.

My Sister, Mother, Friend. They had swapped it back and forth and giggled. It had been a day on which something good had happened.

My Brilliant Brother Santiago. He had passed an exam or found a job.

Dr. Santiago—

Professor Santiago—

Papal Knight and Hero of the World Santiago—

It was her writing. It had been a wonderful day.

Santiago—

Santiago Beo—

There was a last word written in a totally different hand.

Santiago—

Santiago Beo—

It was written, not in pencil, but in ink, hard, so it would not fade.

DESAPARECIDO.

It was Spanish. It was a word in Spanish that had gained currency in Argentina during the mad, vicious reign of the junta.

Desaparecido . . .

It meant *disappeared.*

It was evidence.

It was evidence.

In the street, Elizalde, crushing the glassine envelope and the paper frame in his hand and dropping them into a trash bin, looked down at the words.

Rolly watched. Elizalde, Felix, Lieutenant, Western District Detective Bureau. He knew it would be him. He saw Elizalde put the photo carefully back into his inside pocket and stand thinking.

They had picked the right man. He saw him thinking about it and whatever else he thought about.

In Intramuros around the area of the Casa Manila and the great churches and buildings there were no poor. Since Spanish times they had been kept out by moats or gates or parking police. In Real Street, Elizalde turned to see who was walking behind him.

There was only an anonymous, slightly portly-looking man taking out a wallet from his hip pocket and seemingly about to open it to check that his money was still there. There was no one else. Elizalde began walking toward his car and, when he turned back to unlock the door, the portly man was gone.

Evidence.

He touched at his pocket to make sure it was still there and unlocked the door and got in.

He smiled.

He had places to go.

He looked at his watch. Plenty of time.

In the doorway of a shop selling religious souvenirs and Bibles, as he put his wallet containing the derringer back carefully in his hip pocket and patted at it, Rolly smiled.

It burned. The pile of furniture and bedding, clothes and food, money and everything else that had been in the room, burned to embers.

Back a little from the smoke, the neighbors and friends watched.

They waited.

When everything had been reduced and there were only embers, silently, heavily, with the measured inevitable steps of prisoners walking in circles in a jail exercise yard, they beat them into the ground with their shoes until nothing, nothing remained but ashes.

7

"*D*O RIGHT AND FEAR NOT—AND GET THE PROFITS!"

He knew how to deal with pint-size, puny accountants with bad eyesight and glasses. In her office at the rear of the Gnome Home, Ambrosio, towering over Illuminada like Godzilla, said plainly, efficiently and with purposive interface, "Twenty questions—all right?"

She was a very small person. Her glasses were very large. She had to adjust them on her nose with the fingers of both hands. Illuminada said, "Yes, sir."

"You can call me Mr. Ambrosio." He had never seen a female dwarf close up before. She was about three foot three, perfectly proportioned—on the flat-chested side—wearing a blouse and cotton slacks she must have got from the children's department in a store. She wore only a plain, gold, heart-shaped ring. You couldn't buy rings that size out of the jeweler's tray: someone must have had it made for her. No need to be the gestapo. Ambrosio said, "Or Detective Sergeant, whichever is easier for you."

"Yes, sir."

No need to beat about the bush. "Someone among you, one or more, is setting off these bombs—it isn't a tourist or a gangster or a terrorist, it's one or more of you!"

Illuminada said, "Yes, sir."

"How do you know that?"

"The United Nations man said so."

"You spoke to him, did you?" It was more than Ambrosio

had done. NEVER SURRENDER THE UPPER HAND!
Ambrosio said, "Did you? Oh, yes, *then what was his name?*"

Illuminada said, "Mr. Bjorn Anderson." Illuminada said,
"He was very partial to halo halo in coconut milk."

"How do you know that?"

"I served him while he was here with his team."

Trick questions. Ambrosio said warningly, "I thought you
were the accountant here?" He said tightly, "Hmm?"

"I also waitress and sweep up." Illuminada said, "We all
share jobs. Rodolfo the strong man also does the plumbing and
the dog lady, Carmel—"

"Good." Just testing. Ambrosio said, "You were all part of
a family circus in the provinces, right? You're all the Abala
family?" Ambrosio said, "What was the name of the circus?"

"The Abala Family Circus."

That was question seven. Question eight was the kicker. Ambrosio said darkly, "And what happened to that?"

"It was blown away."

"*By whom?*"

Illuminada said, "Typhoon Vera." Illuminada said, "We
were all left with nothing so we pooled our liquid resources—"

"You mean your money—"

"Our money, took a loan from a development bank at reduc-
ing interest on a heavy two-year payback of the principal
and—"

"You set up here." He didn't need all the facts, ma'am, all
he needed were the facts. Ambrosio said, "Now I want you to
tell me who hates who here."

Illuminada said, "Yes, sir." She was very humble. Maybe he
was frightening her. She was tiny. She looked up at him like a
guilty child. Illuminada said, "We all love each other. Without
each other we couldn't survive."

Ambrosio said, "Sex."

Illuminada said, "Only the married people. Pablo is very
strict."

"Why blow up a kitchen sink and a papier-mâché dragon?"

Illuminada said, "Search me."

"Frustrated desires?"

There was a pause. She was thinking. Illuminada said helpfully, "I wanted to be a nun when I was young." She was thinking hard. "Ignacio always says he wishes he could do cryptic crosswords and Imelda—"

"Real frustrated desires!"

"Is that a question?"

"Yes, that's a question!" She was an accountant and a waitress. She was keeping track. Ambrosio said, "How many have I had?"

Illuminada said, "The last one will be question twelve."

"And what's the answer?" Ambrosio said quickly, "That isn't question thirteen, that's a supplementary question from question twelve." He saw her nod. Behind those eyes there was some sort of pocket calculator tapping his opportunities away one by one.

"What was question twelve again?"

"Who has real, solid, seething frustrated desires here?"

Illuminada said, "No one."

"Are you saying all you people are *nice?*"

She looked away. Maybe that was a free question. Illuminada, smiling, said sweetly, thinking about her family, "We all get on. Families always do." She looked back to him. She asked, "Don't they?" She could have been a nun. She had eyes that turned you to Jell-O. If she had been taller maybe he could have— Illuminada said, "Are you married with a family, Mr. Ambrosio?"

Ambrosio said, "Yes."

"And you love your family, don't you? And they love you?"

Ambrosio said, "Money." Stay on safe ground. Ambrosio said deeply, "Now look, money is the root of all evil and I've been looking at your place from an economic point of view and I can't help feeling that the rent here in the middle of Ermita—"

Illuminada said, "We own the building."

"That the rent here in the middle of Ermita you could get if you rented out the building wouldn't be enough to maintain the living standards of—of—" Ambrosio asked, "How many of you are there?"

"Eleven and we send money back to our distant relatives in the provinces and—"

"All you have here is the tourist trade—"

"Which is very good and made up of such kind and nice people."

"Which may be good and made up of kind and nice people, but—" Ambrosio said suddenly, "What's all this nice? There must be someone who hates someone or someone who wants to screw someone or someone who wants to—"

Illuminada said with genuine surprise, "No."

"In the big world everyone hates everyone!"

"Our world isn't very big."

No. No, it wasn't. He was doing the gestapo bit. NEVER GIVE A DWARF AN EVEN BREAK! Ambrosio said, "No, I didn't mean that—"

"But it isn't."

"Um, where do you all live?"

"Upstairs." Illuminada said, "We all have our own rooms. The ceilings are probably too low for someone as tall as you, but if you'd like to search—"

"No." Ambrosio said, "No, look, I—" Ambrosio said, "I'm not trying to frighten you."

"I know that, sir."

"Don't call me sir!" He was pushing a dwarf around, a person of diminished stature, a female dwarf. Once, he had been kind to small people and females. Ambrosio, feeling awkward, said, "Look, all I want to do is protect you from the mad bomber who's setting off bombs!"

She smiled wonderfully at him. She glowed with love. She would have made the sort of nun who made you slink away in shame and head for the confession box punching yourself in the mouth as you went. Ambrosio said, "People like me—people from the outside world—we have a duty to help our less fortunate fellow citizens. That's why that great and good body the U.N. called us in—"

Illuminada said, "Thank you."

"It doesn't mean we—it means—" Poor dwarves. They were little children. They were happy. They lived in their own little world and played with the flowers. All they had were the tourists. They served. They smiled. They playacted. They swung on trapezes and juggled balls and dreamed of being nuns and doing cryptic crosswords. They loved each other. They worked. They were very helpful to people who had asked them questions. They— Ambrosio asked as question number seventeen, "Do you make money here?"

Illuminada said, "Yes."

Good. At least they had that.

"Enough to live on?" Maybe children's clothes were cheaper. They weren't when his own children had to have them.

Illuminada said, "Yes." That was question number eighteen.

"How much?" He didn't care. He was just making conversation.

"In Philippine pesos or U.S. dollars?" Illuminada said, "We get the tourists almost exclusively. They pay in U.S. dollars." Illuminada said, "We declare it all on our tax."

"I know that."

Illuminada, being helpful, said, "Pesos or dollars?"

"Dollars."

"Gross or net after taxes and expenses for division eleven ways plus small allowances for distant relatives?"

Maybe he could loan her the first Fireball tape. Ambrosio said, "Oh, U.S. dollars."

Illuminada said, "Two hundred ninety-five thousand five hundred average."

Ambrosio said, "What?"

Illuminada said, "Per half year." Illuminada said, "Sometimes, in a good year when the wet season is late, we do better."

Question twenty. Ambrosio said, "*What?*"

"Yes." She smiled.

"Oh."

Illuminada said, "It's nice."

"Ah—"

Illuminada said, "It makes us all very happy."

"Two hundred ninety-five thousand five hundred—American dollars—*profit?*"

He had had all his questions. He saw her, this time, only smile.

Ambrosio said, *"Jesus!"*

He saw her still smiling. She looked up at him like a helpless child with big glasses.

"NEVER BE LOST FOR WORDS!"

He wasn't. He had one. Ambrosio said, *"WHAT?"*

He was a Fireball. He had not one but two words.

Ambrosio, aghast, stunned, wiped out, ruined, defeated, a bum among the ranks of all bums, said in frank, open-wide astonishment, *"JESUS!"*

Above the honor roll outside the Western District Headquarters on United Nations Avenue there was a plaque that read in bold, carved script to commemorate all the dead officers: "Go Spread the Word, Tell the Passersby,/That in This Little World/Men Knew How to Die." It had above it, with the Metro Manila Police crest, the demands, *"Merit. Patriotism. Dignity."*

If he could possibly avoid it, he never went there. It frightened him. Elizalde, in his car on Roxas Boulevard, turned over the photograph. He had found a parking spot a little down from the Manila Hotel near the Deaf-and-Dumb Café. The street was full of trucks and buses belching black diesel smoke and he wound up the window and turned the air-conditioning on low.

Ermalinda R. Beo, Cavite Street.

Santiago Beo, Cavite Street.

My Sister, Mother, Friend.

DESAPARECIDO. It was a word in Spanish. It was not a language either of them would have spoken. It was written in a different hand.

DESAPARECIDO. It meant *disappeared*. It meant gone,

vanished, traceless. In Argentina, where the word had gained common currency during the rule of the junta, it meant death in a ditch. It meant—

It meant someone else had written it.

It meant . . .

In the car, Elizalde touched at the photograph with his thumbnail and looked down hard at the two faces stopped in midconversation on a day so wonderful they had wanted to record their names and their hopes in writing.

My Sister, Mother, Friend.

Ermalinda R. Beo. Santiago Beo.

Across from the Deaf-and-Dumb Café he could see the orchid garden in the park. It was deserted. There was no longer anyone sitting there.

In the car, the police radio was going, calling cars to a traffic pileup somewhere on Taft Avenue and sending a rescue team to an industrial accident out near the airport on a building site. Reaching down, he turned the radio off.

He tapped at the corner of the photograph with his thumbnail. For some reason he touched at the butt of his pistol in its holster to check it was still there.

Cavite Street. Beo.

He had nothing.

He had, only, the photograph and a moment stopped by the photographer's camera that would never come again and was now as if it had never been. He thought, later, he would walk down Roxas Boulevard and look for all the places in the background of the picture.

He thought, probably, it would do him no good at all.

Everywhere, there was the noise and stink and fumes of the city.

Getting out of his car and locking it carefully and obviously in case anyone was watching, Elizalde crossed over the street into the park and, going by way of the orchid garden, went toward the banks of public telephones down by the bay to make a call.

In the kitchen, gluing back the sink with a tube of contact adhesive so he and Bontoc could wash up the lunchtime dishes, Ernesto said conversationally, "You're a Bontoc, hey?" He turned to glance at Bontoc standing behind him waiting, and grinned. Ernesto said, "Have you got any tattoos?"

Maybe he did and maybe he didn't. Bontoc said firmly, "Who do you think is the target here and why?"

"No idea at all." He was engrossed in his task. The tube of cement in his hands looked like a pneumatic drill. Tubes of contact cement were made for people with a minimum hand stretch of seven inches, not four. Ernesto asked, "Have you ever taken a head?"

Bontoc said, "No."

"Me either." Ernesto said, "I like to cook. I think it's one of the great arts of mankind, don't you?"

"Sure."

"Everything. I like to cook Philippino dishes and Chinese dishes and Malay dishes, Indian curries, French cuisine, Austrian veal dishes—" Ernesto said, "But not seafood." Ernesto, still gluing, said dreamily:

> *"tis very seldom i have felt*
> *drawn to a scallop or a smelt*
> *and still more rarely do i feel*
> *love for the electric eel."*

Ernesto said, "That's a poem by Don Marquis. He wrote a book of poems called *archy and mehitabel*. It was about a cat and a cockroach." He went on gluing.

" 'the oyster is useful in his fashion /but has little pride or passion.' " Bontoc said, *"archy and mehitabel* was his first book. The electric eel poem is from his second book called *archy's life of mehitabel."* Bontoc said, "The cockroach used to leave typewritten poems during the nights. He used to jump up and down on the keys to do it, but he couldn't reach the shift keys to make punctuation marks or capital letters. That was why he always wrote in free verse." He thought he was the only person on earth who had ever read it. Bontoc said:

> *"if all the verse what i have wrote*
> *were boiled together in a kettle*
> *twould make a meal for every goat*
> *from nome to popocatepetl mexico."*

He stopped gluing. Ernesto said:

> *"and all the prose what i have penned*
> *if laid together end to end*
> *would reach from russia to south bend*
> *indiana."*

He grinned. He had a nice face when he grinned.

> *"but all the money what i saved*
> *from all them works at which i slaved*
> *is not enough to get me shaved*
> *every morning."*

Bontoc said, shrugging, "All Bontoc males get tattooed on the chest at puberty. It's an initiation thing."

> *"and all the dams which i care*
> *if heaped together in the air*
> *would not much reach out anywhere*
> *they wouldn't."*

Ernesto said warily, "I guess it's a bit like being a dwarf, but in my case you can't cover it with a shirt." He looked down.

Bontoc said, "I guess so." Bontoc said brightly, " 'because i dont shave every day . . .' "

> *"and i write for arts sake anyway*
> *and always hate to take my pay"*

Ernesto said:

> *"man the universal simp*
> *follows lagging with a limp*
> *treading on his neighbors toes*
> *the way the little insect goes*
> *in a million years or more . . ."*

Bontoc said:

> *"man may learn the simple lore*
> *of how bees are organized*
> *and why ants are civilized*
> *may even hope for to approach*
> *the culture of an average roach . . ."*

Ernesto said happily, louder, " 'if he is humble and not smug / may emulate the humble bug!' "

Bontoc said, "I studied in America for a while. I was lonely. I didn't know anybody. I read a lot of poetry." Bontoc said, "They're just cicatrix tattoos. If you're really curious—"

"No.

" '. . .freuds rush in
where angels
fear to tread.' " Ernesto said, "What's that one from?"

Bontoc said, *"songs of los angeles.* That's where archy the cockroach thinks he should be in the movies." Bontoc, thinking hard, said, " 'boss a new book—' "

Ernesto said, " 'book review'!"

> *"boss a new book*
> *has appeared*
> *which should be*

> *read by everyone*
> *it is entitled . . ."*

Bontoc said happily:

> *"the cockroach*
> *its life history*
> *and how to deal*
> *with it and . . ."*

He tossed the ball to Ernesto.

> *"and*
> *the author*
> *is frederick laing*
> *who is assistant*
> *in the department*
> *of entomology in the . . ."*

Ernesto said, "Yes?"

" 'british museum' "

Ernesto asked, "Have you ever been there, Baptiste? To England?"

"No. Have you?"

Ernesto said, "No."

> *"british museum*
> *of natural history*
> *it is one of the best books i ever . . ."*

Bontoc and Ernesto said in unison:

> *"tasted! i am eating*
> *the binding from*
> *a copy with*

a great deal of
relish and . . ."

Bontoc and Ernesto shouted:

> *"and recommend it*
> *to all other insects yours*
> *truly*
> *archy"*

There was a silence. They looked at each other.

Ernesto said quietly, "You were lonely in America?"

Bontoc said, "Yes."

Ernesto said, "You're an ordinary person—how could you be lonely?"

How could he have been? Bontoc said quickly, grinning: "well boss i promised to tell you something of the life story of mehitabel the cat"

He had stopped gluing. He was looking at Bontoc with genuine curiosity. Ernesto said, "Baptiste . . ." He wanted to ask something.

"Um." Bontoc said efficiently, "Ernesto, have you any idea at all who's setting off these bombs?"

There was a silence.

"No." He looked down at the glue tube in his hand. He had never thought that somewhere in the world there was someone else who could quote. He grinned. Ernesto said, " 'wotto hell? wotto hell?' " Ernesto, going back to his gluing said, "No, I haven't the faintest idea on earth." He was still quoting, " 'wotto hell—wotto hell—' "

He had his back to Bontoc. Maybe he had glue on his face. He seemed to touch at his face with his hand.

Ernesto, three foot one and a half inches, gluing back the sink with contact glue, said, shrugging, " 'wotto hell, wotto hell—' "

Ernesto said in a voice so low Bontoc had to strain to hear it, " 'luck may change love / archy.' "

———

He waited.

He watched.

In Rizal Park, down by the bay at dusk, Rolly, sitting in a sidewalk café near the banks of public telephones, watched as Elizalde made his call.

He had no idea who the man was speaking to.

He didn't care. It mattered not at all.

Rolly, watching, waiting, in no hurry, sat at his table drinking coffee and gazing with lazy contentment out at the waters of the bay.

Framed in the setting sun in the harbor was a forty-foot blue-and-white catamaran moored a little way out from the Yacht Club flying an American flag and, dreaming his own little dreams of riches, idly, he wondered whose it was.

Silence. All the dwarves were away for their afternoon siestas in their private quarters. To one side of the darkened ring, Ambrosio watched Bontoc light a cigarette and put his lighter carefully back into his pocket.

Fireball.

archys life of mehitabel.

Bombs. People being nice to each other. Two hundred ninety-five thousand five hundred U.S. dollars per half year.

He saw Bontoc's face looking at him with a look he had never seen before. He saw Bontoc reach into his pocket and take out his lighter again and offer that and his cigarettes to him.

He took one and lit it.

It tasted like dust.

"Baptiste—"

Bontoc said, "Yes?"

Ambrosio said, "Baptiste—" Ambrosio said in a sudden panic, "Baptiste, what the hell is going on here? Do *you* know?"

8

"For God's sake, Felix, *what do you want?*" He seemed terrified. In his glassed-in office at the Joint Services Missing Persons Bureau, Lieutenant Constantino Cafiero, looking for somewhere to go in the tiny room and finding nowhere, said in a whisper, "I told you on the phone: there are no files on missing persons called Barrera or Beo." Outside, through the glass, he could see all the desks and banks of filing cabinets and computer consoles that took up the entire third floor of the building. He could see all the people working at those desks or filing cabinets or consoles looking at him. Cafiero said, "I told you—there's nothing." He had gotten to his feet behind his desk. "What the hell made you come here in person?" Cafiero said, "How did you get in?"

"I'm a cop. I showed my cop badge." He had not seen Cafiero for a long time. Elizalde said, "How's Rosey?"

"I told you! There's no record!" His eyes stayed on the people at the desks and the consoles and at the files. Cafiero said, "I told you!"

"How's your wife?"

"Desaparecido doesn't mean missing—it means disappeared!" Both his hands were working themselves into fists. He was a small Spanish-looking mestizo in his mid-forties. He was sweating. Cafiero said, "Felix, I told you on the phone— The phone call was logged! It's official! You enquired and I told you: we don't have a file on the Barrera or the Beo boy—either of them!"

Elizalde said, "I believe she left you. I was sorry to hear it.

I always thought you two—" He saw the man's face. Elizalde said, "Files go missing or get misplaced."

Cafiero said, "And people get killed."

"Are the files missing? Did you check the numbers and verify the master index?"

"Why the hell are you here?" Out there, the Joint Services personnel included the police, the army, the Secret Service, and God alone knew who else. His jaw was tightening. Cafiero said, *"Why the hell are you here?"*

"What can you tell me?" He was taller by half a head than Cafiero. He stood back to lose the difference. Elizalde said, "I haven't got anywhere else to go. You used to be a—" Elizalde said, "You and Rosey and Marguerita and—" Elizalde said, "Tino, people are dead."

"People are always dead. Every day, there are more of them." Cafiero said tightly, "I read obituaries. Every day in every way people are getting deader and deader. If all the people who ever died were living now—" He could not stop scratching at his thumb. His eyes moved constantly. Cafiero said, "There's no record of the two people you asked about. If you can show cop badges, then act like a cop and go and ask the neighbors of the people who you say are missing! Go and—"

"I have asked them. The barangay people where Barrera lived said nothing. The wife of the dead man—the mother of the missing boy—said his disappearance had been reported. The room where the Beo girl lived with her brother has been cleaned out. The wife of the man who killed the faith healer—the mother of the missing boy—thought I was going to have her killed too!" His voice was rising. He saw people outside look up. Elizalde said, "What do you know about either of the two missing people? If you know anything, tell me!"

"Desaparecido doesn't mean missing, it means 'vanished!' " Cafiero said, "People go missing all the time—"

"Why the hell are you talking in clichés?"

"They are clichés! People go missing because they want to go missing or someone else wants them to go missing! People are commodities—they sell themselves or get sold!" He was talking in clichés. He had never said them out loud before. Cafiero said suddenly, "In the name of God, Felix—!" Cafiero said, "There are people here—in this office who—" He said, "It's meant to be a secret! If you go missing—if you decide to go missing or someone else decides you should go missing—then it's meant to be, by definition, a secret! It's—" He was rambling. He was terrified. He stared out through the glass windows. "People who—people who—" Cafiero said, "You're talking about the barrio people—the slum dwellers—the ones with no brains but only bodies: these people are—" Cafiero said, "Haven't you ever had a fantasy of owning someone completely, doing absolutely what you want with them, and then disposing of them as if they were a commodity?"

"No."

"Don't lie to me!" God alone knew what happened out there in the office. God alone knew what happened to the faces and the lives recorded in the files. God alone knew what— Cafiero said, "Felix, there are things—things that—" He suddenly changed tack. Cafiero said with a grin, "No, you won't get anything out of the barangay people because the barangay people aren't like us. The barangay people are just—"

"What?"

Cafiero said, "Disposable. They don't protest because they don't have any expectations that anyone will listen to their protest and they live, they fuck, they eat, they die, they get sold or go missing without a trace!" Cafiero said, "Sometimes they stage their own disappearances to join the Communists in the mountains or sometimes they stage their own disappearances to go whoring or sometimes they—" His mouth was tight. There was a tic at the side of his jaw with the tension there. "Or sometimes—" He watched, he always watched, he watched what was happening outside in the big room. "Or sometimes—"

Elizalde said with malice, "Or sometimes, they just turn inward, become cowards, and lose everything they had." He waited.

He watched Cafiero's face.

He waited. He saw the man looking out through the glass. There was a silence.

Cafiero said, "Yes. Yes, they do."

"What happened to the Barrera boy and Santiago Beo?"

Cafiero said, "Their files may have gone missing."

"Have they gone missing?"

He watched. Cafiero said, "I answered your question on the phone. Your question and my response were both logged. I won't pursue the matter further at this stage."

"At what stage will you pursue it further?"

"I won't pursue it further at all."

Elizalde said, "*Why not?*"

"Because I won't! Because I—" Cafiero said suddenly, "Felix, do you know what a *pacto de sangre* is?"

"It's a blood pact."

"It's a blood pact." Cafiero said, "Yes. It's a pact where everybody knows what's happening and why something's happening, but nobody says anything. It's a—" He bit at his lip. "It's a—" Cafiero said, "It's where—it's where . . ." Cafiero said, "In Manila altogether, how many people do you think are missing? How many files do you think are gone? How many cases do you think I won't follow through? How many?"

There were two. Elizalde said, "So far—"

"How many? Like this?"

Cafiero said, "The guns these people are using—where did they come from?"

"I'm not sure."

"Aren't you?"

"Gomez thinks—"

Cafiero said, "Cafiero thinks—"

Elizalde said, "They may have come from us."

"May have? Or did?" He had him. His face was set. Cafiero said, "You want something from me. I should give it to you simply because you asked. Now I want something from you.

Give it to me. Did the guns come from us—from the cops—*or didn't they?*"

"Gomez would have to—"

"*Yes or fucking no!*"

Elizalde said, "Yes."

Cafiero said, "My wife left me because I was so afraid I couldn't even pass water!" Cafiero said, "Desaparecido—that's Spanish! Do you really think that some semiliterate barangay peasant wrote that word at the bottom of the photograph? Or do you think maybe it was someone else? Do you think that maybe whoever wrote it thought that the person who would read it could speak Spanish? Do you think—" He said in a voice so low Elizalde had to strain to catch it, " *'Solo Dios sabe lo que viví, Ayer y hoy, y aquí estoy. Mírame—que aquí estoy.'* " Cafiero said, "That's Spanish too. Any idea at all what it means, Lieutenant Felix Elizalde—any idea at all?"

"It means, God alone knows what I lived through, yesterday and today, and here I am. Look at me—here I am."

Cafiero said, "The Spanish on the back of the photograph under the two names and addresses was meant to be read by you." He looked away. Cafiero said, "You were meant to come here." He waited. He gazed sadly out into the big office where people watched.

"And what were you meant to tell me?"

"I don't know." He was not the same man Elizalde had known. He had become someone else. Over and over the nail of his index finger had scratched at the ball of his thumb. The thumb was raw but not bleeding. It never bled. Like his life, all it did was hurt.

"Tino . . ."

"I don't know." He watched all the watchers watching him. In all the files, there were thousands of lives. It was a bank. It was a commodities market. There were riches there. Out in the office, guarding those riches, there were people watching him who never spoke to him. "I don't know." Everything he had ever once been was gone. "I don't know!" Cafiero, his eyes closed, holding back something about to burst that never burst, said desperately, "I don't know! I don't know what it is they even think I *can* tell you!"

Elizalde, Felix, Detective Lieutenant, Western District, Metro Manila Police.

Out in the office of the Joint Services Missing Persons Bureau, under his desk lamp, someone made a note.

It was a man in shirtsleeves. He was well paid for his occasional little bits of information.

These days, every peso counted.

At his desk, he picked up his telephone to make a brief call.

There was a drum roll.

"Ladies and gentlemen, Mesdames et Messieurs . . ." Show time. The diners in the Gnome Home had munched their way through the evening special, *lapu-lapu*—steamed grouper fish garnished with leeks and carrots, salt, butter, and mustard served on rattan plates on banana leaves with helpings of rice—drunk their coffee in demitasses, lit their cigars and cigarettes, had their plates cleared away as they paid their bills and now, now as the lights dimmed to a single diffused blue glow in the center of the ring, Pablo's voice, rolling all his R's, announced above the music, "Our new routine . . . *Un Homme et Une Femme; Ein Mann und eine Frau; Un Hombre y una Mujer'*—there wasn't a paying local in the place so there was no need for Philippino—"*A man and a woman.*"

There was total darkness in the ring.

There was a pause.

There was, on the far side of the sawdust below the kitchen, just for an instant, a single spot.

Nothing.

The customers said, "Oh."

There was another drum roll. There was another spot on the other side of the ring where Bontoc and Ambrosio were with

their coffee and cigarettes. The audience craned. Ambrosio hid
the glow of his cigarette in the cup of his hand.

The audience said—

"Cinderella!" Pablo.

The audience said, "Ah!"

The spot came on in the center of the ring.

Ambrosio said, "Ayo!"

Ar-yo . . . ! It was Cinderella. She stood in the full spot,
beautiful beyond words in black bodice and long ankle-length
yellow skirt, her black hair short and clipped in a fringe above
her dark eyes and rosy cheeks. Her face—was it a mask?—was
yellow with makeup. She was over six feet tall with legs that
must have gone on to her armpits.

The customers said, "Ooohhh."

"Ohhh . . ." If she was a dwarf, she was a very tall one.
Ambrosio, his mouth open to receive the cigarette, said in a
gasp, "Who is it?" She was beautiful. She was Fireball fantasy
stuff. Ambrosio said in a whisper as the vision of loveliness
turned slowly so all could admire her, "Baptiste, who is she?"

"Shh!" In Bontoc they hadn't had Cinderella. He'd been
deprived until he got to America and saw Disneyland. Bontoc
said, "I don't know."

She had a voice like an angel. "I'm so pretty, / I'm so pretty.
/ It's amazing how—" And she mimed well. It was the Natalie
Wood voice from *West Side Story*. She had a hairbrush. It came
out of nowhere. She began brushing her hair. Mirrors appeared
from somewhere, running. Running? They were dwarf mirrors,
box mirrors built around dwarves. The spotlight became a bank
of spotlights. It was the jugglers Ricardo and Jasmine—you
could see their legs in red-and-white-striped stockings under
the cardboard boxes the mirrors were fixed to. They were not
ordinary mirrors: they were glittering, reflecting, sparkling mirrors. The light caught them and they flashed like lasers. There
were more mirrors. The big box mirrors with the striped legs
had hand mirrors in their hands. Their hands stuck out at the
side of the boxes. They were juggling hand mirrors—the hand

mirrors (count them, six—*six*—each) went up and over turning in midair above the headless boxes. The mirrors were juggling mirrors without looking at them. Maybe they had a hole in the top of their boxes. Then they were running and besporting around Cinderella without looking at her. Either way, the customers went, "Sheee—*yee*—!"

Ambrosio said in ecstasy, "My kids would—"

The audience said, "Ah!"

At last, a real dwarf. Out of nowhere, there was a clown. It was Ignacio in a one-piece Grotesque outfit with a single red spot on his otherwise black mouthless white face. It was his nose. He had a bald head. The bald head, out of nowhere, suddenly had a paper flower growing out of it. Pablo's voice yelled over the address system, "Ignacio!" Then another clown, this time in the baggy, ill-fitting Auguste evening dress with boiled shirt and big, toeless, flapping shoes, "Imelda!" They were running, tumbling, pushing and shoving, going over like jumping jacks and vaulting, leaping over each other. They ran from the far spotlight directly toward the main spotlight with the mirrors and Cinderella. Running, falling, cavorting, they saw nothing until they—

Twang! It was a single, heart-breaking note on what sounded like an out-of-tune violin.

Grotesque saw Cinderella.

Cinderella saw only the mirrors.

Twang.

Grotesque fell down clutching at his heart.

Auguste jumped. Grotesque ignored him. Auguste tumbled. Grotesque stared at Cinderella. He went forward and looked into one of the mirrors and saw Cinderella in the mirror. He looked up to see Cinderella's face. He looked up and up to see Cinderella's face. And up . . . and up . . . and up. He fell over backward.

The audience said, "Ah!" Ambrosio said, "Heh!" Bontoc watched Cinderella. He sighed wistfully.

Cinderella brushed at her hair. One by one the juggling hand-held mirrors seemed to grow heavy, to slow down. From some-where, softly, there were the faint strains of the dying swan from Swan Lake. The customers, some of them with popular classic record collections at home themselves, went, "Ahh . . ."

The flying hand-held mirrors one by one slowed down, stopped, and then disappeared.

Grotesque looked up. Grotesque began to rise like Jell-O. He clutched at his heart. Auguste clutched at his sleeve. Grotesque knocked Auguste off his feet and sent him tumbling over and over with a single sweep of his hand. The audience fell about laughing.

Cinderella didn't even look down.

Grotesque looked up. He started forward to touch at Cinder-ella's hem. He stepped back. She looked at the mirrors. Gro-tesque turned and looked at the audience. The audience was silent. He appealed to the audience. They watched. He touched at her hem. It must have been red hot: he fell back over and over grabbing at his wrist. Auguste was back. He touched at Gro-tesque's shoulder. Grotesque floored him. The audience said in relief, "Yaaee!" Ambrosio said in a whisper, happily puffing on his cigarette in the dark, "This is good, isn't it?"

He loved her. In the ring, Grotesque, staring up, loved Cin-derella. He produced, from nowhere, a violin. He played to her a— One of the strings broke and he played a single *twang!*

The audience, replete on grouper fish, coffee, and cigars, said, "Ho! Ho!"

Undaunted, he put his bow up for a second shot.

Twang! Another string.

Twang! And another!

Twang! He threw the violin down and stomped on it. The audience thought that was the yokker of the evening. He took the bits of broken violin and as Auguste came up to offer comfort, solace, and consolation and to get back to a bit of tumbling, falling down and leapfrogging around the place, beat Auguste over the head with it until it exploded into splinters.

"Smile though your heart is breaking . . ." It was the old

Chaplin tune, a guaranteed eye-wiper. In the spotlight, Grotesque was alone. He had nothing. He looked up at Cinderella. He loved her. He took from his pocket a spotted handkerchief the size of a small bedsheet and dabbed at his tears. He had nothing. He appealed to the audience. The audience, getting into the spirit of things, said, "Ohh . . ." So did Ambrosio.

Grotesque had nothing.

He had the flower growing out of his head. He touched at it. Should he try? He looked at the audience. Should he? They hadn't had Cinderella in Bontoc. They'd had flowers and girls. Should he? Bontoc yelled, "Yeah! Yeah!" Should he? He looked to Cinderella. She looked only in the mirrors. Should he? Should he?

Someone with a heavy German accent yelled at the top of his voice, "Offer her der flower!"

"Go on!" It was a woman's voice from somewhere in the back row of tables with an Australian accent. "Give her the weed!"

He appealed. Should he?

The customers yelled as one, "YEAH!!"

He plucked it from his head. It hurt. He bore the pain bravely. The audience applauded him on. Should he?

"YEAH!!"

He gave it to her.

She took it.

The audience clapped.

She looked down at it. Grotesque, his hand clutching his chest, looked as if his heart would break. Auguste came tumbling over and over into the spotlight. Grotesque ignored him. Cinderella looked at the flower. They were back to the Skaters' Waltz. They must have only one or two tapes besides the complete Chuck Berry collection in the entire place.

She looked at the flower.

She looked down at him.

She reached down to touch his hand. The hand was too far away.

The audience said, "Ohh . . ."

Ambrosio yelled, "Jump!"

Grotesque jumped up on his little legs. He jumped about three inches. Love did that to you: you lost all your jump. He jumped again—two inches. He was getting weaker for romance by the moment.

Twang! An idea. He began climbing up the side of one of the cardboard box mirrors. The cardboard box mirror collapsed into a crumpled mess on the sawdust. The other! The other went down like a concertina.

Auguste! Grotesque looked around for Auguste. Auguste was gone. The spotlights tightened. In the spotlight, close together but separated forever by about three foot eight of altitude, Grotesque and Cinderella were alone. The music over the system was a million violins sawing away in minor keys. The audience, heavy with fish and nicotine, made blubbering noises in the darkness. Ambrosio, whispering to Bontoc, said urgently, "Do you know this story? Does it—"

Bontoc said, "Shh!" He sniffed.

They waited. Magic fairy?

There were only Cinderella and Grotesque in the spot.

Right, right. Deus ex machina fairy . . . *godmother*. Right?

Only the sadness, the violins, and the solitary little man and the beautiful face were looking down at him. Someone with a midwestern matron's accent said behind Ambrosio, "Aw . . . gee . . . !"

TWANG!

Fairy godfather! It was Auguste! He was no tumbler, he was a magician. He wore a black cloak and carried a wand!

Applause.

Ambrosio, hopping up and down in his seat, said, "Good! Yeah!"

The tapes started on the theme from the movie *A Man and a Woman*. It was from the bit where the man was a racing-car driver getting things done in a hurry. Auguste offered a magic spell to Grotesque. Grotesque nodded. Auguste, as a Merlin, held a few grudges: he rubbed at his shoulder. Grotesque, rushing to him, fell on his knees and begged. Cinderella put her beautiful hands to her beautiful bosoms and implored.

Applause.

Auguste the magnificent bowed.

Applause.

The music swelled and swelled.

The black cape came off.

The audience went mad with applauding. Along with the coffee they had made inroads into Napoleon brandy. The stuff, in the darkness, was flowing like water.

Auguste postured.

The audience clapped.

Grotesque begged.

Cinderella implored.

Auguste, throwing the cape up into the air, the spotlight chasing it, set off a blinding white light of flashpowder. The cape came down again, turning over and over, bringing the light back to Grotesque and Cinderella.

Where were they? They were yellow and black clothes and a paper flower.

Silence.

The audience, ready to applaud, held their fingertips together like prayers.

Auguste touched at the pile of clothing and rising out of them came Grotesque. The flower began to rise up in someone's hand. It was Cinderella, rising from her long sleep. She rose up and—up no more.

She was a dwarf like Grotesque. Her long yellow skirt was still a long yellow skirt, but it was a shorter long yellow skirt. She was three foot two inches high.

Drum roll.

The audience said, "Yea!" She took off her mask. Below it was a dwarf's face. It was Carmel the dog trainer. She could touch him. She reached out to touch Grotesque. The audience clapped and clapped and clapped. The music swelled and the racing driver and Catherine Deneuve started to go off happily into the sunset together.

She loved him.

He looked at her.

Grotesque looked at Auguste.

She loved him. She held out the flower to give it to him.

"Hooray!" In the audience the Australian woman was blubbering with package-tour happiness.

Grotesque looked at her, like him, a dwarf.

Silence. All the music stopped.

Silence.

Grotesque looked at Auguste.

She loved him. She offered him the flower.

Over the system, Pablo's voice said thickly, "Ah, dreams . . . Dwarves, too, dream of Cinderella. . . ."

In the center of the ring, under the spot, Grotesque, his head bowed, slowly walked away.

In the Gnome Home Acrobatic and One-Ring Sawdust Circus Café; Coffee, Meals, and Entertainment Three Times a Day, there was not a sound.

"Bontoc—" Ambrosio, in the darkness, said in a whisper, "Baptiste, is that it?"

That was it.

In the spot, part of the script or not, Carmel, without makeup, like Auguste—like Imelda—looked into the darkness and waited for the applause.

There was no applause.

In the Gnome Home, without sound, having—mercifully—already paid their bills, one by one or in little family groups, the diners began to get up from their tables and file out.

"Maybelline!" It was their Chuck Berry signature tune. In the ring, coming back, Grotesque and Ignacio, bowing deeply, waited for the laughter and the gales of applause.

It was their new routine. It was the first tryout before a live audience.

At his table in the darkness Bontoc said softly, "Jesus—"

It was what the dwarves thought normal people thought about dwarves. It was their existence. It was what made people laugh.

Utter, complete silence.

In the ring, in the spotlight, Ignacio and Imelda, Carmel and Jasmine grinned and smiled.

Utter, complete, total silence. In the darkness, all the tables where the diners had been were empty. In that darkness, in the emptiness, with nothing else he could think of to say, Bontoc said again, softly, "Jesus, oh Jesus . . ."

He put his hand to his face.

"Smile though your heart is breaking . . ." It was another record, started in the middle. It must have been Pablo somewhere.

"Baptiste . . . ?" It was Ambrosio.

At his table, in the darkness, shaking his head, Bontoc looked away.

He was short himself.

He was not that short.

In the awful, terrible silence, Bontoc covered his eyes.

It was night. In his armory, Gomez, with both the guns laid out on his workshop table, wrote in the section of the report form marked "TYPE OF WEAPON": *Modified Gevarm A7 rifle, shortened and converted to full automatic.*

"MAGAZINE CAPACITY": Gomez wrote, *20.*

"CALIBER": Gomez wrote, *0.22*

"SERIAL NUMBER": Gomez wrote, *None.*

He looked down at the guns. He was alone in the armory.

"Felix . . ." In his office in the Joint Services Missing Persons Bureau in Mabine, the man who had once been Constantino Cafiero and his friend, said quietly, "Go." They had stood in silence for a long time and he had said nothing. Cafiero said, "Go." He said, *"Mírame—que aquí estoy:* look at me . . . here I am . . . and here I am." Cafiero said, "If it's true—If it's true . . ." He said quietly, "If it's true, what I know . . ." Cafiero said suddenly, *"No!* Nothing! Nothing is worth that!"

Cafiero, so loudly that everyone in the outer office could hear him clearly, shouted, "No! I don't know anything! I know nothing at all! Go! *Go!*" Cafiero said suddenly, softly, "Rosey and I—"

Cafiero said, "No! No, I don't know a goddamned thing!" He said, "Go to hell! Go screw yourself ! Go die!" Cafiero shrieked, "Fuck you! Go to hell!" Cafiero yelled as an order so everyone could hear, "For Christ's sake, GET OUT!"

"PLACE OF ORIGIN OR MANUFACTURE": Gomez wrote, *France.*

He had a silver hip flask of Manila rum on the workbench next to the guns. He unscrewed the cap and held the lip up a little from his mouth.

"IS WEAPON TRACEABLE?"

He put the flask to his mouth and took a swig. The rum burned him all the way down.

No. He filled in the space.

He took a second swig from the flask.

No. He was alone in the armory.

Outside, it was night.

He put the silver hip flask to his lips and, his hands shaking, drained it off.

Darkness.

In the Gnome Home Acrobatic and One-Ring Sawdust Circus Café; Coffee, Meals, and Entertainment Three Times a Day there was absolute silence.

Darkness.

In the Gnome Home, after a long while, the Ringmaster, Pablo, came to show them the way out and lock up for the night.

Darkness.

Darkest night.

In the streets and on a boat moored out in the bay, all the lights were burning.

Elizalde, Felix, Lieutenant, Western District, Metro Manila Police.

Cafiero, Constantino, Lieutenant, Joint Services Missing Persons Bureau, Mabine.

Two names. Two things to write down in his file and mull over.

At night, alone on the boat, in the silence, he needed occupation.

He looked at the two names and tapped at them on the page with a pencil.

Secretly, savoring it, lighting a cigarette, on the boat, the Whispering Man smiled.

9

At 9:00 P.M. outside Mrs. Quifano's Serviced Rooms
for Respectable Single Gentlemen in Pagtatapunan Street, there
was a tattooed, half-naked man wearing a headband sitting
under a tree playing a bamboo nose flute and talking to ances-
tral spirits. It was Bontoc. The tune he played was an old
mountain tribe melody called "I Am Not of This World,
Merely Passing Through It" taught to him by his late Uncle
Apo Bontoc. The spirit of his late Uncle Apo Bontoc was up
there in the tree talking to him. The spirit of Uncle Apo said,
"Dwarves?" He pondered it. He had spent his entire life in
Bontoc. Uncle Apo said, "Small people . . . ?"

Bontoc said, "Yes." You sat cross-legged to play the nose
flute. In Bontoc, it was called a *kalaleng*. Two-feet long with
three finger holes and a thumb stop, it was played by a steady
exhaling through the right nostril. It was very popular with the
mothers of small children: it promoted good hygiene. Bontoc
said, "Small people with big foreheads and very short legs and
tufts of black hair and—"

Uncle Apo said, "Japanese!" The happiest days of his life had
been between the years 1941 and 1945 in the jungle. Uncle Apo
said, "Heads!" Uncle Apo said, " '*I Am Not of This World,
Merely Passing Through It!*' " Uncle Apo said, "Japs not pass
by in Bontoc. MacArthur say 'Heads!' We take heads." Uncle
Apo said, discussing his collection, "Three officers, two sergeants, eight soldiers—three with eyeglasses and one—one
with—"

Bontoc said, "Philippinos!"

"MacArthur say no to Philippino heads. Only Japanese

121

heads." In life, Uncle Apo had spoken fluent, melodious Bontoc. In death, on the astral plane, he had lapsed into broken English.

Bontoc said, "Philippino people who are—"

"Manila people!" Uncle Apo said, "No like."

"All sorts of people who are born with a defective—" Bontoc said, "Stunted people."

Uncle Apo said, "Strangle at birth."

His other mentor had been Miss Thomasina Landsborough of the Episcopalian Mission School. Between the ages of eight and fifteen he had loved her with an undying passion. If she were still alive she would be ninety-four years old. She must have still been alive. He had prayed too many times to The One Above—to Intutungtso—to swap her for Uncle Apo for all his prayers to have gone unanswered. Bontoc said tightly, "I'm asking for some advice. I don't know what to do. I don't know why the dwarves are setting off bombs. I don't understand how they think. I want some guidance from someone who has Gone On and who now enjoys All Knowledge, Compassion, and Omniscience!" He had a degree from Harvard. He wondered why he kept doing this sort of thing. Bontoc, putting down his flute and looking up into the leaves, said, *"Well?"*

Uncle Apo said, "Hmm." He was thinking omnisciently.

Bontoc waited.

Uncle Apo said, "Ahh . . ." Noncorporeally, he was scratching his head and looking strained.

"Listen, I'm sitting here in a loin cloth and a headband in the middle of the city asking your advice! The least you can do is—" He definitely wondered why he was doing this sort of thing. Bontoc said, "When I was a kid and you were teaching me how to use a head axe and showing me your collection of chopped-off noggins I thought you were the greatest thing since the Lone Ranger, but you haven't the faintest idea of anything that happens outside the eight square miles around the junglerice husk pile, have you?" Bontoc said, "As soon as Miss Thomasina goes, so do you!"

Uncle Apo said, "Who the Lone Ranger?"

"A man who does good in his life! A man who, on his white horse, gallops through life trying to protect the weak, the poor, the underprivileged, and the short!"

"Why dwarves try to kill people?"

"They're not trying to kill people! They're just setting off bombs to—" To what? Bontoc said, *"That's what I'm asking you!"* Bontoc said, "It's not all the dwarves, it's probably just one of the dwarves!"

"Which one?"

It was hopeless. Bontoc said, "I'm swapping you."

"Can't do!"

"Can do." Bontoc said, "I've been reading up on it. All a Bontoc male has to do is keep himself celibate for three weeks—" Bontoc said bitterly, "Not hard in my case—observe the observances of the Bontoc religion—" He asked Intutungtso to take Miss Thomasina every night— "Find a Bontoc artifact, summon up the spirit, give the spirit the artifact, and say, 'Lengagh!' and the spirit's gone." Bontoc said, "You're here, I've got a kalaleng nose flute Aunt Chollipas Bontoc sent down to keep me company while I suffered through clause number one, I've had enough of you, and all I have to do is toss the artifact up into your general direction and—" Bontoc said, "And you're history."

"Don't do!"

"You're no help to me at all! I'm doing my best to get on in the world and all you can do is—"

"Don't know Manila!"

"Manila is like everywhere else!" It wasn't, but he didn't know that. "Manila is like Bontoc, like New York, like Santiago, and, for all I know, like life in the next world! People here are still people." Bontoc said, "You're supposed to be seventy-nine years old, you lived through the Spanish and the Japanese and the Americans, you loved people, you even killed people—" He said, "You must know about people!" He was getting wound up. He was on his feet abusing the tree. "People! People!

People who like people are the—" Bontoc said, "Don't you know *anything?*"

"Don't cast me out!"

"I am going to cast you out!"

"Apo like Baptiste—!"

Bontoc, determined, said, "No, you're going—"

"No go!"

Bontoc said, "Go."

"No—" He was thinking fast. He wasn't used to it. Uncle Apo said, trying hard, "People—small people—dwarves—people all like other people—people who—" Uncle Apo said, *"People have secret thoughts!"*

"What thoughts? Give me a thought! Give me a thought all people have secretly!" Bontoc, a fair man, giving him a chance, said, "One thought! One thought you and I and the dwarves have in common! One little clue to—" Bontoc said, *"Well?"*

Uncle Apo said, "My thought?"

"Anyone's thought!"

"My thought—"

He waited.

Uncle Apo said quietly, "My thought, thought of all people all time: my thought." He had no idea on earth what a dwarf was. Uncle Apo said, "No cast me out."

"Why not?"

Uncle Apo said from up in the tree somewhere, unseen, like the human heart, concealed and camouflaged and unknowable, "Because lonely. Because you need to talk to, because—" He fell silent.

Uncle Apo said, "Because all day in heaven, only my own kind around—all dead people, all people like me . . ." Suddenly, from the tree, in the darkness, he spoke perfect, fluent Bontoc.

Uncle Apo Bontoc, the man who all his life had sharpened his axe, dreamed of blood, lusted after conquest, and glared, said, pleadingly, "Because in heaven, in life, all the people I ever listened to were people just like me!" Uncle Apo said, "They were me! I listened because they thought what I thought!

Now—now, now I have to listen to me for eternity, I—" Uncle Apo said, "I want to listen to you! I—" Uncle Apo said, "I'm lonely! I'm lonely now for everything I never was! I'm lonely to be like you! I—" Uncle Apo said, "I—" He sounded very upset. "I—" Uncle Apo said, "What did I miss? What did I miss in my life? *What did I miss?*"

"What did you miss not being me?"

Uncle Apo said quietly, "Yes." Uncle Apo said, "Don't cast me out."

Bontoc said, "No."

Uncle Apo said, "Thank you."

"All right."

There was a silence. Uncle Apo said, "You wonder what my life really like, huh?" He was back to the broken English.

Bontoc, nodding, said, "Yes, sometimes."

"Uh!" He was happy. They had gotten somewhere. Good. He was still up in his tree, happy. Uncle Apo said fiercely, joyfully, to his good old nephew, Baptiste, who was obviously not as far gone as he had thought, "Good! Huh! Now Uncle Apo tell you how to salt head lopped off Japanese officer with glasses!"

Uncle Apo, settling himself down in the leaves, said happily, "Play! Play flute and listen to old Apo the Great Head Lopper give you a few good hard-to-get-these-days lessons. . . ."

"You're rich."

"I'm not rich."

In the orchid garden the Barrera woman had thought he was going to have her taken away and killed.

His apartment was filled with books and paintings and objects of no earthly day-to-day use. His five-room apartment was filled with furniture. It was decorated. It had lighting and power and sewage. It had a door that locked.

"You're rich."

Maybe he was. Marguerita was away for a week with her relatives in San Pablo City and, sitting in the darkness smoking a cigar and watching the lights of the cars below in the street reflected in the picture window of his veranda, Elizalde was alone. There was only the steady humming of the air-conditioning in the apartment.

The poor had nothing. The poor were arming themselves.

At the table, watching the lights, he waited for Cafiero to telephone.

They killed people and then died. Barrera had died, the Beo girl had died. And then her neighbors had stripped her room, taken or destroyed everything inside it, and simply melted away.

My Sister, Mother, Friend.

Merit, Patriotism, Dignity: they were the words inscribed above the honor roll of dead officers at the Western District Police Headquarters.

The Barrera woman thought the police were going to take her away and kill her.

Barrera had wanted his face recorded on film before he died.

The Beo girl had carried a photograph, not only of her brother, but of herself.

Ermalinda R. Beo, Cavite Street.

Santiago Beo, Cavite Street.

My Sister, Mother, Friend.

DESAPARECIDO—it meant, in the Spanish neither of them could speak, in a hand neither of them had written, *vanished.*

People died all the time. They were killed, or murdered or they—

The poor were not afraid of death. It was the rich who were afraid of death. It was people like Cafiero, like him. People like him, like Cafiero, were afraid of death, resented it, because it was an event in their lives of gross and insulting unfairness— something unplanned for, unexpected, in the fullness and comfort and predictability of—

It was an event that was part of the lives of the poor and the beasts of this world.

DESAPARECIDO—it meant *gone.*

It was not death. It was not being killed. It was something

else. At the table, gazing at the window and his own reflection in it, Elizalde watched the lights and waited for Cafiero to call.

On the table beside him, his holstered Walther PPK lay beside a box of twenty-five rounds of high-velocity hollow-point cartridges and a little plastic bag containing brushes, a cleaning kit, and oil.

The commodity bank of lives . . . He watched the lights. He watched for one to stop outside in the street. He waited to hear whispers.

Marguerita was away for four more days. He was alone. Someone knew. Outside, in the street, there were, over the minutes, fewer and fewer car headlights. It was a moonless, dark night. Once, a long time ago, he had been shot in the stomach. Sometimes, at night, when he was alone, it hurt. Sometimes, at night, when he was alone, the pain came back in a long burning ache where the bullet had gone in and torn his insides to pieces.

He could not sleep.

In the apartment, there was only the sound of the air-conditioner working.

At the table, by the phone, Elizalde waited for Cafiero to call.

On the phone, Ambrosio said evenly, "I went over to Pag-tatapunan Street to see Bontoc and form a sort of midproject motivation and consolidation forum, but he, um—" It was 10:30 at night. Elizalde must have been right by the phone because he picked it up on the first ring before Ambrosio had lost his nerve about ringing so late. "And I—" Ambrosio said, "I found him sitting out in the street wearing a loin cloth and talking to a tree in some funny language I didn't understand."

Elizalde said, "Right." He waited.

"I suppose it must have been some sort of headhunting thing or some sort of thing he learned when he studied anthropology in America—" He waited. Ambrosio asked, "What did he study in America?"

Elizalde said, "Business administration." Ambrosio must have been ringing from home. In the background there was the sound of a child being energetically shushed. Elizalde asked, "How's the case going?"

"Fine." Ambrosio said hesitantly, "Fine. Just a few little problems, but nothing I can't—" Ambrosio said, "Felix, I didn't know you could play a flute with your nose."

"No." He wondered why he had rung. Elizalde said, "Is there anything I can do, Jesus-Vincente—to help?"

"No! No, no, no, nothing at all. I just thought—I just—" There must have been people in the background listening to his important call to his superior officer. Ambrosio said, "No, many thanks, but no." He made a chuckling sound. Ambrosio said, "I'm a Fireball: there isn't anything I can't solve or over-come given the right determination and resolve and attention to detail and good old horse sense!"

"I believe you."

"Do you?"

"Yes, of course. I have great faith in you and Bontoc."

Ambrosio said, "He's a bit weird, isn't he? Old Bontoc?"

"Have you any idea who the target is at the Gnome Home?"

"Yes." He dropped his voice. Ambrosio said, "Felix, as part of my overall thinking about this, I—" There was a shush in the background, then a giggle, then another shush, and then another giggle. "I've been—" Ambrosio said, "To get into the skins of the dwarves, so to speak—so to speak, I've been walk-ing around the house on my knees all evening seeing what people thought of me." There was a howl of laughter from somewhere in the house. It was not kids. The sound was of a man and a woman falling about in fits of giggling. Ambrosio said, "Nothing demeans the man born to succeed!" He was not talking to Elizalde. Ambrosio said, "I think it's a good, fine, creative example of lateral thinking—what do you think?"

All the lights in his apartment were off. Reflected in the picture window that faced the street, he could see the headlights of cars as they went by or stopped outside. Elizalde said, "I think I have great faith in you, Sergeant Ambrosio."

"Thank you, Felix." Behind him, all the giggling stopped. There was a silence. Elizalde waited.

He waited. He was silent.

"Jesus-Vincente, if you're worried—"

"Right!" He was talking, not to Elizalde but to the people in his house. Maybe now, he was not on his knees, but standing up by the phone glancing back at them. Ambrosio said, "Right. That's right—I'm a Fireball." Ambrosio said, "Right." He sounded sick to his stomach.

Ambrosio said, "OK. Fine. No trouble at all. I just thought—late as it was—I'd put you in the picture."

Ambrosio said, glancing back into his room, "Well, we all have to get to bed sometime. Goodnight, Felix, sleep well." He had never met her. Ambrosio said happily, lightly, "And love, of course, to Marguerita."

He said, predicated on absolutely nothing at all, "Right."

He hung up.

In the faith healer's house, after the killing, they had applauded. They had *clapped*.

On the unloaded PPK pistol, Elizalde pulled down the trigger guard and set it slightly to the left against the frame.

Outside, in the street now, there were fewer and fewer headlights of cars passing or stopping.

They had *clapped*.

He pulled back on the slide of the weapon and raised it clear of the frame and allowed it to move forward under the strength of the spring. The slide came clear, revealing the barrel and receiver of the weapon. Holding it up to the picture window, he looked down the barrel and could not tell in the faint light if it was clean or dirty.

It was clean. He hardly ever fired it except at mandatory monthly practice.

He waited.

He waited for Cafiero to ring.

He would not ring.

In his darkened apartment, alone, watching the lights and listening for noises, carefully, as if his life depended on it, Elizalde began cleaning and oiling his gun.

10

Whispers, rumors of whispers, secrets, voices too far away to hear . . .

It was a little before 6:00 A.M., first dawn. Stopped at an intersection in his car with no other vehicle in sight on any of the long, straight roads going in the three cardinal directions, Cafiero turned on his car radio.

Static, voices, losing and gaining, voices . . . In all the different time zones, in secret places, shadows, echoes, voices . . .

The engine of his Mitsubishi Magna was only a hum.

All the streets were empty.

Whispers, voices, too far away to hear . . .

He felt his breath coming quickly, and his heart, hurting, straining against his chest.

Tombstone may have been the town too tough to die. He was the bum too fat to beg. And now people were making it even harder for him. On the edge of Topacio's salt farm in Las Pinas, Benny the Bum, sucking in his great gut and filling his lungs, yelled at the top of his voice to Topacio, "MY LIVELIHOOD WAS DESTROYED BY THE UNPATRIOTIC EATING HABITS OF PEOPLE LIKE YOU! NOW PEOPLE LIKE YOU ARE HIDING THEIR TRASH!" Benny the Bum yelled, "DID I COMPLAIN WHEN THE GARBAGE YOU PEOPLE LEFT TURNED ME FROM A SLEEK BUT IM-POVERISHED GAZELLE INTO A FAT AND SLUDGY HIPPO? NO, I DIDN'T—I DIVERSIFIED MY WORK PRACTICES! BUT NOW, *TO HIDE YOUR TRASH FROM*

ME . . ." It was the pits. So was he. He looked like a brown olive wearing rags. At the edge of the three-acre salt farm with its cement pools and pipes to bring the water in from the sea, he rocked back and forth to keep his balance. "BUT NOW, TO HURT AND HUMILIATE A MAN WHO . . ." He had an audience of two. A little way from the wooden shack where Topacio lived, near the shed where he bagged his sea salt, there was an eight- or nine-year-old kid wearing a striped T-shirt. The kid was just standing and watching. Benny the Bum shouted, "IT'S ALL JUST TOO MUCH!"

He worked in the heat of the day to get the salt from the evaporated water. At 6:10 A.M. what he did was sleep. It was 6:10 A.M. He wasn't getting any sleep. Topacio, bare chested in his sarong, yelled back, "I DIDN'T HIDE THE TRASH! THE HEALTH INSPECTOR SAID I HAD TO BAG IT IN PLASTIC BAGS AND PUT IT UNDER COVER!" The bags of trash were opened, spilled out. Topacio shouted, "WHAT TRASH? ALL I'VE GOT IS TWO BAGS FULL OF A FEW PATHETIC RICE HUSKS AND BANANA SKINS TO SHOW FOR A WEEK'S HARD WORK!"

"YOU'VE GOT TWO BURGER KING WHOPPER BOXES, A PIZZA HUT THIN 'N' CRISPY TEN-INCH PIE CARTON, AND THREE—THREE—ARTHUR TREACH-ER'S FISH SANDWICH WRAPPERS!"

Topacio said, "That isn't much to show for a lifetime of hard work."

Benny the Bum said tightly, "That's what's killing this country, food like that. We spent years and years getting rid of the Spanish, years and years getting rid of the Japanese, years and years getting rid of the Americans so we could have our own culture, and you eat—what? YOU EAT THE PRECOOKED, PREFROZEN, PREPACKAGED JUNK FOOD OF A ROTTEN CAPITALIST SOCIETY GONE MAD WITH IMPERIALIST DREAMS OF FOISTING CHOLESTEROL ON OUR POOR ASIAN COMMUNITY!" He rocked back. He was about to let fly a great secret. Benny the Bum yelled,

"WHAT DO YOU THINK MADE ME TOO FAT TO BEG? IT WAS EATING FROM TRASH CANS AND FINDING ONLY THIS SORT OF JUNK!" Benny the Bum yelled, "ONCE A MAN COULD RAID TRASH AND FIND NOURISHING RICE AND FISH—NOT FROZEN BITS OF FISH, BUT REAL FISH HEADS WITH EYES—AND STAY THIN AND IN EMPLOYMENT! NOW—" He looked across to the kid watching. Benny the Bum yelled, "WHAT DO YOU THINK THIS IS DOING TO OUR CHILDREN? I'LL TELL YOU WHAT IT'S DOING TO OUR CHILDREN—"

He wasn't a young man anymore. Topacio, sighing, said—

He looked at the kid. The kid was a good-looking kid with thick black hair. He was thin. He was going to grow up bald and fat. The kid looked straight ahead, not saying anything. Nice, respectful kid. Maybe the last one left on earth. Benny the Bum shouted, "IT'S GOING TO TURN OUR CHILDREN INTO A NATION OF BLIMPS WHO CAN'T EVEN RAID A TRASH CAN TO GET A GOOD, NOURISHING MEAL! IT'S GOING TO TURN THEM INTO LITTLE AMERI-CAN ZOMBIES WHOSE IDEA OF THE RESPONSIBILI-TIES OF A TRUE, LOYAL PHILIPPINO IS TO TAKE THE WIFE AND KIDS OUT TO A GREAT, TRADI-TIONAL PHILIPPINO MEAL OF FRENCH FRIES AND TACOS!" The kid looked over. The kid knew all right. Benny the Bum yelled, "J'ACCUSE!" He was an educated bum. "J'ACCUSE TOMAS TOPACIO, SALT FARMER OF MAIN HIGHWAY, LAS PINAS, OF BEING A SUBVER-SIVE ELEMENT OF OUR SOCIETY! J'ACCUSE!"

It was 6:12 A.M. Topacio, wanting to go back inside his house, said, "Give me a break!" He wasn't young; he was fifty-three years old. He liked junk food. It was one of life's little pleasures. Topacio, turning on his heel, yelled, "IN A FREE SOCIETY I CAN EAT WHAT I LIKE!"

"DO YOU KNOW THE PRICE OF COCONUT MILK IN METRO MANILA THESE DAYS?"

Topacio said, "I don't use coconut milk."

"IT'S GONE THROUGH THE ROOF BECAUSE ALL THE PEOPLE WHO USED TO GROW COCONUTS FOR A SOCIETY LOYAL TO ITS ROOTS, TO ITS TRADITIONAL EATING HABITS, HAVE RIPPED UP ALL THEIR COCONUT TREES AND STARTED PLANTING—" He hesitated. He didn't know. He was a city dweller himself. "—STARTED PLANTING THINGS FOR JUNK FOOD THINGS—"

"I FARM SALT!"

Benny the Bum yelled, "EXACTLY!"

Topacio said, "Take the trash, gather up the trash, put the trash in the plastic trash bags, and leave the trash out on the sidewalk for the trash truck. Thank you."

"I'M A FAT BUM!"

Topacio said, "I'm sorry to hear it."

"I GOT FAT EATING TRASH LEFT OUT BY PEOPLE WHO DON'T CARE ANYMORE!"

Topacio said, "Hmm." He was going back to bed.

"I HAVE NO RESPECT LEFT FOR MYSELF ANYMORE! I'M PATHETIC! I'M FAT! ONCE, IN CAMELOT, I HAD DIGNITY AND—" He sniffed. Benny the Bum said, " 'Oh, what profiteth it a man if he gain the whole world but loseth his—' "

The kid was standing by one of the salt pools watching. Topacio wondered who he was. Topacio said on the wooden step of his shack, "Gee whiz . . ."

"I'M A YESTERDAY'S MAN. I'M AN ECHO FROM THE TIME WHEN THIS NATION WAS CLOTHED IN MIST AND LOVE AND GENTLENESS AND—"

Topacio said, "Don't forget to bag up the trash."

"A FISH HEAD! RICE! MY SOUL CRIES OUT FOR—"

Topacio said, "The trash truck comes by the sidewalk. Leave the bags neat, would you?"

"HAVE YOU NO PITY?"

Topacio said, "No."

"IF YOU HAVE TEARS, PREPARE TO SHED THEM NOW!"

Topacio said, "Sorry. Nope." He got to his front door and leaned up to open it.

Benny the Bum said, "ALL THE FATS AND CHOLES-TEROL IN THE GARBAGE YOU PEOPLE EAT IS KILL-ING ME! IF YOU CAN'T CHANGE YOUR DIET, HOW CAN I CHANGE MINE?" Benny the Bum, appealing to Topacio's better nature, said, "I'M CRUSHED LIKE A BUT-TERFLY ON THE UNENDING WHEEL OF FORTUNE!" He looked at the kid. The kid was listening and watching. Good kid. Benny the Bum shouted, "A FISH HEAD! A ROTTEN, DRIED-OUT, PATHETIC MORSEL OF IODINE—CAN YOU DENY THAT TO A DYING MAN?"

He could. He went to go inside.

Benny the Bum said, "Oh . . ."

Benny the Bum said, "Ooohhh . . ."

Benny the Bum said, "Ooohhh . . . ooohh . . ."

Topacio said, *"ALL RIGHT!"*

" 'IF YOU PRICK ME, DO I NOT BLEED—?' "

"ALL RIGHT! I SAID, ALL RIGHT!" Topacio, coming back down his steps and looking at the strewn trash, said, beaten, "How much?"

Benny the Bum said, "One fish."

"Per what?"

"When do you like to get up?"

"Late!"

"Per hour to 7:30 A.M. and thereafter, one cup of coconut milk per every thirty minutes." Benny the Bum said, "That's country rates. In the city—"

"Plus taking the trash away!"

"What do the trash men charge you per bag?"

Topacio said, "Fifty cents for three."

"You've only got two."

"Sometimes I only have one." He wasn't young. He was old. He was too old to fight. Topacio said, "With you around, I'll definitely only have one."

He wasn't a hard man. Oh, yes, he was. Benny the Bum said, "Two fish a week and four cups of coconut milk and—for you only—no money at all—I'll let you sleep in and I'll take your trash to the dump and even sweep up after." Benny the Bum said, "My one and only offer. Yes or no?"

Topacio said, "I don't know what coconut milk costs these days."

Benny the Bum said, "It's dirt cheap."

"All right."

"Today I'll take the trash away for free."

Topacio said, "Thanks very much. Can I go back to bed now?"

"I won't make another sound."

"Thank you."

Benny said, "It's always a pleasure to do business with a good man." Benny the Bum, catching the kid's eye, said, to give him one of life's valuable lessons, "NEGOTIATION! UNDERSTANDING! TOLERANCE! GIVE AND TAKE! THAT'S WHAT MADE OUR COUNTRY GREAT!" It was burgers, tacos, and fries bringing it down. Benny the Bum said, "I'M WORKING TO EARN MYSELF A NEW LIFE!" Benny the Bum said, "UP THERE, AMONG THE STARS, HE'S RIDING ON TO—" He saw Topacio's face. Benny the Bum said, "The trash! Take the trash to the sidewalk!" Benny the Bum said to his latest client, "Yes, sir. At your command, sir. Yes, sir!" He had a nice little racket going. So far, in the course of a month, he had made twenty-seven successful deals. Picking up the trash and stuffing it back into the bags, he hurried to carry out his customer's whim. He didn't hurry that much. Hurrying that much made him lose weight. To keep in trim he was up to eating five Whale Burgers and three Finger Lickin' drumsticks a day. It was hard work but someone had to do it. Benny, waddling for the sidewalk with the trash, said respectfully, "Yes, sir. Thank you, sir." Benny the Bum said, "You look tired, sir. Go back to bed now and enjoy your well-earned rest from toil while you may."

He smiled. He grinned. He sniffed in, not the smell of trash, but of prosperity.

For a moment, on his way to the sidewalk and on to the next

poor bastard on his list he wondered who the kid was. He heard Topacio say curiously to the kid, "Yes, what do you want?"

He heard no reply at all.

Al Capone had got started exactly the same way. On the sidewalk, depositing the trash, Benny, Arturo Oi, Hitler, Marcos—all the self-made men of this world—on his way on and up, said to himself in a grunt, *"Yeah!"*

Tucking the trash bags under his arm, waddling, grinning, doing his civic, patriotic duty, he started traveling resolutely, bravely toward success, toward paradise regained, toward— toward the dump.

He traveled east on Sixto Drive to pick up the road to the south across the river. In his car, Cafiero had turned the radio off and with the air-conditioning on at its lowest level, there was only a faint hum in his car and the sound of the tires on the bitumen. Once, looped around the rearview mirror on a silver chain, there had been a Saint Christopher medal put there by his wife—by Rosey—to protect him. She had gone and now there was only the broken chain. There was no traffic. He reached forward onto the dashboard and took a Pall Mall cigarette from a pack there and lit it with a tiny Pierre Cardin-designed gold lighter. On the seat next to him, under a rug, he had a sawed-off Winchester pump-action riot gun loaded with double O buckshot. He touched at the Walther pistol he carried in a shoulder holster under his coat.

None of it mattered.

She had gone and he was alone and his heart and lungs hurt in his chest and if he died there in the car, it mattered to no one. It was like all the files in his office, all the thousands and thousands of lives: it was merely a matter of record.

He didn't care. He couldn't bring himself to care. All he ever wanted to do was sleep and be away from it.

He touched at the riot gun.

He had no idea whether it was cocked or not and no idea whether or not the charges in the cartridges were still good.

Off the streets, he had moved up into the silver chain and Cardin lighter and good car stratum. He had moved up into the stratum where he was afraid. In his office, they all watched him. In his office, he knew things he was not supposed to know. His chest hurt.

He had no idea what he was frightened of.

The people who frightened him had no idea what he might know.

And she had gone. He had gone home night after night with nothing to say, nowhere to go, and she had left him. Once, once only, after he had not been able to make love, he had told her he was afraid. It had been an excuse. She had left. She had gone.

He had no idea on earth who it was he was afraid of. He had no idea on earth what it was they thought—

In his car, suddenly Cafiero said to no one, to God, to anyone who might listen, "I don't know! *I don't know anything!*"

He touched at his guns.

He never cleaned or checked them and they might not even work.

"I don't!" The sounds were all in his head. Cafiero said desperately, "I don't! *I don't know anything!*"

He was, always, desperately, numbingly frightened.

In his car, seeing the sign, he turned off for the South Super-highway to Las Pinas.

It was 6:14 A.M. He read it on the dial of his Rolex watch.

All his salt farm was was three acres of sandy land near the sea he had lined with row upon row of shallow, twenty-by-twenty cement pools fed by a series of four-inch galvanized iron pipes. He didn't even have a pump. The tide came in, filled his pools through the pipes and, after he had turned off the cocks, the water lay there in the boiling sun and evaporated, leaving the salt in the bottom of the pools. He didn't even have a small tractor. In the heat of the day, when all or most of the water had gone, he merely shoveled up the salt one load at a time, bagged it into hessian bags, and dragged each of the bags back to a wire-mesh sieve to one side of his house and, depending on the grade the wholesale buyer wanted, either left it there in stacks or took it, sifted, into his shed, to sift it even more or boil it out one bag at a time. Topacio glanced first at the kid and then at his property. There was absolutely nothing out there to steal.

The kid was about nine or ten years old wearing a striped T-shirt and khaki shorts and no shoes. He was a pretty little boy with a shock of thick black hair and liquid brown eyes. The eyes, unblinkingly, expressionlessly, stayed on Topacio's shed. Topacio said gently, "Do you want something?" The kid looked pale. "Are you sick?"

The T-shirt was new. It came from one of the markets in Tondo or one of the flea markets in the city. It was something made, not in the Philippines, but in Taiwan. You could tell by the quality that it would not last. The khaki shorts were ironed. They, too, looked almost new. In the left-hand pocket there was the lump of a ball or an orange or some round object the kid must have collected somewhere. His feet were calloused like a kid's.

Topacio said, "What do you want?" He should have thrown the kid off. He had no children of his own. Topacio said, "Are you meeting someone here?" He was a nice-looking kid. He didn't look simple. The eyes, staying on the shed, looked bright and a little sad. Topacio said, "Look, I have to get my sleep—" The kid had hard, work-strong hands. There wasn't much of him, but he looked tough and wiry. He was a kid who didn't go to school, but who worked for his living. Maybe a kid working with him would be nice. Topacio said, touching the boy gently on the shoulder, "What's your name?"

He saw the kid blink.

Topacio said quietly, "You're thinking of going into the salt-farming business and you thought you'd stand here and see what happens in the course of a day—right?" He was fifty-three years old. He had no children, nobody. It occurred to him, standing there towering over the kid, looking at the kid's hands, it occurred to him that he was fifty-three years old and, all day, in the heat, he worked alone. Topacio said, "We can discuss it." Topacio said, "I'm Mr. Tomas Topacio. I own this outright. It gives me a fair living and I don't have to beg from anyone and I can put surplus money away in the bank for emergencies." Topacio said, "If you want to discuss it you can call me Mr. Topacio."

The kid looked at him. There was a sadness in the eyes.

Topacio said in Tagalog, *"Sapagkat kami ay tao lamang."* He nodded encouragingly to the kid. The kid, trying to look tough, was probably terrified. It meant, "We are only human." Topacio said, "Don't worry about the way I talked to the bum. The bum has to make a living too. I would have given him a handout, but he wanted the dignity of work—I let him think he'd tricked work out of me, but I would have given him something anyway." The kid looked up at him. It would be nice to have someone to talk to on the farm, even, even if they were working pools away, someone to call out to—someone to make coffee for and to— Topacio said, "Don't be afraid. I'm really not a bad person when you get to know me."

He had no expression on his face at all. The kid said softly, "I'm alone."

Topacio said, "Yes." He hesitated. He looked at the kid. Topacio said, "Yes, me too." He pursed his lips.

"Tao po." The kid said suddenly, *"Tao po* —a man is here, sir."

"Do you want a job?"

His eyes stayed on the shed. His eyes filled with tears.

Topacio said, "Why are you weeping?" Topacio said, confused, "Why? *Why do you keep staring at my shed?"*

The shed was a long wooden building near the sieves made of mesh where the salt was stored for collection or where the salt was processed. Looking at it, the kid blinked back the tears. His hands were down by his sides, empty. His hands hurt. The salt farmer was gazing at him. He was a head and shoulders taller. Under his chin there were wrinkles and lines of age. He saw the salt farmer's hands. They were calloused and hard, strong. Inside the farmer's body there was a loud voice that had shouted at the bum. The salt farmer was looking at him. At his back, the kid felt a faint breeze in from the sea over the pools and the pipes. He heard water trickling in as the tide must have been coming in. There was the smell of salt and hot, sandy earth. The farmer said anxiously, "Tomas . . . you can call me Tomas."

The kid looked at the shed. Behind his eyes there was a long, painful ache. It was not a kid's feeling—he didn't think it was—it was a feeling grown-ups had. It was a feeling of silence. All the shouting had stopped and there was only a sadness. It was an adult's feeling. He tried to think how everything he had said before had been nothing, had just been words. Now, what he said was to someone else: an adult's feeling. Now, there were things he could not say: things that physically hurt—an adult's feelings. He was nine years old. He gazed at the shed. The kid said softly, "I'm by myself. I can't get fat like him."

"The bum? The bum does it on purpose!" Topacio, grinning, shaking his head, said, "You don't want to get fat! There's more to life than eating. The bum eats because he's got nothing else to do because he's so fat." He was rambling. He felt suddenly, inexplicably happy. Topacio, bending down to rest his hand on the boy's shoulder to give him the benefit of his experience, said, "Don't cry. Anyone can work hard and enjoy this life provided they get a start in life and they keep their needs to a modest level and don't get greedy." Topacio said, "My old father left me this farm—that was my start. If you're prepared to give a good day's value for a fair day's pay and food there's nothing you couldn't—" Maybe the kid wouldn't work hard. He looked at the kid's hands. He worked hard. Topacio said, "The economics of my business have reached a point where the modest expansion of my work force would be a sound move to increase the viability of—" Topacio said suddenly, "You don't think—" Topacio said, "There's no question I'm a *bakla!*" It meant homosexual. Topacio said, "I'm a good, fair man who treats his employees with respect and dignity and only asks that they treat me in the same way!" The kid was lowering his head. His head was dropping on his chest like a shot dog. The kid had nobody. Nobody had ever been kind to him before.

Topacio said, "Please, please consider it." Topacio said, "Don't cry. Please don't cry." Topacio said gently, soothingly, "Hey . . . hey . . ."

The kid had sunk to his knees in the sandy soil, weeping.

Topacio said, "Hey . . . hey, kid . . ."

"Tao po—a man is here, sir. . . ."

Topacio said, "What do you mean? Do you mean you're a man?" Topacio said, "I know that." The kid was weeping. Tears were running down his face. Topacio, kneeling down in front of the boy to talk to him face-to-face, said with his hand resting on his shoulder, pressing a little to give him strength, "My father gave me a chance once and I—and I—" Topacio said, "Let me help you." Topacio said, "We are all only human. We all only have one life. . . ."

> *Resistí todo el año anterior,*
> *Y aquí estoy, todavía:*
> *Solo Dios sabe lo que viví,*
> *Ayer y hoy, y aquí estoy.*
> *Mírame—que aquí estoy.*

> I endured everything that last year,
> And I'm still here. God alone
> Knows what I've lived through,
> Yesterday and today and here I am.
> —Here I am.

His hands were shaking. Lighting another cigarette from the pack on his dashboard, Cafiero's hands shook. He was driving south. His Saint Christopher's medal, a gift from his wife, was gone and lost. It was the medal of the patron saint of travelers.

It was only a broken silver chain hanging from his rearview mirror. The cigarette in his mouth was wet and salty. He thought for a moment he was weeping. His eyes were dry. He could not, any longer, scream. He could not stop. He merely, always, ever, continued on.

He looked not at all at the Winchester riot gun on the seat beside him.

He had no idea whether it was cocked or, if it was, whether the charges in the cartridges were still good.

On the South Superhighway, heading toward an address in Las Pinas, he merely, only, drove on.

"Are you hungry?" Topacio, not knowing what to say, taking his hand away from the boy's shoulder, said, "Are you hungry? Would you like something to eat? Or coffee? Or something?" He felt lost. He felt, moment by moment, he was losing something.

Topacio, shaking his head, trying to think of what to say, said, "Won't you talk to me?"

Topacio said, *"Please! Please talk to me!"*

He stopped. He forced himself to stop at the side of the road. There was a fat bum carrying trash to the dump a little way down the street and, using him as a target, as a point, as something to force his mind to work on, Cafiero stopped the car and took up the shotgun in both hands.

His wife had left him. He had done nothing. He always did nothing. His chest and lungs were hurting with strain. He saw the fat bum waddling away, looking happy. Cafiero was cocooned inside the metal walls of his car. He got his hands onto the stock of the weapon and the pump below the sawed-off barrel. His hands shook. The wood of the stock and the pump were unyielding, confident, strong.

In his car, gritting his teeth, Cafiero drew back the pump and, with a shattering loud double-clacking sound, fed a cartridge into the breech.

His hands shook. He had done it. He sat still for a moment watching the bum.

He put the car back into drive, let off the hand brake, and, accelerating, drove hard and fast the last two hundred yards toward Topacio's salt farm.

"Mr. Topacio—?"

Topacio said urgently, "Yes!" The boy was looking, this time not at the shed or at the ground, but at him. He was only a little boy. Topacio, kneeling with him, said gently, "Yes, I'm here." Somewhere, a little way off there was the sound of an engine. Maybe it was the trash truck. Maybe they would see him. He didn't care. Topacio said, "I don't have anyone—"

"*Tao po.* A man is here, sir."

"I know. I know you're a man." Topacio, aching to gather him up, said, "Life is very hard if you haven't got anyone to care about." He cared, in his own way, for Benny the Bum. He had never thought of it before. Life was long and lonely. Topacio said, "My business has reached an economic crest where the expansion of the work force—" Topacio said, "We could work together. I'm not that young. I can't last forever. I could leave it to you and—" The boy was weeping. Topacio said, "Oh, please, please don't cry. . . ." He had no handkerchief in his sarong to give to the boy. The boy had his own cloth in the pocket of his shorts—he saw the lump it made. He saw the boy reach down for it. Topacio said, "Coffee, or something to eat and you'll—"

The boy reached out for him with his free hand and Topacio, kneeling with him, took him in his arms and held him against his chest.

He heard the boy sniff. He smiled. Kids sniffed all the time. When he had been a boy, all the time, his father had kept telling him to stop sniffing.

"*Tao po*—a man is here, sir."

He meant him. He meant Topacio. He meant that—The boy was dragging out his handkerchief with his free hand. Boys never got things out of their pockets, they dragged them out. When he had been a boy himself, he remembered his father always telling him to— He held the boy hard against his chest. He smiled at all the memories. Topacio said softly, soothingly, "Yes, yes, coffee and then something to eat and then we can—" It was hard, the handkerchief. He felt it for an instant hard against his own chest, like a ball or a lump of metal or— He heard a car. He looked up and saw a man with a gun and he—

"Xavier!" It was the boy. It came from him. He heard the boy screaming, shouting, yelling.

"Xavier Luis . . . !"

Cafiero, at the open door of his car, said, "Oh my God!" He saw it. He saw it in the boy's hand.

"XAVIER!" He heard the boy scream. They were locked together on the ground in some sort of terrible embrace. He saw the man look up, see him. He saw something hard and black in the boy's hand, a grenade. He saw the pin come out with a flick of the boy's thumb. He saw—

He saw the pin drop onto the ground and the lever fly off as the weapon armed itself and, deep inside, a plunger hit a detonator cap and set a fuse burning toward the main charge. He saw—

"XAVIER LUIS *ALONSO!*"

He saw the boy, holding the man, holding him hard, press the grenade between the two of them, against their chests. He saw—

Petrified, frozen, stuck where he was with the loaded and cocked gun held across his chest like a sentry, Cafiero saw the man, for a moment—in the last moment—look at him. He saw his face. He saw— He saw the boy, shaking all over, bury himself into the man's chest with the grenade armed and running. He saw him strain to hold it there. He saw—

Cafiero, uselessly, pointlessly, screamed, *"No!"*

He saw the man look at him with no understanding on his face at all.

Cafiero shrieked, "NO!!"
He saw the blast cut both of them in half simultaneously.

He heard it.
Two streets away, waiting, Rolly heard the blast. It was only
a mild, muffled thump.
It was enough.
Starting his car, having waited there for almost an hour,
merely listening and humming to himself, he smiled, and, carefully, with due care and attention for others on the street, did
a U-turn and began driving back at a measured, legal speed
toward the city.

Whispers, rumors of whispers, secrets, voices too far away to
hear . . .
In the salt farm on South Superhighway, Las Pinas, with the
blast, all the air was full of smoke and buzzing.

11

"It's spreading all over the goddamned city!" By Cafiero's car, Elizalde could see the line of uniformed patrolmen and Watanabe's white-coated coroner's staff and drivers moving across the pools of the salt farm picking up bits of bodies. Where there was blood or flesh in one of the pools, they stepped gingerly, like cats. He was breathing hard. After the Headquarters call he had driven fast from his apartment. It was 7:20 A.M. and in the early morning light, Cafiero was wearing Bollé sunglasses. They hid his eyes. Leaning back a little against the hood of the car, he touched at them to settle them more firmly on the bridge of his nose and swallowed. The smell of high explosives was still in the air. Along the edge of the street, people had come. Soon there would be the TV cameras and the press. Elizalde said tightly, "Who were they?" He saw Cafiero touch again at his sunglasses. Elizalde said, "The salt farmer, according to the patrolmen first on the scene, was Tomas Topacio, aged fifty-three—*who the hell was the kid?*"

"I don't know."

"What the hell happened?"

"He—" Cafiero said, "I don't know."

"What the hell were you doing here?"

"I got a message to come."

"From whom?"

"From Headquarters—from my Headquarters. From the Bureau—"

"To do what?" Gomez from Ballistics was scrabbling around in the dirt by the sieves, putting things into plastic bags. He was

146

finding parts of the grenade. The grenade had blown both their chests apart—the man and the boy—and torn their faces off. Elizalde, starting to shake, demanded, "To do what?" Elizalde said, "Take those goddamned sunglasses off! It isn't bright! You're standing with your back to the rising sun—*take those fucking sunglasses off!*"

"Felix—"

It was everywhere. It was an epidemic. Everywhere, people were arming themselves. Elizalde, looking hard at Cafiero's eyes as he took the glasses off and folded them in his hands, said with ice in his voice, "So help me, Constantino, if you know something, or if in any way at all you're part of this—"

"I got a message from the Bureau to be at the Topacio salt farm on the South Superhighway, Las Pinas, at first light! I got here a little after six! I got a message and I did my duty!"

"Who was the message from?"

"The message was from the Bureau. It came in during the night by phone and the Bureau telephoned me at home at 5:00 A.M. and I drove out here and I—"

"Who was the message from?"

Cafiero said, "The boy saw me and then he—" Cafiero said, "He—" He kept folding and unfolding his sunglasses. Cafiero said tightly, "I saw them both die. . . ."

"Who was the message from?" He glanced into the front seat of the car, "What the hell is the riot gun doing in there?"

"It's my protection!"

"From whom?"

"From—" Cafiero said, "It was a message! It was a message given by phone to be passed on to me! I don't know who left it! It was just a message! The caller didn't want to give his name!"

"Didn't want to—or didn't have to?"

"Felix, I don't know anything! All I know is that—"

"All you know is that someone leaves you a message in the middle of the night, someone who won't or can't or refuses to give his name—you don't care anyway because you're like some fucking dog who lives for his master's pat, anybody's pat, and you go slatheringly happy, wagging your tail out at dawn to a fucking salt farm in the middle of nowhere! IS THAT YOU? IS THAT WHAT YOU DO?"

"Yes! That's what I do!" They were finding bits of meat. The bits of meat had been a man and a boy. Cafiero, crushing the sunglasses in his hand, said, "Yes, that's me! I told you! That's me! I TOLD YOU!"

"If you're in this—if you're even remotely concerned in this . . ." In the orchid garden Mrs. Barrera had thought he was going to take her away and have her killed. All night, in his apartment, thankfully with Marguerita away, he had waited with the gun on the table in front of him. "If you're any part of this—" Elizalde said with his eyes holding Cafiero's, "Believe me, Constantino, you won't have to be afraid of whomever you're afraid of because you'll find what I'll bring down on you will occupy every waking moment of your life—" Elizalde said, "If you know anything, tell me now."

"I don't know any more than I've told you!"

"Then what are you afraid of?"

"Everything!" The riot gun was still on the front seat. It was still cocked. Cafiero, his lips starting to tremble, said, "Everything! I'm afraid of everything!"

"Why did Rosey leave you?"

"She left me because—" Cafiero said, "Go to hell! That's my affair! You go to hell!"

"What are you afraid of? What happened here?"

"He yelled his name—the kid! The moment he pulled the pin and grabbed the old man to him he saw me and he yelled his name!" He was going, beginning to shake. Cafiero said, "I couldn't make it out!"

"What can you make out? What the hell are you afraid of?"

"I don't know! He looked at me!" Cafiero, shaking, shouted, "I don't know! I don't know what I'm afraid of! I'm afraid of that!" She had left because— The truth was— She had left because— Cafiero said, "She left because I sent her away! She left because all the things I heard—all the things people knew I knew—" Cafiero said, *"I was afraid for her!"* He was on the edge. He had not thought there was a point where the days would not go on endlessly, the same, one after another. Thus far and no further. He had reached it. He no longer cared. She was safe. Cafiero, his hands clenching around the expensive sunglasses, crushing them, smashing them with a crack of plastic, said, "She left because I sent her away because if what I know is true then death is nothing! Her death! Mine! All this—all nothing!" He was grinning, smiling, shaking. Cafiero said, "But she's gone! She's in America! She's safe!" He held Elizalde's eyes. "I sent her away because of what they could do to her! After that, after that one moment of heroism or cowardice or whatever, when all the pain came of her not being there anymore—all the godawful, terrible loneliness—I got afraid for myself!" Cafiero said, "Whispers, rumors . . ." Cafiero said, "People are disappearing—hundreds, thousands, every day, every week, all the time—" Cafiero said, *"I can't even look into my own files for fear of what I might find!"*

"The guns used in the killings of Feliciano and the Yuson brothers were supplied by us."

"Don't leave me, Felix." He reached out and touched Elizalde's arm. "Please." Cafiero said, "Please don't leave me alone, Felix."

"The guns in the killings of Feliciano and the Yuson brothers were supplied by us." He waited.

Cafiero said, "Please. I can't go back to the Bureau. Please."

The house on the salt farm had been nothing but a one-room affair with a bed and a kerosene stove and the remnants of junk-food meals on top of the television in the center of the room. No one had yet looked in the shed.

"Felix—"

The shed was locked with a new, strong padlock. In the house when he had searched it, Elizalde had not seen a key.

Cafiero said, "Felix, *in the name of pity*—!"

There was a tire iron in the back of his car that would take care of the lock. He looked at the wooden shed. It was dark and still and everyone on the scene was a long way away from it, picking up pieces of bodies or taking back pieces of the grenade to the Ballistics car.

"Felix—please!" He was sobbing. There were no tears, but he was sobbing. In his hand were the crushed and broken sunglasses. On the seat of his car was the loaded riot gun. His wife was in San Francisco—she was safe. All night, alone, Elizalde had waited at the table, his own wife away in San Pablo City, out of reach. All night—in his case, just one single night—

He drew a breath. Elizalde said quietly, "Come on." With Cafiero a little behind him he went to get the tire iron.

"Thank you, Felix . . ."

"All right."

Unlocking the trunk of the car and getting out the tire iron, he glanced first at the locked door to the shed, then to Cafiero's coat to see if he was armed.

All across the three acres of the salt farm people in uniforms and white coats were picking up the remains of two human beings as if they were litter. In the air, in the growing bright light, he could see wisps of hard gray smoke lying in pockets on the ground. Here and there he could see blood.

He held the tire iron firmly in both hands and felt its weight.

At 7:29 A.M. on the South Superhighway, Las Pinas, with the man who had once been Constantino Cafiero, he went forward to break open the lock of the salt farmer's shed.

It was a Dutch V 40 minigrenade: he had the pin and a piece of the casing. In the front of his car, resting the catalog against the steering wheel, Gomez looked it up in the index and found the picture on page one hundred eighty. The smallest hand grenade in current manufacture, it was half the size of the American Mark II pineapple grenade and the British L2A1. The catalog was an Army Special Forces identification and use manual. It showed each weapon under the heading of Antipersonnel Hand Projected Arms and gave instructions on how it should be used if turned against an enemy. It listed all the world's forces who used each weapon. It listed all the countries which, in the last twenty years or so, had armed their forces with each type of weapon and which arms manufacturers or suppliers had sold or were believed to have sold the weapons to antigovernment forces.

The grenade, with a diameter of only one and a half inches, was a big seller.

Republic of the Philippines . . . He looked it up. On the dashboard of his car was his silver hip flask full of dark Manila rum.

Republic of the Philippines . . . It was too early, even for him, to take a drink.

The converted .22 caliber Gevarm submachine guns had come from his own armory. All together, he had made two hundred eighty-seven of them.

Republic of the Philippines . . . He had thought, he had been told—he had believed all the guns had gone into a furnace to be melted down.

Evaluation Only. Various Government Agencies. Disposition Unknown. Total Number of Grenades Supplied (Manufacturer's Figures); five hundred exactly.

He turned the page.

No further information available.

In his car, he touched at the silver hip flask. He touched at the chopped officer's model Colt 1911AI .45 caliber automatic pistol he carried cocked and locked in a speed holster under his gray dustcoat.

He ran his tongue across his lips. Everywhere, all over the salt farm, there were people in white coats and uniforms, government people.

In the car, hunched down, out of sight, Gomez reached for the silver hip flask and, feeling it burn all the way down, took a drink.

———

The lock came off with a single sharp crack that splintered wood all around it and let light into the old, creaking wooden building through a hundred chinks and holes in its fabric. The hinges had been recently oiled: they moved easily as Elizalde pulled open the door.

The light, flooding in, lit up everything.

He heard Elizalde draw a breath.

Cafiero, a little behind him and to one side, his view momentarily blocked, said anxiously, "Felix? Felix? What's in there?"

FELICIANO, Benigno------ Emmanuel Ernesto Barrera.
YUSON, Sonny--------------Ermalinda R. Beo.
YUSON, Leon-----------------Ermalinda R. Beo.
TOPACIO, Tomas------------Xavier Luis Alonso (aged 9).

On his boat, the Whispering Man had the names written down on a note pinned to a brown manila folder.

FILE NO. He could not read it. He moved the note to one side of the folder.

FILE NO. ZA/6/395/LV/816934/CURRENT/RP6. Bureaucracy, it was wonderful. He opened the file and looked at the black-and-white photograph stapled on the second page.

It showed a dead man lying on a bush trail out in a wood or a jungle somewhere. The man was white, like a blanched chicken. The photograph had as its own caption, a label with a file number printed on it.

It was the same number as the file.

ELIZALDE, Felix.

CAFIERO, Constantino. Both the names were at the very bottom of the note under the long list of other names.

ELIZALDE, Felix.

CAFIERO, Constantino.

The Whispering Man, alone in the semidarkness of his boat, his face yellow and shadowed by the single twelve-volt chart table light he used to read, tapped at both the names with the tip of his pencil and, like God, pondered a decision.

The folder had, stamped on its cover in two colors, a seal. It was the Great Seal of the United States of America.

It had a single word stamped below it in indelible ink from a stamp pad. It was the name of the file.

The name of the file was ASWANG. It meant, in the Tagalog language of the Philippines, *vampire*.

The Whispering Man tapped at the names with his pencil.

He pondered carefully, luxuriously, smiling to himself, a decision.

He watched. In his car, the catalog of weapons still open on the steering wheel of his car, Technical Sergeant Gomez, his hand resting lightly on the butt of his gun, closed his eyes to make it all go away.

It could have been nothing more than the area where he finally desiccated the salt, or sorted it, or graded it, or carried out some process to order for the wholesalers who bought it from him.

It could have been merely that.

Inside the shed, there was a second, inner room. It could have been built merely because the shed itself was old and falling to pieces and structurally unsound. The old shed could merely be hiding the new room because the new room had been built without city-planning permission or because it kept the look of the operation small—it could have been that. He didn't know. He knew nothing about how people worked for every peso they made—he knew nothing about farming three acres or counting profits by stealth or— Elizalde said, "It's an aluminum room within a room." Like a twenty-foot cube of shining metal inside the old barn, the second closed room had no windows. There were funnels and pipes coming out of it, connected to what appeared to be rusty dampening pipes and filters. The pipes and filters led away into a hole in the earth floor to let out fumes, presumably unseen, into some other pipeline that led back to the sea.

The aluminum room was not locked. Where a dented line showed on the material there was a door with an open padlock and hasp on it. Elizalde, with Cafiero a little behind him, pulled off the lock and opened the door.

The past may have been another country where they did things differently: the poor were another nation. They had things done to them.

There was an electric light switch just inside the door. Elizalde turned it on.

Cafiero said, "What is it?"

He knew nothing about them at all. He knew not one thing about how they lived or what they did to survive.

Cafiero said, "Felix—?"

What it was was a sealed aluminum room full of zinc baths, six of them in two rows with pipes running under them to what looked like improvised gas burners. It was like being inside some sort of water tank. Elizalde looked up. On the ceiling there were more pipes and fans and, running along the silver aluminum, green copper lines to take evaporation or fumes away from the fires.

He wouldn't come in. He stood at the door. Cafiero said, "Felix, what is it?"

The zinc baths, each of them, were stained and corroded. It could have been from the evaporation process of the salt. The salt could have been dragged in here, poured still wet from the pools into the baths, and, with all the fires turning the place into a furnace, with all the heat contained and kept in, been dried out, turned to grains, and then shoveled into bags and taken outside to be sold.

The room was scrupulously clean. There was nothing on the floor. Maybe, with the cost of gas, it was only economic using the room once per full harvest. Maybe Topacio collected the salt from his pools a few pounds at a time. Maybe he dried out what he could with the free heat from the sun, hoping maybe the room would only have been to be lit for a few hours, maybe he—

He knew nothing of how more than 80 percent of his own fellow countrymen lived. He knew nothing about them at all.

Getting down on his hands and knees, Elizalde looked under the first of the zinc baths.

"Felix—"

Elizalde said, "Shut up." He put his hand under the bath and felt at the gas ring there. It was cold. The connections were a little loose, improvised.

People who lived like this, in the colonial days, had become soldiers. They were the ones the new weapons were tried out on in the Spanish-American War. They were the ones the Japanese had used for target practice for their troops. They were the ones who—

"Felix—" He was still at the open door. He wanted to go.

Under the zinc bath, Elizalde's hand touched something. It was white, wedged in behind one of the legs bolted to the floor. He pulled it and it came out, white and a little powdery, something curved and thin and broken about six inches long.

The room with the zinc baths was where salt was dried out.

The object was white, a length of something that looked like a curved fragment of china or porcelain three-quarters of an inch thick, jagged at one end where it was broken.

It was a room where salt was desiccated and graded. He touched another, a second object like the first, wedged under the leg of the zinc bath.

The room was somewhere secret, harmless, hidden only from the city zoning laws or from the taxman or—

In his hand, the two objects were cold and dead. They were bone.

It was a room on the South Superhighway, Las Pinas, on a salt farm where—

In the room, Elizalde stood up with the two objects, one in each hand.

It was not two objects, it was one. Each end was jagged. It was one object that had been broken. The two objects came together.

They came together.

In his hands, holding the two white curved things up and bringing them to meet in the middle, they came together.

It was one object.

In the room, as Cafiero looked, there was no dust, no residue, no evidence of what was done in there. There was only the single object brought together in Elizalde's hands.

There was only the look on Cafiero's face as he saw it.

There were only the zinc baths and fires and pipes that took smells and smoke and any sign of what happened back into the sea through hidden, improvised underground ducts.

In the room, the two white objects came together in Elizalde's hands.

The six zinc baths could merely have been used for desiccating salt.

In the room, there, in the light, the two objects formed a single, a broken, jagged, discarded human rib.

He heard Cafiero in a whisper.

In a whisper, frozen to the spot, starting to shake, Cafiero said like a man hurting, "Oh. Oh. Oh—*Jesus!*"

He smashed. He smashed everything.

On the boat, he smashed everything in the engine room with a hammer, all the wires and connections and pipes, everything.

He needed no engine.

He needed nothing.

The file with the photograph of the dead, drained man was still on the chart table in the main saloon of the boat. He knew it was there. All the time, like the hanged child's doll, he carried it around in his head.

He was never, never coming back.

The Whispering Man said, "Do it! Do it!"

Wielding the hammer, he smashed.

He smashed at everything that would ever bring him back from the sea once he had gone.

"Do it! Do it!"

He smashed until everything he could see was broken.

He was shaking with fear.

In his car Gomez, his hands shaking on the wheel, started the engine and putting the lever hard into gear, drove away from that place as fast as he could.

He saw him. He saw Elizalde at the door to the shed. He saw his face. He saw all the people in the pools and around the house, all the people in their uniforms and their white coats turn to look at him.

He saw Cafiero a little to one side. He saw how he looked too. He saw the General coming in his big car with all his minders and underlings. He saw the General wind down the window of the rear passenger seat and lean out to shout an order to someone.

He saw him.

He saw the General coming.

Elizalde, at the open door of the shed, the broken bones still in his hands, shouted at the top of his voice to all of them all over the farm, "Dig it up! Get shovels, spades, anything you need!" He held up the broken rib. *"Dig everything in this place up!"*

Elizalde, taking Cafiero by the scruff of the neck, pushing him, pulling him in the direction of his car a moment before the General could get there, his face white, shaking, trembling, ordered Cafiero with no room for argument at all, "And you— goddamn you—*you come with me!"*

He saw the General coming. He saw the people in the farm go toward their cars and trucks to get the equipment. He saw the General stand, openmouthed and hesitating by the door of his car.

Shoving Cafiero into the side seat of his own car, the expensive Mitsubishi Magna, Elizalde, stopping for nothing, yelled, "Get in! Get in!" He ordered Cafiero, "Drive!" He saw Cafiero look confused. He had no idea where to go at all.

He had not for a very long time.

Elizalde, pushing him in, shoving, wedging him into the driver's seat, his eyes blazing, yelled, "The Yusons!" He knew the General heard.

Elizalde, the two pieces of bone still held in his hand, feeling the cold, awful death of them, ordered Cafiero, "Drive back to the Yusons' shop in Intramuros so I can take that respectable, honest, fair-dealing, nice little fucking establishment apart one goddamned, stinking, fucking brick at a time!"

He saw the General start to say something and then change his mind.

Elizalde, getting into the car and slamming the door hard, ordered Cafiero, "Drive! *Drive!*"

12

*F*ireball yelled in his ear, "THINK! *THINK!*"

He was. He was thinking. Ambrosio, running down the corridor of the dwarves' private quarters at half past seven in the morning, yelled back, "I *am* thinking!"

He was. The whole place was full of smoke, of burning fuses and fizzing powder trains, and he was thinking. Ambrosio screamed, "I *am* thinking!"

"THINK OF THE LONG TERM!"

Screw the long term. The private quarters were like a hotel. There was a long corridor with nothing but doors on both sides, leading away to a blank wall. There were seventeen rooms. The rooms were all full of smoke. There were shouting dwarves running in and out of all the seventeen rooms, eleven of them. There was Bontoc running in and out of the rooms. In the smoke there looked like eight of him.

"THINK OF THE FUTURE—DECADES AHEAD!"

He couldn't even think of the next ten seconds. The smoke was everywhere. They had been let in the front door by Pablo, come in full of resolution and— And the smoke had started the moment they opened their mouths. Someone else had opened his mouth first. Someone had yelled, "Bomb!" and there was the smoke pouring out of the corridor. It was in one of the rooms. He couldn't find which room it was. Ambrosio, wrenching open a door halfway along the corridor and colliding with a papier-mâché tiger's head, two clown slapstick ass whackers, and what looked like an enormous balsa-wood Henry Moore sculpture of a Henry Moore elephant with a hole in its middle, yelled, "It's a storeroom!" The storeroom was full of smoke. It was coming in through the air-conditioning duct and under the door. Ambrosio yelled, "It's not in here!"

It wasn't in room number seven on the right either. Room number seven on the right was a bathroom full of dolls' clothes hanging from the smallest shower rack in the shortest shower in the world. Bontoc, cracking his head as he collided with the rail and getting down, not intentionally, on his hands and knees to search for the bomb, yelled to someone flailing his arms through the smoke behind him, "It's a bathroom!" It was Rodolfo the strong man in neck-to-knee leopard-skin trunks. Rodolfo hadn't opened the door, he had torn it off its hinges. Bontoc, pushing the little fellow out with an easy sweep of his hand and feeling as if his hand had struck solid steel, yelled, "Not in here!"

All the rooms were interconnected. Ambrosio was in room number nine. It was Illuminada's room. If it hadn't been full of smoke it would have been very nice. Ambrosio saw on a little round table a crocheted tablecloth with flowers on it. He saw Illuminada with an armful of ledgers and papers. The smoke was coming up from the floor and swirling. He sniffed. He smelled gunpowder. He didn't smell fire. Ambrosio, sniffing, the lead from the Walkman following him around like a tail, yelled at Illuminada, "Is it in here?"

Illuminada yelled, "No."

"What happened?"

"It just happened!" Illuminada, looking frightened, yelled, "All our money's safe!"

Great. Fireball yelled, "AND THEN PLAN!"

He planned. Ambrosio yelled, "Get out! Get out of here!"

Illuminada said, "All the nice things I've collected—!" The smell of gunpowder was getting stronger. The fuse was burning fast. Illuminada sobbed, "All my poor dead mother's lovely things—!"

Her mother was Imelda. She wasn't dead. Poor thing, all the figures and frustrations had driven her mad. He knew the feeling. Ambrosio, taking her by the shoulder, yelled, "Your mother isn't dead!" She was riveted to the spot. He had a brainstorm. Ambrosio yelled, "Your poor dead mother's waiting for you at the end of the corridor!" Ambrosio yelled, "Go to her! Go to her!"

He was going. He was going straight into room number ten. It was locked. He had Rodolfo. Bontoc, seeing the smoke pouring out from under room number ten and knowing—knowing—the bomb was in there, ordered Rodolfo, "Pull it off its hinges!" Where was Rodolfo? He was gone. Bontoc, standing back and leaping at the door, kicked it in. It was a laundry. The door must have been made of cardboard. Where the hell was Rodolfo? Bontoc, picking himself up out of a stainless-steel basin set eighteen inches from the floor and disentangling himself from the taps, hoses, and what felt like four days' accumulated, soaking, soap-powder-filled washing, yelled, "Rodolfo!" He saw Ambrosio shepherding someone out through the smoke past the door. Bontoc, getting out of the basin like a caterpillar, yelled, "It's not in here!"

He looked in. Bontoc had taken cover in some sort of silver manhole against the wall. He looked as if he were crawling down it to safety. Coward. Ambrosio, shoving Illuminada toward her screaming dead mother at the end of the corridor, ordered him, "Come and help!"

"TAKE CHARGE OF THE SITUATION!"

He was. Ambrosio yelled at Fireball in his ear, "I am!"

Bontoc shouted, "You am what?" He saw Rodolfo. Rodolfo was running. There were dogs in the corridor with him: Carmel's chihuahuas. He saw Rodolfo scoop one up and hurl it down the corridor. He heard Carmel shriek. He heard a yap as either Carmel missed or didn't miss, but either way, the dog wasn't pleased. Bontoc, starting to cough, to sputter as the smoke billowed, yelled to Ambrosio, long gone, "I am helping! I'm stuck in this goddamned basin!" He saw Pablo run by in his top coat and riding boots. He saw Jorge and Ernesto. Good old Ernesto. Bontoc, squeezing himself out of the basin, yelled,

"Ernesto, get Rodolfo! He's with Carmel—" Ernesto didn't stop.

Room number three. It was open. It was full of smoke. It was Josephine's room. It was full of pictures of horses stuck to the walls. It was full of model horses and toy horses and embroideries of horses and it even had a stained-glass window of a horse. It should have smelled horsy. It smelled of gunpowder. Ambrosio, getting to the far corner of the room and moving furniture and kicking chairs and tables out of the way, yelled, "No bomb in here!" He was getting efficient. "No bomb in room number seven on the right."

"No bomb in room number fourteen on the left!" In room number fourteen on the left were Carmel's other—what looked and sounded like—two hundred six chihuahuas. Bontoc, yelling, "Ha!" and stampeding them out into the corridor, yelled, "Where the hell's the center of it?"

"No bomb in room number four!" It was a prop room. It was full of cupboard space and clown costumes and tutus and leopard skins. It was full of Rodolfo pulling out tiny silk dresses and organza frills and petticoats. Illuminada was Ignacio and Imelda's daughter. Carmel was Ricardo's sister. Josephine was Jorge's daughter. Rodolfo was married to— He wasn't married to anyone. *Cherchez la femme.* Ambrosio, grabbing an armful of lace and petticoats, yelled, "Whose clothes are you saving and why?"

Rodolfo yelled, "My own!"

Rodolfo was—well, it took all kinds. Ambrosio said, "Ah!"

Rodolfo said, "Screw you!"

Fireball yelled, "PERSIST! GO!" He took, on balance, Fireball's suggestion. Ambrosio, getting out, yelled to no one in particular, "Room number four clear!"

Who was the target? Bontoc, stopping, pausing, halting, couldn't work out who the target was. There was smoke in all the rooms. If the smoke was only the fuse of the bomb burning, the bomb must have been the size of a house. There was no center point. There should have been fire and fizzing somewhere, but all there was, everywhere, was the smoke. It was as if there were little bombs everywhere. *As if there were little bombs everywhere.* It was not one bomb but—

Bontoc, kicking down door number five with all his might, finding it ajar and ending up on the floor of Ernesto's room amid a pile of pots, pans, woks, spice jars, and an assortment of private kitchenware that would have kept even Imelda Marcos happy between shoe-buying expeditions, yelled, "It's lots of bombs!" He saw Ambrosio go past, still looking disapproving. Bontoc yelled, "I was stuck in a sink!" Bontoc yelled, "It's lots of bombs! Don't look for a big bomb! It's lots of bombs! The bombs are everywhere! The bombs are in all the rooms! Everyone's the target! The whole place is going to be destroyed!" He saw dwarves running through the smoke. They were running like hell. Bontoc, extricating himself from a long-handled frying pan and tripping over an obstacle course of little glass spice bottles and whisks, spatulas, and cleavers, yelled, "The bombs are in all the rooms!" Bontoc yelled, "RUN!"

"What?" Through Fireball exhorting him on, Ambrosio thought he heard, for an instant, the voice of a headhunter, "What?" Fireball yelled, "LIFE IS LOGIC! LOGIC IS POWER! POWER IS—" Ambrosio, heading for the deepest room number eight at the far end of the corridor, said, "What—?"

"EVERY ROOM HAS GOT A BOMB IN IT!"

All the dwarves had run away. The corridor and all the rooms were empty.

Ambrosio, learning as well as how to be powerful, how to be polite, said, "Pardon?"

In the corridor, through the smoke, he saw a small, nutbrown person carring a collander in one hand and a whisk in the other. The small nut-brown person appeared to be covered in bright yellow saffron powder. Ambrosio said—

"THE TARGETS! IT'S NOT THE DWARVES AT ALL!" All the dwarves had gone. Bontoc, starting to hop up and down, yelled, "IT'S US! IT'S US—WE'RE THE GODDAMNED

TARGETS!" Bontoc, wishing Uncle Apo were here to kill something, shrieked in a miasma of smoke and saffron and hopping-mad anger tinged with a very strong desire to be a long way away very quickly, "It's half past seven! Why aren't there any customers?" He saw Ambrosio listen. "There aren't any customers because the goddamned dwarves closed up after we came in! It's us! No one's after any of the dwarves! *Someone's after us!*"

Bontoc said as the first of the bombs went off at the far end of the corridor and blew everything out through the door in a wave of heat and concussion, "Run!" Bontoc said as the second door in room number nine across from room number eight at the far end of the corridor blew everything from room number nine out in the corridor and everything from room number eight back in again, "Run!" He saw room number six go, and then across from it, room number four. He saw Ambrosio taking off his earphones outside room number five looking disappointed. More good money down the tubes. He saw room number ten go. It was the laundry. It was not so much an explosion as a damburst. He saw the laundry go. He saw the stainless-steel basin. He saw Ambrosio open his mouth to say—

Bontoc yelled, "YOU DUMB BASTARD, *RUN!!!*" He saw—

All the rooms went at once and he saw, as he and Ambrosio, running, became airborne, only smoke, and for an instant, as he and Ambrosio hit the sawdust in the ring, still running, going face down, he saw, for an instant—

All the dwarves standing around in a circle watching them, grinning.

7:48 A.M. precisely.

On the corner of Palagayan Street and Georgio Villanueva Street, Tondo, near Chinatown, Rolly looked at his watch. In his pocket he had two keys from Yale padlocks. He put his hand in his pocket and clinked them together.

He smiled to himself. Normally, on a street like this, early in the morning, he would have been afraid. Normally, he would never have come to a street like this.

He smiled. Behind him, twenty yards back, without turning to look at it, he knew there was an old paint-peeling vehicle of some sort trailing him. He guessed it would probably be a Volkswagen Kombi van twenty years old with bald tires and no registration.

He listened and heard its engine straining to keep going.

Palagayan Street was deserted. Once it had been seedily fashionable for the mistresses and servants of the old Spanish regime in Intramuros, but now it was part of the city's slum clearance program and was nothing. It was vacant blocks covered in grass stubble and bushes with only the odd stucco house falling apart at the seams and sidewalks full of unfilled holes and lifting asphalt.

From the van, they watched.

He stopped. He heard the van stop with him.

Number twenty-six, Palagayan Street. It was one of the decaying stucco houses with the remains of an iron spear-point fence around it and a hole in the sidewalk where, a long time ago, there had been a tree planted for the shade.

He touched at the keys in his pocket.

He smiled.

Outside the house, drawing a breath, Rolly, complete, fulfilled—powerful—like a snake, began to make a soft, quiet, hissing sound.

His shoulders were tight, held in hard, tense.

Outside the house, not looking back at the van, Rolly, touching at the two keys in his pocket, pursing his lips, unmusically, to himself, made a series of soft whistling sounds.

He looked at the house.

He stopped whistling.

Powerful, potent, there alone in the street, being watched, he looked in at the decaying house behind the railings and pursed his lips.

———

He *knew*. At his microscope in the police armory, he knew.

The silver hip flash was beside him on the bench where the microscope was and Technical Sergeant Gomez, staring down through the eyepiece at the fragments of the grenade, knew.

The room was full of guns. They lined every wall.

He knew. At his microscope, staring down at the remains of a stamped-on number done with a diesinker, he knew where the grenade had come from.

There were no windows in the room. All the walls were gun racks and compartments—in the room everything was blue-black with oiled and ordered weaponry.

He knew. He knew where the grenade had come from.

He touched at the silver hip flask, but he felt too sick to his stomach to touch it.

God help him, he knew.

His Colt .45 chopped officer's model automatic pistol was on the bench beside him, cocked with the safety catch off, loaded with seven hollow point rounds in the magazine and one in the breech.

He was in a secure and locked steel-doored room with concrete walls two-feet thick lined internally every six inches with stainless steel two-inch-thick bars.

He might as well have been standing out in the open on a rifle range with a target pinned to his chest.

He looked through the microscope and saw again the government department number stamped on the grenade fragment with a diesinker's punch.

He touched again at the silver hip flask.

He knew.

There was nowhere to hide. He was a dead man either way.

In the armory, his hand shaking, Gomez picked up the telephone on his bench to make a call.

In the sawdust, Ambrosio said, "Pablo?" He saw the Ringmaster grinning. Ambrosio said, "Pablo?" That was his name, wasn't it? He had always liked Pablo. The smoke was still billowing over his head and into his eyes so he thought he'd get up. His legs had been blown off: he couldn't move. He looked at his legs. They were still there. He still couldn't get up. Ambrosio, seeing all his friends the dwarves looking down at him and snarling, said in a panic, "Pablo? Ignacio? Ricardo?" There was a dwarf lying on the sawdust next to him struggling to get up and then falling down again. Ambrosio said, *"Baptiste?"*

"The *United Nations* sent us!" The dwarves were moving in. They had things in their hands: black round things. Bontoc, getting up and then falling down, said, "Got that? The United Nations!"

Pablo, nodding, said, "Yes, we called them in."

"So you're in big trouble—all of you!" He wondered where the trapeze artist Jorge was. Jorge was the one with the kind face. The smoke was everywhere. Bontoc, trying to crane his neck around with the strong suspicion that the bombardment in the corridor had neatly disconnected it from his shoulders, said, "Jorge? Ernesto—" He and Ernesto had quoted poetry together. Ernesto had a look on his face that made Bontoc feel like a cockroach about to go under a heel. Bontoc, getting up again, getting down again, said, "Ernesto . . . ? *archy* . . . ?"

"STAND UP AND BE A MAN!" It was Fireball. Somewhere in the corridor, he had survived. "STAND UP AND BE A . . ." He whirred out. He was gone. Ambrosio, seeing a face wearing glasses at the back of the dwarf crush, said, "Illuminada! It's me: Jesus-Vincente!" Ambrosio said, "Illuminada!"

Illuminada said, "Pablo?"

Pablo said, "Yes."

Illuminada went toward the windows near the front entrance to the dining area and, one by one, shuttered them.

Pablo said, "Rodolfo—"

Rodolfo, no longer carrying his nice dresses, but a black leather wrist guard, said, "Here, Pablo."

Pablo said to the sweetest girl in the world, Cinderella, to Carmel, "Carmel?"

"Yes." She had a faraway look in her eyes. Carmel said tightly, "Here, Pablo."

Pablo said, "Check all the doors are locked."

Carmel said, "Yes, Pablo." She went to check.

It clicked. In Ambrosio's mind, it clicked. They were all in it together. Ambrosio, suddenly shouting, yelled, *"You're all in this together!"* He had known it from the start. Ambrosio said, "Why? Why are you doing this?" They were going to murder him. He was a poor broken soul trying to get on in this world and doing no one any harm and they were going to murder him. He had a family. Ambrosio, punching at his legs to get them to work, demanded, "Why? Why are you destroying your own livelihood?" He saw Illuminada at the shutters. *"This place is a goldmine!"*

Bontoc shrieked, "You people are poor dwarves who don't even know what's funny except yourselves!" He had felt so sorry for them he hadn't even brought his gun. He had left it outside in the car. So had Ambrosio. Bontoc, getting up onto his knees and trying to fit his head back on his shoulders, shrieked, "Are you people mad? We came here to help you! We're on your side! We thought and thought about you!" Bontoc yelled, "Ernesto, you and I shared poetry together!" He couldn't see Jorge the trapeze swinger. Bontoc, getting mad, shouted, "What have you done to poor Jorge? Where is he? What have you done to him?"

What the hell were they going to do to him? Ambrosio, fitting one leg under another and hauling himself up, said firmly, warningly, "Now listen, we're police officers. We're very powerful. We're not as nice as you might at first think—"

Pablo said quietly, "Oh, yes, you are."

"Oh, no, we're not." The legs were starting to work. Ambrosio, getting heated, said, "Oh, no, we're not. You're looking at two of the toughest cops this side of—of—" Ambrosio said, "Of anywhere—"

It was Josephine. Josephine said with a soft voice, smiling, "No, both of you are kind and warmhearted and very honest. That's why you're both so poor and you care for the lives of ordinary people—"

Ambrosio said, "No we don't!"

Pablo said, "You do. You're both good."

Ambrosio said, "No, we're—"

Bontoc said, "Right! And we'd like a hand to get up now and then we can continue along life's kind and sympathetic way and we won't say a word about any of this and—"

Pablo said, "Yes, that's what we feared."

"What are you talking about?" Bontoc, his brain starting to work, demanded, *"Where's Jorge?"* He saw Carmel the dog lady over by the wall of mirrors at the master switchboard for the lights. All the shutters were closed. All the doors were locked. Bontoc, trying to work it out, demanded, "What the hell is she—"

"HAAAAA—YAAAA!" It was Jorge on the trapeze. It was Zorro in his gold-lamé suit. It was the posse, the Seventh Cavalry. Jorge, a vision of hope and long johns, swinging upside down by his feet from somewhere high up in the roof, somewhere near heaven, yelled, "JOR--GE!!"

Ambrosio yelled, *"What the hell's going on?"*

Bontoc yelled, "JORGE!"

Jorge yelled, "HAAA—YAAA!" He had two little black things in his hands. The little black things were bombs. He had a burning cigarette in his mouth. He lit both the bombs as he swung. Jorge yelled, "AMBROSIO! BONTOC!"

Pablo yelled to Jorge, "THROW!"

Bontoc yelled to Ambrosio, "DUCK!"

Pablo yelled to Carmel, "LIGHTS!"

Jorge yelled, "HAAAA!" He took aim on the downswing and the two fizzing bombs came falling down in arcs.

Pablo yelled to everyone, "MATCHES!"

They all pulled boxes of matches or lighters from their pockets.

Pablo yelled, "BOMBS!"

They all pulled bombs from nowhere and lit them.

The bombs were falling, falling.

Pablo yelled to Carmel, "LIGHTS!" and in the sawdust ring, as the first of the fizzing objects came sailing down to land on the ground not ten feet from them, as eleven demented, grinning dwarves scattered to find even more bomb-throwing positions, as Ambrosio yelled in a panic, "BAPTISTE—"

—all the lights went out and they were in complete darkness.

In the windows of the Yuson brothers' antique shop all the *santos*—the saints—were watching with painted eyes. Ancient, dried-out, carved wooden figurines and busts, their monochrome paint peeling and flecking, some without arms or legs or noses, they were Saint Peter, Saint John, Luke, Mark, Matthew—all the saints and all the variations of black, brown, Philippino, Spanish, and Chinese of the Holy Mother, the Virgin and Child.

Behind them, deeper into the shop, there were more figures on all the walls and on tables. There were Chinese export porcelain, maps in gold frames, swords, here and there a piece of Spanish conquistadore armor, ancient brassware from Mindanao, and on shelves, behind glass, silverware and gold coins, and everywhere, everywhere in the shop there were the little painted, broken, staring wooden saints.

They had no entry warrant. The keys to the place, with the Yusons themselves, had been taken away. Cafiero, looking shaken, said warningly, "Felix, we can't just—" There was a cast-iron antique foot wiper outside the door to the shop. Something from some nineteenth-century Spanish merchant's house or business, it was an eighteen-inch square filigreed base with two curving dolphins supporting a rectangle of thin metal to wipe away mud. He saw Elizalde lean down and take it up. Cafiero said, "The alarms! The place is probably full of alarms!" He saw Elizalde looking hard at the Yale lock on the door. There were scratch marks around it. Cafiero, glancing back down the arcade to the Casa Manila in case someone was coming, said urgently, "Felix, we can't just—"

He saw the heavy metal object come back in Elizalde's hand. Cafiero shouted, *"Felix—!"* The glass in the door near the lock shattered into fragments. Cafiero, starting to turn to run, said, "The alarm! The goddamned alarm—!"

There was no alarm. After the glass had finished falling, there was no sound at all.

He had no idea at all what he was looking for, but whatever it was, it was in there. Elizalde, touching at his gun, his eyes hard on Cafiero, said in a rasp, "In. You come with me. Now." He saw Cafiero hesitate.

Elizalde, his fist clenched hard, said as an order, his other hand still on the butt of his gun, "Now! *Now!*"

He held, for an instant, Cafiero's eyes with his.

In Elizalde's eyes, there was no argument to be made.

Stepping on the broken glass and hearing it crunch, together, they went into the silent, darkened shop where all the saints were, to find what, hidden, was in there.

"Baptiste?" In the Gnome Home, as the first two bombs blasted sawdust and, as he got up, knocked him down again, Ambrosio, scrambling in the dark, digging a hole in the ground to hide himself, not being able to dig, excavating, yelled, "Baptiste!"

He couldn't see a thing. He saw fuses burning. He saw the burning fuses fly through the air. "Baptiste!"

He ducked. He saw a flash. He saw Bontoc lit up. He saw his eyes. Ambrosio, seeing more burning fuses flying, digging even deeper, getting back into the womb, yelled in total, utter, lost desperation, "Baptiste—*what in God's name have we ever done to them?*"

They were watching. From their van, they watched him. They waited.

He was outside number twenty-six Palagayan Street, Tondo,

near Chinatown. Once, it had been where the mistresses and servants of the rich Intramuros Spanish had lived. The two new keys for two Yale padlocks were in his pocket and he jingled them and pursed his lips.

He pursed his lips. In the street, he did not turn around. He merely smiled to himself.

He raised his hand and pointed once to the house.

"There." Under his breath Rolly said softly, *"There."*

He knew they watched. In the street, Rolly, raising his voice to make sure they heard, said, "There. *There!"*

He knew they watched. He heard the van start behind him.

Once, he jingled his keys. Behind him, he heard the van turn in the street and go back the way it had come.

He smiled.

He began walking away down the street toward MacArthur Avenue to his car.

It was a little after 8:10 A.M. on a clear, cloudless morning.

He walked away unhurriedly, still whistling, to get on with his day.

He heard him. In the darkness, dodging bombs, he heard him. He heard Jorge swinging. He heard him, on his trapeze, sobbing. He was blubbering, wailing, crying, upset. They all were. He heard all the dwarves, as they tried to blow him to tripes, sniffing and blubbering.

In the darkened Gnome Home, dodging death as it flew in toward him in fizzing yellow lines of burning fuses, Bontoc yelled in terrible, total, unarmed confusion, *"Why are you all weeping?"*

13

*E*lizalde had been through the living quarters at the back of the shop. He had found nothing. He was at a filing cabinet by the Spanish mantelpiece pulling out files and folders from a wooden cabinet one by one and opening them—and finding nothing. The air in the shop, with all the wooden saints and the heavy carved furniture, was thick with the smell of wood polish. It was hard to breathe. Cafiero, sunk into a square-backed, carved chair that once must have belonged to a grandee, covering his eyes with his hand, said, swallowing, "Felix, once, when I was young—when I was a child—"

The files were in alphabetical order. They were clients' buying and wants records complete with accounts rendered and paid. There was no typewriter in the room; only on the heavy nara wood desk by the entrance to the living quarters, expensive silver and gold Parker and Sheaffer fountain pens laid out on an English eighteenth-century pewter ship's standish. All the letters and records had been handwritten by one of the brothers.

Cafiero said, "When I was a kid in Tondo . . ."

He saw Elizalde stop at the files and turn to look at him.

Cafiero said, "In Tondo. I was one of them—one of the poor." His face was tight. He was looking away, at all the things that the rich collected. He was smelling the smell of the polish. He had a lit cigarette in his hand. His hand, as he brought it to his mouth, was shaking. He bit at his lip. Cafiero said, "I was one of them. When—when I was one of them, when I lived, when I existed, like a dog with my mother in a house made out of tin sheets and cardboard and bits of old fences, when I was that low, like a dog, there was a man whose name I never knew." The air was close in the packed shop. He was perspiring. He looked down and had nowhere to drop his ash. He flicked it onto the floor, "And the man—the Dark Man—" Cafiero said, "The Dark Man never spoke to me and I never saw him and I never knew his name and I never—" He was shaking. He had not told anyone about it before. "And this man was the man who—" He looked up. Cafiero said, "What? Who did what?" Cafiero said, "Nothing. He did nothing. He said nothing. And I never saw him." Cafiero said, "But he was the man. He was the one who held your life in the palm of his hand."

He saw Elizalde stop to look at him. Elizalde had a business-card folder in his hand. Some of the cards fell out as he held it and fluttered to the floor.

Cafiero said, "People in the barrio got lucky sometimes. It was the man who did that. People in the barrio sometimes fell on hard times—the man did that to them. People died—they were killed. That was the man too." Cafiero said, "Some people—a few—me—succeeded at school, won scholarships, had food delivered to their hovel to keep them from having to go out to work at age ten, and fought their way out—and that was the man too!" He nodded. He touched at his face. Holding the cigarette, his hand was shaking. *The man was everywhere and nowhere because he was the man and because nothing happened in the barrio without the man, like God, doing it!*"

"I thought your family were Spanish mestizos—"

"My father was a Spanish mestizo and my mother was his Philippina servant. He lived in a big house in Mabine and he fucked my mother and after he'd fucked her and got her pregnant he threw her out with nothing!" Cafiero said, "And she brought up her bastard—me—in Tondo." Cafiero said, "I learned my Spanish at school! I went to the local school in Tondo until I was ten and I won a scholarship with just enough money to make it possible to attend a church boarding school. I stayed there until I was fifteen with all the rich boys. When I was fifteen and the scholarship ran out, someone paid to keep me on there for another year until I could win another scholarship to finish, so I could win another scholarship to get into university!" Cafiero said, "I don't know who paid. If it was the man he never wanted anything."

"Where's your mother now?"

"She's dead." Cafiero said, "I did it all myself. I worked day and night and got to be better than all the other children I went to school with because when I got rich and powerful I intended to have my father killed." Cafiero said, "But he died too. He left me money. It was delivered to me one day in my room at university by his attorney. It was a lot of money and I wondered how much of it I owed the man." Cafiero said, "Nothing. There was no man for me then. I was no longer poor, I was no longer one of them, and when I went back to Tondo no one knew me and no one knew anything about the man." Cafiero said softly, "Felix, the man still lives. He's still there. I don't know his name. I've never seen him. I know nothing about him—for all I know—"

"Why did Rosey leave you, Constantino?"

"Because I was afraid."

"Of what?"

"I don't know. Of everything. Of the man. Of the fact that I never repaid whatever it was I should have repaid." There was a tic at the side of his face. "Of the dark. Of the names in all the files, of all the people like me—of the not knowing, of them, of the poor, of—" Cafiero said in a voice so low Elizalde had to strain to catch it, "I thought while my mother lived that if I did anything wrong that the man . . . that my mother was still there to be punished instead of me. I thought, while Rosey was still with me, that if I offended that she—" Cafiero said, "I sent her away. I'm alone. I'm alone all the time now, waiting—waiting for Godot." Cafiero said with a flick of his hand, his mouth set hard, "See? Education."

"Tell me what you know."

"*I don't know what I know!* I don't know who I owe! I don't know when I have to repay! *I don't know!*" Cafiero, on his feet

facing Elizalde, shouted at him, "I'm afraid! Can't you understand that? I'm afraid all the time! I shit myself with fear!
Anything, anything I may have done for the last twenty years—
anything I do in the next twenty seconds, any twenty seconds—
could be wrong! That could be the one thing I was bred,
cultivated, and left alone not to do! I never saw the man! I never
knew his name, but— But he's still there! He's—"

"Tell me what you know!"

"I'm afraid!" Cafiero, shaking, shouted, "I'm afraid!" He saw
Elizalde clearly. He saw his face. He saw the way he stood. He
had seen the way the rich kids at school stood. He had practiced
it. He had heard the way they talked, with just the faintest trace
of Spanish accent in their English. He had practiced that. He
had practiced—it had taken a long while—how to eat properly
at a table. He had practiced to be a grown man and a husband.
He had failed. What he was was a kitchen bastard with a gold
Cardin lighter and a Rolex watch. If he had stayed in the
barrio—if it had been the man's whim—he still would have had
them, but he would have had to have stolen them.

Cafiero, in the shop full of all the saints and the smell of
polish, wishing only that his life, at last, were over, said quietly,
past desperation, "Felix, I can't find the man anywhere! I can't
find who I was anywhere! What if I tell what I think and—and
someone comes out of Tondo and takes me back there to a
street somewhere among all the filth and garbage and kills me
like a dog?" Cafiero said, "I'm afraid! I'm afraid!" Cafiero said,
pleading, "Felix, all my life, through all my childhood, at
school, everywhere, to be someone I wasn't—to be someone
else—to be who I am now . . ."

He saw Elizalde looking at him with contempt. He knew that
look.

Cafiero said, begging, "All my life, all my life . . ." Cafiero
demanded, asking him, "How many times do I have to suffer?
How many times do I have to fight and curl up like a worm,
like an insect, with humiliation, with fear and loathing? How
many times do I have to—"

He had told him. He had never thought he would. Cafiero said quietly, searching for his eyes, "Felix, tell me—someone like me—*how many times do I have to be brave?*"

Item Eighth: The potential opponents of this as yet United
   Nations unprotected classification may be listed as
   the following:
   1. Gangsters
   2. Terrorists
   3. Radicals
   4. Misinformed racists
   5. Tall people with a grudge
   6. Racists
   7. Disgruntled customers of the establishment
      defined in Item First
   8. Religious zealots
   9. Psychopaths
   10. Mad Bombers.

Wrong!

Final Item: Best possible projections and hypotheses based
   on placement, construction, and nonlethality as well
   as total lack of interest previously shown in persons
   of diminished stature by gangsters, terrorists, radicals, misinformed racists, tall people with a grudge,
   fascists, disgruntled customers, zealots, psychopaths,
   and mad bombers suggests that, sadly—making protection by the ORGANIZATION a matter for the
   most careful, cautious, and well-trained officers on
   loan to its service—suggests that—*suggests that one
   or more of the goddamned dwarves are doing it* themselves!

Right!
In the dark, Ambrosio got to his feet. He heard a voice shout, "BE UNSTOPPABLE!" It was Fireball. He was unstoppable.

He was unstoppably getting to his feet. A bomb came from nowhere, went off in a thunderclap on the sawdust, and, in that hail of bomb, sawdust, and stench, he was unstoppably not on his feet, but unstoppably scrambling about like a crab trying to get into a hole. The dwarves were running, sobbing, hurling. He saw nice, mild, timid, shy, reserved, demure Illuminada lit up in a glow of a cigarette lighter. He saw her look away girlishly as she lit a fuse. He saw her blink. He saw the bomb come whizzing over at him in a parabola of sparks and then, scrambling, he was blown up again and went sliding across the ring.

He thought bits had been blown off him.

They hadn't. It was a warm-up bomb. The bits were going to be blown off by Pablo's bomb.

He saw Pablo's face. Pablo's face looked mad. He was weeping. Pablo's bomb came arching over from somewhere near the restaurant tables and, bouncing, landed near the burning bomb Jorge had dropped from aloft on his trapeze like a dive bomber.

The bombs did not go off in blasts. They went off in thumps. Ambrosio, being thumped, inhaling a near-lethal dose of sawdust and gunpowder, going backward, yelled, "Baptiste! Have you got your gun?"

He hadn't. All Baptiste had in the flash of Carmel's bomb and Ricardo's bomb and Ernesto's bomb, thrown simultaneously, was liftoff.

"DO SOMETHING!"

Ambrosio did something. Ambrosio, hopping, falling, clambering up to his feet again and then falling down, scrambling away, yelled, *"Why are you doing this?"* It seemed a reasonable enough question. It brought tears to his eyes. Ambrosio, slapping at his ankle in case, miraculously, his gun had materialized there in its ankle holster and he could haul it out and blow the dwarves into mincemeat with it, yelled, "You're trying to blow up someone who hobbled around on his knees in front of his wife's family just to get an insight into the life-style of a dwarf!" He got blown up by a bomb from Ignacio. Ambrosio screamed, "I love dwarves! I'm a liberal! I'm not even armed!" He saw

Carmel the dog lady, lit up in the scrape of a cigarette lighter, haul back a bomb to her shoulder with a look on her face that he couldn't understand at all, and Ambrosio, ducking, weaving, trying to find someone to strangle with his bare hands, yelled, "I forgive you this aberration! We can talk about it! You haven't hurt anyone! All your bombs were just sound and fury—we can let you off with a good talking to!" He couldn't see Bontoc anywhere. All the dwarves were weeping or howling or sniffing. Ambrosio, trying to catch someone's eye in the light of Carmel's fuse as it came over like a cannonball and landed at his feet, bouncing and fizzing, yelled, "Baptiste! Tell them we're friends! Tell them we're—"

He was already short. He didn't have to be liberal. "YOU BASTARDS ARE GOING FOR TEN YEARS! YOU BASTARDS WHEN WE GET YOU YOU AREN'T GOING TO GET TEN YEARS IN PRISON! YOU BASTARDS ARE GOING TO GET TEN YEARS IN THE BASTILLE! YOU BASTARDS ARE GOING TO THE DUNGEONS WHERE THE ONLY COMPANY YOU'LL HAVE ARE THE GOD-DAMNED COCKROACHES!"

It was Bontoc. He was hopping around, hopping mad. Bontoc shrieked, "YOU BASTARDS ARE GOING TO—" He was blown off his feet. He said, "Aaahhhh!"

"We'll let you off!" All the dwarves were weeping. Ambrosio, trying reason while digging deep in the sawdust for a granite cave somewhere, yelled, "He's kidding! We're nice!"

"WE'RE NOT NICE! WE'RE—"

"You are!" It was Pablo. He was somewhere in the midst of the sobbing, moaning, weeping, sniffing, mad bomb throwers. He sounded desperate. Pablo yelled, "You are! You're nice!" He threw a bomb at the nice people. It blew both of them off their feet together.

Pablo, lighting another bomb, sobbing, shaking with guilt, humiliation, and fury, yelled, "You are! You are! You're both too nice!"

Pablo yelled as the bomb exploded in midair like a daisy

cutter and pummeled Ambrosio another two inches deeper into the sawdust and filled Bontoc's open mouth with smoke and ashes, "You're too nice!"

Pablo yelled to everyone, "The Irish Giant! Remember the Irish Giant!" He threw another bomb. They all did.

Pablo yelled, "Everybody—for your lives—*keep throwing your bombs!*"

"You were sent! You got a phone message to go to the salt farm at that time of morning and you went there!" In the cabinet, Elizalde had found the General's file. The Yusons were good people. They had undercharged him an average of two thousand pesos for each of the first four santos he had bought after he had fixed their parking fines (the saving in fines had been noted in the copperplate hand alongside each transaction), they had given him as a free gift an eighteenth-century carving of Saint Pietro after his third santo, and, finally, on the sheet, in the last two weeks, they had overcharged him by four thousand pesos on a carving of the Christ on the cross and totted up the full six objects and the profit and loss. It came out even on their original selling prices. Elizalde said, "Someone called you and you went!"

"I don't know who!"

Elizalde said, "The boy who died . . . we'll probably never know who he was." Elizalde said quietly, "Maybe, Constantino, he was you." He saw Cafiero looking at him. Elizalde asked, holding his eyes, "What was his name?"

"I told you: I couldn't understand it!"

"Why did he say it?"

He looked down at the floor. The floor was polished Philippine mahogany, like the deck of a ship. It was covered in the gray ash from his cigarette. Cafiero said, looking down at it, "He was just a kid—I don't know what he said!"

"The kid was about ten years old!" Elizalde, moving to the desk away from the filing cabinet, said, still watching Cafiero, "You could tell that by what was left of the lower half of his body after the grenade shrapnel cut through all the flesh and bones in his face and the blast tore his chest out." He was watching, working at him, "You could tell that because—"

"I know what he was! I saw him die!"

"Did he look like anyone you knew? Maybe someone you could have grown up with—maybe a kid in those days you liked or you—"

"I've got no one to protect me now that Rosey's gone!"

"No." Elizalde said, "No, no one at all." He waited. He saw Cafiero, still sunk in the chair, run his hand over the back of his hair. Elizalde said, "Tell me what you know." He went to the desk and opened the center drawer.

"Felix—try to understand—"

"Tell me what you know."

"Try to understand!"

There was nothing in the drawer but invoices and bank statements and stationery, pencils, bottles of ink. There was nothing.

"Felix—"

"Tell me! Tell me now! *Tell me what you know!*"

He had signed the guns out of the armory at 3:37 P.M. on a Friday and they had gone to the foundry where by 4:00 P.M. all the furnaces would have been cold for the weekend and the twenty-five cases of guns would have sat in the foundry storeroom there until Monday morning.

It was on Gomez's day sheet and only the final details of the actual witnessed meltdown would be anywhere else and they would be on the Firearms Disposal files downstairs in Records and, protected by whoever protected them, safe. What, however, was on the day sheet, because Gomez himself had penciled it in for some reason, was the foundry owner's name and home telephone number.

Piscasio, Edgardo, and the home phone number: 77-22-15.

He remembered him. He had met him once out on the rifle range and had had a good lunch from him.

He had got for Edgardo Piscasio, for Edgardo Piscasio's mistress, a nice, unlicensed little .38 caliber Colt Airweight to put in her bedroom side table in case of burglars.

It was still early and Edgardo Piscasio, at home, would probably be having breakfast with his wife.

He was not sure why he did it. In the armory, in the silence of the morning, Gomez, leaning forward at his bench, began dialing the number.

"Jasmine!"

Jasmine threw a bomb.

Bontoc yelled, "Ernesto!"

Ernesto threw a bomb.

"Carmel! Ignacio! Rodolfo!"

Bomb, bomb, bomb.

He was standing up—unsteadily—in the center of the ring, lit up by the sparks and the flashes. Bontoc, planting himself foursquare with his hands on his hips, watching the skies for Jorge on the trapeze, yelled, "Here! I'm here!" All the bombs went wide. Bontoc, holding his ground, lit up again as the second set of bombs got lit, yelled, "What do you mean 'We're too nice'?" That was the easy one. Bontoc yelled, "What Irish Giant?" Bontoc, seeing the new set of infernal devices leave hands and come his way, yelled, "Here! I'm here! Why are you all throwing wide?" They were all sobbing. He felt something on his face from on high. It was a tear from Jorge sailing above him on his trapeze. Bontoc, trying to get to the bottom of things, yelled, "Here I am! Blow me up!" He wasn't nice. Bontoc yelled, "Blow me to pieces! Blow us both to pieces!" Bontoc yelled to Ambrosio, his buddy, his fellow knight on the bridge, "Right? Right? Right, Jesus-Vincente—right? Blow us up properly! Don't piss around throwing the bombs wide! If you've got a good solid 100 percent bomb loaded with rusty nails and bolts full of something a bit tougher than flash powder—say a kilo of TNT—chuck it over and blow us to dog meat!" He was shouting at the top of his voice. Bontoc, not moving a fraction as a stick of flash bombs lit him up like a mad scarecrow shrieked, "Right, Jesus-Vincente—let's have the real bombs! Let's go out in a blaze of guts and glory—RIGHT?"

A voice said, "Ummm . . ." It was Ambrosio's voice.

"HIT ME! BLOW ME UP!"

Ambrosio said, "Umm . . ."

"DISINTEGRATE ME!" He had some sort of awful death wish. "TURN ME TO VAPOR! HIT ME A GOOD ONE RIGHT AT HEAD LEVEL AND TURN ME INTO HARRY THE HEADLESS HORSEMAN!" He was raving. Bontoc yelled, "TUFO! TUFO! DROP A REAL HUM-DINGER, NOT SOME HALF-ASSED LITTLE BANGER, BUT A REAL CHOPPER, A MINCER, A DOOMSDAY DEVICE!" Bontoc yelled, "I'M DEATH! I'M ARMAGED-DON! I'M BAD! I'M THE MEANEST MAN IN TOWN! MAKE MY DAY! BLOW ME TO SHIT!" He was frothing at the mouth. Bontoc yelled, "HERE I AM! HERE!" He had his own cigarette lighter out. He lit it in front of his face. His face looked like something out of a nightmare.

Bontoc shrieked, "I'M THE IRISH GIANT!"

Ambrosio said, "What?"

Bontoc shrieked, "I'M INVINCIBLE! I'M DAUNTLESS! I'M A BONTOC PHANTOM FROM THE DEEPEST TREE BOLE IN THE JUNGLE! I'M—"

He heard them all weeping.

He saw them all light their bombs.

He saw them all arc toward him.

They saw him running to meet them.

They saw—

Bontoc yelled, "I'M READY TO DIE!" He was under three of the falling bombs with his hands out like a catcher to get them. Bontoc shrieked, "Ha! Ha! Ha!" He saw the bombs fall in the light of his cigarette lighter. He flicked the cover down and all he could see were the fizzing fuses.

Ambrosio yelled, "Baptiste—NO!" He saw a single flash that devoured Bontoc in its center, He saw—He saw—

Bontoc yelled, "THE IRISH GIANT!" He wondered what it meant. Bontoc yelled—

All the bombs went off at once and all he said was, ". . . Ohhh!"

On the armory phone Gomez said in disbelief. "Who? Who did you give them to?" He gave Piscasio at the other end of the line no time to answer, "How many did you give him? There were twenty-five cases each with between ten and fifteen individual guns and magazines in them—how many cases were opened?"

There were eight.

There were between eighty and one hundred twenty guns on the streets.

Hand grenade, Dutch mini, Model V40, antipersonnel—he knew where that had come from too.

He listened.

What he heard he knew to be true.

It was true.

It had happened.

He listened.

Gomez shouted suddenly down the line, "God in Heaven, didn't you even ask his *name?*"

There was a silence.

In the Gnome Home Acrobatic and One-Ring Sawdust Circus Café; Coffee, Meals, and Entertainment Three Times a Day, there was a silence.

In the center of the ring, in the silence, there was a shadow, a shape. It was lit by a still burning flame from a cigarette lighter in its outstretched hand.

It was Bontoc.

"Oh, no . . ." It was Pablo. The shape lay twisted on its back, looking up. It was a very small shape, nut brown, Bontoc. Pablo shrieked, "Oh, no!"

"ARCHY! ARCHY!" It was Ernesto.

Jasmine shrieked, "Mr. Bontoc! Mr.—Bontoc—!"

There was not a movement nor a sound from the twisted shape. The twisted shape was dead. There was not even a twitch or a moan. It was deader'n a mackerel.

"BAPTISTE!" It was Ambrosio.

In the Gnome Home all the lights came on. Laid out on the sawdust, ready to go, there were eleven sets of brand-new stainless-steel Smith and Wesson police handcuffs.

He had never known he cared. "You've killed him! You've killed him!" Bruised, battered, besmoked and besawdusted, staggering, reeling, tottering, seeing the handcuffs and all the weeping dwarves with something running about in his head about an Irish Giant that made no sense at all, Ambrosio, going over to touch him, to gently stroke his blackened, deadened forehead, shrieked in utter, total incomprehension, "YOU LOUSY ROTTEN FILTHY MANIACS—YOU'VE KILLED THE POOR LITTLE RUNT!"

He hadn't been, on occasion, too bad a little fellow. Sometimes he had been quite— He hadn't been too bad. Cradling Bontoc's head in his arm, trying to fight back a tear, Ambrosio said quietly, "Oh, no . . . oh, no . . ."

Bontoc stared straight up, his poor dead eyes watching Jorge on the trapeze as, dripping tears, Jorge swung slowly back and forth in the silence.

"Oh, no . . ." Ambrosio, crushing the poor dead fellow's head hard against his chest, said sadly, "How—? How could you do such a thing?"

Poor extinct ex-headhunter. In Ambrosio's arms he looked just like a gentle little child who, at the end of a long, long day, his eyes all heavy with dreams and happiness, had waited patiently for the sandman and, having found him, smiling, his eyes watching the man on the trapeze above his head, had peacefully, happily, softly, gently just gone off to sleep. . . .

"It's all just rumors, whispers! It's just—" Elizalde, at the desk, had found a locked tin box. He had it on top of the desk, working the lock. Cafiero said, "Death squads, private vendettas, people being killed because they have Communist sympathies, unionists, people organizing the poor against—" He kept shaking his head as he said it. "People disappear sometimes simply because they want to, because they—"

In the center drawer with the stationery, there was a heavy Spanish poignard *a main gauche,* the left-handed dagger used in conjunction with the Spanish rapier, the *espada de ropera.* It was in too good condition. It was a copy, a letter opener. Elizalde fitted it in behind the hasp lock on the foot-square tin box from the bottom drawer of the desk.

"—people—"

He pushed. The lock gave a little.

Cafiero said, "Anything else—anything else—it's just rumors! It's just—"

Elizalde said, without looking at him, his mouth hard, "The poor in the barrios are arming themselves with submachine guns and hand grenades."

"If it's true—if it's true—" He had come over. He was at Elizalde's side. He had his hands up to somehow stop him from opening the box, "If it's true—"

It wasn't true. It was the worst of all the things he knew.

Cafiero said, "Don't—" He saw the box was heavy. He heard the lock start to creak and give under the pressure of the knife blade. "If it's true—" Cafiero said, "It isn't! It's a rumor! It isn't—" He heard the lock give.

The box was heavy. In the shed at the salt farm, there had been six zinc baths with gas fires under them. At the salt farm, there had been a broken human rib. "Oh my God . . . oh my God . . ." It was his own voice. Cafiero heard it. He did not know he was saying it.

The lock broke open with a single snap.

"Oh my God . . ." He closed his eyes. All his life had come to this.

"Oh my God . . ."

By Elizalde as he pulled back the lid of the tin box, Cafiero, tight like a spring, his eyes screwed shut, as always, waited, awake, through all his worst nightmares.

14

*W*hen he wasn't bending nails with his teeth, ripping telephone books in half, or just rippling, Rodolfo read the classics. In his leopard-skin neck-to-knee strongman's outfit, gazing down at Bontoc, he was a sad figure. He was in tears. Bontoc was also a sad figure. He was dead. *Sic mea fato canendo solor:* so by my singing am I comforted. It was a medieval ecclesiastical Latin lyric. Rodolfo said softly:

> *"De ramis cadunt folia*
> *nam viror totus periit,*
> *iam calor liquit omnia et aliit;*
> *. . . nam signa coeli ultima sol petiit."*

He sniffed.

> *"Down from the branches fall the leaves,*
> *A wanness comes upon the trees.*
> *The summer's done;*
> *And into his last house in heaven*
> *Now goes the sun."*

He drew a breath. Rodolfo said:

> *"Sharp frost destroys the tender sprays,*
> *Birds are a-cold in these short days;*
> *The nightingale*
> *Is grieving now that the fire of heaven*
> *Is now grown pale."*

Poor dead honest little chap. He had died as he had lived, in perfection. There was no blood or bruising, just a little smoldering where one of the bombs had set the shoulder of his T-shirt on fire. Poor, poor gone blithe spirit. His friend Ambrosio had his wrinkled head cradled in his arms. Ambrosio was looking up to heaven with the whites of his eyes showing like one of the plaster saints you saw in church. What little feet Bontoc had encased in his sawdust-covered sneakers. Rodolfo, fighting back a tear, said:

> *"Nec lympha ceret alveus.*
> *nec prata virent herbida,*
> *sol nostra fugit aureus,*
> *   confinia;*
> *est inde dies niveus,*
> *   nox frigida.*
>
> *The swollen river rushes on*
> *Past meadows whence the green has gone,*
> *The golden sun*
> *Has fled our world. Snow falls by day,*
> *The nights are numb."*

Jasmine said softly, "Poor unfortunate man, I knew him, Pablo—"

Carmel the dog lady said, "He was good."

Ernesto the poet said, "A word from little archibald—" They had had their times together in the kitchen. Ernesto at the death of a kindred soul said quickly, starting to sob:

> *"thank you*
> *for the mittens*
> *socks and*
> *muffler for me*
> *knitted out of*
> *frogs hair by one*

of my admirers which
you so kindly
forwarded i suppose
the reason
i got them was that
they were too
small for you
to wear yourself
yours for rum
crime and riot . . ."

He began blubbering. "—archy"

All the eleven sets of handcuffs were laid out ready on the sawdust. Pablo said desperately to all their faces, "It had to be done! Nobody meant to kill him, but it had to be done! We have to get arrested!" He saw Ambrosio looking at him. Pablo, turning to Illuminada, working out the profit and loss, said, "I'm right, aren't I? We all agreed! We all planned it out together! We all made the bombs together—we agreed we had to get arrested!"

Ignacio said, staring at Bontoc, trying to work himself up to hate him, "He was too nice!" He fixed his eyes on Ambrosio, "You were both too nice!"

Illuminada said, "Arrest us! We did it!"

Jorge, climbing down from his trapeze, yelled, "Put us away for a hundred years!" He saw Bontoc up close. Jorge said, "Oh . . ." Jorge said, "Poor—" Jorge said, shaking his head, "We had to—" He turned to Illuminada. "We had to do it for the sake of—"

Josephine said softly, "Was it worth it?"

He had eleven of them ready to go quietly. It touched his heart. It drove Fireball from his mind and he felt a better person for it. Ambrosio, stroking Bontoc's wiry hair, said as his epitaph, "Good collar, Baptiste." He should have gotten the public-speaking tapes—you had more opportunity to use them. Ambrosio said for his friend, "He was a minority, this man, from one of the savage tribes we here in the Philippines love and nurture and, this day, you have killed him." He nodded, looking up. He looked for his cassette player and wished he had a blank tape. "This man was a good man, a flute player." Ambrosio said, "I myself hobbled on my knees in front of my family to know your souls, but your souls were black. This man sought understanding in music and in palm trees and now he lies dead." Marc Antony had done a good one of these in some play or other he'd had to study at school. He couldn't remember it. Ambrosio said, "He was a cop. He was a cop of the new breed, like myself—honest and kind and always the first to volunteer to spare his friends peril." He looked down at Bontoc. He hadn't realized what a funny color he was: kind of burnt brown. He looked deeper into his staring eyes. They were weird. Ambrosio said, "He was my junior partner—I knew from the start that he was not a man for sordid streets and seedy crime, but a primitive soul from the mountains and the streams and the rocks, but I grew to—" He hesitated. "—I grew to like him quite a lot."

The dwarves looked down at the sawdust.

Ambrosio said, "And you snuffed his life out."

Pablo said, "We had to do—"

"The greatest influence on his life was an old lady who taught him in some squalid school of his childhood called Miss Thomasina Landsborough, a lady of God!" Ambrosio said, "And you killed him!" A few signed confessions would be nice. Ambrosio said, "No man is an island! A single man is not killed! I do not kill one life, I kill a world!" He held the poor dead head in his arms and shook it. Ambrosio said, "O speak to me, Baptiste!" He dropped a single tear down his cheeks. Ambrosio said, "O, for one last time, give us one more gem of your savage wisdom, one last smile from your poor gone eyes, one more—one last—"

Imelda said, "I can't stand this!" Her heart was broken. She hid her face in her handkerchief and sobbed.

Ricardo said, "Ohhh . . ."

Pablo said, "We're sorry . . . we're sorry, but we—" He had to do it. He had a lump in his throat. Pablo said—

Ambrosio said, "Speak to us, Baptiste Bontoc! Come back from the vale to your friends and—"

Jorge said, "Aaahhhh . . ." He fell to his knees howling.

"Miss Thomasina Landsborough, if you are in heaven with your friend Baptiste, now—speak to us!" Ambrosio, starting to feel emotional himself, said, "Baptiste, speak to us!" At least Bontoc being chopped had stopped the dwarves throwing bombs. Ambrosio, slapping Bontoc hard on the face rhythmically, starting to sway, called bootless to heaven, "Oh brave new world that has—" The weeping and tearing of hair was awful. Ambrosio said, "You dwarves, you as yet unofficial United Nations classification, you fellow humans, you beings with fellow feelings for none but your own—"

He blinked. A voice came out and it was not the voice of angels. It was the voice of Uncle Apo.

Bontoc, springing to his feet, clenching his fists, ready to kill, screamed at the top of his voice, "YOU BASTARDS! YOU SCUMBALLS! YOU—YOU—YOU GODDAMNED DWARVES! NOW—*NOW* YOU'RE GOING TO WISH YOU'D NEVER BEEN BORN!" He was hopping up and down. He was, fairly obviously for a dead man, very angry. He wished he had his axe. "NOW! *NOW* . . ."

Bontoc, clenching and unclenching his hands, starting to froth at the mouth, still smouldering a little from the shoulder, shrieked at the top of his voice, "NOW—NOW YOU'RE ALL GOING TO *DIE!*" Bontoc said, "IRISH GIANT? WHAT GODDAMNED, STINKING, LOUSY, GODDAMNED IRISH GIANT?"

Now he was a dead man. The silver hip flask on the armory table was empty and, in the silence and stillness of the empty room, he was a dead man.

His officer's model chopped .45 automatic was on the bench by his hand.

It would do him no good at all. He was a dead man. He had made the calls, identified himself and, in all the whispers and the rumors, in all the secret places where words were exchanged in whispers, he was a dead man. At his bench, Gomez lit a cigarette, but it tasted salty and he put it out.

All the files were downstairs in Records, but he would not go there.

All the little pieces of twisted metal he had picked up at the salt farm were in a pile on a sheet of white paper near his comparison microscope. They were the fragments of a grenade that had blasted out two lives.

He touched at the extinguished cigarette in its ashtray.

His fingers were wet with perspiration and salt.

He was a dead man.

He had no one.

Touching at his face, he tried, desperately, to think.

"How many times, Felix?" In the Yusons', Cafiero saw the box lid coming full open. He saw Elizalde reach down into it to get something out. He could not breathe. He felt his chest tighten and hurt.

"How many times?"

He could not even look at him. Felix would not even look at him. Rosey. She was so far away. Cafiero, standing at the carved wooden chair, his eyes wide and staring, a terrible emptiness in him, seeing something come out of the box in Elizalde's hands, begged at the man, "Felix! How many times—? *How many times do I have to be brave?*"   •

He lived!

Ambrosio, getting up from the sawdust, said, "Oh."

Jorge said, "Thank God!"

"archy—!"

Rodolfo said, *"Ave!"*

Imelda, Josephine, Illuminada, and Carmel, all as one, sighed.

Bontoc shrieked, "WHAT IRISH GIANT?"

Pablo said, "Are you hurt? Are you—"

Bontoc said, "OF COURSE I'M HURT! YOU TRIED TO BLOW US UP! WE'RE BOTH HURT! WE'RE BOTH COVERED IN SAWDUST AND GUNPOWDER! WE'RE BATTERED! WE'RE—"

Pablo said happily, "Then take us away!" He called to Ernesto, "Get the handcuffs!" They were small handcuffs, probably made for the fine-wrist-boned local bondage trade. Pablo said, grinning, rubbing his hands together, looking pleased, "We're all ready to go. We confess. We planted all the bombs—all of us. We endangered life and limb. We threatened two legally appointed police officers. We tried to commit manslaughter—murder—we—"

Bontoc said, "Why are we too nice?"

"What?"

"Why are we too nice?"

Pablo said, "Um—"

Ambrosio said, "Who cares?" He took the handcuffs with a snatch from Ernesto. Ambrosio, taking a deep breath, said, "You are all under arrest. I am obliged to inform you of your rights. Your rights under the Constitution of the Republic of the Philippines include the following—"

"IF WE WERE SO GODDAMNED NICE WHY DID YOU TRY TO BLOW US UP?"

Pablo said, "Um—"

Ernesto said, "Take us away, Baptiste, please—"

Illuminada said, "Mr. Bontoc—"

Ignacio said, "Hate us! We tried to kill you! We deserve to go to prison for a thousand years!"

"WHAT DID YOU MEAN WE'RE TOO NICE?" He saw Ambrosio look hard at him. Ambrosio screwed up his face and nodded urgently. It was a good collar. It was United Nations stuff. It was a Fireball collar. Bontoc, hopping up and down, shrieked, "IF WE WERE SO GODDAMNED NICE WHY DID YOU TRY TO BLOW US TO TRIPES?" Bontoc said suddenly, "You didn't! You didn't try to blow us to tripes. Every bomb was just a harmless flash bang and every bomb was carefully planted to be just—"

He had recently moved on to Shakespeare. Rodolfo, unable to resist a good quote, said, "Full of sound and fury, signifying nothing . . ."

Imelda said suddenly, "Please! Take us to prison! The United Nations will oversee our prison term and with you and Mr. Ambrosio we'll get there safely and—"

Bontoc said, "You'll be safe?"

Imelda said, "Yes."

"From what?"

"From—" Imelda said, "From—from—"

Ambrosio asked helpfully, "The Irish Giant?"

Imelda said, "Yes! *No!*"

Bontoc said, "WHAT IRISH GIANT?"

Ambrosio said, "You guys aren't going to go to jail for just a few years, you know. Attacking police officers is a serious offense. You guys are going to—"

Carmel, weeping, said, "Oh thank you, thank you—"

Imelda said, "Oh dear, sweet Ambrosio and Bontoc . . ."

Pablo said, "Take us away. We're ready."

Bontoc said, "Why did you call the United Nations in?" He looked hard at Pablo's face. "Why do you think we're both too nice? What are you afraid of if you don't go to jail? Why are you ready to give up everything you've worked for? Who is the Irish Giant? Why are you afraid of him? What is it you think— *because you've worked it all out!—Jesus-Vincente and I are going to do with you?*" Bontoc, starting to see it at last, said, "Because we're nice!" He said, "Ahh!" He slapped himself on the forehead. Bontoc, seeing it, said, "We're not too nice! We're too nice to do something you feared we might do! We're too nice to be what you're afraid of!" Maybe it was the explosions. He thought he was making sense. He looked at Ambrosio's face and wasn't sure, "We're too nice not to oblige you! We're too nice to be cruel and—" Bontoc, suddenly grasping Ambrosio by the shoulder and spilling his armful of handcuffs, yelled,

"Don't you see? We're too nice not to throw them in the darkest deepest dungeon where they'll be safe!"

BE POSITIVE. Ambrosio said, "Um—yes."

Bontoc, stepping up to Pablo, to all of them, yelled, "You want to go to jail?"

Pablo said, "Yes!"

"You want full police escort to the pokey and full fingerprinting and photographs—"

Imelda said, heartfelt, "Oh sweet Baptiste, dear good Baptiste—"

Ernesto, man to man, said, "Thank you, archy—"

"IS THAT IT?"

Rodolfo said, "Veni, vidi—"

Bontoc said evenly, smiling, "No."

Jorge said, "What?"

Bontoc said, "No." Bontoc, smiling, said, "No, you're right. We're nice. We'll let you off." Bontoc, patting Ambrosio on the shoulder, said, smiling, "We're nice. You're right. We're so nice we're going to forgive you." Bontoc said, "Right, Jesus-Vincente?"

It was a wonderful collar. It was the sort of collar that got into the newspapers and then into—maybe there was a movie in it. Ambrosio said, "Aye?"

Bontoc said in a whisper, "What *junior* partner?"

Ambrosio said, "Right! That's right!"

Pablo said, "NO—!"

He waited. In the center of the sawdust ring, watching all the dwarves' faces, smelling success, smelling terror, he waited. He hummed a little tune. He let it sink in. His eyes were no longer the kind, watery, soft eyes of Miss Thomasina Landsborough. He was Uncle Apo. He burned with cruelty.

Bontoc, waiting, waiting, said after a long while, very quietly, "The Irish Giant—The . . . Irish . . . Giant . . ." He waited again.

Bontoc said, "One last chance: tell me who the Irish Giant is *now*—OR I SWEAR TO GOD YOU'LL STAY HERE SAFE, FORGIVEN, AND OUT OF PRISON UNTIL HE COMES TO GET YOU ONE BY ONE!"

He started to turn on his heel, taking Ambrosio with him by the arm.

Bontoc, meaning it, starting for the locked main doors wondering how the hell to open them once he got there, shouted back over his shoulder, "You've got exactly five seconds, starting now!" He heard a sound that sounded like a terrible low animal moan of pain. It came from all of them at once. He was cruel. He was Apo. He had no pity.

Bontoc, going for the door, ignoring whatever it was Ambrosio was muttering hard in his ear, starting to count, said unstoppably, "NINE SECONDS NOW . . . EIGHT . . . SEVEN . . . SIX . . . FIVE . . . FOUR—"

His only hope was Elizalde. He had called Scientific on a radio telephone patch at the salt farm and they had told him where they thought the man was. He was in the Yusons' shop in Intramuros. In the police armory Gomez nodded. The shop had not been opened—it had been kept closed, protected. In the armory, Gomez, lighting another cigarette, stared straight ahead, thinking. In the armory, alone, with nothing, he was a dead man.

He glanced at his watch.

Taking up his chopped officer's model Colt and pulling back the slide with a sharp, metallic click and setting the hammer to the cocked and locked position, Technical Sergeant Jorge Gomez of the Metro Manila Western District Police, starting to fight back for his life, slipping the gun into a Speed-Draw holster on his belt, went toward the other side of the room to get the keys to his car.

There were wads of money, pesos, U.S. dollars, deutsche marks, a fully loaded nine-millimeter damascened engraved gold, pearl-handled, Llama model XI automatic pistol, and, at the bottom of the tin box, a small, leatherbound notebook held closed with an elastic band.

On the cover of the notebook, typed on a stick-on label, there was the legend OSSINC.

Below it, typed in, were the letters C/F. It was the latest ledger of perhaps many. It meant *Carried Forward.*

In the book, on the first page, there was a handwritten list of names in columns and, below it, as if it represented on a business document all the people entitled to a copy, a list of initials.

The names were: *Barrera*
Beo
Alonso
Segundo
Ramirez
Rey
Gueverra
Kilusang

The initials listed were: *B. F.*
S. Y.
L. Y.
T. T.
Pal 'n St, T.M.N.

The initials meant *Benigno Feliciano*—dead
Sonny and Leon Yuson—dead
The salt farmer Tomas Topacio—dead
and a street abbreviation, *Palagayan Street, Tondo, Metro Manila.*

OSSINC. It was the name of some sort of company. Barrera, Beo—they were names of a fruit vendor who had killed and a dead girl killed by a policeman with no shoes.

Alonso was probably the name of the nine-year-old boy with the grenade.

They were the names, also, of the missing.

OSSINC. It was the name of a company somewhere that would not be in any phonebook or business directory.

Palagayan Street. Where on Palagayan Street?

"Oh my God—" In the shop, Elizalde heard Cafiero's voice in a whisper. At the desk, Elizalde had all the answers in his hand. He did not even know the question.

"Oh my God, Felix!"

He knew. Cafiero knew what it was. This time, now, he was sure. He had never, never thought that it could be that. He had never, never believed . . . Amid all the rumors, the whispers, the uncertainties, he had never, never believed that it could have been true.

Elizalde said quietly, directly, "Constantino, what does it mean?" He saw the man's face. He saw him touch his hand to his eyes. Elizalde said evenly, quietly, "Do you know what it means?"

"Yes." He knew how many times he had to be brave. Now, finally, when it had come, he knew. Once, only once. At the end, because it was the end, he only had to find it in himself to be brave once.

Cafiero said, "Yes, I know what it means." Cafiero said, "I never, never thought it could be that. I never, never really—" He looked down at the money and the gold gun on the desk and then at the open notebook in Elizalde's hands.

He looked up and held Elizalde's eyes.

In the heavy, musty room, Cafiero said with no expression on his face at all, all the color in it drained away, "What it means . . . what it means is the worst thing in the world. What it means is a rumor so awful, so horrible that no one who ever heard it without proof ever thought it could be true."

Cafiero said, "It means—It means—" Cafiero said, "It's a list. It's the *desaparecido* list: the disappeared. It's a list of what happened to them—and who did it—"

Cafiero said, "OSSINC—it's the name of the place where they are now." Cafiero, his hands clenched tight at his mouth, his eyes staring, said, "It's a list straight from *hell!*"

Pablo said, trembling, "The Irish Giant. *The Irish Giant*— The Irish Giant was a man called Patrick Cotter O'Brian, who was born in Kinsale in County Cork in 1760. He was some-where between seven-feet-ten-inches and eight-feet-eight-inches tall, and he lived until 1806, when he died in Bristol in En-gland." Pablo said tightly, "He was forty-six years old when he died and before he died he made a long, carefully witnessed and publicized will that his body was to be put, first inside a lead coffin and sealed, then inside a wooden one—with an attorney's seal—and then, finally, both coffins together were to be buried, not in a grave at the local cemetery, but in a vault with stone foundations *lined in four layers of best quality brick.*" Pablo said, "Until his body rotted, the grave was to be guarded day and night by two armed men." They were all silent, the dwarves. Pablo said, "That was the Irish Giant. Now you know. We read about him somewhere and now you know, now you understand." Pablo said, "Nightmares. The Irish Giant—"

He saw their faces. Pablo, his face a mask of terror, said, "You do know what I'm talking about? You do know, both of you—don't you?"

Bontoc said, "No."

Ambrosio said, "Huh?" He looked at Bontoc.

Pablo said in case they hadn't heard it clearly, "The Irish Giant—Patrick Cotter O'Brian—they—after he had done all that, they still—they still—they—"

It was beyond his comprehension that they did not know. It was unbelievable, wrong, impossible. It was—

Pablo, his eyes bulging, looking at his family around him, said in total, complete bewilderment, "Don't you know? You—you're *cops!* You're—" It wasn't possible.

Pablo, his hands out to them, pleading, his mouth trying to form the words, shrieked, "Don't you know? Don't you know? Don't you even know what I'm talking about *at all?*"

In the Yusons' shop Cafiero said quickly, "Rumors, whispers, the things everybody knows but nobody can prove, all the stories of things that have happened not to the person telling you the story, but to a friend of a friend, to someone remote, shadowy, someone you can never—" Cafiero, touching at his face, then taking his hand away again, then touching at it, said, "All my—all my—" He saw Elizalde's face. He saw the book in his hand and the tin box and, by the tin box, the gun and the wads and wads of money. Cafiero said, "How many times, Felix? *How many times do I have to be brave? How many times?*"

Cafiero said, "Felix—*Felix!*" He knew how many times. It was once, once in a lifetime. Cafiero said—

Cafiero said—

Elizalde ordered him, "Tell me! Tell me what you know!"

He could not catch his breath. Of all the things, he had never believed it could be this one.

He could not catch his breath to speak.

"*Tell me what you know!*"

He saw it. He saw Cafiero's car parked outside the main gate to the Casa Manila and he knew that he, at least, was in the Yusons' shop and it was all too late.

He should have turned and gone back. There was nowhere to go back to.

Getting out of his car, touching at his pistol in its Speed-Draw holster, Gomez began running toward the arcade where the shop lay.

Pablo, on the edge of hysteria, shouted, "We're dwarves! Look at us—look at what we are, whatwealwayswere,andwhat we always will be! We're dwarves! We're unique! We're—"

Bontoc said, "What? What is it you're afraid of?" He couldn't understand. He couldn't get it out of them. He couldn't—

Bontoc shouting, desperate to know, demanded, "What? *What is it you're afraid someone will do to you?*"

Cafiero said with all the nerves in his arms and shoulders tingling and hurting, rising, starting to explode out of his body, "The people—the people who have nothing—the poor, the defenseless, the people of no value other than as commodities for work or sex or—the people who are . . ." Cafiero said tightly, "There is a story that there are people—that there are people who are lifting them and drugging them and killing them and taking them somewhere and then are—" Cafiero said, nodding, in extremis, "The salt farm! The zinc baths at the salt farm!— and, with acid or whatever it is they use . . . with whatever it is they use—"

In his hand Elizalde held the book with all the names of the missing in it and in another column the initials of all the people who got copies of the list.

Cafiero said suddenly, evenly, "A human skeleton, in the medical supply world, in America and Europe, brings in approximately five thousand U.S. dollars to the supplier." Cafiero said, "People a penny each." Cafiero said, "People who have no value. People who—" Cafiero said suddenly out of control, "They're taking people nobody cares about off the streets and rendering them down like cattle and selling their skeletons—all shapes and sizes, on order—just tell us what you want—to anyone who will buy them!" Cafiero screamed, "I never believed it! It was the one horror story I never brought myself to believe! I believed all the rest about the killings and the disappearances, but I never believed that there were people who could do—" Cafiero said, "And you've got all their names in your hand!" Cafiero shrieked, "And you're dead! You're as dead as me because the people who are doing it—the people who are doing it—" He could hardly stop from laughing.

Cafiero said, "Felix, in the name of Christ, the people doing it—it's *us!*"

Pablo said softly, "Have you ever seen in a museum a little glass case of stuffed and mounted squirrels? Rare ones? Ones like us?" They were the crème de la crème of an anatomical collection. They were eleven, perfect dwarves, six male, five female. He was sobbing gently. Pablo said, "Help us. Keep us safe somewhere. We're afraid to even go out." He came forward and put his hands on Bontoc's chest. Pablo said, "Please, please, we couldn't think of any other way of saving ourselves— please." He was weeping on Bontoc's T-shirt. Bontoc put his hand out gently and held his head. Pablo said, "It's you. You're the ones doing it. We heard. We heard—we heard . . ."

Pablo, sobbing like a child, safe in the arms of someone guaranteed to be nice, to be safe, to be their protector, said in desperation, "In the name of pity, please, you and Jesus-Vincente, put us somewhere safe!"

Pablo said, *"The people doing it are the cops!"*

In the shop he had his gun out. Gomez, covering them both, said desperately, "I don't know who to trust!" He saw their faces. He saw the book and the money and the gun and the tin box on the desk and he saw, most of all, Elizalde's face.

Now he was a dead man. Gomez, lowering the gun, said evenly, "I know who's been supplying the machine guns and the grenades to the poor to kill people." He put the gun back into his holster and did not look up, "I know who it is."

In the shop, there was no sound at all.

Gomez said, "It's us. It's the police. It's someone with an identification so high, a gold badge—joint Police-Secret Service liaison—no one even bothers to ask his name." Gomez said, "A Spanish speaker, a man of importance—" Gomez said, "One of us." He looked up at Elizalde and Cafiero. "One of you—one—one of the rich!"

Now he was a dead man.

Gomez, like Cafiero, no longer caring, no longer afraid, at last past that, said with all the muscles in his facing moving, "That's right! The man arming the poor with fucking submachine guns and grenades is for some God-only-knows reason—one of the rich!"

Gomez said quietly, "Now we're dead—all of us. Now we know and, like the poor, we haven't got a hope in hell and we're dead. And we can't ask anyone else any more because they'd be gone too and we wouldn't have a hope in hell."

OSSINC.

Palagayan Street. It was an address. It was a place. It was somewhere to go. There was nothing to say. In the shop smelling of wood and antiquity, with all the painted eyes of all the wooden saints everywhere, Elizalde could find nothing to say. His wife was away in San Pablo City for a few days. It was all the hope he had.

He had the name of a street in Tondo.

He had, when he wanted them, Ambrosio and Bontoc.

All he had to do was close the book and burn it.

Alonso. That must have been the name of the nine-year-old boy who had blown himself to bits with the grenade.

He had blown one of them to bits.

Alonso—that had been his name. He had been no more than nine years old.

Elizalde ordered Gomez, "Go home, Jorge. Protect your family. Go home and stay there." Elizalde said softly, "Constantino?"

"I haven't anybody left to protect."

Palagayan Street, Tondo.

Elizalde, stuffing the black book quickly into the pocket of his coat and touching at the butt of his gun, said abruptly, unarguably to Gomez, "Go. Now. Don't go back to Headquarters, speak to nobody, just go. Go home now!"

15

DATED AS: 11 December 1981.

THIS IS A COPY
THIS COPY TO: FILE NO. ZA/6/395/LV/816934/CUR-
RENT/RP6
ORIGINAL TO: PERSONNEL JACKET EMPLOYEE E.
E. MOLLISON

TEXT FOLLOWS:

RECOMMENDATION FOR HONOR AND MERIT AWARD FOR MR. EDWARD ("TED") E. MOLLISON

It is recommended that MR. EDWARD EUGENE MOLLI-
SON be awarded the Central Intelligence Agency Intelligence Medal of Merit.

Mr. Mollison was a senior intelligence analyst in the
Manila Station's Liaison Branch from September 1978
until April 1980, with special responsibilities to assist,
advise, and liaise with the counterterrorist activities of the
Long Range patrols of the Philippines armed forces and
paramilitary Philippines Constabulary units. During this
period Mr. Mollison acquitted his tasks with great energy
and originality, gaining the trust of the Philippines' units
he assisted, and was instrumental in several successful
counterterrorist operations capturing or killing important
leaders of the Communist rebel New People's Army on
the island of Negros. His recent promotion to the grade
of GS-13 is a testament to his outstanding service in this
posting.

Previous to his posting in the Republic of the Philippines, Mr. Mollison served in Taiwan from 1952 to 1954 as an adviser to the Government of General Chiang Kaishek and was successful in forming many valuable contacts for later use by the Agency.

Following retraining, Mr. Mollison then served in Hong Kong from 1958 to 1960 until his posting to the U.S. Army's special PsyWar facility in Maryland. In 1970 Mr. Mollison was posted to Saigon, South Vietnam, where he served with distinction until the evacuation of the U.S. Embassy on 29 April 1975. (SEE CROSS-REFERENCE FILE SOUTH VIETNAM OPERATIONS JO/9/7890678/395/PB/67881 to PB/45666789421.)

Following a short posting to Bangkok, Thailand, to assist in debriefing duties, Mr. Mollison received his final posting to Manila on 9 September 1978.

On 23 March 1980 Mr. Mollison was on special advisory attachment to the Long Range patrol of the Philippines Constabulary on the island of Negros during a protracted operation to neutralize a particularly successful unit of the Communist New People's Army led by the rebel Marxist priest known as "Father Antonio."

Repeated sweeps by the Philippines' authorities had been unsuccessful in locating this terrorist unit, and with each victory the Father Antonio unit had been gaining valuable support from local villages and tribesmen in the area. The morale of the Long Range Unit and the local military authorities, when Mr. Mollison joined them, had reached a low ebb and desertions were common.

Mr. Mollison, realizing that the presence of a "man of God" in the leadership of the rebel unit was a large factor in the minds of the superstitious local people, using his experience gained in Vietnam and other Asian stations, devised a plan to neutralize this influence.

Forming a small PsyWar unit from within the counterterrorist forces he was liaising with, Mr. Mollison planted rumors in the local villages and meeting places that a Philippine *aswang* or vampire had been sighted in the jungle. Giving the rumors time to circulate and bribing certain uncommitted members of the ruling cliques in the area to claim sightings of the mythical creature, Mr. Mollison then laid an ambush for an NPA patrol. As the patrol passed, the last man was quietly lifted by the ambushing party, killed silently without leaving marks on the body, and removed from the immediate area. The corpse was then punctured, vampire fashion, with two holes in the neck and hung upside down until the blood was drained out of the body and his complexion became stark white. The corpse was then taken back to the area of the ambush and left on the trail to be discovered.

The rebels, like all Philippinos, superstitious to an extraordinary degree, fled from the area, no longer believing in the more orthodox power of "Father Antonio" to protect them.

For this, and other operations, Mr. Mollison is awarded the Intelligence Medal of Merit.

DOCUMENT ENDS. THIS IS A COPY.

On *Goosewing,* the Whispering Man turned over the page in the file. He had read it many times before and he knew there was nothing typed on the back, but he turned it over. He read the next document in the file. It was a clipping from a newspaper, pasted onto a sheet of quarto paper and marked with the same reference number for the file and the same cross-reference into the personnel jacket.

OBITUARY   12 July 1982
E. E. ("Ted") Mollison

Mr. Ted Mollison, who died today in Elizabeth City, will be greatly missed by all those in our town including this Editor who came to know and love him in the last years of his life. A good friend to all, he was a pillar of St. Mary's

Church and Rotary as well as being an active member of various local fishing, boating, and conservation organizations.

Indéed, as the vice-president of the North Carolina Woods Association, he will be best known both for his love of the woods and countryside of his state and for his many successful fund-raising activities.

Ted was not married, but was loved by his family of friends as a man of tireless enthusiasm for his pet projects, a gentle companion, and a deeply religious member of his church.

Ted, in typical fashion, never spoke of his own achievement, but served as a high-ranking member of the State Department for many years prior to his recent retirement.

His death, after a short illness, bravely borne, is a loss to us all.

DOCUMENT ENDS. THIS IS A COPY.

He was dead. He had died in 1982. He had no family, no one. He had, only, all the lies. At his chart table, the Whispering Man turned the document over. There was nothing on the back.

CENTRAL INTELLIGENCE AGENCY

THIS IS A COPY.
REF: "Aswang Operation"
       Mollison E.
       Philippines Theatre
       23 March 1980
INSERT INTO FILE NO.
ZA/6/395/LV/816934/CURRENT/RP6
12 November 1980

FOLLOW-UP ASSESSMENT TO OPERATION

NAME OF ASSESSOR: E. E. MOLLISON *GRADE*: GS-12.
ASSESSMENT FOLLOWS:

This operation can be judged entirely successful. The "Father Antonio" unit of the Communist New People's

Army operating in sector 67 on the island of Negros, by this operation, was almost entirely neutralized with a minimum expenditure of funds and personnel. This operation terminated a highly successful and effective unit and resulted in enhanced morale among the counterterrorist forces and the increased cooperation of villagers in supplying high-grade tactical intelligence for later successful operations resulting in the capture of many middle-ranking Communist organizers in the area and the assassination by his own people of the Marxist priest known as "Father Antonio."

Not only was the use of psychological warfare effective in this area, but once compromised for the sake of morale among the counterterrorist troops, it effectively transferred superstitious terror into a belief in the troops' own efficiency and ability to succeed without religious dread.

During the brief period between the method of operation being compromised and the realization that the "aswang" was nothing but a childish figment of imagination, it was found necessary to protect the instigators of the scheme by giving up a minor pawn in the game.

It was therefore suggested by rumor, once the proverbial cat was let out of the bag, that a minor local official had in fact organized the operation. It was hoped to remove this official from the immediate area before any reprisals could be taken against him, but this was not found to be possible and, judgmentally, the official was not protected. This was an unfortunate, but unavoidable, corollary to the success of the operation, but one which was found to be acceptable.

The official's name, in this report, has been suppressed. Details will be inserted in fifty-year file and may be viewed on production of the usual need-to-know basis.

ASSESSMENT ENDS. THIS IS A COPY.

They had come out of the jungle a little before dawn to where the hill house was. There were eight of them. At the chart table of the catamaran, amid the ruins of everything he had smashed, the Whispering Man touched at the file.

They had come with knives. Not guns. Not at that time of the morning. Knives.

There were eight of them. They were the terrorists. They were a death squad, and they had, first, killed his wife and then they had half-killed him and—and then they had dragged his five-year-old daughter into the room where he lay gasping and heaving for breath—and they had killed his five-year-old daughter in front of him.

All the time, through all the years, he still heard her screams.

There were eight of them. They had eyes like coals.

And they had taken the rag doll from his daughter's hand and put a noose around its neck and jerked it and then—then, after a long while, after he had gone mad and all his soul had gone out of him, one of them had stood over him with his long knife and killed him.

He could not get his breath. On the boat, the Whispering Man, touching at the scar across his throat where the knife had gone, panted and gasped to get his breath.

Mollison.

His death, after a short illness, bravely borne, is a loss to us all.

DOCUMENT ENDS. THIS IS A COPY.

Mollison!

He was dead. He had died. He was safe.

On the boat, the Whispering Man, alive, said in a rasp, "Mollison—"

He was dead. He had died peacefully in bed.

All the Whispering Man and his family had been in Negros were unavoidable corollaries.

GENERAL INFORMATION FOR RECIPIENTS OF HONORS

It is the policy of the Agency that all and any honors won by personnel shall not be worn in any area or venue other than those designated by the Agency to be acceptable areas or venues for the wearing or display of honors.

This includes all and any medals, citations, including social and sports trophies, which may serve to identify the winner or holder as a member of this Agency.

This policy will be without exception.

It is recommended that any honors or medals awarded by the Agency or in any way connected with the Agency be donated back to the Agency where they will be displayed in the Agency Museum.

The Director regrets this policy, but this policy will be enforced with sanctions for noncompliance.

Mollison. In Elizabeth City, North Carolina, at home, he had been the doyen of the wilderness set. In Negros, Republic of the Philippines, he had been the man who decided who died and who lived.

Now, he himself was dead.

No matter.

No . . . matter.

On the catamaran, that dawn years ago taking all the soul out of his body, the Whispering Man, a ghost, step by step, planned to go down into the heart of hell and bring Mollison back and then, when he had him . . .

When he had him . . .

He had him now. Step by step . . .

"MOLLISON!"

Step by step, bit by bit, he was bringing him back from the dead to kill him.

He had hobbled about in his living room in front of his relatives to try to understand what it was like to be a dwarf.

He understood now. In 1806, three days after he had been buried in a lead coffin in a stone and brick vault, the anatomists had bribed his guards and dug up the Irish Giant and spirited his corpse away to render him down like a dead horse to get at the bones for their collection. He stayed in a glass case in

London, a freak until a German bomb in World War II destroyed him.

On the phone to the United Nations, Ambrosio said, "Yep, we got 'em."

The United Nations man said, "How many of them?"

Ambrosio said, "All of them. You were right. It was the goddamned dwarves all right." Ambrosio said, "Great report you did. If it hadn't been for you giving us the clue we might never have thought of it." They were all behind him, listening. Ambrosio, swallowing hard, said, "Just psychos—just plain old half-pint psychos. Just the usual collection of goddamned inferior personality traits you get with any minority group: niggers, kikes, coons, Zulus, Arabs, Jews, Catholics, women—"

The United Nations man said, *"Hey!"*

"—the sort of scum we love putting in our jails." Ambrosio said, "The sort of subhumans our jails are designed to sort out for once and for all." Ambrosio said, "In our jails, where the good, pure Philippino race—"

The United Nations man said, "Steady on here!"

"—where they know what to do with the *untermensch.*" Ambrosio said, "Hitler was right. The only way to keep a nation and a race pure—" Ambrosio said, "Heh, heh, it's like that little savage Bontoc: that little savage Bontoc—"

The United Nations man said, "The dwarves are under United Nations protection!"

"Crapola! You said yourself they weren't classified." Ambrosio, warming to it, said with a cackle, "Amnesty International doesn't get into our jails! Here in the exotic East we still have a few tricks to make people suffer—"

"The dwarves are under U.N. protection!" The United Nations man said with his Swedish accent getting thicker and thicker, "The dwarves, if they're going to be arrested—" The United Nations man said, "Exactly what are you arresting them for?"

"Public nuisance, wasting police time—"

"If they didn't hurt anyone—" The United Nations man

said, "I can telephone your General and by God, when I put it to him, the dwarves will be protected!"

Ambrosio said, snarling, "No one's protected from me!" He said, "Me and my sort, we—" Ambrosio said, "Where are you going to hide them? Where can you hide them? About the only place you could hide them from me and my fellow bigots would be—" Ambrosio said, "I hate dwarves! Everyone hates dwarves!" He said, "About the only place you could hide eleven dwarves would be in the General's house in Forbes Park!" Ambrosio said, "And the General wouldn't agree to that." Ambrosio said, "It's a nice house in Forbes Park with big gardens and lots of guards." He was a Fireball. There was nothing more important in this world than reputation and success. Oh, wasn't there? Ambrosio said, "Number ten, Zabala Avenue. You can't miss it. It's the one with the barbed wire and the tank parked outside."

The United Nations man said, "It's already done." The United Nations man said, "Put that in your pipe and smoke it, you Nazi!" The United Nations man said, "You bigot! You scum! You fascist! You—"

"Detective Sergeant." He felt Bontoc's hand on his shoulder. It wasn't bad being a nothing. At least other nothings liked you.

Ambrosio said, "Detective Sergeant Jesus-Vincente Ambrosio." Ambrosio said helpfully, "You'll send a bus? I'll tell the dwarves to start packing. . . ."

Palagayan Street, Tondo, Metro Manila. From a safe distance, in a safe area, Rolly, smoking a cigarette, leaned against his car and watched the sky. He touched at the little derringer in its leather wallet and smiled.

He thought of money.

Watching the sky, he hummed to himself, smoking his cigarette, smiling.

"YOU BUM! YOU FAILURE! YOU NE'ER-DO-WELL!" Half buried in the sawdust, the tape was still running. They were good batteries. Fireball shrieked, "DO ANY

OF THESE DESCRIPTIONS FIT YOU, YOU CRUD?"

Nope. He saw Bontoc, watching the dwarves packing, look over at him and smile. Nope, not a bit.

"YOU LOSER! YOU MOOCHER! YOU *PHILIPPINO!* YOU KNOW WHAT YOU HAVE TO DO NOW—DO YOU? *OR DON'T YOU?*"

He did. Ambrosio said softly, "I do." He picked up the expensive cassette tape player and its expensive cassette tapes.

"WHAT YOU HAVE TO DO IS—"

He did it. Ambrosio said, "AH, SHUT UP WHY DON'T YOU!"

He did the only thing a real success at life would do.

Smiling back at Bontoc and the dwarves, nodding, he switched the *Play* button finally, firmly, to *Off*.

He smiled.

Safe, watching the sky above Palagayan Street, dreaming of riches, making plans, Rolly smiled.

On the radio patch from his car to Watanabe at the salt farm, Elizalde said, "Anything?"

They had found nothing. Watanabe said, "Nothing. Nothing at all. They've dug up the salt pans and at the moment there's an earth mover coming in to take up the ground around the shed, but there's nothing." Watanabe said, "The soil hasn't been disturbed for a long while and they're going to find nothing." Watanabe said, "I'm sorry, Felix, but there's nothing here at all." He asked, "How about you?"

"No." He was outside 26 Palagayan Street, Tondo, parked in the street outside the iron railings that surrounded the place. He saw Cafiero standing at the open gates looking in. Elizalde said evenly, softly, "No, nothing at all."

Inside the railings, set alight by a dozen Molotov cocktail gasoline bombs an hour and a half before, as the Fire Service worked to try to stop it spreading, 26 Palagayan Street and everything that might have been in it—derelict, deserted, dry as tinder, unsavably—*burned*.

16

In Palagayan Street the fire was still out of control. The house was going to burn to the ground and all the Fire Service could do was keep it from spreading. At the smashed-down iron fence where the units had gotten into the grounds, the Fire Chief, at the back of a communications van calling for more appliances, shouted to Ambrosio above the roar of the pumps and the crashing building, "General Vega Street! He ordered me to patch into the police frequency and get them to call you! He's gone to General Vega Street!" He was a man in his fifties, he was not sure he was supposed to take orders from a police lieutenant at the scene of a fire. "He and another cop—called Constantino something—waited until my headquarters got back to me on the radio with the name of the owner and keyholder of this place and then they took off like lunatics!" The Fire Chief, seeing someone waiting by Ambrosio's car in the smoke who looked like some sort of Bontoc headhunter in mufti, yelled, "Who's that?" The smoke was all around Bontoc. It looked like he was part of the smoke. The Fire Chief said, "What the hell's the matter with you cops?" He didn't want to know. The Fire Chief yelled, "Your boss Elizalde had a tin box in his hand! I saw it open! It had a goddamned gold pistol in it and enough money to pay half the national debt!"

"Who does own this place?" At the burning building, there was a shout as a wall came down and an explosion of sparks and smoke. "Who is the key holder?"

"There isn't one! There's no one listed as being responsible!" He was starting to go toward his men. The Fire Chief yelled,

"The place hasn't been used for years! It looks like a house, but it's some sort of storage facility!" He had a clipboard with numbers and codes scribbled on it, the information from Headquarters.

The Fire Chief shouted, "Pan Pacific Corporation—that's all I know! It hasn't been used for years! At least there's nothing we don't know about stored inside it!"

The Fire Chief, glancing at Bontoc by the car and believing in smoke-devils, yelled back to fulfill his duty to cops who gave him orders, "General Vega Street—that's all your boss said! Pan Pacific!" The Fire Chief said again, looking at Bontoc, "Holy Mother of God, the people who turn up at fires—!"

"They *applauded!* They knew! They knew all of them otherwise they wouldn't have done it! They knew the names of all of them—they knew what they did and that's why they were part of the killing of the first one, of the faith healer Feliciano! They were part of it because whoever told them about him told them about all the others!" He was in the main area of a banana-ripening warehouse at the far end of General Vega Street. Everywhere in the huge tin building there were bunches and hands of bananas hanging down from bamboo tracks, turning ripe under the eerie light of movable blue-tinted windows in the roof. At the rough wooden table were the barangay captain, Emilio, and Mrs. Barrera and Mang Eleuterio. They were the only people he could see. In the darkness, what he could hear were other people hiding. Mrs. Barrera had said nothing. There were papers on the table and signed documents and a cash box: she had been making some arrangement with the barangay to sell her husband's effects and route. Mang Eleuterio had been there, as he always was, to see fairness. The barangay captain, picking up his blue sweatband from the table, put it carefully on his head. This time, he was not afraid. This time he had more than his forged picture of John Wayne. This time, in the darkness, hidden, there were people with machetes and knives and guns.

She had been weeping. At the table, Mrs. Barrera looked hard at Mang Eleuterio.

In the closed tin warehouse the smell of the ripening fruit was heavy and sweet, the bananas in the strange light from the tinted roof windows all the wrong colors. Cafiero was outside in the car. Facing the table and the people watching him, hearing the sounds of movement, Elizalde said tightly, "Benigno Feliciano, dentist, Rio Cocodrilo Street: if it's all true, he was the one who selected the suitable specimens to be killed." He watched Mrs. Barrera's face. She knew nothing. They had told her nothing. "Specimens with no broken bones or physical disabilities; with, probably, a reasonably good set of teeth if the order was for a special one for a skull." He saw the barangay captain run his tongue slowly across his lips and then wipe at his mouth with his crooked finger. "Sonny and Leon Yuson, antique dealers of Intramuros—they were the ones who contacted the killer and probably helped with the transport." He asked the barangay captain, "How was it done? Any idea? Was it done with poison? Probably not. Too expensive. Or maybe a gunshot to the back of the neck? Too much damage to the merchandise." Elizalde said, "Maybe it was done with something like a long knitting needle rammed through the ear or the temple! Maybe it was done—"

Mang Eleuterio said, "Enough!" He had his hand resting on Mrs. Barrera's shoulder. He felt her shaking.

"Maybe it was done by drowning! Maybe it was done out there on the salt farm at night by both the Yuson brothers holding the victim down until he died and then—"

Mrs. Barrera said, "*I don't know what he means!*"

"And then your son, after he was dead—after he was just a carcass—was taken into the shed and all his flesh was dissolved away in the zinc bath, and then, after that was done, and all he was was bone and gristle—!"

"*What is this man talking about?*"

"After all that, the farmer, Tomas Topacio—"

The barangay captain said, "We know nothing."

"—after all that, the farmer Tomas Topacio—what? Bagged the remains up, labeled them and sent them—how?—to Palagayan Street where they were finished and sorted and wired together and crated and then shipped out!" He was right. He knew it. Elizalde asked the barangay captain, "Is that what he told you, the man who told you? Is that the order, the method, the system? Is what he told you so convincingly, so undeniably, that you believed him? Is that why the people who had once loved the things that were put in crates like dog meat were so willing to kill? *Is that why they were so willing to die?*" Elizalde said, "Your people: Emmanuel Ernesto Barrera, fruit vendor, your husband, is dead. Ermalinda Beo, factory worker—dead. Some nine-year-old boy with only a surname—Alonso—dead." Elizalde said, "Who else? Who else is ready to go? Who else has been given a gun or a grenade or a gasoline bomb? *The man who told you all this: who else has he convinced to die?*"

Mrs. Barrera said, "Mang—"

Elizalde said tightly, formally, "Your son is dead. So is the brother of Ermalinda Beo. So probably is the father of the boy Alonso. They were examined, taken, killed, defleshed and then shipped out as skeletons and now, wired together like dolls, they are somewhere in other countries where they are going to stay forever, where people are going to pick at them and exhibit them and use them and—" Elizalde said, "The man who came to tell your husband this, the man who came to tell all the relatives of the dead—"

"Mang Eleuterio—?"

Mang Eleuterio said softly, "I believe it is true."

"—told you that you could tell no one, seek help from no one, because the people doing it were the cops!"

The barangay captain said in a whisper, "It is the cops."

"—he told your husband—he told all of them—"

The barangay captain said, "It was the cops."

"He armed you. He got the guns and the grenades and he armed you!" Elizalde said, "Where do you think he got the guns?" Elizalde said, *"He got them from the cops!"*

From somewhere in the darkness, he heard a sound. Cafiero was outside. He was alone in the warehouse facing them. Elizalde said, "He spoke Spanish, this man. He was a man of substance. He wrote desaparecido on the back of Ermalinda Beo's photograph of her brother. Probably, he had documents and papers and photographs to prove what he said. He told you to trust nobody. He told you—"

The barangay captain said in a snarl, "He was our friend—he is our friend! He knew! He knew it was the cops! He's a cop himself!"

"It isn't the cops!"

"It is the cops! The cops killed Ermalinda Beo in Intramuros for a start!"

"Ermalinda Beo was killed by a patrolman who thought she was going to kill him! Ermalinda Beo was killed by a man with a rusty gun who under normal circumstances couldn't shoot a dying dog in the street!" Elizalde said, "OSSINC—did he tell you about that? Did he tell you that was the name of the organization the 'cops' were running?"

"Maybe!"

"Did he tell you what it meant?"

"It meant something in Latin! It meant something to do with 'bone'! It meant—"

Elizalde said, "The Spanish speaker. The man of education. The man who—"

"He was the only man who ever came here to help us!"

Elizalde said evenly, "And now I am here."

There was a silence. The woman did not understand. All she had was Mang Eleuterio's hand on her shoulder. The barangay captain said, "If you believe in God, make your peace with Him—"

"*Emilio!*" Mang Eleuterio said, "Emilio, you—"

"OSSINC has nothing to do with Latin!" Elizalde said, "You cannot win. They are not words, but initials. The initials are O.S.S. The house in Palagayan Street was owned by the Pan Pacific Corporation. O.S.S. is the name of something from a long time ago. It is almost a joke. It is certainly a cruel and cynical—"

The barangay captain said, "We have no education here! We are on our own!"

"It stands for Office of Strategic Services. Pan Pacific Corporation is the name of the front organization in Asia for the O.S.S.'s successor, the American CIA." Elizalde said, "The man came to talk to you. Did he tell you any of that? I am here now—*I am telling you that!* The man came to tell you you could win. The man told you it was the cops. It is not the cops. You cannot win. It is—"

"How do we know any of this is true?"

"Because I am here!" He was afraid. There were worse things than death. Elizalde said, "Because I am here."

"Because you are rich and powerful and your friends in the cops—"

Elizalde said, "I am unarmed. My gun is in the car with my friend outside. My friend is also unarmed. His gun and mine are locked in the trunk of his car. There are no other guns hidden." Elizalde said suddenly to Mrs. Barrera, "Your husband would not tell you anything because he didn't want you to know what had happened to your son. All he wanted was that his face be photographed and his name known so it would not happen to him. Maybe, if he knew for a long time, he tried to stop you loving him to make it easier for you." There was no sound in the warehouse. Elizalde said, "I don't know."

Mang Eleuterio said gently, "I didn't know him. Perhaps his soul was deep." He rested his hand on the woman's shoulder and looked at the barangay captain. Mang Eleuterio said, "You cannot win. You can only react after something has happened, but you cannot stop it happening."

Elizalde said evenly, "Tell me the name of the man who told you about OSSINC. Tell me what he told you. This man is causing all your people to be killed!" Elizalde said, "The man who killed Ermalinda Beo was a man like you! The only reason he was even there in Intramuros in the first place was that he had taken off his shoes to rest his feet!" Elizalde said, pleading, "For the love of God, tell me the name of the man who told you to do all this!"

Outside in the street, they were forming, coming together in little groups and knots of people, the young men of the barrio, the ones with knives. Both his and Elizalde's guns were in the back of the car, impossible to get at. In the car, Cafiero, starting to sweat, put both hands on the wheel and watched.

They were forming, coming, gathering.

He saw them start to talk in whispers.

He saw them.

He saw them starting to gather.

In the car traveling north, Bontoc, the street map on his lap, said, "Where? Where on General Vega Street?" Ambrosio, driving, caught in traffic on Roxas Boulevard, took a sudden right down a lane. The lane was unmarked. It was not on the street map. On the map, General Vega Street, a winding green river through the heart of the slum area, seemed to go on forever.

Ambrosio, swerving to find another lane, found an alley.

Bontoc, being flung against the car door, losing his place, demanded for the second time, *"Where? Where on General Vega Street?"*

He had reached the limit of his endurance. The barangay captain like all the barangays, the barrios, was fighting back. Standing facing Elizalde, his hands clenched into fists, Emilio shouted to anyone who would listen, "They took people off the streets and they were gone! There were no bodies where they had killed people for revenge or for politics! There was no blood or broken bones! They didn't even rob or rape—they just took people off the streets—they picked them, selected them, took only the healthy ones—and they farmed them!" Emilio said, "We are the poor, the animals! We have no humanity, we are not people like the rich and the powerful with voices and lives and hopes: all we are to them are objects to be sold!" Emilio said, "Even a race you hate, even people you kill in a war, after that war you allow to have humanity—you say after a war that it was a pity that the people you killed lost their lives—you say that! But we are the poor, we are impure, we have done something wrong, God does not love us as He loves the rich. He has not given us something He gave you—we have no names, no faces—all we are is a great, single, unlimited, constant supply of flesh and bone and muscle!" Emilio said, "We do not have children like the rich, we breed! We do not have hopes like people, we covet like criminals!" He said, "All my life, and through all the lives of my parents and my grandparents and through all the lives of my children, we have nothing—we have always had nothing—all we have is each other, and that is not thought to be companionship, that is thought to be the gang mentality!" Emilio said, "They took everything! They took our bodies and then they threw them away! They took our humanity! They reduced us to bones! They—" Emilio shouted, "The poor are not like other people! The poor are not even worth *pity!*"

"The man who came—"

"The man who came helped!"

"I am helping!"

"I don't know you!" Emilio, his mouth trembling, taking a step forward, on the very edge, said, "Look at you! You probably think that I see you as a man like me! You are not a man like me!" His fists were clenching and unclenching. Mang Eleuterio, starting to say something, reached out to touch him. Emilio shook his head to stop him. "You have more in your pocket now—more in your change and your credit cards that you only carry around to get through the day—than I can comprehend one man having in his life!" He said, "We live in a city like rats in a sewer! We cannot escape! We have no education because we have no money for education! We have no businesses because we have no money for capital! We have—we have nothing!" Emilio said, "The man who came—"

"The man who came—"

"The man who came at least gave us the truth!"

"He gave you guns!"

Emilio said tightly, "No, he gave us targets." He saw Mrs. Barrera's face. Emilio said, "Look at her—her son is gone! What else can she feed on except revenge?"

"All your people are dying!"

"My people have always died!"

"All your people are being taken and all the people who are left behind who are killing people they think took them are being killed themselves!"

"We are just animals to be slaughtered."

Elizalde said, "Thousands of people have gone! If it's all true thousands of people have gone! You cannot win! All the man is telling you is the names of the few people at the bottom of it all! He has not told you the names of the people at the top! You can kill the people at the bottom because they are nobodies, unprotected—the people at the top are unreachable by you!"

"Are they reachable by you?"

"*Yes!*"

Mang Eleuterio asked suddenly, "Are they?" He said softly to Emilio, "I know this man's soul."

"*It is the CIA! You cannot win!*" Elizalde said, "I swear to you, you cannot win!" Elizalde, shaking his head, shouted back at the man, "I swear to you—*you cannot win!*" He heard sounds in the darkness, movement. He heard whispers. He heard—

He heard, in the sudden hush, Mrs. Barrera sobbing.

Elizalde said suddenly, at last, "Yes! You're right! I'm rich! I can afford it! I'm safe! No one can touch me and I can do what I like!"

He knew them. He knew their faces. They were the faces of his childhood. In his car, Cafiero saw their eyes, their hands. He saw, without seeing them, the knives they carried in their pockets. From his car, he smelled the smell of the rotting filth of the unsewered houses and the streets full of garbage, the places children played for the few years before they were old enough to work, and he smelled the smell of sweat and he heard again, from his childhood, the sounds of coughing and sickness from the houses. He remembered, from his childhood, dark nights, nights darker than he had ever seen since—he remembered the sounds of whispering, of whispering in dark places, of whispering in dark secret places hidden away, hidden almost underground. He remembered the smell and the touch and the feel of having nothing.

They were watching him. In herds, they were watching and whispering.

In his car, Cafiero, his eyes straight ahead on them, touched at the handle of the door.

He watched their faces.

He read their eyes.

He touched at the car door gently and unlocked it with a click.

"Rosey." Cafiero, his hand still on the door, blinking back something he could not explain, said softly to his gone wife, "Oh, Rosey . . ."

He wondered, this day, where she was.

In the street, sitting alone in the car, he watched the poor watching him.

He wondered who they thought he was and where he had come from.

General Vega Street. At the northern end, traveling fast, Ambrosio yelled, "Where does it go? It looks like it goes straight on!" It was mile after mile of slums, of filth and decay and hopelessness. Ambrosio, looking from side to side, yelled, "What do we do? What do we do?"

"Look for the car!" On the seat beside him, Bontoc had his gun in its ankle holster. No time to strap it on. He pulled the weapon out and cocked it with a single snap. Bontoc said, "Here!" He got Ambrosio's pistol from the glove compartment and cocked it hard and put it in Ambrosio's lap. He could see not one parked car on the entire street. It was as if the entire street were deserted. Bontoc said again, quickly, the gun ready on his lap, "The car! Look for the car!" The Irish Giant. The thought chilled him to the bone. Bontoc, shouting in case Ambrosio had not heard, yelled as an order, "Look for the goddamned car!"

Mrs. Barrera shrieked, "Is it true?" All she had was the barangay captain and Mang Eleuterio. All she had was Mang Eleuterio. Mrs. Barrera, silent no more, silent too long, shrieked at the man, "Is it true?"

"It's true." It was Elizalde.

"*Is it true?*"

Mang Eleuterio said, "Yes."

"Is it true that—"

Emilio said, "Yes, it's true! This man—"

Elizalde said, "Tell me the man's name and I can—"

Mrs. Barrera said, "This man is rich! All the things this man is saying—"

He saw them coming. In his car, Cafiero saw them coming. They began walking toward him, all the people from his fears. There were twenty, twenty-five of them, more. He saw a car at the far end of the street. He saw the poor coming and he saw the car moving fast toward, not him, but them. He saw Ambrosio and Bontoc. He saw, for an instant, in Bontoc's hand, a pistol.

He saw the poor coming.

He opened the car door and stood out in the street, unarmed.

He saw Bontoc and Ambrosio coming. He saw the poor.

He saw the cops coming for the poor and he saw their guns.

"The man who came—*what did he give you in return?*" He was running out of time. He had been there too long, given them too long to think about it. Elizalde, unarmed, alone in the warehouse, demanded, "Did he give you anything in return? Did he give you a hostage to prove that what he was saying was true? Or was he rich like me and he gave you nothing?"

Mang Eleuterio said to Emilio, "This man is a good man—"

"Or did he simply tell you and show you? Did he speak Spanish and use words you didn't understand and, for the first time in your lives, talk to you as if you were his equals, as if your lives counted, and did he—"

Emilio said, "He gave us his trust!"

"He gave you a death list and he gave you a list of people to slaughter the names on that death list and then die themselves!"

"Their deaths were an escape!" Emilio said, "This woman's husband: death was nothing to him! His son—his only son— was taken like an animal and turned into nothing like trash and then—" Emilio said, "He will never be buried, never have his soul saved! His bones will stay in some sort of filthy museum for centuries and everything that was human about him, all his life and his hopes—" Emilio said, "The bone takers, they took all our souls and threw them away! This woman's husband died because he could no longer live!" Emilio said, "The man who came—"

Mang Eleuterio said, "Emilio—"

Emilio said, "No!"

Mang Eleuterio said, "Emilio, perhaps—"

"No!" Emilio said, "I can kill this man! I have the people and the guns and the knives and if we hide his body no one will ever come here to look for him!" His eyes held Elizalde's. Emilio said coldly, suddenly, "Are you prepared to die? Are you afraid?" Emilio said, "Give us your life and we will believe you!"

Cafiero. He had thought what Cafiero had done had been easy. It was not easy. It was the hardest thing to do in the world. It was the hardest thing to give because it was not his to give. It turned his stomach to water.

In the warehouse, in the sudden silence, Elizalde said, "All

I have in my life is my wife. She is what I hold precious. Her name is Marguerita and she can be found, now, today, at 46 Gabriel Pascua Street, San Pablo City, where she has gone to visit her family." He closed his eyes. Elizalde said, "Marguerita Elizalde. Her family name—the name of her family in San Pablo City is Lanternero. If the men you send are afraid to ask, what she looks like, how you will recognize her on the street, is—"

Mang Eleuterio shouted, "Emilio, I know this man's soul! What this man is telling you is true!"

"She is twenty-nine years old, younger than me, and—"

Mang Eleuterio said, "Emilio, it is all true." Mang Eleuterio said, "All our people are dying!"

"—and—and—" He was shaking. Elizalde said, "And—and she—and she—"

Mrs. Barrera said in a voice so low he had to strain to catch it, "Emilio, do you know the name of the man who came to speak to my husband?"

"—and—and—"

In the street, Cafiero ordered Ambrosio and Bontoc, "Wait!" He saw the fear on all the faces of the people. He saw— He was out of the car walking toward them. He thought he saw in those faces, a face from such a long time ago. He thought he saw—

In the street, at the top of his voice, Cafiero shouted to anyone who would listen, "These people are good people! These are my people!" He ordered Ambrosio and Bontoc, "Put your guns away! These people are only poor!" God help them, that was all they were.

Cafiero shouted, "They are my people! All they want is to be allowed to hope!"

He screamed at the top of his voice, not in the English of his life or the Spanish he had learned at night, but in the Tagalog of the streets he had grown up in, "These people—these people—" Cafiero screamed, "All these people are is *poor!*"

———

In the silence, in the hush, Mrs. Barrera asked Elizalde directly, "Is all you say true?"

Elizalde said, "Yes, it is all true." Elizalde said softly, unable to swallow, "Now, like you, I have nothing. Now, like you—"

Mang Eleuterio asked quietly, "What is it you want?"

He had lost everything. All he wanted now was what the poor wanted. There was nothing else to hope for. He waited. He looked at Emilio's face and could not read what was there. It was all he had left. Elizalde said in a whisper, "A miracle."

There was no sound at all.

Elizalde said softly, "A miracle."

He waited.

He was alone on the street. He was alone with everything he had ever feared and he was not afraid.

"Rosey . . ." Cafiero said softly, "Rosey . . ." In all the years they had been married he had never told her where he had come from. In all the years he had lied.

He was alone.

He was not afraid.

Cafiero, touching at his face, shaking his head, said in a whisper, a prayer, "Rosey . . . Rosey . . ."

Mrs. Barrera said to Emilio, "The man this man wants. The man who came to see my husband. The man who came to see all the other people in all the other barangays and barrios, do you know who he is?"

Emilio said, "Yes."

Mang Eleuterio pleaded, "Emilio—"

Mrs. Barrera said, "Tell him! Tell him! *Tell this man his name!*"

17

*A*t his desk in his office at Police Headquarters, the General said in disbelief into his phone, "Eleven male and female *what?*" His housekeeper must have been drunk. The General said, *"Dwarves?* Did you say—" The General shouted down the line, "Are you *mad?*"

The other phone on his desk rang. The General, wrenching it up, shouted, "What? What do you want? Who is this?"

It was the man from the United Nations, the one who, before he handed out medals for service to suffering humanity, called you up for a little friendly chat.

The General, getting back to his housekeeper, said tersely, "I'll call you back."

The General, fixing his uniform collar with his free hand, said sweetly to the man from the United Nations, "Sir, what an honor to hear from you. In what way can I or any of my staff assist you in any of your noble and selfless causes?"

In the street, Elizalde said, "Fontanilla. Police Lieutenant Raymundo Fontanilla, Special Services." Elizalde said to Cafiero, "He was a balding, nondescript man, slightly rotund, and he had all the papers and documents and photographs he needed to convince people he was telling the truth, and he had a list of people. In this barangay he had at the top of his list the faith healer Feliciano. He saw, first, three times, Barrera about his missing son and when Barrera started to believe him he made a fourth visit to see not only Barrera, but the barangay captain and the neighborhood council. The barangay captain says he was convinced. The barangay captain says he had nothing to do with the gun Fontanilla gave Barrera and nothing to do with Barrera killing himself." The people in the street had gone. As if by a secret signal, by telepathy, they had melted away and the street was empty. Elizalde said, "I've never heard of Fontanilla. If he's really a cop—"

Cafiero said, "I have."

"Who is he?" Elizalde glanced at Ambrosio and Bontoc. They both shook their heads.

Cafiero said, "Special Services. He's a liaison officer between the police and the Secret Service and the army. He's counterintelligence. He isn't paid by the cops." Cafiero said, "God only knows who pays him. He's got Secret Service rank as well as police rank." He said quickly, "I don't know what it is." Cafiero said, "He's untouchable. It's known that he was with the old right-wing death squads and it's known that—"

"He had police photos. He had police photographs of the missing people—the photographs that were given to the police by the relatives." Elizalde said, "He's a Spanish speaker. He—" He had been the one who had written the single word in Spanish on the back of the Beo girl's picture. The picture had been the one the Beo girl had given to the police when she had reported her brother missing. Elizalde said, "He told the barangay people that the ones behind it were the cops—the ones at the top."

Cafiero said, "Fontanilla is the man in charge of the files of missing people the intelligence services think have gone into the mountains with the New People's Army." His voice was even, expressionless. He felt a great weight leaving him. Cafiero said, "He's the one who—" Cafiero said, "I know him. He isn't a cop, he isn't even Secret Service—" Cafiero said, "Once, once I heard—" All his life he had heard things, all his life he had—

Cafiero said, "He's CIA. His name is Raymundo Rolando Fontanilla. He's got the police rank of lieutenant, but people . . . people just call him 'Rolly.'" Cafiero said, "He kills people. He's untouchable. He works at the Joint Services Missing Persons Bureau with me." Cafiero said simply, "He's my deputy." He glanced at Bontoc and Ambrosio and then at Elizalde. They were in the street. All the time he had waited in the car for

Elizalde, he had been unarmed. At night, every night, he half slept with his gun ready for shadows. Today he had waited in the car with nothing. For some reason, stupidly, he could not stop smiling. He almost giggled.

Cafiero, in the street, said joyously, fiercely, "Felix, in the Bureau . . . Rolly . . . Lieutenant Raymundo Rolando Fontanilla—"

Cafiero said, "I know where he keeps his private files!"

On the phone, Rolly said, "He knows. Gomez in the police armory knows where the guns came from. I got a message from the guy at the foundry and I rang him, but he's lost his nerve and he wouldn't talk to me. I rang his mistress and she told me he'd come to get some pistol or other back that Gomez at the police armory had given her and to give her money and he was preparing to leave the country." Rolly said, "Gomez knows. He's tracked it down through records and by leaning on the guy at the foundry and he knows where the guns came from and who took them." Rolly said, "I'm calling from near Chinatown. I'm about to set the next one in motion and I—" Rolly said suddenly, "You're the man. You tell me what to do!"

On his boat the Whispering Man said, "The Segundo woman—"

"Gomez knows! I'm not activating the next one on the list without dealing with Gomez first! I know Gomez! He's a frightened man! He spends his life locking doors and protecting his back so half the killers and psychopaths in Manila don't cut him to pieces for his guns! He'll protect himself! He'll cover himself and dissipate the information so that everyone will know and he'll be safe!" Rolly said, "He'll contact Elizalde, he'll—" Rolly said, "I'm not activating the Segundo woman to kill some minor cog at Customs until I know I'm safe from Gomez!"

"What barrio is the Segundo woman from?"

"Forget the Segundo woman!"

"What barrio?"

"Barrio Saint Pietro."

"And the one after that? The next on the list?"

"Barrio Saint Maria!" Rolly said, "You've got the list! What the hell am I going to do about Gomez?"

There was a silence. On the boat, the Whispering Man drew a deep, cleansing breath. He put his hand to his forehead and, for the first time in a long while, felt a little peace. It was happening. It was coming. It was—

Rolly said warningly, "I'm not activating more of these killings unless—"

The Whispering Man said pleasantly, "Yes, you're quite right to worry." It was coming, happening. He almost wept with relief. The Whispering Man said, "No, something has to be done."

"You're the one with all the money and power!" Rolly said, "And this, this is going to cost you more!"

"Yes, anything you like." The Whispering Man said, only half listening, "Gomez?"

"Technical Sergeant Jorge Gomez at the police armory Western District!"

The Whispering Man said, "Yes." The Whispering Man said, "It's almost 4:00 P.M."

"So?"

The Whispering Man said, "It'll be dark soon." The Whispering Man said, "I want to see it. This one. I want to see it." The Whispering Man, almost blubbering with relief, transferring all his love and gratitude to Rolly, said, "Rolly, good old Rolly—" The Whispering Man said tersely and suddenly efficiently, "Get him to the dock, get him to where I can see it! Get him there! There are lights! Get him under the lights! Get him there! Tell him everything! Tell him everything so he knows everything! Tell him he's safe! Tell him it's all, all safe! Tell him it's—" He was laughing like a maniac, his breath coming in fast, shallow gasps like a lover. "At night, tonight, make it as soon as it's dark!" The Whispering Man said, "Where I can see it! Where I can see it!"

The Whispering Man said, "Tonight, under the lights, you, yourself—*kill him!*"

In the car traveling north, Bontoc said, "Felix, the dwarves—" Ambrosio and Cafiero were in Cafiero's car, ahead of them with the siren going, clearing the way. Bontoc, trying to work it out, said, "Cafiero, he—" It was all just names, nothing made sense. Bontoc said as another name, "Rolly—"

"It's him." Elizalde's gun was on the dashboard in front of him. As he drove he glanced at it. Elizalde said, "It's him. Somehow he's gotten hold of all the names of all the victims and he's cross-referenced them with the missing persons reports— taken them and destroyed any reference to them—and he's gone around over God knows how long to all the relatives and he's told them what happened. According to the barangay captain he had photographs and invoices—he had photographs of human beings being defleshed in some sort of slaughterhouse, some sort of death house, and he's—" Elizalde said, "He told a boy of nine years old that his parents had been taken off the street like cattle and killed in a salt farm out on the highway and he gave the boy the name and address of the man who did it and he gave the boy a hand grenade and told him how to use it." He could not take his eyes off his gun on the dashboard. Elizalde said, "And a fruit vendor, Barrera—he told him that a faith healer named Feliciano was the cattle grader: the man who, when people came to him for treatment for their teeth, casually asked them about their general health, whether they'd ever had any broken bones, and, if they hadn't, if they were prime specimens, passed their names on to someone else for slaughter—maybe even took them there himself."

It was Rolly. He had told the poor the truth. He had told them—what? About the Yuson brothers?

He had told Ermalinda Beo that her brother, her friend—*My brilliant brother Santiago, Dr. Santiago, Professor Santiago, Papal Knight and Hero of the World Santiago*—he had told her that everything, everything he had ever been or would ever become had been reduced to nothing by the Yuson brothers in Intramuros. Maybe he had told her about the money in the tin box. He had given her a machine gun.

He had told the people who had burned the storehouse or the holding house or whatever it was on Palagayan Street how to make self-igniting petrol bombs.

Bontoc said desperately, "Felix, this man Fontanilla—if it's the cops—" He was not listening. His eyes were fixed on the gun. Bontoc said, "Felix, if he's CIA—"

Elizalde said, "The house in Palagayan Street belongs to the CIA—"

"Then if—" Ahead of him, Cafiero's car was moving fast through the traffic, "Then if—" Bontoc, being thrown against the car door as Cafiero made a hard, fast right onto Roxas Boulevard against the lights and Elizalde followed, said in desperation, then minutes from the Joint Services Missing Persons Bureau and Fontanilla's private files, "Felix, this guy Rolly—*whose side is he on?*"

He saw Elizalde reach forward and touch the gun to steady it.

He saw the look in Elizalde's eyes.

Bontoc said, knowing he would get no answer, "Felix, in the name of God—whose side are *we* on?"

All done. Almost all done.

He wept.

On the boat, on the *Goosewing,* the Whispering Man, his head in his hands at the chart table, wept.

Mollison. *Aswang* . . . almost all, all done.

On the table in front of him was the little rag doll with the noose around its neck. He touched at it and spoke silently to the child who, a long, long time ago, had held it.

Almost all, all done. The Whispering Man, taking his hand away from his face, looked at his palm. Almost all, all done. He saw his hand, as if disembodied, reach out with all the fingers outstretched for the wooden instrument shelf at the edge of the chart table.

The shelf was teak with a low-turned fiddle around it to stop things rolling out at sea.

The fiddle, also teak, once oiled and rubbed to a glow, was dusty and covered with little specks of dust and pollution from the smog blowing across the harbor from the city.

His hand touched at something on the shelf. It was a key with a lanyard attaching it to a cork ball so, if dropped overboard, the key would float.

Parts of the cork float had been attacked by insects and, as he took it up, some of the substance came away in his hands and felt soggy and rotten.

Mollison. He was at the gateway to hell, going after him to drag him back to send him back to hell again.

Mollison.

The Whispering Man shrieked, *"Mollison!"*

He was coming. He was coming for him.

The key was crushed hard in his fist. It was the ignition key to the sixty-five-horsepower auxiliary engine of the boat. The ignition lock was on the bulkhead behind his head.

The Whispering Man, rising, said, smiling, "Time to go."

Almost all, all done.

"Time to go."

He thought of Gomez and Elizalde and Cafiero. He thought, briefly, only briefly, of Rolly.

The Whispering Man, gazing at the ignition lock for the engine, not seeing it, said softly, "Time to die."

The Whispering Man smiled.

On the boat, an hour and a half before dark the Whispering Man clicked the change lever over to his spare, unused battery and put the ignition key for the engine carefully and firmly into its starting position.

On the phone Rolly said pleasantly, "Technical Sergeant Gomez, this is Lieutenant Raymundo Fontanilla of the Joint Services Missing Persons Bureau. I'm calling you from near the Yacht Club on the harbor."

There was a silence. There, in his house, in his home, with his family, safe, Gomez was listening.

Rolly said, "Fontanilla, badge number 45789, Special Services." Rolly said, "Most people just call me Rolly." He paused for a moment, "I believe we have someone in common who runs the government foundry and occasionally makes his blast furnaces available as a public service." He waited.

Within reach, propped up against the steel-reinforced front door of his apartment, there was a fully automatic U.S. M16 Armalite assault rifle with two thirty-round magazines taped together ready in it. The rifle was cocked with the safety off, ready. It was not the only weapon Gomez had in the apartment.

Gomez said with no expression in his voice, "Yes?"

"I believe I can help you out of your predicament."

There was no reply. His wife and children were in the bedroom. They had no notion of what was happening. The bedroom window was shuttered and they waited together in the dark.

Gomez said, "What are you offering?"

"What is it you want?"

Gomez said nothing.

Rolly said, "Gomez? Jorge? Sergeant? Are you still there?" *"People are being killed!"*

"Yes." Rolly said quietly, "Maybe, for once, it's all the right people." Rolly asked, "Are you armed?"

Gomez said, "Yes."

"Your family is safe. Your wife, your two girls and your son, they're all safe." Rolly asked calmly, quietly, "What choice have you got?" Rolly said, "All I want to do is talk. Bring your weapon if you want." Rolly said again, "All I want to do is talk." Rolly said, "We're on the same side. This time, for once, we can be on the side of the angels."

Rolly said, "Think of your family."

Rolly said easily, unhurriedly, serenely, one professional policeman to another, "Jorge—Sergeant—all we need to do together is talk."

In the third floor office of the Joint Services Missing Persons Bureau, Cafiero said in the terrible, hushed silence, "Anyone—

anyone who picks up a phone to make a call *dies!*" He had the
riot gun from the back of his car in his hands. All the people
at all the desks and consoles were silent where they sat, frozen.
Behind him, Ambrosio and Bontoc had their pistols out, pointing at the floor. Behind him, Elizalde was in Rolly's glass-
partitioned office at the bank of filing cabinets. Cafiero, his eyes
taking in all the floor, said with no room for argument, "Anybody who thinks of making a call—" He saw a movement at
one of the desks. He saw out of the corner of his eye Ambrosio
start to raise his gun to curb it. Cafiero said, "I've got nothing
to lose." He saw the movement at the desk stop. Cafiero said,
"Nobody even blinks!" He ordered Elizalde in the partitioned
office, "That one! The green cabinet by the door! That one!" He
saw Elizalde wrench at it and try to break the lock. Cafiero,
stepping back, said, "Anybody—anybody who works for anybody else—" He ordered Elizalde from the open door, "Step
back! Step back now!" He thought, for some strange reason, for
an instant, of Rosey. It was just her face. There was no place
or time or event to it, it was just a flash.

Cafiero ordered the man, "Felix!" He saw Elizalde step back
quickly from the locked cabinet.

Her face. It was just a flash. He had never known if the riot
gun he had carried all those years in the car to protect himself
was even still good.

Swinging the barrel into the room, he pulled at the trigger
and blew the lock on the filing cabinet into pieces with a single,
shattering, deafening blast.

In his apartment, Gomez, after a long while considering, said
softly, "Yes."

He swallowed hard, his mind racing. His family was in the
shuttered bedroom, trembling with fear.

Gomez said definitely, finally, into the phone, "Yes. All
right."

Gomez said, "I'll be there in an hour."

———

The first thing Elizalde saw in the top drawer of the burst-open filing cabinet was the bones.

They were identical to the ones he had found at Topacio's salt farm, two pieces of a broken human lower rib.

He saw a word in thick black type on a manila folder under the bones.

The word was *ASWANG.*

He saw a name. The name was *MOLLISON.*

It was a file. It was a scenario.

MOLLISON: it was the name of the author of the file.

It was a file on how to kill a great number of people.

It was more.

It was a file from the Manila Station of the Central Intelligence Agency.

ASWANG. It meant *vampire.*

It was a file straight from hell.

Goosewing. It was the name of his boat. It was the name of all his dreams. He had had the boat and the dreams for, sometimes it seemed, all his life.

The spare battery for the ignition was on line.

On the boat, staring straight ahead, the Whispering Man, holding the old hanged doll in his other hand, turned the key once, firmly, in the lock.

18

On the boat, staring straight ahead, the Whispering Man, holding the old hanged doll in his other hand, turned the key once, firmly, in the lock.

In the Bureau, from their desks and consoles as they came forward, they saw first laid out on the desk, the envelopes of money. They saw the five .22 caliber submachine guns. They saw, as Elizalde took them from the folders, the pictures of butchered people, of skeletons. They saw the files of people, their photographs: Barrera, Beo, Alonso, others—someone, a man named Segundo—they saw the Great Seal on the covers of files. They saw the CIA emblem. They saw the bones.

All the people Cafiero feared, all the people who watched him at their consoles and telephones, they began to come forward to see. They stopped at the glass windows and by the open door watching. They saw what was being laid out on the desk from the burst-open filing cabinet. They still smelled the smell of cordite and burned paint of the shotgun blast.

He looked at them. He saw them.

They were all, like him, afraid.

At the open door, his eyes, too, on the desk, Cafiero lowered his gun.

He was reading some of it. He saw the photographs. Ambrosio, trying to see Elizalde's face as he opened a file, said with a rising sickness in his stomach, "Felix—?"

The photographs were of human carcasses hanging on hooks

like slaughterhouse cattle. The photographs were of skulls laid out on a dirt floor in rows. The photographs were of—

Ambrosio said softly, "Holy Mother of . . ."

The photographs in all the missing persons files were of men and women like him. The photographs were of—

He saw Elizalde flip open one of the CIA jackets with a pencil.

Ambrosio said in a whisper, "Oh, Holy Jesus . . ."

On the boat, staring straight ahead, the Whispering Man, holding the old hanged doll in his other hand, turned the key once, firmly, in the lock.

PASS TO: CENTRAL INTELLIGENCE AGENCY, MANILA

Dated as: January 26, 1981.

Field Operatives and Others Authorized to View This File:

HEAD OF STATION ONLY

Precis and Scope of File:

THIS IS AN OPERATING MANUAL AND BACKGROUND-ING FOR THE COVERT DESTABILIZATION OF ASIAN NA-TIONS BY THE CREATION AND DIRECTION OF MASS PSYCHOTIC BEHAVIOR BY UNVERIFIABLE RUMOR

Author:

E. E. Mollison (Grade GS-13)

This Manual Has Been Passed by the Covert Opera-tions Committee and Been Authorized As: ACTIVE STATUS.

Current Operational Classification: PENDING. AVAILABLE.

INDEX AND PRECIS FOLLOW

THIS IS A BLUEPRINT FOR VIOLENT POPULAR REV-OLUTION

THIS MANUAL IS GRADED: DENY TOTALLY

He turned the key and everything, everything in the engine was smashed or rotted or seized up and there was no sound at all.

On the deck of the catamaran, all the galvanized rigging had rusted and begun to come loose from the turnbuckles and chainplates that secured it and, along the fiberglass deck there were cracks and cobwebs of fractures where the sun had gotten into the glass and split it.

He turned the key in the lock and there was no sound at all.

Below the waterline, along the twin hulls, hanging down in the water there was a jungle of trailing weeds and barnacles and fouling.

He had had the boat and the dream for it seemed all his life. It went nowhere. It rotted.

In his hand the Whispering Man held the hanged rag doll. His boat was a ghost ship. It rotted beneath him, eroded, got eaten away by living things, was smashed. The boat smelled, everywhere, in every corner, of rot and corruption.

He touched at the doll.

They had come that morning, not with guns, but with knives.

In his chart table, the Whispering Man had an oiled and loaded Ingram Model 11 machine pistol. It was a gun that fired at full automatic over twelve hundred rounds of steel-jacketed 105 grain .380 caliber ammunition a minute.

At the dead and silent lock, the Whispering Man still had the doll in his hand.

On his boat, in all his dreams—

Time—

Time . . .

He touched softly, gently at the doll and laid it down gently on the seat at the chart table as if it were a sleeping child.

Time . . .

That morning, they had come with knives.

He touched at his scarred throat with the faintest touch of his fingertips. He put the useless key for the boat by the doll and looked at it and saw the rust on it.

He had come to it, finally, at last.

It was time . . .

"Mollison . . ."

On the boat, finally, at last come to it, the Whispering Man, his breath coming fast, went to get his gun.

In Rolly's office, Elizalde read aloud, " 'Paragraph Headings. Item: Use of Terror in Asian Countries (History and Relation to Cultural Background); Item: British Army Use of Misinformation and PsyWar in Malayan Emergency in the 1950s; Item: Hong Kong Riots 1959–1965; Item: Propaganda and Selective Assassination, South Vietnam 1965–1975; Item: Selective Terror Operations Against Communist Insurgent Units, Republic of the Philippines, 1979–1980.' " Elizalde read aloud, " 'Item: The Poor.' "

Elizalde read aloud. " 'The poor—those deemed to be under-privileged and politically unrepresented in Asian communities—have traditionally been rural workers on large estates owned and operated by foreign (usually U.S.) capital. These traditional estates in Asian countries have been based largely on products for which synthetic replacements have now been found, e.g., sugar, coconut, and rubber or products already in oversupply, e.g., rice and fish. Some nations, e.g., Japan have replaced this traditional rural production with modern high-tech export items, e.g., electronics, and moved quickly into a politically stable position, but, in the main, all other Asian countries have not.

" 'The collapse of world markets and the demise of the large estates has seen the creation of a new, even more intense poverty and given rise to a mass migration to the cities.

" 'In the main, the cities are unable to accommodate or reem-ploy these untrained people and vast slum areas have grown up to accommodate them.' "

The file meant places like Tondo. The file meant places where people lived in cardboard boxes or tin shacks with no sewage or electricity or hope.

" 'These people have no hope.

" 'These people are caught in an endless cycle of crushing poverty and abuse by minor officials.

" 'These people, in say, the Philippines, supply their young women for prostitution and their males for violent, petty crime.' "

Mollison. It was the author's name. There was an award citation for the man in the file. He had been awarded the Intelligence Medal of Honor for killing a rebel and draining all his blood. At the door Elizalde saw all the people from the Bureau watching.

" 'Item: *It cannot be too highly emphasized that these people are safe to use for the simple reason that they are too unimportant and too numerous for officials to care about them.*' "

Elizalde said aloud from the file, " 'These people have, by long practice, learned to endure the unendurable. All they have as their hope is the hope of the worker of the Middle Ages: a peaceful death and a new life in the next world.' "

He read the file. " 'It is this single hope, I propose, we should destroy and so unleash the violence inherent in such an existence.' "

Bontoc said softly, "The skeletons. After everything, people are taken from the streets like dogs and melted down to—"

Elizalde said from the file, " 'Death is of paramount importance in Asia. The death and quiet rest of the individual is all he has to look forward to. Many societies have as their central tenet respect and veneration of the dead—' "

In Bontoc, the dead were placed on thrones until they became corrupt and then they were part of the panoply of life. His uncle, Uncle Apo had died. He still lived. His bones lay beneath a cairn on a mountain where all his favorite trees grew and—

Ambrosio said, "I'm a good Catholic, Felix, I—"

" 'The legal and illegal skeleton market, active mainly in India, supplies on average fifty thousand specimens a year to

Western research and medical markets. It is worth, at a con-
servative estimate, seven million dollars a year to its operators.
Local Asian agents and businessmen, as well as corrupt officials, will find this an irresistible renumeration for any assistance they may be called upon to give.' "

It was a file from hell.

Elizalde read aloud, " *'Western-cultured officers and agents
may find aspects of this operation personally distasteful, but it
must be emphasized that the stakes here are of fomenting a
violent, national revolution to topple or install a government, and
notions of compassion and/or pity or humanity should not be
allowed to cloud the firm and smooth operation of this plan.*

" *'Inherently, an operation of this nature will involve death
and suffering on the part of apparently innocent people, but it
must be remembered that there are no innocent people in an
operation of this nature. There is only the realization of a national and global result in line with the current requirements and
strategies of the government of the United States of America.'* "

Ambrosio said, "Why? Why us? What have we done to
them?" Ambrosio said, not understanding at all, *"Why us?"*

His mouth was twisted, hard. Elizalde said tonelessly from
the pages, " *'Minimum Number of Casualties Expected to
Achieve Result: Fifty-Seven.'* "

Ambrosio said, "But the Yusons, Feliciano, Topacio, all the
people you said were killed—" Ambrosio said, "It's the plan,
isn't it? The plan is to take the skeletons, terrify people, and
then give them the names of—" Ambrosio said, "The killing's
begun! The poor are killing their betters! They're killing—"
Ambrosio said, "It's us! We're doing it! It's the cops! The
dwarves said it was the cops! The poor first kill the cops and
then, as they move deeper into the chain and find the people at
the top—the ones who are financing it—then they—"

Bontoc said, "Who's giving them the guns?" It was the CIA.
It was Rolly.

" *'Scapegoats must be carefully chosen—'* "

Ambrosio said, "Why are they doing this to us? We're on
their side! Why are they doing this to the Philippines?"

Elizalde said from the file, " 'In an operation in Negros in April 1980, the author was forced to cast around for a scapegoat to take pressure off the real instigators of a plan to instill terror by the creation of a mythical "aswang" or vampire. The scapegoat chosen was of minor importance to the region, but just of sufficient guilt to be accepted by a reprisal squad as their victim. This policy is to be recommended in operations of this nature.' "

It was all a lie.

Feliciano, the Yusons, Topacio—it was all a lie.

It was all, all a lie.

Elizalde said suddenly, "It's a lie! It's all, all of it, a *lie!*"

He was moving fast now. On the boat, using the Seaphone, the Whispering Man said, "I know the man's name. The man's name is Lieutenant Raymundô Rolando Fontanilla. He'll be at the old Vito Cruz dock near the yacht club in twenty minutes!" He had the barangay captain of the barrio of Santa Maria del Rosa on the line. He was speaking in Tagalog, very fast.

The Whispering Man said, "He's a rotund man in his thirties, Philippino, wearing a shirt and slacks."

The Whispering Man said, "Be quick! It's almost dark. You won't have another chance!"

The Whispering Man said, "He's armed. He carries a little gun in his wallet."

The Whispering Man said, offhandedly, brushing off the barangay captain's gratitude, "Be quick! Go now! Just—be quick!"

On the phone to Cafiero's office, Gomez said quickly to Cafiero, "Tell Felix the Vito Cruz dock! Tell him Rolly telephoned me and he wants to meet me there!" He did not know if he could trust Cafiero or not. He had seen him with Elizalde. He thought he was Elizalde's friend.

Gomez said, "I've got to go! I have to go! I have to!"

Gomez said, "My family—I have to—I—"

Gomez said, "Cafiero. Sir. Lieutenant, please—Tell Felix. You're the only hope I've got. *Tell Felix now!*"

It was all, all a lie. The photographs of the skeletons were photographs from India, retouched. They were the photographs the people in the barangays had been shown. The ribs were old, broken. They had been planted at Topacio's as the black book and all the money had been planted at the Yusons' and it was all, all a lie.

It did not exist. It was PsyWar. It was a plan, a plot, it was a scenario. It was from a man called Mollison.

> *Grief and Mourning in Asian Societies*
> *Illiteracy among the Underprivileged*
> *The Influence of the Nonexistent "Dark Man" in Ghetto*
> *   Groups*
> *The Fear of Death*
> *The Fear of Mutilation of the Body after Death*
> *Utilizing These Fears on a One-to-One Basis*
> *Local Personnel Profiles for Informants*
> *Payment of Police and Minor Government Officials in the*
> *   Smaller Picture*
> *The Arming of the Poor and Procurement of Appropriate*
> *   Stolen Government Weapons*
> *The Death of Hope*
> *Violence and Frustration in Poor Ghetto Communities*
> *Prime Targets*

It was all, all laid out, all of it, and all of it, all of it, was *lies.* It was a plan to destroy a country by turning the poor loose in the streets with guns. It was a plan to destroy a country by turning the poor loose in the streets with rumors. With lies. There was no trade in skeletons in the Philippines. It was all, all just a lie.

Mollison. The man who had written the file, planned it, gloated over it, was a man called Mollison. He had, for this and for other things, been awarded a medal.

This Manual Has Been Passed by the Covert Operations Committee and Been Authorized As: ACTIVE STATUS. *Current Operational Status:* PENDING. AVAILABLE.

He had no idea on earth why the CIA should be doing it to them. He had no notion on earth.

Mollison, Eugene, Edward. There was the photostat of an obituary from an American newspaper in with the citation for the medal. Elizalde saw the citation. It was all, all hidden. It was all, all lies.

Aswang. It was something he had done years ago. It was a rehearsal for this. Then, too, he had killed innocent people.

Scapegoats. It was a chapter heading. Then, back then, he had used them too. No compassion, no pity. He had killed someone whose name was hidden for fifty years under executive order.

HEAD OF STATION ONLY. Elizalde saw Cafiero coming fast from his office. HEAD OF STATION ONLY. It was a scrap of paper with the name of someone on it.

FIFTY-YEAR RULE. HEAD OF STATION MANILA.

It was the name of the scapegoat in the Aswang Operation. Elizalde read the name.

The name was Peter Alfred Vogelsang. He had been, at that time, attached to the Agricultural Advisory Section of the U.S. Embassy, and the killer squad had come for him one morning before dawn with knives.

He knew the name.

He knew who it was.

"*Felix—!*" He heard Cafiero shout.

Mollison.

It was all, all lies.

In the office with all of it spread out on the desk in front of him—with all the people from the Bureau there who, by a telephone call here and there or a lost file, had helped, doing nothing wrong, doing only little un-understood favors, making money, killing people—Elizalde in a single awful moment, knew who was doing it all.

———

It was happening. It was happening again.

On the phone in the barangay Santa Maria del Rosa, as the poor assembled, as they came out this time, not one or two of them, but in a moving mass of people, Mang Eleuterio shrieked down the line to Police Headquarters, "Elizalde! Get me Elizalde! I won't talk to anyone else! Get me Felix Elizalde *now!*"

19

*I*t wasn't right. There was something wrong with it. They were moving fast along Roxas Boulevard toward the docks through all the traffic and the neon lights and the life toward the darkness of the harbor to the south. In the back of the car Elizalde could hear Bontoc and Ambrosio loading cartridges into the magazines of weapons, into Cafiero's shotgun and into the Swedish Carl Gustav M45B submachine gun they had gotten from the Bureau armory. It wasn't right. Elizalde, making a hard right to avoid a jeepney changing lanes, as Cafiero beside him in the front seat drew his pistol to check it, said above the noise, "It isn't right! There just aren't enough people! Even if it isn't really happening there just aren't enough victims for it to work!" It was being contained. There was no popular revolution starting. He saw in the rearview mirror Ambrosio snap a loaded magazine into the submachine gun and draw back the cocking bolt. There were no skeletons. Everything had been planted: the bones at the salt farm, the book and the money at the Yusons—it was too obvious. The padlock at the farm had been too obviously new, the shop had been clearly jemmied. It was all, all too obvious. The car was moving fast through the traffic, into Malate. It was dark night. Down at the harbor, all the lights would peter out and there would be only the faint illumination of widely spaced lamps along the shore. He heard a click as Bontoc got the shotgun fully loaded and shucked a shell into the breech ready. Elizalde, trying to think, moving too fast, running out of time, going somewhere to kill, shouted above the sound of the engine, "All the stuff we found was meant to be found! We were meant to talk to all the people we talked to!"

248

"All the files Rolly had were real!" Beside him, checking the pistol, Cafiero, not wanting to stop, not wanting to pause, *moving*, said, "I've seen CIA files before, Felix!"

"So have I!"

"The files were real! The pictures of the skeletons were fakes, but that file was real! We weren't meant to find Rolly's private files!"

"We did find them!"

"He's being paid by the CIA! He's being paid by whoever's doing it!"

"I know who's doing it! What I don't understand is why! What I don't understand is why it isn't working! What I don't understand is why we've had clues scattered throughout it! What I don't understand is why you or I haven't been killed as soon as we got close—even as soon as we started talking to the barangay captain! What I don't understand is why they didn't nip us off before we could—" Elizalde said, *"What I don't understand is why the CIA is doing it to the Philippines!"*

He had his Armalite. At his car parked back in the darkness away from the dock, Gomez, crouching down with the weapon across his knees, waited. To his right, he could see the lights of the city reflected off the water. The tide was high: he could hear it lapping against the stone retaining walls at the foreshore and, a little farther out, at the hull of a darkened catamaran yacht anchored in the bay. His breathing hurt. He could not seem to fill his lungs with enough air. The entire area was due for redevelopment—there were no buildings anywhere, only unlit, vacant land.

He waited.

He touched at the gun. He heard a sound and he tensed, ready.

He tried to swallow, but his mouth was too dry.

He listened. Frozen like a statue, crouched down against the car, he listened.

He heard a sound, a click.

———

He saw him. There was a storm-water drain running down from under Santa Cruz Dock Road into the harbor and in its shadow, Rolly saw him by the car. He saw the rifle in his hands. He smiled. Rolly, so quietly it could not be heard, said in a child-coaxing voice, in the voice of a phantom, "Go . . . mez . . ." His heart was thumping with excitement.

Rolly said in a whisper, "Go . . . mez . . ." Before he had shot people in the back of the head when he had been with the right-wing death squads, he had always, once, called their names. They had always, invariably, wet themselves in terror.

He liked it.

"Go . . . mez . . ."

He had one of the modified .22 caliber Gevarm submachine guns cradled in his hands. He had his derringer in the wallet in his hip pocket.

"Go . . . mez . . ."

It excited him. It always did.

At the drain, Rolly, standing up, still a shadow—Death— coming forward, said softly, unheard, into the darkness, "Go . . . *mez* . . ."

He started the engine. A Johnson twelve-horsepower out-board on the back of the Zodiac inflatable boat, it burst into life with the first pull. There was only one line holding the inflatable boat to the seaward side of the stern of the catamaran and the Whispering Man cast it off quickly and let the inflatable drift in neutral until it was clear. In the boat he had his Ingram and two plastic packets containing long, colored cylinders. In the city, all the lights were on. He saw all the lights of cars moving. He saw lights moving quickly toward the docks turnoff. He had the doll in his hand. He touched at it hard, once.

He put the engine into forward drive and, twisting at the throttle, set it to full power toward the docks, leaning back in the stern as the bow, starting to plane, lifted off the water and turned the dark bay around him white with foam.

He was moving fast.

Time to die.

He turned the helm landward and went for the dock.

They were at the end of Roxas Boulevard, looking for the turn. In the car Elizalde said above Ambrosio giving directions, "Constantino—"

"No!" Cañero, ready, said, "No, I know that man! That man is a paid killer! You saw the money!"

"I don't know why this is being done! There's something wrong and I don't know why it's being done! If we kill everyone we find there we'll never know!" It made no sense. It had all been handed to him, all the police guns and the bones and the black book, everything. Even Palagayan Street. Palagayan Street was owned by Pan Pacific Corporation—even the Fire Service had it on their register. Even a schoolboy, even anyone who had read one history of the Vietnam war, even someone who had read the newspapers, knew Pan Pacific was the CIA. And what was there in Palagayan Street? There had been a derelict house. There had been nothing.

There had been no skeletons or skeleton-shipping factory.

There had been no skeletons or skeleton-shipping factory because there were no skeletons to be shipped!

It was all, all a lie.

It was all, all of it, not true.

It was—

Ambrosio, at the map with a pen flashlight in the back of the car, shouted, "There! There! That turn there!"

It was—

He made the turn.

It made no sense.

It suddenly made sense.

In the car, spinning the wheel hard to make the turn as all the streetlights seemed to run out at once and he moved through darkness, Elizalde said, knowing it all, "Oh my God! Oh my God!" He had thought there could have been nothing worse than it all being true. He had thought there could have been nothing worse than the plan being implemented to topple a government. He had thought that there could have been nothing worse than them picking the Philippines to destroy one piece at a time. He had thought there could have been nothing worse than—

Elizalde shouted, "It's an experiment! It's a tryout on a small scale to see if the plan works! We're part of it! We've been given free rein, helped along, manipulated to see how long it takes— what?—takes average dumb cops to work it out! Somewhere there's a file on every one of us! We've all been selected, chosen, set into motion and moved about! We've been put in place, sent to deal with the dwarves because of who we are and what we are, pushed along, coaxed, prodded— It's not happening! Not only is the skeleton thing not happening, but even the misinformation isn't happening! The plan, the scheme, the scenario isn't being taken to its end by the CIA because there is no end to it—what the bastard who's doing this wants to know is—"

Elizalde said unarguably, "What this all is is a laboratory experiment in a friendly country where money and influence can buy the CIA out of any trouble it might cause to friendly people whose lives don't matter a shit!"

It was all, all true. It was the only explanation.

All they were were laboratory rats.

In the car, going hard for the dock, Elizalde, in a sudden realization that turned his stomach over, shouted to anyone who might listen in the armed car, "All it is to the people who are running it is just a lousy, minor experiment in PsyWar! It's an exercise! It's just an exercise! It's a goddamned *exercise!*"

"Go . . . mez . . ."

He saw him. At the car Gomez saw him stand up at the foreshore with the gun in his hands. He heard an engine coming fast from somewhere out on the water. He saw Rolly with the gun outstretched in his hands.

"Go . . . mez . . ."

It froze him. He felt his breath tighten, stop. He felt something like a hand stop his heart. He heard—

"Go—mez . . ."

Standing out, coming toward him with the gun as an offering, Rolly said in a quiet, coaxing tone, "Lieutenant Fontanilla. It's only me. I've brought you one of the guns you made. It isn't to hurt you with. . . ." He started to bend down to put the weapon carefully on the ground. Rolly said as to a child, gently, "I've got my wallet in my pocket with all my identification in it. I'll put the gun down on the ground here and step back and then I'll take my wallet out and give it to you. . . ." Rolly said, "Easy . . . easy . . ." He was wearing only a shirt and slacks.

Rolly said soothingly, "You can see I'm not carrying any other weapons."

Rolly said, "Trust me. I've got something important to show you in my wallet. Rolly said, "Gomez! Technical Sergeant Gomez?" Rolly said, "Lower the gun. Trust me." Rolly said, starting to put the Gevarm on the ground, "Trust me. . . ."

Rolly said, smiling, "Gomez . . . ?"

Momentarily, as the boat made headway to the dock, he was drifting. The engine was off. The boat drifted toward the steps to the wharf itself and he saw them. He saw the lights. He saw the people coming. They were along the foreshore, moving along the edge of the tide through the sand and he saw them and caught hold of the edge of the dock and pulled himself ashore.

He heard them. They were a moving mass and he heard them the way you heard animals coming.

He saw them. He saw them start to clamber over the seawall back behind the car.

He was out of the boat. It was drifting back into the harbor, lost. He saw them coming. It mattered not at all about the boat. He had his doll and his gun and his two plastic packets.

Time to die.

He had the doll in his pocket.

Time to die.

He saw lights coming. Far off, turning fast into the street to the dock, he saw lights coming.

Felix. It was Felix.

Time to die.

He heard a click.

"Gomez!" He heard Rolly give an order.

"NO!" By his car, Gomez shrieked, "NO!" He heard sounds, people. There were shadows, sounds, people. He heard a car coming fast. He saw Rolly start to put the gun down on the ground and reach for his wallet. He knew about wallets like that. He knew about his family. Gomez, bringing the Armalite up on full automatic and reaching for the safety catch, ready to cut the man to pieces where he stood, yelled, "No!"

"There!" In the car, Cafiero yelled, "There! I see a car! There!" He had his gun out, his other hand on the door handle pushing it open. He was filled with a bursting, a rage, a volume of something welling up swelling his body, making it start to crack, to give way, to shatter, to explode. *"There!"* He saw shadows, movements. There were people coming over the sea-wall like ants. Cafiero, shouting, screaming, yelled, "There! There!" Cafiero screamed at the top of his voice, "THERE! THERE! *THERE!"*

He saw the car coming. In an awful moment, Rolly saw the car and the Whispering Man on the dock and he saw and heard all the ants, the herd, the animals, coming. Gomez's gun was coming up. He saw it in slow motion. He was God: he saw everything from every angle all at once.

He saw on the dock the man who had sold him out. He saw him with something in his hand. He saw him pull it from a plastic packet and turn it in his hand like a baton. He saw him pull some sort of plastic cap from it and hold it up.

He saw the ants, the animals, the filth from the barangays coming for him like spiders.

He saw—

He saw the Whispering Man fire a single, forty-thousandcandlepower, Schermuly, white-magnesium parachute flare straight up above him. He saw, as it burst, in that awful milli-second between darkness and light, as the poor came over the seawall toward him, all the faces of all the dead. He saw Gomez with the Armalite. He saw—

He saw the car with Elizalde and Cafiero in the front seats, moving fast. He saw the windshield glitter with light. Every-where, all along the seashore, armed with knives and bolos, he saw dead men rising, all the dead he had ever killed, all their faces. He saw—

He saw for an instant Cafiero and Elizalde clearly outlined as the car came to a halt and, ducking away from Gomez as the man staggered, blinded by the falling white light, Rolly, getting the Gevarm submachine gun up in both hands and shooting it outstretched, emptied the full magazine at the car windshield, turned it to splinters, and in the explosion of glass and blood and shouting—he thought—killed instantly everyone inside.

20

*T*he flare, crackling, dropping sparks, was falling in an umbrella of shimmering white light visible at night for over ten miles. The umbrella lit up all of Vito Cruz Street and the water around it, contained it in a dome of light. In the absence of wind, the flare was falling straight down, its center too bright to look at; above it, all the lines and silk of the parachute were frozen like ice-covered cobwebs. It lit up all of Manila. It was visible from everywhere in the city. In Vito Cruz Street it was a brilliant white light that washed out all color. In the car, Cafiero, his neck and face running with blood from the exploded windshield, felt someone grab him by the shoulders and jerk him toward an open door. With the flare and the blood he was half-blind. He saw an outline, a shape, a black shadow with the brilliant white light behind him—Elizalde—and he felt himself go bodily out of the shattered car and onto the ground. His legs weren't working: he came out like a dead body. There was no pain. He felt glass grating and cutting into his face and neck, but there was no pain. There were people moving, running— he heard sounds. He saw, for an instant, either Bontoc or Ambrosio with the barrel of a submachine gun and he was rolling, being pushed hard against the car for protection and he heard Elizalde shout to someone. He heard gunfire. He saw, from somewhere, people everywhere—the poor—he saw the poor swarming in the light like ants. He heard glass breaking—the rest of the windshield falling out—and then he heard a burst of small-caliber automatic fire that exploded all around him and sent Elizalde ducking and dragging him harder against the car. He heard running, shouting, movement. He was blind. He could not see for the blood.

He was running, twisting, and turning to find somewhere to go. There was nowhere. In the light, there was nothing. All the ground was clear and empty and there was nowhere to hide. All the ground around him was covered in glittering, fired brass cartridge cases from the .22. It was empty. He had only one other magazine for it in his pants pocket. It was only an eight-shot magazine. Ejecting the spent magazine, reaching in for the eight shot and getting it into the gun, Rolly, trying to find somewhere to run, saw Gomez on the ground reaching for his Armalite. He could not cover the distance between them in time. He had only eight shots for the .22. If he wasn't careful, the eight shots would all go in one burst. Rolly, twisting, turning, trying to find somewhere, starting for the seawall, saw the poor coming for him. He had only eight shots. They had knives and bolos. He saw their faces. The flare was falling, spitting sparks and burning magnesium: he saw for an instant, forty yards away, a mound of rubble and a bulldozer. He had only eight shots. Yanking the cocking bolt back, swinging the gun on the poor and halting them in their tracks, he ran for cover.

"Gomez!" The man was on the ground, scrambling for the Armalite. At the car, trying to see Rolly running, seeing him only as a blackness in the light, Elizalde, trying to find Cafiero's wounds with his hand, ordered the man, "Over here! Get over here with the rifle and cover Cafiero!" He saw Gomez look around. He saw him grab for the rifle as Ambrosio went past him with the submachine gun with Bontoc only a step behind. He saw him get to his knees and swing the gun toward—
Elizalde yelled, *"Gomez! Over here! Here! Now!"* He saw Rolly running for the bulldozer and the cover. He saw Ambrosio, lost in the brightness, take the wrong direction after him. He saw a shadow at the far end of the street, at the dock, and he knew who it was.

Elizalde, getting to his feet to get the man bodily over to the car as the poor swarmed over the seawall, shouted to Ambrosio a moment before the poor cut him off, "Ambrosio! Jesus-Vincente! To the left! He's gone to the left!" He saw Gomez fix his voice, identify him, and Elizalde, standing up with his pistol in his hand, watching not Rolly but the figure standing on the dock, yelled, "Here! Get yourself here and help Cafiero!"

The flare had a full burning time of forty seconds. It had been burning at the apogee for five seconds. It was falling, coming down on the parachute, swinging. It lit up all of Manila. It had thirty-five seconds left to burn. It was directly above him, dropping fire. He had been sold out. Rolly, running hard for the rubble, had been sold out. He was going to be killed. There was nowhere to hide. He saw the poor coming for him from the seawall and there was nowhere to hide and he knew who had fired the flare and he had been sold out.

His breath was coming hard. He was running and running toward the rubble, going around in circles, running for the shadow the rubble made and he was getting nowhere. There was bile in his throat. He was running with only eight shots in the submachine gun and he heard behind him running men, and he was getting nowhere in the light, going around and around and the rubble mound was not getting any closer and there was nowhere to go.

He was lost. He was running with Bontoc and he was going nowhere. In the center of the street, running hard for nowhere, Ambrosio, the retinas of his eyes tiny pinpricks in the blinding light, was running nowhere. He could not stop. He ran. He was running for the seawall. He saw shadows, shapes, things coming over the wall and, his finger on the trigger of the submachine gun, ready to shoot, he was running for the sea.

"*No!*" Mang Eleuterio, at the seawall trying to stop his people going over, was yelling in Tagalog. Mang Eleuterio yelled, "No!" They were amok, it was *napasubo,* the point of no return, what the Spanish had called *juramentado,* committed unto death. They were his people. They were screaming, shrieking. They were going over the seawall like ants, like a stampede.

At the wall, Mang Eleuterio, praying to God, to any force that might listen, shrieked, "No! It's all wrong! It's all wrong! *Believe me! Believe what I told you!"*

"Take him!" At the car Elizalde, grabbing Gomez by the neck and forcing him down to the ground beside Cafiero, ordered the man, "Stay here! Stay here and find his wound!" He could not find anything. There was blood, but he could not find a bullet wound. He saw Cafiero's eyes in the light. They were gone, lost, rolling back. The man was hard hit somewhere and in shock. He could not find a bullet wound. Elizalde yelled above a sudden unearthly shriek as one of the poor, drawing back his razor-sharp bolo, saw Rolly. "Don't leave him! Find the wound and stop the blood and don't leave him!"

It was a dead man. It was the face of one of the dead men he had killed over the years. It was the face of one of the men he had taken when he had been in the right-wing death squads and killed with a single bullet wound in the back of the neck. He saw him coming. He saw his eyes. He saw the bolo.

He had nowhere to go. There was no mound. It was a shadow.

He saw him coming ahead of the others. He heard him shriek.

He had nowhere to go.

Rolly, turning, his finger on the trigger hard and controlled, touching off the gun with the gentlest, the most careful of pressures, fired a burst of three shots and killed the man where he ran.

He saw a flash. It was to the right. He saw the flash and the red sparks from the breech of the gun and he knew where Rolly was.

Bontoc, twisting, yanking Ambrosio by the shoulder to turn

him, seeing shadows, hearing someone scream in pain as the bullets ripped into him and tore living tissue, yelled, "There! There!" He must have turned away from the drifting flare. He saw, in a moment, clearly, all the shadows and movements. He saw a man with a cut-down .22 rifle. He saw—

He saw people falling to the ground to take cover. He saw one of them get up with a knife in his hand and then, ahead of him, running toward the end of the street, he saw Rolly. It was him. He had the gun. He saw him turn back and he saw his face. Bontoc, getting his pistol up, shooting like a competitor on the dueling range, fired shot after shot. He saw Ambrosio getting his footing beside him, get the Swedish SMG up. He was shooting one round after another at the man, not hitting him.

The air all around him shattered into sound as Ambrosio loosed off the SMG and destroyed all the ground around Rolly's feet in a long, sweeping area burst that sent empty cases flying all around in the air in a single falling mass of red-hot glittering brass.

Elizalde saw him shoot. He saw the area around Ambrosio and Bontoc light up in a different, sharper color and he saw Rolly seem to skip as the ground around him exploded into dust. Ahead, a little between the exploding ground and where the light ran out into shadows, Elizalde saw a dead man twitching and kicking on the ground. He saw, as the corpse convulsed and seemed to turn backward, that all his face had been blown away into splinters and there was only stark white bone.

He was running toward the jetty. The poor were coming, appearing between him, and he shouted at them in Tagalog to get back. They were crazed, out of their minds, all their hate and frustration loose and free. They were running, shrieking. He saw Mang Eleuterio on his feet shouting at them and then Rolly, miraculously running out of the destroyed ground and all the bullets around him, turn and fire a quick burst that killed the closest running man in midstride.

Bontoc was shooting with his pistol. He had reloaded and taken aim but the bullets were going nowhere and however he anchored his feet, he could not keep the gun from wavering and missing.

Elizalde saw Mang Eleuterio. He was shouting, touching at some magic amulet at his neck. He was praying, shouting an orison at the top of his voice to a diety who would not listen. The flare was falling. It had been burning for fifteen seconds. It was all happening too fast to take in. He saw the man Rolly had killed going down in slow motion and then Ambrosio loose off an entire magazine from the submachine gun and Rolly was running through that and twisting back with the gun to fire. Elizalde, taking aim, trying to follow him with the barrel of his PPK, fired a single shot that he thought should have killed the man. He saw Rolly seem to skip, to look down, and he thought he had hit him hard in the chest, but nothing would stop him and he was still running. He was running under the exact center of the falling flare and being blurred out, disappearing, getting away into the light, and Elizalde, firing again, fired into nothing.

He was in the light, safe. He was in the exact center of the light and everything was washed out and he was safe. He had been sold out. He knew who had done it, fired the flare, sold him out—he knew who it was who watched from the jetty and he tried to orient himself to get there. Out there, outside the center of the light, the pinpoint of white light that hid him, he saw shadows; he saw the shadows of the poor. He was killing them. He was killing them as he had always killed them and he was getting away. He had seen a bulldozer. He knew he had seen it. It was out there somewhere. He knew it was there.

The flare was falling, burning and crackling and coming closer. It could not burn forever. It had burned for fifteen or twenty seconds and it could only burn another twenty seconds or so and it would be gone and there would be darkness. He knew the bulldozer was out there. He knew everyone would be blind. He knew, in the darkness when the flare went, that the darkness—

He saw a shape, a shadow. He saw an old woman appear

suddenly like a nightmare at the corner of the light and Rolly, yanking at the trigger of the gun, shot her cleanly in the face and she was gone again.

He was killing all his people. He heard shrieks, yelling, and all his people were being killed. "GET BACK!" At the seawall, Mang Eleuterio, everything he loved being destroyed, being murdered, pushing, shoving at people, shrieked, "GET BACK! YOU CAN'T WIN! *GET BACK!*" The man nearest him was an old, old man with a long glittering bolo. The leather-bound hilt of the weapon was loose. It was second rate. It was all second rate. It was the poor. Everything, everything was—

Mang Eleuterio, weeping, sobbing, trying to wrench the poor, useless weapon from the man's hand, shrieked blinded by the light and the tears, "Please! *Please!* PLEASE!" He saw Elizalde. He saw him standing up with a pistol in his hand, searching with the barrel of the gun in the light, and Mang Eleuterio, fighting the old man, trying to save at least him, shrieked in Tagalog, "It doesn't work! All my protection! All my faith—IT DOESN'T WORK ANYMORE!" He saw a shape, a shadow at the very center of the light. He saw the Devil in the pinpoint of Hell. He saw every nightmare as a single shape, an outline. He saw—

Mang Eleuterio, fighting, grappling with the old man to save at least him—the man of peace—screamed at Elizalde, "Kill him! Kill him! *Kill him before he kills everything in the world!*"

He was in shock. The glass had hit him in the face and in that second he had thought he was dead and all he could see through the blood was the face of his wife and it was all, all too late.

At the car, Cafiero, trying to push Gomez away, reaching for the Armalite lying next to the man, said over and over, "Glass. It's glass. It's just glass." He was bleeding profusely from his face and neck, but there was no pumping feeling and none of the arteries had been severed and he was still alive. "Glass. Glass." He said it over and over, trying to force his body to get up. Gomez was saying something, trying to soothe him. Cafiero saw only the black outline of the Armalite rifle on the ground beside him. He tried to get it, kept trying to get it, but it seemed a long way away.

"Glass." It was only glass.

Everywhere he heard gunfire and the sounds of people running.

He waited.

At the end of the jetty with the Ingram gun held loosely by his side, the Whispering Man merely . . . waited.

He waited.

He was there. The light in the sky was drifting sideways and he was there and he saw it, the bulldozer: the darkness, something, somewhere to hide until the light had gone.

The gun was empty and he threw it down and reached into his back pocket for his derringer and got it out. He was there, he had found it. He could wait. He could wait, safe in the light until the light went and then he was in darkness and the concealment of the bulldozer and he could get away and he was safe. There were lights, sounds, shouting. He heard a siren a long way off and the whole of Manila was coming and he could get away.

He waited. On the jetty, counting the moments the Whispering Man waited. He heard a siren. It was coming from the sea. It was a Coast Guard boat, and all the sea around it was lit up as it swung its searchlight. For a moment, looking back, he saw the *Goosewing* lit up and he was counting. He was standing on the jetty holding the Ingram gun loosely by his side, counting the moments and waiting.

He was waiting for Elizalde.

"Behind you!" Ambrosio, seeing suddenly the mass of people moving, yelled to Bontoc, "Behind you!" Bontoc had his pistol out. He turned and the poor were almost upon him and Ambrosio yelled, "Behind you!" He could have killed them all with

a single burst of the SMG. A Fireball would have killed them all with a single burst of the SMG. He was no Fireball. He was a man. Ambrosio, getting the gun up in the air and loosing off a full magazine as the poor all went for the ground, shrieked, "Police! I'm a police officer! For God's sake clear the area or you'll—" Or you'll what?

BE HARD, UNCOMPROMISING, RUTHLESS!

Ambrosio, begging, yelled, "Or you'll all be—"

Or you'll all be—

Ambrosio shrieked, "For God's sake, for your families—for God's sake, *save yourselves!*"

The flare had eighteen seconds left to burn. It was falling faster, dying, spitting flame and sparks as the charge burned down to the base of the casing.

They were coming. From all over the city, people were coming. Rolly heard sirens, he heard sounds, the sounds of fire engines and ambulances. He heard the hooting of the Coast Guard cutter. He heard—

He was safe.

The flare was dying and he was lost in its center and he was safe.

The flare was spitting hard, crackling, getting closer, falling away, going out and he was safe.

He heard—

He heard—

He saw a shape, a shadow.

He saw something moving slowly, almost unhurriedly into the light and he brought up his little gun to kill it.

He was there. He saw him. Moving fast toward the jetty, as the catamaran was lit up in the searchlight from the Coast Guard cutter, as the cutter turned away to circle it, Elizalde saw him. He saw him standing there.

He saw a man at the end of the jetty with a gun in his hand, waiting. He saw his mouth moving.

He saw him counting out the moments.
He saw him smile.

The Whispering Man said almost conversationally, "Felix."

They had turned. They were going back. At the seawall, with all the sounds and the lights and the sirens, the poor were going back.

They were going away like ants, disappearing along the seawall, almost going into its stones and they were going away, going back to their barong-barongs—their shanties, their slums—and they were safe and they were going away.

The flare was falling, dropping faster with only eight seconds left to burn. The parachute was only a square of something, not silk, and it was dropping the burning casing fast onto the ground and it would be—

He heard a single shot, something from a short-barreled weapon firing high-velocity magnum-length .22 and then another and if it was from Rolly's derringer then he had fired both shots and he was finished.

He saw the Whispering Man at the end of the jetty and he heard him call his name.

"Felix . . ." It was a greeting. It was a soft acknowledgment of a planned meeting and Elizalde, his gun in his hand, went forward to the jetty in the last of the light.

They were gone. Both shots were gone and he had hit the shadow and the shadow was still coming for him and he had not hit the shadow. He was on the ground. He had two more rounds for the little gun but he had dropped them getting them out of his pocket and with the action of the gun empty and broken, he was scrambling around trying to find them with the palms of his hands. He had killed the shadow. He had killed all the shadows.

He saw the shadow above him and for a moment Rolly thought it was—

It was Mang Eleuterio. He had a bolo with a broken hilt in his hand and he was looking down.

"Felix."

At the end of the jetty, with the gun held loosely against his side the Whispering Man, shaking his head, was counting the seconds.

"Felix . . ."

For a moment, he smiled.

They were gone. They were safe.

All the poor were running, escaping, and they would not die and they were safe. The flare was dying. There was almost no sound and Ambrosio and Bontoc were standing by the seawall and all the poor had gone and they would not die. The dwarves would not die and all the poor—they, themselves, also the poor—

He had it. At the car Cafiero had the Armalite in his hand and he was getting up. He felt Gomez's hands on his shoulders and the man was helping him and he would not die and there would be time—and he would not die.

The Whispering Man said quietly, "Hullo, Felix . . ."

He counted the last seconds out silently, moving his lips.

On his knees, begging, Rolly shrieked, *"NO!"*

The flare was going. It had reached the end of its pyrotechnic load and it was falling as a dying yellow light and everywhere, in the last moments, the darkness was coming in. He was a man of religion and of hope and of miracles. He was seventy years old. He had been a fisherman. All his life he had been strong. In the last light Mang Eleuterio raised the long bolo above his head.

Rolly shrieked, *"NO!"*

He was a man who looked into souls. In the last moment of light, in that light, Mang Eleuterio looked into Rolly's soul to see what was there.

He heard the scream.

At the jetty the Whispering Man, at the end of all his counting, at the end of everything, smiled.

In the last moment, Mang Eleuterio, driving down hard with the bolo, decapitated the squirming, screaming man with a single blow.

One. All the counting was done and in that moment as the flare fell to earth and died in the darkness, the Whispering Man said softly to Elizalde, "Well . . ."

Perhaps he smiled.

In that moment, at the last moment, as the firebomb set on board the *Goosewing* detonated in a single sheet of flame that set the boat alight from stem to stern, the Whispering Man, wifeless and childless for what seemed like a very long time, like eternity, said in a rasp, touching at the scar on his throat where the killer squad in Negros had thought that dawn they had killed him, "Well, Felix . . ."

In that moment, Peter Alfred Vogelsand, the Head of Station, CIA, Manila, said in a rasp, "Kill me, Felix. That's why you're here."

The Whispering Man said earnestly, "Kill me, Felix! Shoot me dead!"

The Whispering Man, lit up in the glow of the burning boat like something from hell, said urgently, "Kill me! You must know by now that's the reason you're here! I'm relying on you! I've been relying on you from the start! Do it! Do it now!"

The Whispering Man ordered him, "Now! For the love of God, *do it now!*"

Out in the bay, lit up by the searchlights of the Coast Guard cutter as it radioed urgently for assistance, from one end to the other, the *Goosewing* burned.

21

*H*e was moving in a blur of darkness and the light from the burning boat on the bay. At the car, on his feet, pushing at Gomez with his free hand, Cafiero ordered the man, "Get away! Leave me!" He had the Armalite held by the pistol grip. He kept trying to bring it up to port, but it was heavy and it kept swinging back down in his hand. He saw Gomez's face in the yellow light: it was ashen. Cafiero, moving toward the jetty and Elizalde, thinking he was going straight, dragging the gun, ordered Gomez, "I know who it is! I can see him! Get away from me!" The man was talking, trying to say something to him, touching at him, almost patting him to pull him back. His face was white with fear. Cafiero, shoving him away, forcing his legs to work, brushing at the blood on his face and around his eyes, demanded, "Go! Get away! You're out of it! Go home to your family!" He got the gun up to port and swung the butt to warn Gomez off. The yellow light and the sirens and the sound of the Coast Guard boat on the bay were a hundred yards away, getting closer. He was moving, getting there.

Cafiero, getting his hand to Gomez's shoulder and pushing the man hard, shouted, "Go! Get out! Don't stay! *Go!*"

"Keep away!" Ambrosio and Bontoc were coming up fast. Elizalde, glancing back quickly, saw Ambrosio fitting another magazine into the submachine gun. He saw Bontoc—

Elizalde shouted, "Get back! Don't come here!" The Whispering Man on the dock had the Ingram still held loosely by his side. He was watching, lit up by the yellow light. He stopped them. Elizalde, only daring to look back to them for an instant, yelled, "Don't come here!" The sirens were coming from all over Manila. He could hear them. Elizalde, facing the Whispering Man, watching the gun, shouted, "Get back down the street and stop the first marked police car and get them to set up a road block! Don't let anyone come here!"

The man at the end of the jetty was only a man. He was a European, an American. He was only a man in his early fifties with a single little gun that was not even held ready to fire. In the glow of the burning boat, he was only a slim, slightly built man with a receding hairline and a lined face. He was a man with deep, sunken eyes. He was a man holding a gun in his right hand and what looked like a broken rag doll in the other. He was a man dressed in slacks and a shirt. He was nothing. He was only a man.

He was a caged tiger. Elizalde shouted, "Baptiste! Jesus-Vincente—"

Ambrosio said, "Who is he?"

"Do as you're ordered!" He was the Head of CIA Station, Manila. Elizalde, shaking his head, commanded them, "Don't come near him! Put your guns down! Don't come near him! Get out! Get out and set up the road block and don't let anyone past!"

"Who—?"

In the bay the catamaran was burning from end to end. On the boom, the furled sails had caught and, dry and rotted, went up in a single sheet of bright flame that set the deck on fire and ruptured a fuel tank. There was a dull thud from somewhere below decks and then another, brighter flame, and then black smoke began rolling out with flames still burning in it. It was lit up by the searchlights of the Coast Guard cutter. The cutter was circling, searching for people in the water. At the jetty the Whispering Man did not even turn around.

Elizalde shouted, "Now! Go now!" He was shaking with fear. He looked at Vogelsang and saw—

Elizalde yelled, *"Go!"*

It burned. It went to nothing the same way that everything he had ever had had gone to nothing. Behind him, the *Goosewing,* all his dreams, burned. He heard the fiberglass crackle and burst in the heat. He felt the heat at his back. There was a bang as one of the spare jerry cans of fuel for the Zodiac's outboard motor exploded and then there was a roar as a compartment below decks must have burst open and paint or thinner or some chemical in there went up. The Whispering Man, looking at his face, said softly, entreatingly, "Felix—"

He had never met him, but he knew who he was. He knew the name. He knew who he was. He knew what he represented. He knew the power he had.

He was shaking. On the jetty, facing him, in the heat, Elizalde was shaking with fear. The PPK pistol in his hand was a toy. It was nothing. He knew who he was.

"Kill me, Felix!"
Elizalde shouted, *"You go to hell!"*

The Whispering Man smiled. He touched at his throat with the hand that held the broken rag doll. The Whispering Man said in a rasp, like a demon, "I know you, Felix. I've got a file on you. I know what you are." He was smiling, letting the Ingram gun swing a little in his hand. "I knew Gomez would go to you and you'd come because I know everything about you." The Whispering Man said, "I chose you. I worked out when you'd be on duty and I worked out where you'd be when the faith healer died and I worked out that'd have to be you and I—" The Whispering Man said, "I know everything about you." He said, "You've killed one man in your career. You don't kill easily. You need an excuse." The Whispering Man said, "I could have given you Rolly, but then it would have had to be just you and him and I needed the people from the barangays to kill him." The Whispering Man, smiling, said, "Rolly worked for money. Poor Rolly worked so hard for money he thought there was nothing else in the world but money and it never occurred to him that while he was working hard in the barangays earning his money with the files and the photographs and the bits of bone that I could be going around other barangays, with just my identification, doing the same thing for nothing."

"It's all a lie! Everything!"

"Yes." The Whispering Man said, "I knew you'd come to it. It was easy enough and I know what sort of man you are and that eventually someone in the barangays would trust you and you'd come to it." The Whispering Man said, "But is it a lie? What's a lie?" The Whispering Man said, "All you have to do to finish it to my satisfaction is kill me." He said, "You don't kill easily. You need a reason. That's all part of it. The reason is the main thing. The reason has been taken into account too and that's all part of it." The Whispering Man said tightly, "You'll do what's expected of you because I know everything about you."

"There were no skeletons!"

"No."

"And no conspiracy! All of them—all the people you had killed—Feliciano, the Yuson brothers, Topacio—all of them— *they'd done nothing at all!*"

The Whispering Man said, "No. I chose them at random from the electoral rolls."

Elizalde said, "The missing people, the husbands and the brothers and the— *Where are the bodies?*"

"Bodies are just bodies."

"They were people!"

The Whispering Man said, "I knew you'd get the job, the work, because I made a file on you and I know all about you." He watched Elizalde's face. "You're honest. I found it hard to believe and I still haven't worked out the reason, but your one shining feature, Felix, is that you're not corrupt. A rarity. I don't know why, but I—"

Elizalde said, "I'm rich. I don't need to steal."

"No." The Whispering Man said, "I offered Rolly a half a

million dollars and a new, protected life in America. That's rich. What you have—" The Whispering Man said suddenly, smiling, "Maybe you are. I thought I was once, but it all turned out—"

"You've killed at least eight people I know of!"

The Whispering Man said, "Once, in Negros, I thought—" The Whispering Man said, "No, it isn't a lie, it's the truth. The lie is the truth and it's all real." The Whispering Man said, smiling, almost laughing, "No, rich is what I have control of." The Whispering Man said, "This whole operation was authorized by me and paid for under *Miscellaneous*—that's what rich means! That's what I am!"

"What you are is the CIA!"

The Whispering Man said, "Yes. Debtor to the U.S. Government. CIA. Destruction of Philippino Society, a few million dollars, hardly worth itemizing. Paid for under *Miscellaneous.*" The Whispering Man said, "It isn't much of a country. There's no reason to bother the accountants with it."

"You're not destroying the Philippines! You're trying to destroy a dead man called Mollison! You're trying to destroy the man who told a Communist killer squad that you planned the Aswang Operation! You're trying to destroy the man who had your wife and child killed and wrote them off as minor casualties and locked their names away for fifty years until anyone who might care was dead!" Elizalde, watching the gun still pointing down at the ground, said, losing control, "This isn't a CIA operation! It's your operation!"

"I am the CIA!"

"The CIA knows nothing about this and they—"

"The CIA doesn't have to know anything about any of this!" The Whispering Man, shaking his head, said, "You don't understand, do you? You're so used to getting the shit jobs, the ones where there's absolutely no risk of you compromising anyone important, that you don't even know, do you?" The Whispering Man said, "The Mollison file is real! The photographs in it are real—"

"The photographs are retouched pictures of the skeleton trade in India!"

"The photographs are photographs good enough to make the poor and the stupid and the brutish believe! The photographs for that purpose are real!" The Whispering Man said, "The file is real! It's an operational file!" The Whispering Man, shouting, demanded, *"Can't you read?* Didn't you read the classification, the status of the file at the top? It says ACTIVE STATUS. It says PENDING. It says AVAILABLE!" The Whispering Man said abruptly, "They came a little before dawn for me, Felix, out in Negros. There were, I think, eight of them and they came in through, not the window, but the front door as if they were callers. They all had bandannas around their heads so they wouldn't drop sweat onto their hands, and in their hands they had knives and bolos because guns would make too much noise." The Whispering Man said, "My wife's name was Susie and they killed her first and then, in front of me, they killed my five-year-old daughter. They held me down on the bed while they killed her, while my wife's blood was still pumping out, and then they brought in her doll with a noose around its neck and they held it swinging there for a very long time." The Whispering Man said, not to Elizalde, but to himself, curiously, "It stopped. Time. It just stopped. It was happening, time was passing, but nothing moved. It was like . . . like . . ." The Whispering Man said, "And then one of them, one with a red bandanna just leaned down with a butterfly knife and laid it across my throat and then—" The Whispering Man said, "I felt it slice me. I felt it slice me as if it were someone else and I thought—" The Whispering Man said, "And then one of them I didn't see stabbed hard into my neck with something else and I died there." The Whispering Man said, "I drowned. I drowned in all the blood on the bed and I floated away and I—I went—" The Whispering Man said, "I just—" The Whispering Man said, "And my wife's face was different, dead. It was white and empty and—" His voice was rasping, ruined. The Whispering Man said, "I never saw my daughter's body because by the time I'd been sewn up and come back from the dead she was buried and rotting."

"The people you had killed had wives and children too!"

" *'Western-cultured officers and agents may find aspects of this operation personally distasteful, but it must be emphasized the stakes here are of fomenting a violent national revolution—'* " The Whispering Man said tonelessly, "I quote selectively: *'and notions of compassion or pity or humanity should not be allowed to cloud . . . There are no innocent people. There is only the realization of a national and global result in line with the current requirements and strategies of the government of the United States of America.'* " The Whispering Man said, " *'Minimum Number of Casualties Expected to Achieve Result: Fifty-seven.'* "

He was moving, getting stronger. The pain was dissipating and all the strength was moving into his arms and legs and, with the Armalite held up, feeling the power coming into his muscles and hands and legs, Cafiero was moving. He moved toward the light from the flames. He moved toward the jetty. He moved toward Elizalde.

"It's all a lie! Mollison is dead!"

"It's an experiment. It's an experiment to see if Mollison's plan works. It does." The Whispering Man said almost happily, "It does. It works well. It's just an experiment done on a country that doesn't matter very much that we could placate if the experiment had gone wrong—something we could pay our way out of—but lo and behold, it worked." The Whispering Man said, "Good old Ed Mollison, what a guy. He got all his experience in Asia, killing people, helping to assassinate Diem in Vietnam, starting riots in Hong Kong, torturing people in Taiwan, neutralizing Communist killer teams in the Philippines without too many casualties and, lo and behold, by God, he deserved his medal and his retirement days full of honors and glory and good reputation in the autumnal wilds of North Carolina—and it works!" The Whispering Man said, "The Mollison Plan works!"

"It hasn't worked."

"It has. You're here, but that was me. I did that. If I hadn't brought you here—" The Whispering Man said, "I've got a file on you, Felix. I know all about you. It works, you're here. The Mollison Plan works—!" The Whispering Man said, "And when you've worked up enough hate to kill me or I have to kill you and find someone else, then it will have worked full circle and—"

Elizalde said tightly, one word at a time, "And then you will have destroyed Mollison for what he did to your family!"

"No." The Whispering Man said, "No." He lifted the gun a little to test its weight. The Whispering Man said, "No." The Whispering Man said, "Watergate, Felix. Rumors. Lies. Whispers. Rumors." The Whispering Man said, "No, Felix, no. No, when you kill me, when you—when I'm dead, when the file is made public—" He said quickly, "Where did you get the file?"

"From the Missing Persons Bureau, from Rolly's safe—"

"Ah." The Whispering Man said, "Ah. Well, there was another in Rolly's house and another—" The Whispering Man said, "No. No, what I propose to destroy, what it will destroy, what it will shatter into pieces—"

The Whispering Man said, "Here you are at a historic moment, Felix, a watershed—"

The Whispering Man said, lifting up the gun a little in his hand and smiling, "No, what all this—what all this was designed to do—by me—was—"

The Whispering Man, his face drained of all color, his eyes bright in the yellow light of the burning boat, said easily, unemotionally, "Felix, between us, courtesy of the Mollison plan that you're going to tell everybody about because the place is so littered with bodies that no one can ignore it—because so many people already know so many little bits of it—what you and I are going to do, forever, finally, at last, is totally, 100 percent—"

The Whispering Man said, at last, "Felix, you and I, here, now, you and I are going to destroy forever the entire CIA!"

"You're CIA yourself! There weren't any agricultural advisers living alone in some house on a hill at the height of the Communist activity in Negros! You were CIA yourself even then!"

"I was a minor agent! I was a part-time agent! I was—"

"You're a goddamned liar! You were—"

"I was Mollison's Number Two! I was Mollison's good boy he held in reserve in case he needed me! I was needed when he needed me to die! If I was CIA, I was there to—" The Whispering Man said, "My wife wasn't! My child wasn't! I was just a minor—" The Whispering Man said, "No photo of Mollison in the file! There never are photos of us in files because we're—" The Whispering Man, holding the doll hard in his hand, shrieked, "Mollison was a nice, white-haired man who talked with a gentle Southern accent, and when he smiled his eyes crinkled up and he looked like—" He was grimacing, fighting for control. "To my daughter—he was Uncle Ed. She said when he smiled he looked like—" The Whispering Man said, "He was an evil, toothless, gummy killer! He was every worst nightmare in the world. He was a man who played with lives on bits of paper—"

"And what do you do?"

"I work for the greatest good!"

"You work for—"

"I'm one of them! I'm him!" The Whispering Man said, "I know that! Look at me! I know what I am! But I'm—"

"You're doing the same thing!"

"I'm destroying an organization so evil, so callous, so calculating that—"

"You're working out some sort of private revenge with the lives of people who want to do nothing more than live and have hope!" *My brilliant brother—My Sister, Mother, Friend.* One day, there in Roxas Boulevard, one day when a street photograph had been taken—Elizalde shouted at the man in the light of the burning boat, "I won't kill you! You won't make me part of it because I—"

"What are you going to do—*take me in?*"
"Yes!"

At the two bodies, kneeling by them, Mang Eleuterio saw Cafiero's face.

For a moment, with the gun in his hand, Cafiero looked down at him.

For a moment, from a long time ago, from somewhere on the streets, among the poor, Mang Eleuterio thought he recognized him.

For a moment—

He saw his face.

Mang Eleuterio, at the bodies of the two dead people, of the man and woman shot dead by Rolly, saw Cafiero's face.

He saw his eyes.

He saw what was in them.

"*Are you insane?*" At the jetty, the Whispering Man, almost on the point of laughing, said incredulously, "Are you completely *insane?* Have you any idea what will happen to you if you try that, if even the faintest whisper gets back to the CIA that you're trying to take in a Head of Station? Have you any idea how long you'll last? Have you any idea how many people we pay; how many people telephone us and give us little tidbits or— Have you any notion on earth how many people we own?" The Whispering Man yelled, "Are you crazy? How much does it take to get through to you?" The Whispering Man shrieked, "Hear me! Listen to me! *Read my lips!* The Mollison Plan is available! It exists! It can be used! It can be used against a hostile country and it can be tried out in a friendly one! It's active, pending—it's available! All it takes is someone like me, like Mollison! All it takes to activate it is a Head of Station saying yes and it works! All I had to do was work it through to a point where cops, where politicians—where anyone I cared to suggest—was shipping out the skeletons of the poor for profit, where the targets were being killed and everyone back home, reading my report would have applauded a good little experiment brought to a valid conclusion and the plan would have been moved up to the top of the pile!" The Whispering Man said, "You don't win by getting led to uncover this one little plot on the part of the naughty CIA—there are rooms, vaults full of things even worse than this—you win by destroying the entire enterprise! You win by bringing down the CIA the way Watergate brought down Nixon! You win by discrediting them so thoroughly that it'll take a hundred years before they dare raise their heads again! You win by shackling the CIA so tight with checks and balances—by making sure that nothing gets done under the heading of *Miscellaneous*—that they're a spent force! That they're like the dodo! That they're dead!" The Whispering Man shouted, "Look around you! This isn't America! This is another country! This is your country!

"Mollison—" The Whispering Man said, "What he did to me, I've done to you!"

He was there. He was within range. Behind him, he could hear the sirens coming. Behind him, there were two dead people being tended by a man of God. Behind him, there was all his life. There was blood on his face, going hard. He was weeping. Staggering, closing the gap, the rifle held hard in his hands, Cafiero was weeping for everything that had ever been.

At the end of the road, standing in the glare of the car lights like a traffic policeman, Bontoc yelled, "Stop!" They were coming from all over Manila. Back along Roxas Boulevard, under all the streetlights, he could see them coming.

"Halt!" Ambrosio had the submachine gun in his hands. He had his badge pinned to his shirt pocket. He was side by side with Bontoc in the lights. Far back behind him, on the jetty Elizalde was alone with the man with the Ingram and the rag doll.

"*Stop!*"

They saw the lights turn to stop in front of them.

He was turning; he was half turning away toward the burning boat. Facing him, Elizalde saw the gun coming up. He saw the Whispering Man so gently drop the rag doll onto the ground and slowly, the movement made obvious, reach over with his free hand and draw back the cocking bolt of the Ingram until it clicked.

It was happening in slow motion. It had come to it. *My Sister, Mother, Friend—* It had come to it. It had come to a point where there was nothing left in the world but to die, where the horror of the days and the light was more than— At the salt farm they had found the remains of what had once been a nine-year-old boy. Mrs. Barrera . . . in the orchid garden she had thought he was going to— He had his gun up, the PPK. The PPK was coming up and pointing. Out on the bay the boat was burning, crackling, dying down. It was— Marguerita was safe with her— It had come to it. It had come to it—

He came back. He was coming back with the Ingram gun coming up and he was smiling with a fierce smile in the light and his eyes were alive and he was at the last moment. The Whispering Man, his eyes lit up, the gun coming up, coming up, yelled, "For the love of God, Elizalde, for the love of God— *take your country back!*" The Whispering Man, shrieking, bringing the gun up, screamed, "Take it back! Take your fucking country—BACK!"

"FELIX!" He was a poor man. He was a poor man who had grown up in the barangays and who had never become anything, never learned Spanish, never, never owned anything like a Rolex watch or a Cardin cigarette lighter and he was a poor man from the barangays and all his life, all his life had come to this. Cafiero, standing up, the gun up at his shoulder, his finger moving on the trigger, shrieked, "FELIX—FELIX!"

"Now! Take it back now!"

He had never told Rosey anything of what he was or what he had done. He would tell her this.

"Felix—!"

He saw Elizalde go down in a crouch with his PPK out and pointing at the man at the end of the jetty. He saw the gun in his hands.

"FELIX—!" All his life he had been afraid to die. "Felix—!" It was a shout, a warning, it was for someone else. He saw the man on the end of the jetty, he saw the head of the CIA Station, Manila, he saw him full on.

He saw him see him.

He saw him look.

He saw, at last, the Dark Man. He saw—

Clear, his face like the face of a devil, a nightmare, lit up by the burning boat out in the bay, Cafiero, in an orison, a prayer, calling to someone else, to his friend, the Armalite set on full automatic exploding in a burst of light and sound, emptying the entire magazine, unerringly, full of power, killed the Whispering Man where he stood.

My Sister, Mother, Friend . . .

Voices.

They were the voices of the poor. They were everywhere. They were numerous. They were the victims.

At 6:00 A.M. when the Coast Guard divers went down at first light to check the underwater damage to the hull of the catamaran, weighted down, one by one, each shot once cleanly in the back of the head by a short-barreled large-caliber hideout gun, they began finding the bodies of the missing.

There were nineteen of them. Most of them, because of the action of the water, were unidentifiable.

They were nobodies, like soldiers dead only at random.

Perhaps, in the grand, great scheme of things, perhaps . . .

Perhaps they mattered not at all.

Bestselling Crime

☐ Moonspender	Jonathan Gash	£2.50
☐ Shake Hands For Ever	Ruth Rendell	£2.50
☐ A Guilty Thing Surprised	Ruth Rendell	£2.50
☐ The Tree of Hands	Ruth Rendell	£2.50
☐ Wexford: An Omnibus	Ruth Rendell	£5.95
☐ Evidence to Destroy	Margaret Yorke	£2.50
☐ No One Rides For Free	Larry Beinhart	£2.95
☐ In La La Land We Trust	Robert Campbell	£2.50
☐ Suspects	William J. Caunitz	£2.95
☐ Blood on the Moon	James Ellroy	£2.50
☐ Roses Are Dead	Loren D. Estleman	£2.50
☐ The Body in the Billiard Room	H.R.F. Keating	£2.50
☐ Rough Cider	Peter Lovesey	£2.50

Prices and other details are liable to change

ARROW BOOKS, BOOKSERVICE BY POST, PO BOX 29, DOUGLAS, ISLE OF MAN, BRITISH ISLES

NAME . . . .

ADDRESS . . . .

. . . .

. . . .

Please enclose a cheque or postal order made out to Arrow Books Ltd. for the amount due and allow the following for postage and packing.

U.K. CUSTOMERS: Please allow 22p per book to a maximum of £3.00.

B.F.P.O. & EIRE: Please allow 22p per book to a maximum of £3.00

OVERSEAS CUSTOMERS: Please allow 22p per book.

Whilst every effort is made to keep prices low it is sometimes necessary to increase cover prices at short notice. Arrow Books reserve the right to show new retail prices on covers which may differ from those previously advertised in the text or elsewhere.